Praise for
PETER ROBINSON and
A NECESSARY END

"P.D. James, Reginald Hill, and Ruth Rendell may be writing
as fast as they can. But what are devotees of the English
country mystery supposed to be reading betweentimes?
This superior series by Peter Robinson should do nicely."
The New York Times Book Review

"A fluidly written, superior mystery . . .
Robinson has created a stalwart cop in Alan Banks."
Publishers Weekly

"His characters are so believable you'll find yourself
wondering what they're doing after Robinson stops writing."
San Jose Mercury News

"An absorbing tale . . . Peter Robinson
gets you intensely involved."
United Press International

"A winner . . . a top-flight procedural with no pretensions . . .
the characters are finely etched, the dialogue chatty,
the small-town North England setting flawlessly evoked."
Booklist

"A tantalizing puzzle."
Mostly Murder

PETER ROBINSON

A NECESSARY END

AN
INSPECTOR ALAN BANKS
MYSTERY

AVON BOOKS
An Imprint of HarperCollinsPublishers

This is a work of fiction. Names, characters, places, and incidents are products of the author's imagination or are used fictitiously and are not to be construed as real. Any resemblance to actual events, locales, organizations, or persons, living or dead, is entirely coincidental.

AVON BOOKS
An Imprint of HarperCollinsPublishers
195 Broadway
New York, NY 10007

Copyright © 1989 by Peter Robinson
Inside cover author photo by Clifford Robinson
Published by arrangement with Charles Scribner's Sons
Library of Congress Catalog Card Number: 91-24521
ISBN: 0-380-71946-0
www.avonbooks.com

First Avon Twilight printing: January 2000
First Avon Books printing: August 1993

Avon Trademark Reg. U.S. Pat. Off. and in Other Countries, Marca Registrada, Hecho en U.S.A.
HarperCollins® is a trademark of HarperCollins Publishers Inc.

Printed in the U.S.A.

10

For Martin, Chris, Steve and Paul—
old friends who all contributed.

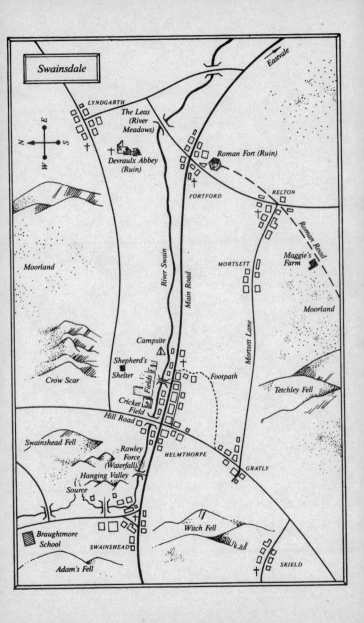

Swainsdale

Easvale

LYNDGARTH

The Leas
(River Meadows)

Roman Fort (Ruin)

Devraulx Abbey
(Ruin)

RELTON

FORTFORD

N
E
W
S

Moorland

MORTSETT

Maggie's
Farm

Roman Road

River Swain

Main Road

Moorland

Mortsett Lane

Crow Scar

Campsite

Shepherd's
Shelter

Footpath

Fields

Tetchley Fell

Cricket
Field

Hill Road

Swainshead Fell

Rawley Force
(Waterfall)

HELMTHORPE

GRATLY

Hanging Valley

Source

Braughtmore
School

Witch Fell

SWAINSHEAD

SKIELD

Adam's Fell

ONE

I

The demonstrators huddled in the March drizzle outside Eastvale Community Centre. Some of them held home-made placards aloft, but the anti-nuclear slogans had run in the rain like the red lettering at the beginning of horror movies. It was hard to make out exactly what they said any more. By eight-thirty, everyone was thoroughly soaked and fed up. No television cameras recorded the scene, and not one reporter mingled with the crowd. Protests were *passé*, and the media were only interested in what was going on inside. Besides, it was cold, wet and dark out there.

Despite all the frustration, the demonstrators had been patient so far. Their wet hair lay plastered to their skulls and water dribbled down their necks, but still they had held up their illegible placards and shifted from foot to foot for over an hour. Now, however, many of them were beginning to feel claustrophobic. North Market Street was narrow and only dimly lit by old-fashioned gaslamps. The protestors were hemmed in on all sides by police, who had edged so close that there was no-where left to spread out. An extra line of police stood guard at the top of the steps by the heavy oak doors, and opposite the hall more officers blocked the snickets that led to the winding back streets and the open fields beyond Cardigan Drive.

Finally, just to get breathing space, some people at the edges began pushing. The police shoved back hard. The agitation rippled its way to the solidly packed heart of the crowd, and suppressed tempers rose. When someone brought a placard down on a copper's head, the other demonstrators cheered. Someone else threw a bottle. It smashed harmlessly, high against the wall. Then a few people began to wave their fists in the air and the crowd started chanting, "WE WANT IN! LET US IN!" Isolated scuffles broke out. They were still struggling for more ground, and the police pushed back to contain them. It was like sitting on the lid of a boiling pot; something had to give.

Later, nobody could say exactly how it happened, or who started it, but most of the protestors questioned claimed that a policeman yelled, "Let's clobber the buggers!" and that the line advanced down the steps, truncheons out. Then all hell broke loose.

II

It was too hot inside the Community Centre. Detective Chief Inspector Alan Banks fidgeted with his tie. He hated ties, and when he had to wear one he usually kept the top button of his shirt undone to alleviate the choking feeling. But this time he toyed with the loose knot out of boredom, as well as discomfort. He wished he was at home with his arm around Sandra and a tumbler of good single-malt Scotch in his hand.

But home had been a cold and lonely place these past two days because Sandra and the children were away. Her father had suffered a mild stroke, and she had taken off down to Croyden to help her mother cope. Banks wished she were back. They had married young, and he found that the single life, after almost twenty years of (mostly) happy marriage, had little to recommend it.

But the main cause of Banks's ill humour droned on and on, bringing to the crowded Eastvale Community Centre a particularly nasal brand of Home Counties monetarism. It was the Honourable Honoria Winstanley, MP, come to pour oil on the troubled waters of North-South relations. Eastvale had been blessed with her presence because, though not large, it was the biggest and most important town in that part of the country between York and Darlington. It was also enjoying a period of unprecedented and inexplicable growth, thus marking itself out as a shining example of popular capitalism at work. Banks was present as a gesture of courtesy, sandwiched between two taciturn Special Branch agents. Superintendent Gristhorpe had no doubt assigned him, Banks thought, because he had no desire to listen to the Hon Honoria himself. If pushed, Banks described himself as a moderate socialist, but politics bored him and politicians usually made him angry.

Occasionally, he glanced left or right and noticed the restless eyes of the official bodyguards, who seemed to be expecting terrorist action at any moment. For want of their real names, he had christened them Chas and Dave. Chas was the bulky one with the rheumy eyes and bloated red nose, and Dave was blessed with the lean and hungry look of a Tory cabinet minister. If a member of the audience shifted in his or her seat, raised a fist to muffle a cough or reached for a handkerchief, either Chas or Dave would slip his hand under his jacket towards his shoulder-holster.

It was all very silly, Banks thought. The only reason anyone might want to kill Honoria Winstanley would be for inflicting a dull speech on the audience. As motives for murder went, that came a long way down the list—though any sane judge would certainly pronounce it justifiable homicide.

Ms Winstanley paused and took a sip of water while the audience applauded. "And I say to you all," she continued in all-out rhetorical flight, "that in the fullness of time, when the results of our policies have come to fruition and every vestige of socialism has been stamped out, all divisions will be healed, and the north, that revered cradle of the Industrial Revolution, will indeed prosper every bit as much as the rest of our glorious nation. Once again this will be a *united* kingdom, united under the banner of enterprise, incentive and hard work. You can already see it happening around you here in Eastvale."

Banks covered his mouth with his hand and yawned. He looked to his left and noticed that Chas had become so enrapt by Honoria that he had momentarily forgotten to keep an eye open for the IRA, the PLO, the Baader-Meinhof group and the Red Brigade.

The speech was going down well, Banks thought, considering that members of the same government had recently told the north to stop whining about unemployment and had added that most of its problems were caused by poor taste in food. Still, with an audience made up almost entirely of members of the local Conservative Association—small businessmen, farmers and landowners, for the most part—such whole-hearted enthusiasm was only to be expected. The people in the hall had plenty of money, and no doubt they ate well, too.

It was getting even hotter and stuffier, but the Hon Honoria showed no signs of flagging. Indeed, she was off on a laudatory digression about share-owning, making it sound as if every Englishman could become a millionaire overnight if the government continued to sell off nationalized industries and services to the private sector.

Banks needed a cigarette. He'd been trying to give up smoking again lately, but without success. With so little happening at the station and Sandra and the children away, he had actually increased his intake. The only progress he had made was in switching from Benson & Hedges Special Mild to Silk Cut. He'd heard somewhere that breaking brand loyalty was the first step towards stopping entirely. Unfortunately, he was beginning to like the new brand more than the old.

He shifted in his seat when Honoria moved on to the necessity of maintaining, even expanding, the American military presence in Britain, and Chas gave him a challenging glance. He began to wonder if perhaps this latest digression was a roundabout way of approaching the issue the many people present wanted to hear about.

There had been rumours about a nuclear-power station across the North York Moors on the coast, only about forty miles from Eastvale. With Sellafield to the west, that was one too many, even for some of the more right-wing locals. After all, radioactivity could be quite nasty when you depended on the land for your prosperity. They all remembered Chernobyl, with its tales of contaminated milk and meat.

And as if the peaceful use of nuclear power weren't bad enough, there was also talk of a new American airforce base in the area. People were already fed up with low-flying jets breaking the sound barrier day in, day out. Even if the sheep did seem to have got used to them, they were bad for the tourist business. But it looked as if Honoria was going to skirt the issue in true politician's fashion and dazzle everyone with visions of a new Golden Age. Maybe the matter would come up in question time.

Honoria's speech ended after a soaring paean to education reform, law and order, the importance of military strength, and private ownership of council housing. She had made no reference at all to the nuclear-power station or to the proposed air base. There was a five-second pause before the audience realized it was all over and began to clap. In that pause, Banks thought he heard signs of a ruckus outside. Chas and Dave seemed to have the same notion too; their eyes darted to the doors and their hands slid towards their left armpits.

III

Outside, police and demonstrators punched and kicked each other wildly. Parts of the dense crowd had broken up into small skirmishes, but a heaving, struggling central mass remained. Everyone seemed oblivious to all but his or her personal battle. There were no individuals, just fists, wooden sticks, boots and uniforms. Occasionally, when a truncheon connected, someone would scream in agony, fall to his knees and put his hands to the flow of blood in stunned disbelief. The police got as good as they gave, too; boots connected with groins, fists with heads. Helmets flew off and demonstrators picked them up to swing them by the straps and use as weapons. The fallen on both sides were trampled by the rest; there was no room to avoid them, no time for compassion.

One young constable, beset by two men and a woman, covered his face and flailed blindly with his truncheon; a girl, blood flowing down the side of her neck, kicked a policeman, who lay in the rain curled up in the foetal position. Four people, locked together, toppled over and crashed through the window of Winston's Tobacco Shop, scattering the fine display of Havana cigars, bowls of aromatic pipe tobacco and exotic Turkish and American cigarette packets onto the wet pavement.

Eastvale Regional Police Headquarters was only a hundred yards or so down the street, fronting the market square. When he heard the noise, Sergeant Rowe dashed outside and sized up the situation quickly. He then sent out two squad cars to block off the narrow street at both ends, and a Black Maria to put the prisoners in. He also phoned the hospital for ambulances.

When the demonstrators heard the sirens, most of them were aware enough to know they were trapped. Scuffles ceased and the scared protestors broke for freedom. Some managed to slip by before the car doors opened, and two people shoved aside the driver of one car and ran to freedom across the market square. A few others hurled themselves at the policemen who were still trying to block off the snickets, knocked them out of the way, and took off into the safety and obscurity of the back alleys. One muscular protestor forced his way up the steps towards the Community Centre doors with two policemen hanging onto the scruff of his neck trying to drag him back.

IV

Loud and prolonged applause drowned out all other sounds, and the Special Branch men relaxed their grips on their guns. The Hon Honoria beamed at the audience and raised her clasped hands above her head in triumph.

Banks still felt uneasy. He was sure he'd heard sounds of an argument or a fight outside. He knew that a small demonstration had been planned, and wondered if it had turned violent. Still, there was nothing he could do. At all costs, the show must go on, and he didn't want to create a stir by getting up and leaving early.

At least the speech was over. If question time didn't go on too long he'd be able to get outside and smoke a cigarette in half an hour or so. An hour might see him at home with that Scotch, and Sandra on the other end of the telephone line. He was hungry, too. In Sandra's absence, he had decided to have a go at *haute cuisine*, and though it hadn't worked out too well so far—the curry had lacked spiciness, and he'd overcooked the fish casserole—he was making progress. Surely a Spanish omelette could present no real problems?

The applause died down and the chairman announced question time. As the first person stood up and began to ask about the proposed site of the nuclear-power station, the doors burst open and a hefty, bedraggled young man lurched in with two policemen in tow. A truncheon cracked down, and the three fell onto the back row. The young man yelped out in pain. Women screamed and reached for their fur coats as the flimsy chairs toppled and splintered under the weight of the three men.

Chas and Dave didn't waste a second. They rushed to Honoria, shielding her from the audience, and with Banks in front, they left through the back door. Beyond the cluttered store-rooms, an exit opened onto a complex of back streets, and Banks led them down a narrow alley where the shops on York Road dumped their rubbish. In no time at all the four of them had crossed the road and entered the old Riverview Hotel, where the Hon Honoria was booked to stay the night. For the first time that evening, she was quiet. Banks noticed in the muted light of the hotel lobby how pale she had turned.

Only when they got to the room, a suite with a superb view over the terraced river-gardens, did Chas and Dave relax. Honoria sighed and sank into the sofa, and Dave locked the door and put the chain on while Chas headed over to the cocktail cabinet.

"Pour me a gin-and-tonic, will you, dear?" said Honoria in a shaky voice.

"What the hell was all that about?" Chas asked, also pouring out two stiff shots of Scotch.

"I don't know," Banks said. "There was a small demonstration outside. I suppose it could have—"

"Some bloody security you've got here," said Dave, taking his drink and passing the gin-and-tonic to Honoria.

She gulped it down and put her hand to her brow. "My God," she said, "I thought there was nobody but farmers and horse-trainers living up here. Look at me, I'm shaking like a bloody leaf."

"Look," Banks said, hovering at the door, "I'd better go and see what's happening." It was obvious he wasn't going to get a drink, and he was damned if he was going to stand in as a whipping boy for the security organizers. "Will you be all right?"

"A damn sight safer than we were back there," Dave

said. Then his tone softened a little and he came to the door with Banks. "Yes, go on. It's your problem now, mate." He smiled and lowered his voice, twitching his head in Honoria's direction. "Ours is her."

In the rush, Banks had left his raincoat in the Community Centre, and his cigarettes were in the right-hand pocket. He noticed Chas lighting up as he left, but hadn't the audacity to ask for one. Things were bad enough already. Flipping up his jacket collar against the rain, he ran down to the market square, turned right in front of the church and stopped dead.

The wounded lay groaning or unconscious in the drizzle, and police still scuffled with the ones they'd caught, trying to force them into the backs of the cars or into the Black Maria. Some demonstrators, held by their hair, wriggled and kicked as they went, receiving sharp blows from the truncheons for their efforts. Others went peacefully. They were frightened and tired now; most of the fight had gone out of them.

Banks stood rooted to the spot and watched the scene. Radios crackled; blue lights spun; the injured cried in pain and shock while ambulance attendants rushed around with stretchers. It defied belief. A full-blown riot in Eastvale, admittedly on a small scale, was near unthinkable. Banks had got used to the rising crime rate, which affected even places as small as Eastvale, with just over fourteen thousand people, but riots were surely reserved for Birmingham, Liverpool, Leeds, Manchester, Bristol or London. It couldn't happen here, he had always thought as he shook his head over news of Brixton, Toxteth and Tottenham. But now it had, and the moaning casualties, police and demonstrators alike, were witness to that hard truth.

The street was blocked off at the market square to the south and near the Town Hall, at the junction with Elmet Street, to the north. The gaslamps and illuminated window displays in the twee tourist shops full of Yorkshire woollen wear, walking gear and local produce shone on the chaotic scene. A boy, no more than fifteen or sixteen, cried out as two policemen dragged him by his hair along the glistening cobbles; a torn placard that had once defiantly read NO NUKES flapped in the March wind as the thin rain tapped a faint tattoo against it; one policeman, helmet gone and hair in disarray, bent to help up another, whose moustache was matted with blood and whose nose lay at an odd angle to his face.

In the revolving blue lights, the aftermath of the battle took on a slow-motion, surrealistic quality to Banks. Elongated shadows played across walls. In the street, odd objects caught the light for a second, then seemed to vanish: an upturned helmet, an empty beer bottle, a key-ring, a half-eaten apple browning at the edges, a long white scarf twisted like a snake.

Several policemen had come out of the station to help, and Banks recognized Sergeant Rowe standing behind a squad car by the corner.

"What happened?" he asked.

Rowe shook his head. "Demo turned nasty, sir. We don't know how or why yet."

"How many were there?"

"About a hundred." He waved his hand at the scene. "But we didn't expect anything like this."

"Got a cigarette, Sergeant?"

Rowe gave him a Senior Service. It tasted strong after Silk Cut, but he drew the smoke deep into his lungs nonetheless.

"How many hurt?"

"Don't know yet, sir."

"Any of ours?"

"Aye, a few, I reckon. We had about thirty or so on crowd-control duty, but most of them were drafted in from York and Scarborough on overtime. Craig was there, and young Tolliver. I haven't seen either of them yet. It'll be busy in the station tonight. Looks like we've nicked about half of them."

Two ambulance attendants trotted by with a stretcher

between them. On it lay a middle-aged woman, her left eye clouded with blood. She turned her head painfully and spat at Sergeant Rowe as they passed.

"Bloody hell!" Rowe said. "That was Mrs Campbell. She takes Sunday School at Cardigan Drive Congregationalist."

"War makes animals of us all, Sergeant," Banks said, wishing he could remember where he'd heard that, and turned away. "I'd better get to the station. Does the super know?"

"It's his day off, sir." Rowe still seemed stunned.

"I'd better call him. Hatchley and Richmond, too."

"DC Richmond's over there, sir." Rowe pointed to a tall, slim man standing near the Black Maria.

Banks walked over and touched Richmond's arm.

The young detective constable flinched. "Oh, it's you, sir. Sorry, this has got me all tense."

"How long have you been here, Phil?"

"I came out when Sergeant Rowe told us what was happening."

"You didn't see it start, then?"

"No, sir. It was all over in fifteen minutes."

"Come on. We'd better get inside and help with the processing."

Chaos reigned inside the station. Every square inch of available space was taken up by arrested demonstrators, some of them bleeding from minor cuts, and most of them complaining loudly about police brutality. As Banks and Richmond shouldered their way towards the stairs, a familiar voice called out after them.

"Craig!" Banks said, when the young constable caught up with them. "What happened?"

"Not much, sir," PC Craig shouted over the noise. His right eye was dark and puffed up, and blood oozed from a split lip. "I got off lucky."

"You should be at the hospital."

"It's nothing, sir, really. They took Susan Gay off in an ambulance."

"What was she doing out there?"

"They needed help, sir. The men on crowd control. We just went out. We never knew it would be like this. . . ."

"Is she hurt badly?"

"They think it's just concussion, sir. She got knocked down, and some bastard kicked her in the head. The hospital just phoned. A Dr Partridge wants to talk to you."

A scuffle broke out behind them and someone went flying into the small of Richmond's back. He fell forward and knocked Banks and Craig against the wall.

Banks got up and regained his balance. "Can't anyone keep these bloody people quiet!" he shouted to the station in general. Then he turned to Craig again. "I'll talk to the doctor. But give the super a call, if you're up to it. Tell him what's happened and ask to come in. Sergeant Hatchley, too. Then get to the hospital. You might as well have someone look at your eye while you pay a sick call on Susan."

"Yes, sir." Craig elbowed his way back through the crowd, and Banks and Richmond made their way upstairs to the CID offices.

First Banks reached into his desk drawer, where he kept a spare packet of cigarettes, then he dialled Eastvale General Infirmary.

Reception paged the doctor, who picked up the phone about a minute later.

"Are there any serious injuries?" Banks asked.

"Most of them are just cuts and bruises. A few minor head wounds. On the whole, I'd say it looks worse than it is. But that's not—"

"What about PC Gay?"

"Who?"

"Susan Gay. The policewoman."

"Oh, yes. She's all right. She's got concussion. We'll keep her in overnight for observation, then after a few days' rest she'll be right as rain. Look, I understand your concern, Chief Inspector, but that's not what I wanted to talk to you about."

"What is it, then?" For a moment, Banks felt an icy prickle of irrational fear. Sandra? The children? The results of his last chest X-ray?

"There's been a death."

"At the demonstration?"

"Yes."

"Go on."

"Well, it's more of a murder, I suppose."

"Suppose?"

"I mean that's what it looks like. I'm not a pathologist. I'm not qualified—"

"Who's the victim?"

"It's a policeman. PC Edwin Gill."

Banks frowned. "I've not heard the name. Where's he from?"

"One of the others said he was drafted in from Scarborough."

"How did he die?"

"Well, that's the thing. You'd expect a fractured skull or some wound consistent with what went on."

"But?"

"He was stabbed. He was still alive when he was brought in. I'm afraid we didn't . . . There was no obvious wound at first. We thought he'd just been knocked out like the others. He died before we could do anything. Internal bleeding."

Banks put his hand over the receiver and turned his eyes up to the ceiling. "Shit!"

"Hello, Chief Inspector? Are you still there?"

"Yes. Sorry, doc. Thanks for calling so quickly. I'll send down some more police guards. Nobody's to leave, no matter how minor their injuries. Is there anyone from Eastvale station there? Anyone conscious, that is."

"Just a minute."

Dr Partridge came back with PC Tolliver, who had accompanied Susan Gay in the ambulance.

"Listen carefully, lad," Banks said. "We've got a bloody crisis on our hands back here, so you'll have to handle the hospital end yourself."

"Yes, sir."

"There'll be more men down there as soon as I can round some up, but until then do the best you can. I don't want anyone from tonight's fracas to leave there, do you understand?"

"Yes, sir."

"And that includes our men, too. I realize some of them might be anxious to get home after they've had their cuts dressed, but I need statements, and I need them while things are fresh in their minds. Okay?"

"Yes, sir. There's two or three more blokes here without serious injuries. We'll see to it."

"Good. You know about PC Gill?"

"Yes, sir. The doctor told me. I didn't know him."

"You'd better get someone to identify the body formally. Did he have a family?"

"Don't know, sir."

"Find out. If he did, you know what to do."

"Yes, sir."

"And get Dr Glendenning down there. We need him to examine the body. We've got to move quickly on this, before things get cold."

"I understand, sir."

"Good. Off you go."

Banks hung up and turned to Richmond, who stood in the doorway nervously smoothing his moustache. "Go downstairs, would you, Phil, and tell whoever's in charge to get things quietened down and make sure no one sneaks out. Then call York and ask if they can spare a few more men for the night. If they can't, try Darlington. And you'd better get someone to rope off the street from the market square to the Town Hall, too."

"What's up?" Richmond asked.

Banks sighed and ran a hand through his close-cropped hair. "It looks like we've got a murder on our hands and a hundred or more bloody suspects."

TWO

I

The wind chimes tinkled and rain hissed on the rough moorland grass. Mara Delacey had just put the children to bed and read them Beatrix Potter's *Tale of Squirrel Nutkin*. Now it was time for her to relax, to enjoy the stillness and isolation, the play of silence and natural sound. It reminded her of the old days when she used to meditate on her mantra.

As usual, it had been a tiring day: washing to do, meals to cook, children to take care of. But it had also been satisfying. She had managed to fit in a couple of hours throwing pots in the back of Elspeth's craft shop in Relton. If it was her lot in life to be an earth mother, she thought with a smile, better to be one here, away from the rigid rules and self-righteous spirituality of the ashram, where she hadn't even been able to sneak a cigarette after dinner. She was glad she'd left all that rubbish behind.

Now she could enjoy some time to herself without feeling she ought to be out chasing after converts or singing the praises of the guru—not that many did now he was serving his stretch in jail for fraud and tax evasion. The devotees had scattered: some, lost and lonely, had gone to look for new leaders; others, like Mara, had moved on to something else.

She had met Seth Cotton a year after he had bought

the place near Relton, which he had christened Maggie's
Farm. As soon as he showed it to her, she knew it had
to be her home. It was a typical eighteenth-century Dales
farmhouse set in a couple of acres of land on the moors
above the dale. The walls were built of limestone, with
gritstone corners and a flagstone roof. Recessed windows looked north over the dale, and the heavy door-
head, supported on stacked quoins, bore the initials
T. J. H.—standing for the original owner—and the date
1765. The only addition apart from Seth's workshop, a
shed at the far end of the back garden, was a limestone
porch with a slate roof. Beyond the back-garden fence,
about fifty yards east of the main house, stood an old
barn, which Seth had been busy renovating when she
met him. He had split it into an upper studio-apartment,
where Rick Trelawney, an artist, lived with his son, and
a one-bedroom flat on the ground floor, occupied by Zoe
Hardacre and her daughter. Paul, their most recent ten-
ant, had a room in the main house.

Although the barn was more modern inside, Mara preferred the farmhouse. Its front door led directly into the
spacious living-room, a clean and tidy place furnished
with a collection of odds and sods: an imitation Persian
carpet, a reupholstered fifties sofa, and a large table and
four chairs made of white pine by Seth himself. Large
beanbag cushions lay scattered against the walls for
comfort.

On the wall opposite the stone fireplace hung a huge
tapestry of a Chinese scene. It showed enormous moun-
tains, their snow-streaked peaks sharp as needles above
the pine forests. In the middle-distance, a straggling line
of tiny human figures moved up a winding path. Mara
looked at it a lot. There was no overhead light in the
room. She kept the shaded lamps dim and supplemented
them with fat red candles because she liked the shadows
the flames cast on the tapestry and the whitewashed
stone walls. Her favourite place to curl up was near the
window in an old rocking chair Seth had restored. There,

she could hear the wind chimes clearly as she sipped wine and read.

In her early days, she had devoured Kerouac, Burroughs, Ginsberg, Carlos Castaneda and the rest, but at thirty-eight she found their works embarrassingly adolescent, and her tastes had reverted to the classics she remembered from her university days. There was something about those long Victorian novels that suited a place as isolated and slow-moving as Maggie's Farm.

Now she decided to settle down and lose herself in *The Mill on the Floss*. A hand-rolled Old Holborn and a glass of Barsac would also go down nicely. And maybe some music. She walked to the stereo, selected Holst's *The Planets*, the side with "Saturn," "Uranus" and "Neptune," then nestled in the chair to read by candlelight. The others were all at the demo, and they'd be sure to stop off for a pint or two at the Black Sheep in Relton on the way back. The kids were sleeping in the spare room upstairs, so she wouldn't have to keep nipping out to the barn to check on them. It was half-past nine now. She could probably count on at least a couple of hours to herself.

But she couldn't seem to concentrate. The hissing outside stopped. It was replaced by the steady dripping of rain from the eaves-troughs, the porch and the trees that protected Maggie's Farm from the harsh west winds. The chimes began to sound like warning bells. There was something in the air. If Zoe were home, she'd no doubt have plenty to say about psychic forces—probably the moon.

Shrugging off her feeling of unease, Mara returned to her reading: "And this is Dorlcote Mill. I must stand a minute or two here on the bridge and look at it, though the clouds are threatening, and it is far on in the afternoon. . . ." It was no good; she couldn't get into it. George Eliot's spell just wasn't working tonight. Mara put down the book and concentrated on the music.

As the ethereal choir entered towards the end of "Neptune," the front door rattled open and Paul rushed in. His combat jacket was dark with rain and his tight jeans stuck to his stick-insect legs.

Mara frowned. "You're back early," she said. "Where are the others?"

"I don't know." Paul was out of breath and his voice sounded shaky. He took off his jacket and hung it on the hook at the back of the door. "I ran back by myself over the moors."

"But that's more than four miles. What's wrong, Paul? Why didn't you wait for Seth and the others? You could have come back in the van."

"There was some trouble," Paul said. "Things got nasty." He took a cigarette from his pack of Players and lit it, cupping it in his hands the way soldiers do in old war films. His hands were trembling. Mara noticed again how short and stubby his fingers were, nails bitten to the quick. She rolled another cigarette. Paul started to pace the room.

"What's that?" Mara asked, pointing in alarm to the fleshy spot at the base of his left thumb. "It looks like blood. You've hurt yourself."

"It's nothing."

Mara reached out, but he pulled his hand away.

"At least let me put something on it."

"I told you, it's nothing. I'll see to it later. Don't you want to hear what happened?"

Mara knew better than to persist. "Sit down, then," she said. "You're driving me crazy pacing around like that."

Paul flopped onto the cushions by the wall, taking care to keep his bloodied hand out of sight.

"Well?" Mara said.

"The police set on us, that's what. Fucking bastards."

"Why?"

"They just laid into us, that's all. Don't ask me why. I don't know how cops think. Can I have some wine?"

Mara poured him a glass of Barsac. He took a sip and pulled a face.

"Sorry," she said. "I forgot you don't like the sweet stuff. There's some beer in the fridge."

"Great." Paul hauled himself up and went through to the kitchen. When he came back he was carrying a can of Carlsberg lager and he'd stuck an Elastoplast on his hand.

"What happened to the others?" Mara asked.

"I don't know. A lot of people got arrested. The police just charged into the crowd and dragged them off left, right and centre. There'll be plenty in hospital, too."

"Weren't you all together?"

"We were at first, right up at the front, but we got separated when the fighting broke out. I managed to sneak by some cops and slip down the alley, then I ran all the way through the back streets and over the moor. I'm bloody knackered." His Liverpudlian accent grew thicker as he became more excited.

"So people did get away?"

"Some, yes. But I don't know how many. I didn't hang around to wait for the others. It was every man for himself, Mara. The last I saw of Rick he was trying to make his way to the market square. I couldn't see Zoe. You know how small she is. It was a bleeding massacre. They'd everything short of water cannons and rubber bullets. I've seen some bother in my time, but I never expected anything like this, not in Eastvale."

"What about Seth?"

"Sorry, Mara. I've no idea what became of him. Don't worry, though, they'll be all right."

"Yes." Mara turned and looked out of the window. She could see her own reflection against the dark glass streaked with rain. It looked like a candle flame was burning from her right shoulder.

"Maybe they got away," Paul added. "They might be on their way back right now."

Mara nodded. "Maybe."

But she knew there'd be trouble. The police would soon be round, bullying and searching, just like when Seth's old friend Liz Dale ran away from the nut-house and hid out with them for a few days. They'd been looking for heroin then—Liz had a history of drug abuse—but as far as Mara remembered they'd just made a bloody mess of everything in the place. She resented that kind of intrusion into her world and didn't look forward to another one.

She reached for the wine bottle, but before she started pouring, the front door burst open again.

II

When Banks went downstairs, things were considerably quieter than they had been earlier. Richmond had helped the uniformed men to usher all the prisoners down to the cellar until they could be questioned, charged and released. Eastvale station didn't have many cells, but there was plenty of unused storage space down there.

Sergeant Hatchley had also arrived. Straw-haired, head and shoulders above the others, he looked like a rugby prop-forward gone to seed. He leaned on the reception desk looking bewildered and put out as Richmond explained what had happened.

Banks walked up to them. "Super here yet?"

"On his way, sir," Richmond answered.

"Can you get everyone together while we're waiting?" Banks asked. "There's a few things I want to tell them right now."

Richmond went into the open-plan office area, the domain of the uniformed police at Eastvale, and rounded up everyone he could. The men and women sat on desks or leaned against partitions and waited for instructions. Some of them still showed signs of the recent battle: a bruised cheekbone, torn uniform, black eye, cauliflower ear.

"Does anyone know exactly how many we've got in custody?" Banks asked first.

"Thirty-six, sir." It was a constable with a split lip and the top button torn off his jacket who answered. "And I've heard there's ten more at the hospital."

"Any serious injuries?"

"No, sir. Except, well, Constable Gill."

"Yes. So if there were about a hundred at the demo, there's almost a fifty-fifty chance we've already caught our killer. First, I want everyone searched, fingerprinted and examined for Gill's bloodstains. Constable Reynolds, will you act as liaison with the hospital?"

"Yes, sir."

"The same procedure applies there. Ask the doctor to check the ten patients for blood. Next we've got to find the murder weapon. All we know so far is that PC Gill was stabbed. We don't know what kind of knife was used, so anything with a blade is suspicious, from a kitchen knife to a stiletto. There's some extra men on the way from York, but I want a couple of you to start searching the street thoroughly right away, and that includes having a good look down the grates, too. Clear so far?"

Some muttered, "Yes, sir." Others nodded.

"Right. Now we get to the hard work. We'll need a list of names: everyone we've got and anyone else we can get them to name. Remember, about sixty people got away, and we have to know who they were. If any of you recall seeing a familiar face we don't have here or at the hospital, make a note of it. I don't suppose the people we question will want to give their friends away, but lean on them a bit, do what you can. Be on the lookout for any slips. Use whatever cunning you have. We also want to know who the organizers were and what action groups were represented.

"I want statements from everyone, even if they've

nothing to say. We're going to have to divide up the interrogations, so just do the best you can. Stick to the murder; ask about anyone with a knife. Find out if we've got any recorded troublemakers in the cells; look up their files and see what you come up with. If you think someone's lying or being evasive, push them as far as you can, then make a note of your reservations on the statement. I realize we're going to be swamped with paperwork, but there's no avoiding it. Any questions?"

Nobody said a word.

"Fine. One last thing: we want statements from all witnesses, too, not just the demonstrators. There must have been some people watching from those flats over-looking the street. Do the rounds. Find out if anyone saw anything. And rack your own brains. You know there'll be some kind of official enquiry into why all this happened in the first place, so all of you who were there might as well make a statement now, while the events are fresh in your minds. I want all statements typed and on Superintendent Gristhorpe's desk first thing in the morning."

Banks looked at his watch. "It's nine-thirty now. We'd better get cracking. Anything I've overlooked?"

Several officers shook their heads; others stood silent. Finally a policewoman put her hand up. "What are we to do with the prisoners, sir, after we've got all the state-ments?"

"Follow normal procedure," Banks said. "Just charge them and let them go unless you've got any reason to think they're involved in PC Gill's death. They'll appear before the magistrate as soon as possible. Is that all?" He paused, but nobody said anything. "Right. Off you go then. I want to know about any leads as soon as they come up. With a bit of luck we could get this wrapped up by morning. And would someone take some of the prisoners upstairs? There'll be three of us interviewing up there when the super arrives." He turned to Richmond. "We'll want you on the computer, Phil. There'll be a lot of records to check."

"The super's here now, sir." PC Telford pointed to the door, which was out of Banks's line of vision.

Superintendent Gristhorpe, a bulky man in his late fifties with bushy grey hair and eyebrows, a red pock-marked face and a bristly moustache, walked over to where the three CID men were standing by the stairs. His eyes, usually as guileless as a baby's, were clouded with concern, but his presence still brought an aura of calm and unhurried common sense.

"You've heard?" Banks asked.

"Aye," said Gristhorpe. "Not all the details, but enough. Let's go upstairs and you can tell me about it over a cup of coffee." He put his hand on Banks's arm gently.

Banks turned to Sergeant Hatchley. "You might as well get started on the interviews," he said. "We'll help you out in a minute when I've filled the super in." Then the four CID men trudged upstairs and PC Telford ush-ered a brace of wet, frightened demonstrators up after them.

III

"Zoe! Thank God you're all right!"

Paul and Mara stared at the slight figure in the glis-tening red anorak. Her ginger hair was stuck to her skull, and the dark roots showed. Rain dripped onto the straw mat just inside the doorway. She slipped off her jacket, hung it next to Paul's and walked over to hug them both.

"You've told her what happened?" she asked Paul.

"Yes."

Zoe looked at Mara. "How was Luna?"

"No trouble. She fell asleep when Squirrel Nutkin started tickling Mr Brown with a nettle."

Zoe's face twitched in a brief smile. She went over to the bookcase. "I threw an I Ching this morning," she said, "and it came up 'Conflict.' I should have known what would happen." She opened the book and read from the text: " 'Conflict. You are being sincere and are being obstructed. A cautious halt halfway brings good fortune. Going through to the end brings misfortune. It furthers one to see the great man. It does not further one to cross the great water.' "

"You can't take it so literally," Mara said. "That's the problem. It didn't tell you what would happen, or how." Though she was certainly interested in the I Ching and tarot cards, herself, Mara often thought that Zoe went too far.

"It's clear enough to me. I should have known something like this would happen: 'Going through to the end brings misfortune.' You can't get any more specific than that."

"What if you *had* known?" Paul said. "You couldn't call it off, could you? You'd still have gone. Things would still have worked out the same."

"Yes," Zoe muttered, "but I should have been prepared."

"How?" asked Mara. "Do you mean you should have gone armed or something?"

Zoe sighed. "I don't know. I just should have been prepared."

"It's easy to say that now," Paul said. "The truth is nobody had the slightest idea the demo would turn nasty, and there wasn't a damn thing they could do about it when it did. There were a lot of people involved, Zoe, and if they'd've all done the I Ching this morning they'd've all got different answers. It's a load of cobblers, if you ask me."

"Sit down," said Mara. "Have a glass of wine. Did you see what happened to the others?"

"I'm not sure." Zoe sat cross-legged on the carpet and accepted Paul's glass. "I think Rick got arrested. I saw him struggling with some police at the edge of the crowd."

"And Seth?"

"I don't know. I couldn't see." Zoe smiled sadly. "Most people were bigger than me. All I could see was shoulders and necks. That's how I managed to get away, because I'm so little. That and the rain. One cop grabbed my anorak, but his hand slipped off because it was wet. I'm a Pisces, a slippery fish." She paused to sip her Barsac. "What'll happen to them, Mara, the ones who got caught?"

Mara shrugged. "I should imagine they'll be charged and let go. That's what usually happens. Then the magistrate decides what to fine them or whether to send them to jail. Mostly they just get fined or let off with a caution."

Mara wished she felt as confident as she sounded. Her uneasiness had nothing to do with the message Zoe had got from the I Ching, but the words of the oracle somehow emphasized it and gave her disquietude a deeper dimension of credibility: "Going through to the end brings misfortune. It furthers one to see the great man." Who was the great man?

"Shouldn't we do something?" Paul asked.

"Like what?"

"Go down there, down to the police station and find out what's happened. Try and get them out."

Mara shook her head. "If we do that, it's more likely they'll take us in for obstructing justice or something."

"I just feel so bloody powerless, so useless, not being able to do a damn thing." Paul's fists clenched, and Mara could read the words jaggedly tattooed just below his knuckles. Instead of the more common combination, LOVE on one hand and HATE on the other, his read HATE on both hands. Seeing the capitalized word so ineptly tattooed there reminded Mara how hard and violent Paul's past had been and how far he had come since they'd found him sleeping in the open, early the past winter on their way to a craft fair in Wensleydale.

"If we had a phone we could at least call the hospital," Zoe said. "Maybe one of us should walk down to Relton and do it anyway."

"I'll go," Mara said. "You two have had enough for one night. Besides, the exercise will do me good."

She got to her feet before either of the others could offer to go instead. It was only a mile down to Relton, a village high on the southern slope of Swainsdale, and the walk should be a pleasant one. Mara looked out of the window. It was drizzling lightly again. She took her yellow cyclist's cape and matching rainhat out of the cupboard and opened the door. As she left, Paul was on his way to the fridge for another beer, and Zoe was reaching for her tarot cards.

Zoe worried Mara sometimes. Not that she wasn't a good mother, but she did seem too offhand. True, she had asked about Luna, but she hadn't wanted to go and look in on her. Instead she had turned immediately to her occult aids. Mara doted on both children: Luna, aged four, and Julian, five. Even Paul, just out of his teens, seemed more like a son than anything else at times. She knew she felt especially close to them because she had no children of her own. Many of her old schoolfriends would probably have kids Paul's age. What an irony, she thought, heading for the track—a barren earth mother!

The rain was hardly worth covering up for, but it gave an edge to the chill already present in the March air, and Mara was glad for the sweater she wore under her cape. The straight narrow track she followed was part of an old Roman road that ran diagonally across the moors above the dale right down to Fortford. Just wide enough for the van, it was dry-walled on both sides and covered with gravel and small chips of stone that crunched and crackled underfoot. Mara could see the lights of Relton at the bottom of the slope. Behind her the candle glowed in the window, and Maggie's Farm looked like an ark adrift on a dark sea.

She shoved her hands through the slits in her cape, deep into the pockets of her cords, and marched the way she imagined an ancient Roman would have done. Beyond the clouds, she could make out the pearly sheen of a half moon.

The great silence all around magnified the little sounds—the clatter of small stones, the rhythmic crunch of gravel, the swishing of her cords against the cape— and Mara felt the strain on her weak left knee that she always got going downhill. She raised her head and let the thin, cool rain fall on her closed eyelids and breathed in the wet-dog smell of the air. When she opened her eyes, she saw the black bulk of distant fells against a dark grey sky.

At the end of the track, Mara walked into Relton. The change from gravel to the smooth tarmac of Mortsett Lane felt strange at first. The village shops were all closed. Television sets flickered behind drawn curtains.

Just to be sure, Mara first popped her head inside the Black Sheep, but neither Seth nor Rick was there. A log fire crackled in the corner of the cosy public bar, but the place was half-empty. The landlord, Larry Grafton, smiled and said hello. Like many of the locals, he had come to accept the incomers from Maggie's Farm. At least, he had once told Mara, they weren't like those London yuppies who seemed to be buying up all the vacant property in the Dales these days.

"Can I get you anything?" Grafton called out.

"No. No, thanks," Mara said. "I was looking for Seth. You haven't seen him, have you?"

Two old men looked up from their game of dominoes, and a trio of young farm labourers paused in their argument over subsidies and glanced at Mara with faintly curious expressions on their faces.

"No, lass," Grafton said. "They've not been in since

lunchtime. Said they were off to that there demonstration in Eastvale."

Mara nodded. "That's right. There's been some trouble and they haven't come back yet. I was just wondering—"

"Is it right, then?" one of the farm labourers asked. "Tommy Exton dropped in half an hour sin' and said there'd been some fighting in Market Street."

Mara told him what little she knew, and he shook his head. "It don't pay to get involved in things like that. Best left well alone," he said, and returned to his pint.

Mara left the Black Sheep and headed for the public telephone-box on Mortsett Lane. Why they didn't have a phone installed at the farm she didn't know. Seth had once said he wouldn't have one of the things in the house, but he never explained why. Every time he needed to make a few calls he went down to the village, and he never once complained. At least in the country you could usually be sure the telephones hadn't been vandalized.

The receptionist at Eastvale General Infirmary answered and asked her what she wanted. Mara explained that she was interested in news of a friend of hers who hadn't come home from the demonstration. The receptionist said, "Just a minute," and the phone hiccupped and burped a few times. Finally a man's voice came on.

"Can I help you, miss?"

"Yes. I'd like to know if you have a patient called Seth Cotton and one called Rick Trelawney."

"Who is this calling?"

"I . . . I'd rather not say," Mara answered, suddenly afraid that if she gave her name she would be inviting trouble.

"Are you a relation?"

"I'm a friend. A very close friend."

"I see. Well, unless you identify yourself, miss, I'm afraid I can't give out any information."

"Look," Mara said, getting angry, "this is ridiculous.

It's not as if I'm asking you to break the Official Secrets Act or anything. I just want to know if my friends are there and, if so, how badly they're injured. Who are you, anyway?"

"Constable Parker, miss. If you've any complaints you'd better take them up with Chief Inspector Banks at Eastvale CID Headquarters."

"Chief Inspector Banks? CID?" Mara repeated slowly. She remembered the name. He was the one who had visited the farm before, when Liz was there. "Why? I don't understand. What's going on? I only want to know if my friends are hurt."

"Sorry, miss. Orders. Tell me your name and I'll see what I can do."

Mara hung up. Something was very wrong. She'd done enough damage already by mentioning Seth and Rick. The police would surely take special note of their names and push them even harder than the rest. There was nothing to do but wait and worry. Frowning, she opened the door and walked back into the rain.

IV

"Feel like a broke-down engine, ain't got no drivin' wheel," sang Blind Willie McTell.

"I know exactly what you mean, mate," Banks mumbled to himself as he poured a shot of Laphroaig single-malt, an indulgence he could scarcely afford. It was almost two in the morning and the interrogations had produced no results so far. Tired, Banks had left the others to it and come home for a few hours' sleep. He felt he deserved it. *They* hadn't had to spend the morning in court, the afternoon on a wild-goose chase after a stolen tractor, and the evening listening to the Hon Honoria, who would no doubt by now be sleeping the sleep

of the truly virtuous before heading back, with great relief, down south in the morning.

Banks put his feet up, lit a cigarette and warmed the
glass in his palm. Suddenly the doorbell rang. He
jumped to his feet and cursed as he spilled a little valuable Scotch on his shirt front. Rubbing it with the heel
of his hand, he walked into the hall and opened the door
a few inches on the chain.

It was Jenny Fuller, the psychologist he had met and
worked with on his first case in Eastvale. More than that,
he had to admit; there had been a mutual attraction between them. Nothing had come of it, of course, and
Jenny had even become good friends with Sandra. The
three of them had often been out together. But the attraction remained, unresolved. Things like that didn't
seem to go away as easily as they arrived.

"Jenny?" He slipped off the chain and opened the
door wider.

"I know. It's two o'clock in the morning and you're
wondering what I'm doing at your door."

"Something like that. I assume it's not just my irre-
sistible charm?"

Jenny smiled. The laugh lines around her green eyes
crinkled. But the smile was forced and short-lived.

"What is it?" Banks asked.

"Dennis Osmond."

"Who?"

"A friend. He's in trouble."

"Boy-friend?"

"Yes, boy-friend." Jenny blushed. "Or would you prefer beau? Lover? Significant other? Look, can I come
in? It's cold and raining out here."

Banks moved aside. "Yes, of course. I'm sorry. Have
a drink?"

"I will, if you don't mind." Jenny walked into the
front room, took off her green silk scarf and shook her
red hair. The muted trumpet wailed and Sara Martin
sang "Death Sting Me Blues."

"What happened to opera?" Jenny asked.

Banks poured her a shot of Laphroaig. "There's a lot of music in the world," he said. "I want to listen to as much as I can before I shuffle off this mortal coil."

"Does that include heavy metal and middle-of-the-road?"

Banks scowled. "Dennis Osmond. What about him?"

"Ooh, touchy, aren't we?" Jenny raised her eyes to the ceiling and lowered her voice. "By the way, I hope I haven't disturbed Sandra or the children?"

Banks explained their absence. "It was all a bit sudden," he added, to fill the silence that followed, which seemed somehow more weighty than it should. Jenny expressed her sympathy and shifted in her seat. She took a deep breath. "Dennis was arrested during that demonstration tonight. He managed to get in a phone call to me from the police station. He's not come back yet. I've just been there and the man on the desk told me you'd left. They wouldn't tell me anything about the prisoners at all. What's going on?"

"Where hasn't he come back to?"

"My place."

"Do you live together?"

Jenny's eyes hardened and drilled into him like emerald laser beams. "That's none of your damn business." She drank some more Scotch. "As a matter of fact, no, we don't. He was going to come round and tell me about the demonstration. It should have been all over hours ago."

"You weren't there yourself?"

"Are you interrogating me?"

"No. Just asking."

"I believe in the cause—I mean, I'm against nuclear power and American missile bases—but I don't see any point standing in the rain in front of Eastvale Community Centre."

"I see." Banks smiled. "It *was* a nasty night, wasn't it?"

"And there's no need to be such a cynic. I had work to do."

"It was a pretty bad night inside, too."

Jenny raised her eyebrows. "The Hon Hon?"

"Indeed."

"You were there?"

"I had that dubious honour, yes. Duty."

"You poor man. It might have been worth a black eye to get out of that."

"I take it you haven't heard the news, then?"

"What news?"

"A policeman was killed at that peaceful little demonstration tonight. Not a local chap, but one of us, nonetheless."

"Is that why Dennis is still at the station?"

"We're still questioning people, yes. It's serious, Jenny. I haven't seen Dennis Osmond, never even heard of him. But they won't let him go till they've got his statement, and we're not giving out any information to members of the public yet. It doesn't mean he's under suspicion or anything, just that he hasn't been questioned yet."

"And then?"

"They'll let him go. If all's well you'll still have some of the night left together."

Jenny lowered her head for a moment, then glared at him again. "You're being a bastard, you know," she said. "I don't like being teased that way."

"What do you want me to do?" Banks asked. "Why did you come?"

"I . . . I just wanted to find out what happened."

"Are you sure you're not trying to get him special treatment?"

Jenny sighed. "Alan, we're friends, aren't we?"

Banks nodded.

"Well," she went on, "I know you can't help being a policeman, but if you don't know where your job ends and your friendships begin . . . Need I go on?"

Banks rubbed his bristly chin. "No. I'm sorry. It's been a rough night. But you still haven't answered my question."

"I'd just hoped to get some idea of what might have happened to him, that's all. I got the impression that if I'd lingered a moment longer down at the station they'd have had me in for questioning, too. I didn't know about the death. I suppose that changes things?"

"Of course it does. It means we've got a cop killer on the loose. I'm sure it's nothing to do with your Dennis, but he'll have to answer the same questions as the rest. I can't say exactly how long he'll be. At least you know he's not in hospital. Plenty of people are."

"I can't believe it, Alan. I can understand tempers getting frayed, fists flying, but not a killing. What happened?"

"He was stabbed. It was deliberate; there's no getting around that."

Jenny shook her head.

"Sorry I can't be any more help," Banks said. "What was Dennis's involvement with the demo?"

"He was one of the organizers, along with the Students Union and those people from Maggie's Farm."

"That place up near Relton?"

"That's it. The local women's group was involved, too."

"WEEF? Dorothy Wycombe?"

Jenny nodded. Banks had come up against the Women of Eastvale for Emancipation and Freedom before—Dorothy Wycombe in particular—and it gave him a sinking feeling to realize that he might have to deal with them again.

"I still can't believe it," Jenny went on. "Dennis told me time and time again that the last thing they wanted was a violent confrontation."

"I don't suppose anybody wanted it, but these things have a way of getting out of hand. Look, why don't you go home? I'm sure he'll be back soon. He won't be mistreated. We don't suddenly turn into vicious goons when things like this happen."

"*You* might not," said Jenny. "But I've heard how you close ranks."

"Don't worry."

Jenny finished her drink. "All right. I can see you're trying to get rid of me."

"Not at all. Have another Scotch if you want."

Jenny hesitated. "No," she said finally. "I was only teasing. You're right. It's late. I'd better get back home." She picked up her scarf. "It was good, though. The Scotch. So rich you could chew it."

Banks walked her to the door. "If there are any problems," he said, "let me know. And I could do with your help, too. You seem to know a bit about what went on behind the scenes."

Jenny nodded and fastened her scarf.

"Maybe you could come to dinner?" Banks suggested on impulse. "Try my gourmet cooking?"

Jenny smiled and shook her head. "I don't think so."

"Why not? It's not that bad. At least—"

"It's just . . . it wouldn't seem right with Sandra away, that's all. The neighbours . . ."

"Okay. We'll go out. How does the Royal Oak in Lyndgarth suit you?"

"It'll do fine," Jenny said. "Give me a call."

"I will."

She pecked him on the cheek and he watched her walk down the path and get into her Metro. They waved to each other as she set off, then he closed his door on the wet, chilly night. He picked up the Scotch bottle and pulled the cork, thought for a moment, pushed it back and went upstairs to bed.

THREE

I

COP KILLED IN DALES DEATH-DEMO, screamed
the tabloid headlines the next morning. As he glanced
at them over coffee and a cigarette in his office, Banks
wondered why the reporter hadn't gone the whole hog
and spelled cop with a "k."

He put the paper aside and walked over to the window. The market square looked dreary and desolate in
the grey March light, and Banks fancied he could detect
a shell-shocked atmosphere hovering around the place.
Shoppers shuffled along with their heads hung low and
glanced covertly at the site of the demonstration as they
passed, as if they expected to see armed guards wearing
gas masks, and tear-gas drifting in the air. North Market
Street was still roped off. The four officers sent from
York had arrived at about four in the morning to help
the local men search the area, but they had found no
murder weapon. Now, they were trying again in what
daylight there was.

Banks looked at the calendar on his wall. It was
March 17, St Patrick's Day. The illustration showed the
ruins of St Mary's Abbey in York. Judging by the sunshine and the happy tourists, it had probably been taken
in July. On the real March 17, his small space-heater
coughed and hiccupped as it struggled to take the chill
out of the air.

He turned back to the newspapers. The accounts varied a great deal. According to the left-wing press, the police had brutally attacked a peaceful crowd without provocation; the right-wing papers, however, maintained that a mob of unruly demonstrators had provoked the police into retaliation by throwing bottles and stones. In the more moderate newspapers, nobody seemed to know exactly what had happened, but the whole affair was said to be extremely unfortunate and regrettable.

At eight-thirty, Superintendent Gristhorpe, who had been up most of the night interviewing demonstrators and supervising the search, called Banks in. Banks stubbed out his cigarette—the super didn't approve of smoking—and wandered into the book-lined office. The shaded table-lamp on Gristhorpe's huge teak desk cast its warm glow on a foot-thick pile of statements.

"I've been talking to the Assistant Chief Constable," Gristhorpe said. "He's been on the phone to London and they're sending a man up this morning. I'm to cover the preliminary inquiry into the demo for the Police Complaints Authority." He rubbed his eyes. "Of course, someone'll no doubt accuse me of being biased and scrap the whole thing, but they want to be seen to be acting quickly."

"This man they're sending," Banks asked, "what's he going to do?"

"Handle the murder investigation. You'll be working with him, along with Hatchley and Richmond."

"Do you know who he is?"

Gristhorpe searched for the scrap of paper on his desk. "Yes . . . let me see . . . It's a Superintendent Burgess. He's attached to a squad dealing with politically sensitive crimes. Not exactly Special Branch, but not quite your regular CID, either. I'm not even sure we're allowed to know *what* he is. Some sort of political trouble-shooter, I suppose."

"Is that Superintendent Richard Burgess?" Banks asked.

"Yes. Why? Know him?"

"Bloody hell."

"Alan, you've gone pale. What's up?"

"Yes, I know him," Banks said. "Not well, but I worked with him a couple of times in London. He's about my age, but he's always been a step ahead."

"Ambitious?"

"Very. But it's not his ambition I mind so much," Banks went on. "He's slightly to the right of . . . Well, you name him and Burgess is to the right."

"Is he good, though?"

"He gets results."

"Isn't that what we need?"

"I suppose so. But he's a real bastard to work with."

"How?"

"Oh, he plays his cards close to his chest. Doesn't let the right hand know what the left hand's doing. He takes short cuts. People get hurt."

"You make him sound like he doesn't even have a left hand," Gristhorpe said.

Banks smiled. "We used to call him Dirty Dick Burgess."

"Why?"

"You'll find out. It's nothing to do with his sexual activities, I can tell you that. Though he did have a reputation as a fairly active stud-about-town."

"Anyway," Gristhorpe said, "he should be here around midday. He's taking the early Intercity to York. There's too long a wait between connections, so I'm sending Craig to meet him at the station there."

"Lucky Craig."

Gristhorpe frowned. Banks noticed the bags under his eyes. "Yes, well, make the best of it, Alan. If Superintendent Burgess steps out of line, I won't be far away. It's still our patch. By the way, Honoria Winstanley called before she left—at least one of her escorts did. Said all's well, apologized for his brusqueness last night and thanked you for handling things so smoothly."

"Wonders never cease."

"I've booked Burgess into the Castle Hotel on York Road. It's not quite as fancy or expensive as the Riverview, but then Burgess isn't an MP, is he?"

Banks nodded. "What about office space?"

"We're putting him in an interview room for the time being. At least there's a desk and a chair."

"He'll probably complain. People like Burgess get finicky about offices and titles."

"Let him," Gristhorpe said, gesturing around the room. "He's not getting this place."

"Any news from the hospital?"

"Nothing serious. Most of the injured have been sent home. Susan Gay's on sick-leave for the rest of the week."

"When you were going through the statements," Banks asked, "did you come across anything on a chap called Dennis Osmond?"

"The name rings a bell. Let me have a look." Gristhorpe leafed through the pile. "Yes, I thought so. Interviewed him myself. One of the last. Why?"

Banks explained about Jenny's visit.

"I took his statement and sent him home." Gristhorpe read through the sheet. "That's him. Belligerent young devil. Threatened to bring charges against the police, start an enquiry of his own. Hadn't seen anything, though. Or at least he didn't admit to it. According to records he's a CND member, active in the local anti-nuclear group. Amnesty International, too—and you know what Mrs Thatcher thinks of *them* these days. He's got connections with various other groups as well, including the International Socialists. I should imagine Superintendent Burgess will certainly want to talk to him."

"Hmmm." Banks wondered how Jenny would take that. Knowing both her and Burgess as he did, he could guarantee sparks would fly. "Did anything turn up in the statements?"

"Nobody witnessed the stabbing. Three people said

they thought they glimpsed a knife on the road during the scuffles. It must have got kicked about quite a bit. Nothing I've heard so far brings order out of chaos. The poor lighting didn't help, either. You know how badly that street is lit. Dorothy Wycombe's been pestering us about it for weeks. I keep putting her onto the council, but to no avail. She says it's an invitation to rape, especially with all those unlit side alleys, but the council says the gaslamps are good for the tourist business. Anyway, PC Gill was found just at the bottom of the Community Centre steps, for what that's worth. Maybe if we can find out the names of the people on the front line we'll get somewhere."

Banks went on to tell Gristhorpe what he'd discovered from Jenny about the other organizers.

"The Church for Peace group was involved, too," Gristhorpe added. "Did I hear you mention Maggie's Farm, that place near Relton?"

Banks nodded.

"Didn't we have some trouble with them a year or so ago?"

"Yes," Banks said. "But it was a storm in a teacup. They seemed a harmless enough bunch to me."

"What was it? A drug raid?"

"That's right. Nothing turned up, though. They must have had the foresight to hide it, if they had anything. We were acting on a tip from some hospital social workers. I think they were over-reacting."

"Anyway," Gristhorpe said, "that's about it. The rest of the people we picked up were just private citizens who were there because they feel strongly about nuclear power, or about government policy in general."

"So what do we do now?"

"You'd better look over these statements," Gristhorpe said, shoving the tower of paper towards Banks, "and wait for the great man. Sergeant Hatchley's still questioning those people in the flats overlooking the street. Not that there's much chance of anything there. They can't have seen more than a sea of heads. If only the bloody TV cameras had been there we'd have had it on video. Those buggers in the media are never around when you need them."

"Like policemen," Banks said with a grin.

The phone rang. Gristhorpe picked it up, listened to the message and turned back to Banks. "Sergeant Rowe says Dr Glendenning's on his way up. He's finished his preliminary examination. I think you'd better stay for this."

Banks smiled. "It's a rare honour indeed, the good doctor setting foot in here. I didn't know he paid house-calls."

"I heard that," said a gruff voice with a distinct Edinburgh accent behind him. "I hope it wasn't meant to be sarcastic."

The tall, white-haired doctor looked down sternly at Banks, blue eyes twinkling. His moustache was stained yellow with nicotine, and a cigarette hung from the corner of his mouth. He was wheezing after climbing the stairs.

"There's no smoking in here," Gristhorpe said. "You ought to know better; you're a doctor."

Glendenning grunted. "Then I'll go elsewhere."

"Come to my office," Banks said. "I could do with a fag myself."

"Fine, laddie. Lead the way."

"Bloody traitor." Gristhorpe sighed and followed them.

After they'd got coffee and an extra chair, the doctor began. "To put it in layman's terms," he said, "PC Gill was stabbed. The knife entered under the rib-cage and did enough damage to cause death from internal bleeding. The blade was at least five inches long, and it looks like it went in to the hilt. It was a single-edged blade with a very sharp point. Judging by the wound, I'd say it was some kind of flick-knife."

"Flick-knife?" echoed Banks.

"Aye, laddie. You know what a flick-knife is, don't you? They come in all shapes and sizes. Illegal here, of course, but easy enough to pick up on the continent. The cutting edge was extremely sharp, as was the point."

"What about blood?" Gristhorpe asked. "Nobody conveniently covered in Gill's type, I suppose?"

Dr Glendenning lit another Senior Service and shook his head. "No. I've checked the tests. And I'd have been very surprised if there had been," he said. "What most people don't realize is that unless you open a major vein or artery—the carotid or the jugular, for example— there's often very little external bleeding with knife wounds. I'd say in this case that there was hardly any, and what there was would've been mostly absorbed by the man's clothing. The slit closes behind the blade, you see—especially a thin one—and most of the bleeding is internal."

"Can you tell if it was a professional job?" Gristhorpe asked.

"I wouldn't care to speculate. It could have been, but it could just as easily have been a lucky strike. It was a right-handed up-thrust wound. With a blow like that on a dark night, I doubt that anybody would have noticed, unless they saw the blade flash, and there's not enough light for that on North Market Street. It would have looked more like a punch to the solar plexus than anything else, and from what I hear, there was plenty of that going on. Now if he'd raised his hand above his head and thrust downwards . . ."

"People aren't usually so obliging," Banks said.

"If we take into account the kind of knife used," Gristhorpe speculated, "it could easily have been a spontaneous act. Pros don't usually use flick-knives—they're street weapons."

"Aye, well," said Glendenning, standing to leave, "that's for you fellows to work out. I'll let you know if I find anything more at the post-mortem."

"Who identified the body?" Banks asked him.

"Sister. Pretty upset about it, too. A couple of your lads did the paperwork. Luckily, Gill didn't have a wife and kids." A quarter inch of ash fell onto the linoleum. Glendenning shook his head slowly. "Nasty business all round. Be seeing you."

When the doctor had left, Gristhorpe stood up and flapped his hand theatrically in front of his face. "Filthy bloody habit. I'm off back to my office where the air's clean. Does this Burgess fellow smoke, too?"

Banks smiled. "Cigars, if I remember right."

Gristhorpe swore.

II

Over the valley from Maggie's Farm, mist clung to the hillsides and limestone scars, draining them of all colour. Soon after breakfast, Seth disappeared into his workshop to finish restoring Jack Lippett's Welsh dresser; Rick did some shopping in Helmthorpe, then went to his studio in the converted barn to daub away at his latest painting; Zoe busied herself in her flat with Elsie Goodbody's natal chart; and Paul went for a long walk on the moors.

In the living-room, Mara kept an eye on Luna and Julian while she mended the tears in Seth's jacket. The children were playing with Lego bricks and she often glanced over, awed by the look of pure concentration on their faces as they built. Occasionally, an argument would break out, and Julian would complain that the slightly younger Luna wasn't doing things right. Then Luna would accuse him of being bossy. Mara would step in and give them her advice, healing the rift temporarily.

There was nothing to worry about really, Mara told herself as she sewed, but after what Seth and Rick had said about the dead policeman, she knew they could expect to come under close scrutiny. After all, they were different. While not political in the sense of belonging to any party, they certainly believed in protection of the environment. They had even allowed their house to be used as a base for planning the demo. It would only be a matter of time before the knock at the door. There was something else bothering Mara, too, hovering at the back of her mind, but she couldn't quite figure out what it was.

Seth and Rick had been tired and hungry when they got back just after two in the morning. Seth had been charged with threatening behaviour and Rick with obstructing a police officer. They hadn't much to add to what Mara had heard earlier except for the news of PC Gill's murder, which had soon spread around the police station.

In bed, Mara had tried to cheer Seth up, but he had been difficult to reach. Finally, he said he was tired and went to sleep. Mara had stayed awake listening to the rain for a long time and thinking just how often Seth seemed remote. She'd been living with him for two years now, but she hardly felt she knew him. She didn't even know if he really was asleep now or just pretending. He was a man of deep silences, as if he were carrying a great weight of sadness within him. Mara knew that his wife, Alison, had died tragically just before he bought the farm, but really she knew nothing else of his past.

How different from Rick he was, she thought. Rick had tragedy in his life, too—he was involved in a nasty custody suit with his ex-wife over Julian—but he was open and he let his feelings show, whereas Seth never said much. But Seth was strong, Mara thought—the kind of person everyone else looked up to as being really in command. And he loved her. She knew she had been foolish to feel such jealousy when Liz Dale had run away from the psychiatric hospital and come to stay. But Liz had been a close friend of Alison's and had known Seth for years; she was a part of his life that was shut off from Mara, and that hurt. Night after night Mara had lain awake listening to their muffled voices downstairs until the small hours, gripping the pillow tightly. It had been a difficult time, what with Liz, the plague of social workers and the police raid, but she could look back and laugh at the memory of her jealousy now.

As she sat and sewed, watching the children, Mara felt lucky to be alive. Most of the time these days she was happy; she wouldn't change things for the world. It had been a good life so far, though a confusing one at times. After her student days, she had thrown herself into life—travel, communal living, love affairs, drugs— all without a care in the world.

Then she had spent four years with the Resplendent Light Organization, culminating in nine long months in one of their ashrams, where all earnings were turned over to the group and freedom was severely limited. There were no movies, no evenings in the pub, no frivolous, chatty gatherings around the fire; there was very little laughter. Mara had soon come to feel trapped, and the whole episode had left her with a bitter taste in her mouth. She felt she had been cheated into wasting her time. There had been no love there, no special person to share life with. But that was all over now. She had Seth—a solid dependable man, however distant he could be—Paul, Zoe, Rick and, most important of all, the children. After wandering and searching for so long, she seemed at last to have found the stability she needed. She had come home.

Sometimes, though, she wondered what things would be like if her life had been more normal. She'd heard of business executives dropping out in the sixties: they took off their suits and ties, dropped LSD and headed for Woodstock. But sometimes Mara dreamed of dropping in. She had a good brain; she had got a first in English Literature at the University of Essex. At moments, she could see herself all crisp and efficient in a business suit, perhaps working in advertising, or standing in front of a blackboard reading Keats or Coleridge to a class of spellbound children.

But the fantasies never lasted long. She was thirty-eight years old, and jobs were hard to come by even for the qualified and experienced. All those opportunities had passed her by. She knew also that she would no more be able to work in the everyday world, with its furious pace, its petty demands and its money-grubbing mentality, than she would be able to join the armed forces. Her years on the fringes of society had distanced her from life inside the system. She didn't even know what people talked about at work these days. The new BMW? Holidays in the Caribbean? All she knew was what she read in the papers, where it seemed that people no longer lived their lives but had "life-styles" instead.

The closest she came to a normal middle-class existence was working in Elspeth's craft shop in Relton three days a week in exchange for the use of the pottery wheel and kiln in the back. But Elspeth was hardly an ordinary person; she was a kindly old silver-haired lesbian who had been living in Relton with her companion, Dottie, for over thirty years. She affected the tweedy look of a country matron, but the twinkle in her eyes told a different story. Mara loved both of them very much, but Dottie was rarely to be seen these days. She was ill—dying of cancer, Mara suspected—and Elspeth bore the burden with her typical gruff stoicism.

At twelve o'clock, Rick knocked and came in through the back door, interrupting Mara's wandering thoughts. He looked every inch the artist: beard, paint-stained smock and jeans, beer belly. His whole appearance cried out that he believed in himself and didn't give a damn what other people thought about him.

"All quiet on the western front?" he asked.

Mara nodded. She'd been half listening for the sound of a police car above the wind chimes. "They'll be here, though."

"It'll probably take them a while," Rick said. "There

were a lot of others involved. We might not be as important as we think we are."

He picked up Julian and whirled him around in the air. The child squealed with delight and wriggled as Rick rubbed his beard against his face. Zoe tapped at the door and came in from the barn to join them.

"Stop it, Daddy!" Julian screamed. "It tickles. Stop it!"

Rick put him down and mussed his hair. "What are you two building?" he asked.

"A space station," answered Luna seriously.

Mara looked at the jumble of Lego and smiled to herself. It didn't look like much of anything to her, but it was remarkable what children could do with their imaginations.

Rick laughed and turned to Zoe. "All right, kiddo?" he asked, slipping his arm around her thin shoulder. "What do the stars have to say today?"

Zoe smiled. She obviously adored Rick, Mara thought; otherwise she would never put up with being teased and treated like a youngster at the age of thirty-two. Could there be any chance of them getting together? she wondered. It would be good for the children.

"Elsie Goodbody's wasted as a housewife," said Zoe. "By the looks of her chart she should be in politics."

"She's in domestic politics," Rick said, "and that's even worse. Anyone for the pub?"

They usually all walked down to the Black Sheep on Saturday and Sunday lunchtimes. The landlord was good about the children as long as they kept quiet, and Zoe took along colouring books to occupy them. Mara fetched Seth from his workshop, Julian got up on his father's shoulders, and Luna held Zoe's hand as they walked out to the track.

"Just a minute, I'll catch you up," Mara said, dashing back into the house. She wanted to leave a note for Paul to tell him where they were: a formality, really, an affectionate gesture. But as she wrote and her mind turned back to him, she suddenly realized what had been nagging her all morning.

Last night, Paul's hand had been bleeding and he had put an Elastoplast on it. This morning, when he came down, the plaster had slipped off, probably when he was washing, and the base of his thumb was as smooth as ever. There was no sign of a cut at all.

Mara's heart beat fast as she hurried to catch up with the others.

III

"Detective Superintendent Burgess, sir," PC Craig said, then left.

The man who stood before them in Gristhorpe's office looked little different from the Burgess that Banks remembered. He wore a scuffed black leather sports jacket over an open-necked white shirt, and close-fitting navy-blue cords. The handsome face with its square determined jaw hadn't changed much, even if his slightly crooked teeth were a little more tobacco-stained. The pouches under his cynical grey eyes still suited him. His dark hair, short and combed back, was touched with grey at the temples, and by the look of it he still used Brylcreem. He was about six feet tall, well-built but filling out a bit, and looked as if he still played squash twice a week. The most striking thing about his appearance was his deep tan.

"Barbados," he said, catching their surprise. "I'd recommend it highly, especially at this time of year. Just got back when this business came up."

Gristhorpe introduced himself, then Burgess looked over at Banks and narrowed his eyes. "Banks, isn't it? I heard you'd been transferred. Looking a bit pasty-faced, aren't you? Not feeding you well up here?"

Banks forced a smile. It was typical of Burgess to

make the transfer sound like a punishment and a demotion. "We don't get much sun," he said.

Burgess looked towards the window. "So I see. If it's any consolation, it was pissing down in London when I left." He clapped his hands together sharply. "Where's the boozer, then? I'm starving. Didn't dare risk British Rail food. I could do with a pint, as well."

Gristhorpe excused himself, claiming a meeting with the Assistant Chief Commissioner, and Banks led Burgess over to the Queen's Arms.

"Not a bad-looking place," Burgess said, glancing around and taking in the spacious lounge with its dimpled copper-topped tables with black wrought-iron legs, and deep armchairs by the blazing fire. Then his eyes rested on the barmaid. "Yes. Not bad at all. Let's sit at the bar."

Some of the locals paused in their conversations to stare at them. They knew Banks already, and Burgess's accent still bore traces of his East End background. As right-wing as he was, he didn't come from the privileged school of Tories, Banks remembered. His father had been a barrow-boy, and Burgess had fought his way up from the bottom. Banks also knew that he felt little solidarity with those of his class who hadn't managed to do likewise. To the locals, he was obviously the London big-wig they'd been expecting after the previous night's events.

Banks and Burgess perched on the high stools. "What'll you have?" Burgess asked, taking a shiny black leather wallet from his inside pocket. "I'm buying."

"Thanks very much. I'll have a pint of Theakston's bitter."

"Food?"

"The hot-pot is usually good."

"I think I'll stick to plaice and chips," Burgess said. He ordered the food and drinks from the barmaid. "And a pint of Double Diamond for me, please, love." He lit a Tom Thumb cigar and poked it at Banks's glass.

"Can't stand that real ale stuff," he said, rubbing his stomach and grimacing. "Always gives me the runs. Ah, thank you, love. What's your name?"

"Glenys," the barmaid said. She gave him a coy smile with his change and turned to serve another customer.

"Nice," Burgess said. "Not exactly your buxom-barmaid type, but nice nonetheless. Lovely bum. A fiver says I'll bonk her before this business is over."

Banks wished he would try. The muscular man drying glasses at the far end of the bar was Glenys's husband, Cyril. "You're on," he said, shaking hands. Though how Burgess would prove it if he won, Banks had no idea. Perhaps he'd persuade Glenys to part with a pair of panties as a trophy? The most likely outcome, though, would be a black eye for Burgess and a fiver in Banks's pocket.

"So, I hear you had a riot on your hands last night."

"Not quite a riot," Banks said, "but bad enough."

"It shouldn't have been allowed."

"Sure. It's easy to say that from hindsight, but we'd no reason to expect trouble. A lot of people around here have sympathy with the cause and they don't usually kill policemen."

Burgess's eyes narrowed. "Including you? Sympathy with the cause?"

Banks shrugged. "Nobody wants any more air-base activity in the Dales, and I'm no great fan of nuclear power."

"A bloody Bolshy on the force, eh? No wonder they sent you up here. Like getting sent to Siberia, I'll bet?" He chuckled at his own joke, then sank about half a pint in one gulp. "What have you got so far, then?"

Banks told him about the statements they'd taken and the main groups involved in organizing the protest, including the people at Maggie's Farm. As he listened, Burgess sucked on his lower lip and tapped his cigar on the side of the blue ashtray. Every time Glenys walked by, his restless eyes followed her.

"Seventy-one names," he commented when Banks

had finished. "And you think there were over a hundred there. That's not a lot, is it?"

"It is in a murder investigation."

"Hmmm. Got anyone marked out for it?"

"Pardon?"

"Local trouble-maker, shit-stirrer. Let's be honest about this, Banks. It doesn't look like we'll get any physical evidence unless someone finds the knife. The odds are that whoever did it was one of the ones who got away. You might not even have his name on your list. I was just wondering who's your most likely suspect."

"We don't have any suspects yet."

"Oh, come on! No one with a record of political violence?"

"Only the local Conservative member."

"Very good," Burgess said, grinning. "Very good. It seems to me," he went on, "that there are two possibilities. One: it happened in the heat of the moment; someone lost his temper and lashed out with a knife. Or, two: it was a planned deliberate act to kill a copper, an act of terrorism calculated to cause chaos, to disrupt society."

"What about the knife?" Banks said. "The killer couldn't be sure of getting away, and we've found no traces of it in the area. I'd say that points more towards your first theory. Someone lost his temper and didn't stop to think of the consequences, then just got lucky."

Burgess finished his pint. "Not necessarily," he said. "They're kamikaze merchants, these bloody terrorists. They don't care if they get caught or not. Like you said, whoever it was just got lucky this time."

"It's possible, I suppose."

"But unlikely?"

"In Eastvale, yes. I told you, most of the people involved were fairly harmless; even the groups they belonged to have never been violent before."

"But you don't have everyone's name."

"No."

"Then that's something to work on. Sweat the ones you've got and get a full list."

"DC Richmond's working on it," Banks said, though he could hardly see Philip Richmond sweating anyone.

"Good." Burgess gestured to the barmaid. "Another two pints, Gladys, love," he called out.

"It's Glenys," she said, then she blushed and lowered her head to keep an eye on the pint she was pulling.

"Sorry, love, I'm still train-lagged. Have one for yourself, too, Glenys."

"Thank you very much." Glenys smiled shyly at him and took the money for a gin and tonic. "I'll have it later when we're not so busy, if you don't mind."

"As you will." Burgess treated her to a broad smile and winked. "Where were we?" he asked, returning to Banks.

"Names."

"Yes. You must have a list of local reds and what not? You know the kind I mean—anarchists, skinheads, bum-punchers, women's libbers, uppity niggers."

"Of course. We keep it on the back of a postage stamp."

"You mentioned three organizations earlier. What's WEEF?"

"Women of Eastvale for Emancipation and Freedom."

"Oh, very impressive. Touch of the Greenham Common women, eh?"

"Not really. They mostly stick to local issues like poor streetlighting and sexual discrimination in jobs."

"Still," Burgess said, "it's a start. Get your man—Richmond, is it?—to liaise with Special Branch on this. They've got extensive files on Bolshies everywhere. He can do it through the computer, if you've got one up here."

"We've got one."

"Good. Tell him to see me about access." Their food arrived, and Burgess poured salt and vinegar on his fish and chips. "We can set them against each other, for openers," he said. "Simple divide-and-conquer tactics. We tell those WEEF people that the Students Union has fingered them for the murder, and vice versa. That way if anyone does know anything they'll likely tell us out of anger at being dropped right in it. We need results, and we need them quick. This business can give us a chance to look good for once. We're always looking like the bad guys these days—especially since that bloody miners' strike. We need some good press for a change, and here's our chance. A copper's been killed—that gets us plenty of public sympathy for a start. If we can come up with some pinko terrorist we've got it made."

"I don't think setting the groups against each other will get us anywhere," Banks said. "They're just not that aggressive."

"Don't be so bloody negative, man. Remember, *somebody* knows who did it, even if it's only the killer. I'll get myself acclimatized this afternoon, and tomorrow"— Burgess clapped his hands and showered his plate with ash—"we'll swoop into action." He had a nasty habit of sitting or standing motionless for ages, then making a sudden jerky movement. Banks remembered how disconcerting it was from their previous meetings.

"Action?"

"Raids, visits, call them what you will. We're looking for documents, letters, anything that might give us a clue to what happened. Any trouble getting warrants up here?"

Banks shook his head.

Burgess speared a chip. "Nothing like a Sunday morning for a nice little raid, I always say. People have funny ideas about Sundays, you know. Especially churchy types. They're all comfortable and complacent after a nice little natter with the Almighty, and then they get pissed off as hell if something interrupts their routine. Best day for raids and interrogations, believe me. Just wait till they get their feet up with the Sunday papers.

You mentioned some drop-outs at a farm earlier, didn't you?"

"They're not drop-outs," Banks said. "They just try to be self-sufficient, keep to themselves. They call the place Maggie's Farm," he added. "It's the title of an old Bob Dylan song. I suppose it's a joke about Thatcher, too."

Burgess grinned. "At least they've got a sense of humour. They'll bloody need it before we're through. We'll pay them a visit, keep them on their toes. Bound to be drugs around, if nothing else. How about dividing up the raids? Any suggestions?"

Banks had no desire to tangle with Dorothy Wycombe again, and sending Sergeant Hatchley to WEEF headquarters would be like sending a bull into a china shop, as would sending Burgess up to Maggie's Farm. On the other hand, he thought, meeting Ms Wycombe might do Dirty Dick some good.

"I'll take the farm," he said. "Let Hatchley do the church group, Richmond the students, and you can handle WEEF. We can take a couple of uniformed men to do the searches while we ask the questions."

Burgess's eyes narrowed suspiciously, then he smiled and said, "Right, we're on."

He knows I'm setting him up, Banks thought, but he's willing to go along anyway. Cocky bastard.

Burgess washed down the last of his plaice and chips. "I'd like to stay for another," he said, "and feast my eyes more on the lovely Glenys, but duty calls. Let's hope we'll have plenty of reason to celebrate tomorrow lunch-time. Why don't you catch up on a bit of paperwork this afternoon? There's not a lot we can do yet. And maybe this evening you can show me some of these quaint village pubs I've read about in the tourist brochures?"

The prospect of a pub crawl with Dirty Dick Burgess, following hot on the heels of an evening with the Hon Honoria Winstanley, appealed to Banks about as much as a slap in the face with a wet fish, but he agreed politely. It was a job, after all, and Burgess was his senior officer. They'd be working together for a few days, probably, and it would do no harm to get on as good terms as possible. Make the best of it, Gristhorpe had said. And Banks did have a vague recollection that Burgess wasn't such bad company after a few jars.

Burgess slid off his chair and strode towards the door. "Bye, Glenys, love," he called out over his shoulder as he left. Banks noticed Cyril scowl and tighten his grip on the pump he was pulling.

Banks pushed his empty plate aside and lit a Silk Cut. He felt exhausted. Just listening to Burgess reminded him of everything he had hated about his days on the Met. But Burgess was right, of course: they were looking into a political murder, and the first logical step was to check out local activist groups.

It was the obvious relish with which the superintendent contemplated the task that irked Banks and reminded him so much of his London days. And he remembered Burgess's interrogation technique, probably learned from the Spanish Inquisition. There were hard times ahead for a few innocent people who simply happened to believe in nuclear disarmament and the future of the human race. Burgess was like a pit-bull terrier; he wouldn't let go until he got what he wanted.

Oh, for a nice English village murder, Banks wished, just like the ones in books: a closed group of five or six suspects, a dodgy will, and no hurry to solve the puzzle. No such luck. He drained his pint, stubbed out the cigarette and went back across the street to read more statements.

IV

Mara sipped at her half of mild without really tasting it. She couldn't seem to relax and enjoy the company as usual. Seth sat at the bar chatting with Larry Grafton about some old furniture the landlord had inherited from his great-grandmother, and Rick and Zoe were arguing about astrology. By the window, the children sat colouring quietly.

What did it mean? Mara wondered. When she had tackled Paul about the blood on his hand the previous evening, he had gone into the kitchen and put on a plaster without showing her the cut. Now, it turned out, there was no cut. So whose blood had it been?

Of course, she told herself, anything could have happened. He could have accidentally brushed against somebody who had been hurt in the demo, or even tried to help someone. But he had clearly run all the way home; when he had arrived he had been upset and out of breath. And if the explanation was an innocent one, why had he lied? Because that's what it came down to in the end. Instead of telling the simple truth, he had let her go on believing he was hurt, albeit not badly, and she couldn't come up with a convincing reason why he had done that.

"You're quiet today," Seth said, walking over with more drinks.

It's easy for you, she felt like saying. You can cover up your feelings and talk about hammers and planes and chisels and bevels and chamfering as if nothing has happened, but I don't have any small talk. Instead, she said, "It's nothing. I'm just a bit tired after last night, I suppose."

Seth took her hand. "Didn't you sleep well?"

No, Mara almost said, No I didn't bloody sleep well. I was waiting for you to share your feelings with me, but you never did. You never do. You can talk about work to any Tom, Dick and Harry, but not about anything else, not about anything important. But she didn't say any of that. She squeezed his hand, kissed him lightly and said she was all right. She knew she was just irritable, worried about Paul, and the mood would soon pass. No point starting a row.

Rick, his conversation with Zoe finished, turned to the others. Mara noticed streaks of orange and white paint in his beard. "They were all talking about the Eastvale demo," he said. "Plenty of tongues started clucking in the grocer's when I walked in."

"What did they think about it?" Mara asked.

Rick snorted. "They don't think. They're just like the sheep they raise. They're too frightened to come out with an opinion about anything for fear it'll be the wrong one. Oh, they worry about nuclear fall-out. Who doesn't? But that's about all they do, worry and whine. When push comes to shove they'll just put up with it like everything else and bury their heads in the ground. The wives are even worse. All they can do if anything upsets the nice, neat, comfortable little lives they've made for themselves is say tut-tut-tut, isn't it a shame."

The door creaked open and Paul walked in.

Mara watched the emaciated figure, fists bunched in his pockets, walk over to them. With his hollow, bony face, tattooed fingers, and the scars, needle-tracks and self-inflicted cigarette burns that Mara knew stretched all the way up his arms, Paul seemed a frightening figure. The only thing that softened his appearance was his hair-style. His blond hair was short at the back and sides but long on top, and the fringe kept slipping down over his eyes. He'd brush it back impatiently and scowl but never mention having it cut.

Mara couldn't help thinking about his background. Right from childhood, Paul's life had been rough and hard. He never said much about his real parents, but he'd told Mara about the emotionally cold foster home where he had been expected to show undying gratitude for every little thing they did for him. Finally, he had run away and lived a punk life on the streets, done whatever he'd had to to survive. It had been a life of hard drugs and violence and, eventually, jail. When they had met

him, he had been lost and looking for some kind of
anchor in life. She wondered just how much he really
had changed since he'd been with them.

Remembering the blood on his hand, the way he had
lied, and the murdered policeman, she began to feel
frightened. What would he do if she were to question
him? Was she living with a killer? And if she was, what
should she do about it?

As the conversation went on around her, Mara began
to feel herself drifting off on a chaotic spate of her own
thoughts. She could hear the sounds the others were
making, but not the words, the meaning. She thought of
confiding in Seth, but what if he took some kind of action? He might be hard on Paul, even drive him away.
He could be very stern and inflexible at times. She didn't
want her new family to split apart, imperfect as she knew
it was. It was all she had in the world.

No, she decided, she wouldn't tell anyone. Not yet.
She wouldn't make Paul feel as if they were ganging up
on him. The whole thing was probably ridiculous anyway. She was imagining things, filling her head with
stupid fears. Paul would never hurt her, she told herself,
never in a million years.

FOUR

I

Sunday morning dawned clear and cold. A brisk March wind blew, restoring the sun and the delicate colours of early spring to the lower hillsides. Women hung on to their hats and men clutched the lapels of their best suits as they struggled to church along Mortsett Lane in Relton. The police car, a white Fiesta Popular, with the official red and blue stripes on its sides, turned and made its way up the bumpy Roman road to Maggie's Farm. PC McDonald drove, with Craig silent beside him and Banks cramped in the back.

The view across the dale was superb. Banks could set Fortford on the valley bottom and Devraulx Abbey below Lyndgarth on the opposite slope. Behind them all, the northern daleside rose, baring along its snowy heights scars of exposed limestone that looked like rows of teeth gleaming in the light.

Banks felt refreshed after an evening at home reading *Madame Bovary*, followed by a good night's sleep. Luckily, Dirty Dick had phoned to cancel their pub crawl, claiming tiredness. Banks suspected he had decided to drop in at the Queen's Arms—just around the corner from his hotel—to work on Glenys, but Burgess looked relatively unscathed the next morning. He seemed tired, though, and his grey eyes were dull, like champagne that had lost its fizz. Banks wondered how he was getting on with Dorothy Wycombe.

As the car pulled onto the gravel outside the farm-house, someone glanced through the window. When Banks got out, he could hear the wind chimes jingling like a piece of experimental music, harmonizing strangely with the wind that whistled around his ears. He had forgotten how high on the moorland Maggie's Farm was.

His knock was answered by a tall, slender woman in her mid- to late-thirties wearing jeans and a rust-coloured jumper. Banks thought he remembered her from his previous visit. Her wavy chestnut hair tumbled over her shoulders, framing a pale, heart-shaped face, free of make-up. Perhaps her chin was a little too pointed and her nose a bit too long, but the whole effect was pleasing. Her clear brown eyes looked both innocent and knowing at once.

Banks presented his warrant and the woman moved aside wearily. They knew we were coming sometime, he thought; they've just been waiting to get it over with.

"They'd better not damage anything," she said, nodding towards McDonald and Craig.

"Don't worry, they won't. You won't even know they've been here."

Mara sniffed. "I'll get the others."

The two uniformed men started their search, and Banks sat in the rocking chair by the window. Turning his head sideways, he scanned the titles in the pine book-case beside him. They were mostly novels—Hardy, the Brontës, John Cowper Powys, Fay Weldon, Graham Greene—mixed in with a few more esoteric works, such as an introduction to Jung's psychology and a survey of the occult. On the lower shelves rested a number of older, well-thumbed paperbacks—*The Teachings of Don Juan, Naked Lunch, The Lord of the Rings*. In addition, there were the obligatory political texts: Marcuse, Fanon, Marx and Engels.

On the floor beside Banks lay a copy of George El-

iot's *The Mill on the Floss*. He picked it up. The book-
mark stood at the second page; that was about as far as
he'd ever got with George Eliot himself.

Mara came back from the barn with the others, three
of them vaguely familiar to Banks from eighteen months
ago: Zoe Hardacre, a slight, freckle-faced woman with
frizzy ginger hair and dark roots; Rick Trelawney, a big
bear of a man in a baggy paint-smeared T-shirt and torn
jeans; and Seth Cotton, in from his workshop, wearing
a sand-coloured lab coat, tall and thin with mournful
brown eyes and neatly trimmed dark hair and beard
framing a dark-complexioned face. Finally came a
skinny, hostile-looking youth Banks hadn't seen before.

"Who are you?" he asked.

"Paul's not been here long," Mara said quickly.

"What's your last name?"

Paul said nothing.

"He doesn't have to say," Mara argued. "He's done
nothing."

Seth shook his head. "Might as well tell him," he said
to Paul. "He'll find out anyway."

"He's right, you know," Banks said.

"It's Boyd, Paul Boyd."

"Ever been in trouble, Paul?"

Paul smiled. It was either that or a scowl, Banks
couldn't decide. "So what if I have? I'm not on probation or parole. I don't have to register at the local nick
everywhere I go, do I?" He fished for a cigarette in a
grubby ten-pack of Players. Banks noticed that his
stubby fingers were trembling slightly.

"Just like to know who we've got living among us,"
Banks said pleasantly. He didn't need to pursue the matter. If Boyd had a record, the Police National Computer
would provide all the information he wanted.

"So what's all this in aid of?" Rick said, leaning
against the mantelpiece. "As if I need ask."

"You know what happened on Friday night. You were
arrested for obstructing a police officer." Rick laughed.

Banks ignored him and went on. "You also know that a policeman was killed at that demonstration."

"Are you saying you think one of us did it?"

Banks shook his head. "Come on," he said, "you know the rules as well as I do. A situation like this comes up, we check out all political groups."

"We're not political," Mara said.

Banks looked around the room. "Don't be so naïve. Everything you have here, everything you say and do, makes a political statement. It doesn't matter whether or not any of you belong to an official party. You know that as well as I do. Besides, we've got to act on tips we get."

"What tip?" Rick asked. "Who's been talking?"

"Never mind that. We just heard you were involved, that's all." Burgess's trick seemed at least worth a try.

"So we were there," Rick said, "Seth and me. You already know that. We gave statements. We told you all we knew. Why come back pestering us now? What are you looking for?"

"Anything we can find."

"Look," Rick went on, "I still don't see why you're persecuting us. I can't imagine who's been telling you things or what they've been saying, but you're misinformed. Just because we employed our right to demonstrate for a cause we happen to believe in, it doesn't give you the right to come around with these Gestapo tactics and harass us."

"The Gestapo didn't need a search warrant."

Rick sneered and scratched his straggly beard. "With a JP like the one you've got in your pocket, I'd hardly consider that a valid argument."

"Besides," Banks went on, "we're not persecuting you or harassing you. Believe me, if we were, you'd know it. Do any of you remember anything else about Friday night?"

Seth and Rick shook their heads. Banks looked around at the others. "Come on, I'm assuming you were all

there. Don't worry, I can't prove it. I'm not going to
arrest you if you admit it. It's just that one of you might
have seen something important. This is a murder investigation."

Still silence. Banks sighed. "Fine. Don't blame me if
things do get rough. We've got a man up from London.
A specialist. Dirty Dick, his friends call him. He's a hell
of a lot nastier than I am."

"Is that some kind of threat?" Mara asked.

Banks shook his head. "I'm just letting you know
your options, that's all."

"How can we tell you we saw something if we
didn't?" Paul said angrily. "You say you know we were
there. Okay. Maybe we were. I'm not saying we were,
but maybe. That doesn't mean we saw anything or did
anything wrong. It's like Rick says, we had a right to
be there. It's not a fucking police state yet." He turned
away sullenly and drew on his cigarette.

"Nobody's denying your right to be there," Banks
said. "I just want to know if you saw anything that could
help us solve this murder."

Silence.

"Does anyone here own a flick-knife?"

Rick said no and the others shook their heads.

"Ever seen one around? Know anyone who does have
one?"

Again nothing. Banks thought he saw an expression
of surprise flit across Mara's face, but it could have been
a trick of the light.

In the following silence, Craig and McDonald came
downstairs, shook their heads and went to search the
outbuildings. Two small children walked in from the
kitchen and hurried over to Mara, each taking a hand.
Banks smiled at them, but they just stared at him, sucking their thumbs.

He tried to imagine Brian and Tracy, his own children, growing up under such conditions, isolated from
other children. For one thing, there didn't seem to be a

television in the place. Banks disapproved of TV in general, and he always tried to make sure that Brian and Tracy didn't watch too much, but if children saw none at all, they would have nothing to talk to their pals about. There had to be a compromise somewhere; you couldn't just ignore the blasted idiot-box in this day and age, much as you might wish you could.

On the other hand, these children certainly showed no signs of neglect, and there was no reason to assume that Rick and the rest weren't good parents. Seth Cotton, Banks knew, had a reputation as a fine carpenter, and Mara's pottery sold well locally. Sandra even had a piece, a shapely vase glazed in a mixture of shades: green, ultramarine and the like. He didn't know much about Rick Trelawney's paintings, but if the local landscape propped up by the fireplace was his, then he was good, too. No, he had no call to impose his own limited perspective on them. If the children grew up into creative, free-thinking adults, their minds unpolluted by TV and mass culture, what could be so wrong about that?

Apart from the sounds of the wind chimes, they sat in silence until Rick finally spoke. "Do you know," he said to Banks, "how many children come down with leukaemia and rare forms of cancer in areas around Sellafield and other nuclear-power stations? Do you have any idea?"

"Look," said Banks. "I'm not here to attack your views. You're entitled to them. I might even agree. The thing is, what happened on Friday night goes beyond all that. I'm not here to argue politics or philosophy; I'm investigating a murder. Why can't you get that into your heads?"

"Maybe they can't be as neatly separated as you think," Rick argued. "Politics, philosophy, murder—they're all connected. Look at Latin America, Israel, Nicaragua, South Africa. Besides, the police started it. They kept us penned in like animals, then they charged with their truncheons out, just like some Chilean goon squad. If some of them got hurt, too, they bloody well deserved it."

"One of them got killed. Is that all right?"

Rick turned away in disgust. "I never said I was a pacifist," he muttered, looking at Seth. "There'll be a local police inquiry," he went on, "and the whole thing'll be rigged. You can't expect us to believe there's going to be any objectivity about all this. When it comes to the crunch you bastards always stick together."

"Believe what you like," Banks said.

Craig and McDonald came back in through the kitchen. They'd found nothing. It was eleven o'clock. At twelve Banks was to meet Burgess, Hatchley and Richmond in the Queen's Arms to compare notes. There was nothing to be gained by staying to discuss nuclear ethics with Rick, so he stood up and walked over to the door.

As he held his jacket closed and pushed against the wind to the car, he felt someone staring at his back through the window. He knew he had sensed fear in the house. Not just fear of a police raid they'd been expecting, but something different. All was not as harmonious as it should have been. He filed away his uneasiness to be mulled over later along with the thousand other things—concrete or nebulous—that lodged themselves in his mind during an investigation.

II

"Nothing," Burgess growled, grinding out his cigar viciously in the ashtray at the centre of the copper-topped table. "Absolutely bugger all. And that woman's crazy. I'll swear I thought she was going to bite me."

For the first time ever, Banks felt a sudden rush of affection for Dorothy Wycombe.

All in all, though, the morning had been disappointing

for everyone. Not surprisingly, the searches had produced no murder weapon or documents attesting to the terrorist plot that Burgess suspected; none of the witnesses had changed their statements; and the reaction to Burgess's divide-and-conquer tactic had been negligible.

Sergeant Hatchley reported that the Church for Peace group seemed stunned by the murder and had even offered prayers for PC Gill in their service that morning. The Students Union, according to DC Richmond, who had visited the leaders—Tim Fenton and Abha Sutton—at their flat, thought it typical of the others to blame them for what happened, but insisted that assassination was not part of their programme for a peaceful revolution. While Burgess thought Dorothy Wycombe quite capable of murder—especially of a member of the male species—she had stuck to her guns and ridiculed any such suggestion.

"So it's back to square one," Hatchley said. "A hundred suspects and not one scrap of evidence."

"I did find out from one of the lads on duty," said Richmond, "that Dorothy Wycombe, Dennis Osmond and some of the people from Maggie's Farm were close to the front at one time. But he said everything went haywire when the fighting started. He also said he noticed a punkish-looking kid with them."

"That'd be Paul Boyd," Banks said. "He seems to live up at the farm, too. Run him through the computer, will you, Phil, and see what comes up. I wouldn't be surprised if he's done time. While you're at it, find out what you can about the lot of them up there. I've got a funny feeling that something's not quite right about that place."

He glanced at Burgess, who seemed to be staring abstractedly over at Glenys. Her husband was nowhere in sight.

"Maybe we should have a look into Gill's background," Banks suggested.

Burgess turned. "Why?"

"Someone might have had a reason for wanting him

dead. We'll get nowhere on means and opportunity unless the knife turns up, but if we could find a motive—"

Burgess shook his head. "Not in a crime like this. Whether it was planned or spur-of-the-moment, the victim was random. It could have happened to any of the coppers on duty that night. It was just poor Gill's bad luck, that's all."

"But still," Banks insisted, "it's something we can do. Maybe the demo was just used as a cover."

"No. It'll look bad, for a start. What if the papers find out we're investigating one of our own? We've got enough trouble already with an enquiry into the whole bloody mess. That'd give the press enough ammo to take a few cheap shots at us without us making things easier for them. Jesus, there's enough weirdos and commies to investigate already without bringing a good copper into it. What about this Osmond character? Anyone talked to him yet?"

"No," said Banks. "Not since Friday night."

"Right, this is what we'll do. Get another round in, Constable, would you?" Burgess handed Richmond a fiver.

Richmond nodded and went to the bar. Burgess had switched from Double Diamond to double Scotch, claiming it was easier on his stomach, but Banks thought he was just trying to impress Glenys with his largesse. And now he was showing her he was too important to leave the conference and that he had the power to order others to do things for him. Good tactics, but would they work on her?

"You and I, Banks," he said, "will pay this Osmond fellow a visit this afternoon. DC Richmond can check up on those drop-outs you went to see and feed a few more names into the PNC. Sergeant Hatchley here can start making files on the leaders of the various groups involved. We want every statement cross-checked with the others for inaccuracies, and all further statements checked against the originals. Someone's going to slip up at some point, and we're going to catch the bugger at it. Bottoms up." He drank his Scotch and turned to wink at Glenys. "By the way," he said to Banks, "that bloody office you gave me isn't big enough to swing a dead cat in. Any chance of another?"

Banks shook his head. "Sorry, we're pushed for space. It's either that or the cells."

"What about yours?"

"Too small for two."

"I was meaning for one. Me."

"Forget it. I've got all my files and records in there. Besides, it's cold and the blind doesn't work."

"Hmmm. Still . . ."

"You could do most of the paperwork in your hotel room," Banks suggested. "It's close enough, big enough, and there's a phone." And you'll be out of my way, too, he thought.

Burgess nodded slowly. "All right. It'll do for now. Come on!" He jumped into action and clapped Banks on the back. "Let's see if anything's turned up at the station first, then we'll set off and have a chat with Mr Dennis Osmond, CND."

Nothing had turned up, and as soon as Richmond had located Paul Boyd's record and Banks had had a quick look at it, the pair set off for Osmond's flat in Banks's white Cortina.

"Tell me about this Boyd character," Burgess asked as Banks drove.

"Nasty piece of work." Banks slipped a Billie Holiday cassette in the stereo and turned the volume down low. "He started as a juvenile—gang fights, assault, that kind of thing—skipping school and hanging around the streets with the rest of the dead-beats. He's been nicked four times, and he drew eighteen months on the last one. First it was drunk and disorderly, underage, then assaulting a police officer trying to disperse a bunch of punks frightening shoppers in Liverpool city centre. After that it was a drugs charge, possession of a small amount of amphetamines. Then he got nicked breaking into a chemist's to steal pills. He's been clean for just over a year now."

Burgess rubbed his chin. "Everything short of soccer hooliganism, eh? Maybe he's not the sporting type. Assaulting a police officer, you say?"

"Yes. Him and a couple of others. They didn't do any real damage, so they got off lightly."

"That's the bloody trouble," Burgess said. "Most of them do. Any political connections?"

"None that we know of so far. Richmond hasn't been onto the Branch yet, so we haven't been able to check on his friends and acquaintances."

"Anything else?"

"Not really. Most of his probation officers and social workers seemed to give up on him."

"My heart bleeds for the poor bastard. It looks like we've got a likely candidate. This Osmond is a social worker, isn't he?"

"Yes."

"Maybe he'll know something about the kid. Let's remember to ask him. Where's Boyd from?"

"Liverpool."

"Any IRA connections?"

"Not as far as we know."

"Still . . ."

Dennis Osmond lived in a one-bedroom flat in northeast Eastvale. It had originally been council-owned, but the tenants had seized their chance and bought their units cheaply when the government started selling them off.

A shirtless Osmond answered the door and led Banks and Burgess inside. He was tall and slim with a hairy chest and a small tattoo of a butterfly on his upper right arm. He wore a gold crucifix on a chain around his neck. With his shaggy dark hair and Mediterranean good looks, he looked the kind of man who would be attractive to women. He moved slowly and calmly, and didn't seem at all surprised by their arrival.

The flat had a spacious living-room with a large plate-glass window that overlooked the fertile plain to the east of Swainsdale: a checkerboard of ploughed fields, bordered by hedgerows, rich brown, ready for spring. The furniture was modern—tubes and cushions—and a large framed painting hung on the wall over the fake fireplace. Banks had to look very closely to make sure the canvas wasn't blank; it was scored with faint red and black lines.

"Who is it?" A woman's voice came from behind them. Banks turned and saw Jenny Fuller poking her head around a door. From what he could tell, she was wearing a loose dressing-gown, and her hair was in disarray. His eyes caught hers and he felt his stomach tense up and his chest tighten. Meeting her in a situation like this was something he hadn't expected. He was surprised how hard it hit.

"Police," Osmond said. But Jenny had already turned back and shut the door behind her.

Burgess, who had watched all this, made no comment. "Can we sit down?" he asked.

"Go ahead." Osmond gestured to the armchairs and pulled a black T-shirt over his head while they made themselves as comfortable as possible. The decal on the front showed the CND symbol—a circle with a widespread, inverted Y inside it, each branch touching the circumference—with NO NUKES written in a crescent under it.

Banks fumbled for a cigarette and looked around for an ashtray.

"I'd rather you didn't," Osmond said. "Second-hand smoke can kill, you know." He paused and looked Banks over. "So you're Chief Inspector Banks, are you? I've heard a lot about you."

"Hope it was good," Banks said, with more equilibrium than he felt. What had Jenny been telling him? "It'll save us time getting acquainted, won't it?"

"And you're the whiz-kid they sent up from London," Osmond said to Burgess.

"My, my. How word travels." Dirty Dick smiled. He had the kind of smile that made most people feel nervous, but it seemed to have no effect on Osmond. As Banks settled into the chair, he could picture Jenny dressing in the other room. It was probably the bedroom, he thought gloomily, and the double bed would be rumpled and stained, the *Sunday Times* review section spread out over the creased sheets. He took out his notebook and settled down as best he could for the interrogation.

"What do you want?" Osmond asked, perching at the edge of the sofa and leaning forward.

"I hear you were one of the organizers of Friday's demonstration," Burgess opened.

"So what if I was?"

"And you're a member of the Campaign for Nuclear Disarmament and the International Socialists, if I'm not mistaken."

"I'm in Amnesty International, as well, in case you don't have that in your file. And as far as I'm aware it's not a crime yet."

"Don't be so touchy."

"Look, can you get to the point? I haven't got all day."

"Oh yes, you have," Burgess said. "And you've got all night, too, if I want it like that."

"You've no right—"

"I've every right. One of your lot—maybe even you—killed a good, honest copper on Friday night, and we don't like that; we don't like it at all. I'm sorry if we're keeping you from your fancy woman, but that's the way it is. Whose idea was it?"

Osmond frowned. "Whose idea was what? And I don't like you calling Jenny names like that."

"You don't?" Burgess narrowed his eyes. "There'll be a lot worse names than that flying around, sonny, if you don't start to co-operate. Whose idea was the demonstration?"

"I don't know. It just sort of came together."

Burgess sighed. " 'It just sort of came together,' " he repeated mockingly, looking at Banks. "Now what's that supposed to mean? Men and women come together, if they're lucky, but not political demonstrations—they're planned. What are you trying to tell me?"

"Exactly what I said. There are plenty of people around here opposed to nuclear arms, you know."

"Are you telling me that you all just happened to meet outside the Community Centre that night? Is that what you're trying to say? 'Hello, Fred, fancy meeting you here. Let's have a demo.' Is that what you're saying?"

Osmond shrugged.

"Well, balls is what I say, Osmond. Balls to that. This was an organized demonstration, and that means somebody organized it. That somebody might have also arranged for a little killing to spice things up a bit. Now, so far the only somebody we know about for sure is you. Maybe you did it all by yourself, but I'm betting you had some help. Whose tune do you dance to, Mr Osmond? Moscow's? Peking's? Or is it Belfast?"

Osmond laughed. "You've got your politics a bit mixed up, haven't you? A socialist is hardly the same as a Maoist. Besides, the Chairman's out of favour these days. And as for the IRA, you can't seriously believe—"

"I seriously believe a lot of things that might surprise you," Burgess cut in. "And you can spare me the fucking lecture. Who gave you your orders?"

"You're wrong," Osmond said. "It wasn't like that at all. And even if there was somebody else involved, do you think I'm going to tell you who it was?"

"Yes, I do," Burgess said. "There's nothing more certain. The only question is when you're going to tell me, and where."

"Look," Banks said, "we'll find out anyway. There's no need to take it on yourself to carry the burden and get done for withholding information in a murder investigation. If you didn't do it and you don't think your mates did, either, then you've nothing to worry about, have you?" Banks found it easy to play the nice guy to Burgess's heavy, even though he felt a strong, instinctive dislike for Osmond. When he questioned suspects with Sergeant Hatchley, the two of them switched roles. But Burgess only had one method of approach: head on.

"Listen to him," Burgess said. "He's right."

"Why don't you find out from someone else, then?" Osmond said to Banks. "I'm damned if I'm telling you anything."

"Do you own a flick-knife?" Burgess asked.

"No."

"Have you ever owned one?"

"No."

"Know anybody who does?"

Osmond shook his head.

"Did you know PC Gill?" Banks asked. "Had you any contact with him before last Friday?"

Osmond looked puzzled by the question, and when he finally answered no, it didn't ring true. Or maybe he was just thrown off balance. Burgess didn't seem to notice anything, but Banks made a mental note to check into the possibility that Osmond and Gill had somehow come into contact.

The bedroom door opened and Jenny walked out. She'd brushed her hair and put on a pair of jeans and an oversized plaid shirt. Banks bet it belonged to Osmond and tried not to think about what had been going on earlier in the bedroom.

"Hello, love," Burgess said, patting an empty chair beside him. "Come to join us? What's your name?"

"In the first place," Jenny said stiffly, "I'm not 'love,' and in the second, I don't see as my name's any of your damn business. I wasn't even there on Friday."

"As you like," Burgess said. "Just trying to be friendly."

Jenny glanced at Banks as if to ask, "Who is this bastard?" and Burgess caught the exchange.

"Do you two know each other?" he asked.

Banks cursed inwardly and felt himself turning red. There was no way out. "This is Dr Fuller," he said. "She helped us on a case here a year or so back."

Burgess beamed at Jenny. "I see. Well, maybe you can help us again, Dr Fuller. Your boy-friend here doesn't want to talk to us, but if you've helped the police before—"

"Leave her alone," Osmond said. "She had nothing to do with it." Banks had felt the same thing—he didn't want Burgess getting his claws into Jenny—and he resented Osmond for being able to defend her.

"Very prickly today, aren't we?" Burgess said. "All right, sonny, we'll get back to you, if that's the way you want it." But he kept looking at Jenny, and Banks knew he was filing her away for future use. Banks now found it hard to look her in the eye himself. He was only a chief inspector and Burgess was a superintendent. When things were going his way, Burgess wouldn't pull rank, but if Banks let any of his special feeling for Jenny show, or tried in any way to protect her, then Burgess would certainly want to humiliate him. Besides, she had her knight in shining armour in the form of Osmond. Let him take the flack.

"What were you charged with on Friday?" Burgess asked.

"You know damn well what I was charged with. It was a trumped-up charge."

"But what was it? Tell me. Say it. Just to humour me." Burgess reached into his pocket and took out his tin of Tom Thumbs. Holding Osmond's eyes with his own all the time, he slowly took out a cigar and lit it.

"I said I don't want you smoking in here," Osmond protested on cue. "It's my home and—"

"Shut up," Burgess said, just loudly enough to stop him in his tracks. "What was the charge?"

"Breach of the peace," Osmond mumbled. "But I told you, it was trumped up. If anyone broke the peace, it was the police."

"Ever heard of a lad by the name of Paul Boyd?" Banks asked.

"No." It was a foolish lie. Osmond had answered before he'd had time to register the question. Banks would have known he was lying even if he hadn't already learned, via Jenny, that Osmond was acquainted with the people at Maggie's Farm.

"Look," Osmond went on, "I'm starting an inquiry of my own into what happened on Friday. I'll be taking statements, and believe me, I'll make sure your behaviour here today goes into the final report."

"Bully for you," said Burgess. Then he shook his head slowly. "You don't get it, do you, sonny? You might be able to pull those outraged-citizen tactics with the locals, but they won't wash with me. Do you know why not?"

Osmond scowled and kept silent.

"I said, do you know why not?"

"All right, no, I don't bloody well know why not!"

"Because I don't give a flying fuck for you or for others like you," Burgess said, stabbing the air with his cigar. "As far as I'm concerned, you're shit, and we'd all be a hell of a lot better off without you. And the people I work with, they feel the same way. It doesn't matter if Chief Inspector Banks here has the hots for your Dr Fuller and wants to go easy on her. It doesn't matter that he's got a social conscience and respects people's rights, either. I don't, and my bosses don't. We don't piss around, we get things done, and you'd do well to remember that, both of you."

Jenny was flushed and speechless with rage; Banks himself felt pale and impotent. He should have known that nothing would slip by Burgess.

"I can't tell you anything," Osmond repeated wearily. "Why can't you believe me? I don't know who killed that policeman. I didn't see it, I didn't do it, and I don't know who did."

A long silence followed. At least it seemed long to Banks, who was aware only of the pounding of his heart. Finally Burgess stood up and walked over to the window, where he stubbed out his cigar on the white sill. Then he turned and smiled. Osmond gripped the tubular arms of his chair tightly.

"Okay," Burgess said, turning to Banks. "We'll be off, then, for the moment. Sorry to spoil your afternoon in bed. You can get back to it now, if you like." He looked at Jenny and licked his lips. "That's a fetching shirt you've got on, love," he said to her. "But you didn't need to leave it half-unbuttoned just for me. I've got plenty of imagination."

Back in the car, Banks was fuming. "You were way out of line in there," he said. "There was no reason to insult Jenny, and there was especially no need to bring me into it the way you did. What the hell were you trying to achieve?"

"Just trying to stir them up a bit, that's all."

"So how does making me out to be a bloody lecher stir them up?"

"You're not thinking clearly, Banks. We make Osmond jealous, maybe he lets his guard down." Burgess grinned. "Anyway, there's nothing in it, is there, you and her?"

"Of course there isn't."

"Methinks this fellow doth protest too much."

"Fuck off."

"Oh, come on," Burgess said calmly. "Don't take it so seriously. You use what you need to get results. Christ, I don't blame you. I wouldn't mind tumbling her, myself. Lovely pair of tits under that shirt. Did you see?"

Banks took a deep breath and reached for a cigarette. There was no point, he realized, in going on. Burgess was an unstoppable force. However angry and disoriented Banks felt, it would do no good to let more of it show. Instead, he put his emotions in check, something he knew he should have done right from the start. But the feelings still rankled as they knotted up below the surface. He was mad at Burgess, he was mad at Osmond, he was mad at Jenny, and he was mad, most of all, at himself.

Starting the car with a lurch, he shoved the cassette back in and turned up the volume. Billie Holiday sang "God Bless the Child," and Burgess whistled blithely along as they sped through the bright, blustery March day back to the market square.

III

They were all a bit drunk, and that was unusual at Maggie's Farm. Mara certainly hadn't been so tipsy for a long time. Rick was sketching them as they sat around the living-room. Paul drank lager from the can, and even Zoe had turned giggly on white wine. But Seth was the worst. His speech was slurred, his eyes were watery, and his co-ordination was askew. He was also getting maudlin about the sixties, something he never did when he was sober. Mara had seen him drunk only once before, the time he had let slip about the death of his wife. Mostly, he was well-guarded and got on with life without moaning.

Things had begun well enough. After the police visit, they had all walked down to the Black Sheep for a drink. Perhaps the feeling of relief, of celebration, had encouraged them to drink more than usual, and they had splurged on a few cans of Carlsberg Special Brew, some white wine and a bottle of Scotch to take home. Most of the afternoon Seth and Mara had lounged about over the papers or dozed by the fire, while Paul messed about in the shed, Rick painted in his studio, and Zoe amused the children. Early in the evening they all got together, and the whisky and wine started making the rounds.

Seth stumbled over to the stereo and sought out a scratchy old Grateful Dead record from his collection. "Those were the days," he said. "All gone now. All people care about today is money. Bloody yuppies."

Rick looked up from his sketch-pad and laughed. "When was it ever any different?"

"Isle of Wight, Knebworth . . ." Seth went on, listing the rock festivals he'd been to. "People really shared back then. . . ."

Mara listened to him ramble. They had been under a lot of stress since the demo, she thought, and this was clearly Seth's way of getting it out of his system. It was easy to fall under the spell of nostalgia. She remembered the sixties, too—or more accurately the late sixties, when the hippie era had really got going in England. Things *had* seemed better back then. Simpler. More clear-cut. There was us and them, and you knew *them* by the shortness of their hair.

". . . Santana, Janis, Hendrix, the Doors. Jesus, even the Hare Krishnas were fun back then. Now they all wear bloody business suits and wigs. I remember one time—"

"It's all crap!" Paul shouted, banging his empty can on the floor. "It was never like that. It's just a load of cobblers you're talking, Seth."

"How would you know?" Seth sat up and balanced unsteadily on his elbow. "You weren't there, were you? You were nought but a twinkle in your old man's eye."

"My mum and dad were hippies," Paul said scornfully. "Fucking flower children. She OD'd, and he was too bloody stoned to take care of me, so he gave me away."

Mara was stunned. Paul had never spoken about his true parents before, only about the way he had been badly treated in his foster home. If it was true, she thought, did he really see Seth and her in the same light? They were about the right age. Did he hate them, too?

But she couldn't believe that. There was another side to the coin. Maybe Paul was looking for what he had lost, and he had found at least some of it at Maggie's Farm. They didn't take drugs and, while she and Seth might have grown up in the sixties and tried to cling on to some of its ideals, they neither looked nor acted like hippies any longer.

"We're not like that," she protested, looking over at Zoe for support. "You know it, Paul. We care about you. We'd never desert you. It was fun back then for a lot of people. Seth's only reminiscing about his youth."

"I know," Paul said grudgingly. "I can't say I had one worth reminiscing about, myself. Anyway, I'm only saying, Mara, that's all. It wasn't all peace and love like Seth tells it. He's full of shit."

"You're right about that, mate," Rick agreed, putting down his sketch-pad and pouring another shot of Scotch. "I never did have much time for hippies myself. Nothing but a moaning, whining bunch of little kids, if you ask me. Seth's just pissed, that's all. Look at him now, anyway—he's a bloody landowner, a landlord even. Pretty soon it'll be baggy tweeds and out shooting pheasant every afternoon. Sir Seth Cotton, Squire of Maggie's Farm."

But Seth had slumped back against a beanbag and seemed to have lost all interest in the conversation. His eyes were closed, and Mara guessed that he was either asleep or absorbed in the soaring Jerry Garcia guitar solo.

"Where's your father now?" Mara asked Paul.

"I don't fucking know. Don't fucking care, either." Paul ripped open another can of lager.

"But didn't he ever get in touch?"

"Why should he? I told you, he was too zonked out to notice me even when I was there."

"It's still no reason to say everyone was like that," Mara said. "All Seth was saying was that the spirit of love was strong back then. All that talk about the Age of Aquarius meant something."

"Yeah, and what's happened to it now? Two thousand years of this crap I can do without, thanks very much. Let's just forget the fucking past and get on with life." With that, Paul got up and left the room.

Jerry Garcia played on. Seth stirred, opened one blood-shot eye, then closed it again.

Mara poured herself and Zoe some more white wine, then her mind wandered back to Paul. As if she weren't confused enough already, the hostility he'd shown to-night and the new information about his feelings for his parents muddied the waters even more. She was scared of approaching him about the blood on his hand, and she was beginning to feel frightened to go on living in the same house as someone she suspected of murder. But she hated herself for feeling that way about him, for not being able to trust him completely and believe in him.

What she needed was somebody to talk to, somebody she could trust from outside the house. She felt like a woman with a breast lump who was afraid to go to the doctor and find out if it really was cancer.

And what made it worse was that she'd noticed the knife was missing: the flick-knife Seth said he had bought in France years ago. Everybody else must have noticed, too, but no one had mentioned it. The knife had been lying on the mantelpiece for anyone to use ever since she'd been at Maggie's Farm, and now it was gone.

IV

Banks ate the fish and chips he had bought on the way home, then went into the living-room. Screw gourmet cooking, he thought. If that irritating neighbour, Selena

Harcourt, didn't turn up with some sticky dessert to feed him up "while the little woman's away," he'd have the evening to relax instead of mixing up sauces that never turned out anyway.

He had calmed down soon after leaving Burgess at the station. The bastard had been right. What had happened at Osmond's, he realized, had not been particularly serious, but his shock at finding Jenny there had made him exaggerate things. His reaction had been extreme, and for a few moments, he'd lost his detachment. That was all. It had happened before and it would happen again. Not the end of the world.

He poured a drink, put his feet up and turned on the television. There was a special about the Peak District on Yorkshire TV. Half-watching, he flipped through Tracy's latest copy of *History Today* and read an interesting article on Sir Titus Salt, who had built a Utopian community called Saltaire, near Bradford, for the workers in his textile mills. It would be a good place to visit with Sandra and the kids, he thought. Sandra could take photographs; Tracy would be fascinated; and surely even Brian would find something of interest. The problem was that Sir Titus had been a firm teetotaller. There were no pubs in Saltaire. Obviously one man's Utopia is another man's Hell.

The article made him think of Maggie's Farm. He liked the place and respected Seth and Mara. They had shown antagonism towards him, but that was only to be expected. In his job, he was used to much worse. He didn't take it personally. Being a policeman was like being a vicar in some ways; people could never be really comfortable with you, even when you dropped into the local for a pint.

The TV programme finished, and he decided there was no point putting off the inevitable. Picking up the phone, he dialled Jenny's number. He was in luck; she answered on the third ring.

"Jenny? It's Alan."

There was a pause at the other end. "I'm not sure I want to talk to you," she said finally.

"Could you be persuaded to?"

"Try."

"I just wanted to apologize for this afternoon. I hadn't expected to see you there."

Only the slight crackle of the line filled the silence. "It surprised me, too," Jenny said. "You keep some pretty bad company."

I could say the same for you, too, Banks thought. "Yes," he said, "I know."

"I do think you should keep him on a leash in future. You could maybe try a muzzle on him as well." She was obviously warming to him again, he could tell.

"Love to. But he's the boss. How did Osmond take it?" The name almost stuck in his throat.

"He was pissed off, all right. But it didn't last. Dennis is resilient. He's used to police harassment."

There was silence again, more awkward this time.

"Well," Banks said, "I just wanted to say I was sorry."

"Yes. You've said that already. It wasn't your fault. I'm not used to seeing you in a supporting role. You're not at your best like that, you know."

"What did you expect me to do? Jump up and hit him?"

"No, I didn't mean anything like that. But when he said what he did about us I could see you were ready to."

"Was it so obvious?"

"It was to me."

"I blew up at him in the car."

"I thought you would. What did he say?"

"Just laughed it off."

"Charming. I could have killed him when he said that about my shirt being undone."

"It was, though."

"I dressed in a hurry. I wanted to know what was going on."

"I know. I'm not trying to make out you did it on purpose or anything. It's just that, well, with a bloke like him around you've got to be extra careful."

"Now I know. Though I hope I won't have the pleasure again."

"He doesn't give up easily," Banks said gloomily.

"Nor do I. Where are you? What are you doing?"

"At home. Relaxing."

"Me, too. Is Sandra back?"

"No." The silence crackled again. Banks cleared his throat. "Look," he said, "when I mentioned dinner the other day, before all this, I meant it. How about tomorrow?"

"Can't tomorrow. I've got an evening class to teach."

"Tuesday?"

Jenny paused. "I suppose I can break my date," she said. "It had better be worth it, though."

"The Royal Oak is always worth it. My treat. I need to talk to you."

"Business?"

"I'm hoping you can help me get a handle on some of those Maggie's Farm people. Seth and Mara are about my age. It's funny how we all grew up in the sixties and turned out so different."

"Not really. Everybody's different."

"I liked the music. I just never felt I fit in with the long-haired crowd. Mind you, I did try pot once or twice."

"Alan! You didn't?"

"I did."

"And here's me thinking you're so strait-laced. What happened?"

"Nothing, the first time."

"And the second?"

"I fell asleep."

Jenny laughed.

"Still," Banks mused, "Burgess is about my age, too."

"He was probably sitting around in jackboots and a

leather overcoat pulling the wings off flies."

"Probably. Anyway, dinner. Eight o'clock all right?"

"Fine."

"I'll pick you up."

Jenny said good night and hung up. Still friends. Banks breathed a sigh of relief.

He went back to his armchair and his drink, but he suddenly felt the need to call Sandra.

"How's your father?" he asked.

Sandra laughed. "Cantankerous as ever. But mother's coping better than I'd hoped." The line was poor and her voice sounded far-away.

"How much longer will you be down there?"

"A few more days should do it. Why? Are you missing us?"

"More than you know."

"Hang on a minute. We had a day in London yesterday and Tracy wants to tell you about it."

Banks talked to his daughter for a while about St. Paul's and the Tower of London, then Brian cut in and told him how great the record shops were down there. There was exactly the guitar he'd been looking for. . . . Finally, Sandra came back on again.

"Anything happening up there?"

"You could say that." Banks told her about the demo and the killing.

Sandra whistled. "I'm glad I'm out of it. I can imagine how frantic things are."

"Thanks for the support."

"You know what I mean."

"Remember Dick Burgess? Used to be a chief inspector at the Yard?"

"Was he the one who pawed the hostess and threw up in the geraniums at Lottie's party?"

"That's the one. He's up here, in charge."

"God help you. Now I'm really glad I'm down here. He had his eyes on me, too, you know, if not his hands."

"I'd like to say it was good taste, but don't flatter

yourself, love. He's like that with everyone in a skirt."

Sandra laughed. "Better go now. Brian and Tracy are at it again."

"Give them my love. Take care. See you soon."

After he'd hung up, Banks felt so depressed that he almost regretted phoning in the first place. Why, he wondered, does a phone call to a distant loved one only intensify the emptiness and loneliness you were feeling before you called?

At a loose end, he turned off the television in the middle of a pop-music special that Brian would have loved and put on the blues tape an old colleague had sent him from London. The Reverend Robert Wilkins sang "Prodigal Son" in his eerie voice, unusually thin and high-pitched for a bluesman. Banks slouched in the armchair by the gas fire and sipped his drink. He often did his best thinking while drinking Scotch and listening to music, and it was time to put some of his thoughts about Gill's murder in order.

A number of things bothered him. There were demonstrations all the time, much bigger than the one in Eastvale, and while opposing sides sometimes came to blows, policemen didn't usually get stabbed. Call it statistics, probability, or just a hunch, but he didn't believe in Burgess's view of the affair.

And that was a problem, because it didn't leave much else to choose from. He still had uneasy feelings about some of the Maggie's Farm crowd. Paul Boyd was a dangerous character if ever he'd met one, and Mara had seemed extremely keen to come to his defense. Seth and Zoe had been especially quiet, but Rick Trelawney had expressed more violent views than Banks had expected. He didn't know what it added up to, but he felt that somebody knew something, or thought they did, and didn't want to communicate their suspicions to the police. It was a stupid way to behave, but people did it all the time. Banks just hoped that none of them got hurt.

As for Dennis Osmond, putting personal antipathy

aside, Banks had caught him on two lies. Osmond had said he didn't know Paul Boyd, when he clearly did, and Banks had also suspected him of lying when he denied knowing PC Gill. It was easy enough to see why he might have lied: nobody wants to admit a connection with a murdered man or a convicted criminal if he doesn't have to. But Banks had to determine if there was anything more sinister to it than that. How could Osmond have known PC Gill? Maybe they'd been to school together. Or perhaps Gill had had occasion to arrest Osmond at some previous anti-nuclear protest. If so, it should be on the files. Richmond would have the gen from Special Branch in the morning.

Nothing so far seemed much like a motive for murder, though. If he was really cautious, he might be able to get something out of Jenny on Tuesday. She didn't usually resent his trying to question her, but she was bound to be especially sensitive where Osmond was concerned.

Perhaps he had reacted unprofessionally on finding Jenny in Osmond's bedroom and to Burgess's approach to interrogation. But, he reminded himself, Dirty Dick had made him look a proper wally, and what was more, he had insulted Jenny. Sometimes Banks thought that Burgess's technique was to badger everyone involved in a case until someone was driven to try to throttle him. At least then he could lay a charge of attempted murder.

Halfway through his third Laphroaig and the second side of the tape, Banks decided that there was only one way to get back at the bastard, and that was to solve the case himself, in his own way. Burgess wasn't the only one who could play his cards close to his chest. Let him concentrate on the reds under the bed. Banks would do a bit of discreet digging and see if he could come up with anyone who had a motive for wanting PC Edwin Gill, and not just any copper, dead.

But if Gill the person rather than Gill the policeman was the victim, it raised a number of problems. For a start, how could the killer know that Gill was going to be at the demo? Also, how could he be sure that things would turn violent enough to mask a kill? Most puzzling of all was how could he have been certain of an escape? But at least these were concrete questions, a starting point. The more Banks thought about it, the more the thick of a political demonstration seemed the ideal cover for murder.

FIVE

I

The funeral procession wound its way from Gordon Street, where Edwin Gill had lived, along Manor Road to the cemetery. Somehow, Banks thought, the funeral of a fellow officer was always more solemn and grim than any other. Every policeman there knew that it could just as easily have been him in the coffin; every copper's wife lived with the fear that her husband, too, might end up stabbed, beaten or, these days, shot; and the public at large felt the tremor and momentary weakness in the order of things.

For the second time in less than a week, Banks found himself uncomfortable in a suit and tie. He listened to the vicar's eulogy, the obligatory verses from the *Book of Common Prayer*, and stared at the bristly necks in front of him. At the front, Gill's immediate family— mother, two sisters, uncles and aunts, nephews and nieces—snuffled and slipped each other wads of Kleenex.

When it was over, everyone filed out and waited for the cars to take them to the funeral lunch. The oaks and beeches lining the cemetery drive shook in the brisk wind. One moment the sun popped out from behind the clouds, and the next, a five-minute shower took everyone by surprise. It was that kind of day: chameleon, unpredictable.

Banks stood with DC Richmond by the unmarked black police Rover—his own white Cortina was hardly the thing for a funeral—and waited for someone to lead the way. He wore a light grey raincoat over his navy-blue suit, but his head was bare. With his close-cropped black hair, scar beside the right eye, and lean, angular features, he thought he must look a suspicious figure as he held his raincoat collar tight around his throat to keep out the cold wind. Richmond, rangy and athletic, wearing a camel-hair overcoat and trilby, stood beside him.

It was early Tuesday afternoon. Banks had spent the morning reading over the records Richmond had managed to gather on Osmond and the Maggie's Farm crowd. There wasn't much. Seth Cotton had once been arrested for carrying an offensive weapon (a bicycle chain) at a mods-and-rockers debacle in Brighton in the early sixties. After that, he had one marijuana bust to his credit—only a quid deal, nothing serious—for which he had been fined.

Rick Trelawney had been in trouble only once, in St Ives, Cornwall. A tourist had taken exception to his drunken pronouncements on the perfidy of collecting art, and a rowdy argument turned into a punch-up. It had taken three men to drag Rick off, and the tourist had ended up with a broken jaw and one permanently deaf ear.

The only other skeleton in Rick's cupboard was the wife from whom he had recently separated. She was an alcoholic, which made it easy enough for Rick to get custody of Julian. But she was now staying with her sister in London while undergoing treatment, and there was a legal battle brewing. Things had got so bad at one point that Rick had applied for a court order to prevent her from coming near their son.

There was nothing on Zoe, but Richmond had checked the birth registry and discovered that the father of her child, Luna, was one Lyle Greenberg, an American student who had since returned to his home in Eau Claire, Wisconsin.

On Mara there was even less. Immigration identified her as Moira Delacey, originally from Dublin. With her parents, she had come to England at the age of six, and they had settled in Manchester. No known Republican connections.

Most interesting and disturbing of all was Dennis Osmond's criminal record. In addition to arrests for his part in anti-government demonstrations—with charges ranging from breach of the peace to theft of a police officer's helmet—he had also been accused of assault by a live-in-girl-friend called Ellen Ventner four years ago. At the woman's insistence, the charges had later been dropped, but Ventner's injuries—two broken ribs, a broken nose, three teeth knocked out and concussion—had been clearly documented by the hospital, and Osmond came out of the affair looking far from clean. Banks wasn't sure whether to bring up the subject when he met Jenny for dinner that evening. He wondered if she already knew. If she didn't she might not take kindly to his interference. Somehow, he doubted that Osmond had told her.

They were still waiting for the information from Special Branch, who had files on Osmond, Tim Fenton, the student leader, and five others known to have been at the demo. Apparently, the Branch needed Burgess's personal access code, password, voice-print and genetic fingerprint, or some equally ludicrous sequence of identification. Banks didn't expect much from them, anyway. In his own experience, Special Branch kept files on everyone who had ever bought a copy of *Socialist Weekly*.

Today, while Banks and Richmond were attending Gill's funeral, Burgess was taking Sergeant Hatchley to do the rounds again. They intended to revisit Osmond, Dorothy Wycombe, Tim Fenton and Maggie's Farm. Banks wanted to talk to the students himself, so he de-

cided to call on them when he got back that evening—
if Burgess hadn't alienated them beyond all communi-
cation by then.

Burgess had been practically salivating at the prospect
of more interrogations, and even Hatchley had seemed
more excited about work than usual. Perhaps it was the
chance to work with a superstar that thrilled him, Banks
thought. The sergeant had always found "The Sweeney"
much more interesting than the real thing. Or maybe he
was going to suck up to Dirty Dick in the hope of being
chosen for some special Scotland Yard squad. And the
devil of it was, perhaps he would be, too.

Banks had mixed feelings about that possibility. He
had got used to Sergeant Hatchley sooner than he'd expected to, and they had worked quite well together. But
Banks had no real feeling for him. He couldn't even
bring himself to call Hatchley by his first name, Jim.

In Banks's mind, Hatchley was a sergeant and always
would be. He didn't have that extra keen edge needed
to make inspector. Phil Richmond did, but unfortunately
there wasn't anywhere for him to move up to locally
unless Hatchley was promoted, too. Superintendent Gristhorpe wouldn't have that, and Banks didn't blame him.
If Burgess liked Hatchley enough to suggest a job in
London, that would solve all their problems. Richmond
had already passed his sergeant's exams—the first stage
on the long road to promotion—and perhaps PC Susan
Gay, who had shown remarkable aptitude for detective
work, could be transferred in from the uniformed branch
as a new detective constable. PC Craig would be opposed, of course. He still called policewomen "wopsies,"
even though the gender-specific designation, WPC, had
been dropped in favour of the neutral PC as far back as
1975. But that was Craig's problem; Hatchley was
everyone's cross to bear.

Finally, the glossy black cars set off. Banks and Richmond followed them through the dull, deserted streets
of Scarborough to the reception. There was nowhere

quite as gloomy as a coastal resort in the off-season. If it hadn't been for the vague whiff of sea and fish in the air, nobody would have guessed they were at the seaside.

"Fancy a walk on the prom after lunch?" Banks asked.

Richmond sniffed. "Hardly the weather for that, is it?"

"Bracing, I'd say."

"Maybe I'll wait for you in a nice cosy pub, if you don't mind, sir."

Banks smiled. "And put your notes in order?" He knew how fussy Richmond was about notes and reports.

"I'll have to, won't I? It'll not stick in my memory that long."

On the way to Scarborough, Banks had put forward his theory about Gill's murder not being quite what it seemed. While Richmond had expressed reservations, he had agreed that it was at least worth pursuing. They had decided to chat up Gill's colleagues at the reception and see what they could pick up about the man. Burgess, of course, was to know nothing about this.

Richmond had argued that even if there was something odd about Gill, none of his mates would say so at his funeral. Banks disagreed. He thought funerals worked wonders on the conscience. The phony platitudes often stuck in people's craws and made them want to tell someone the truth. After all, it wasn't as if they were trying to prove corruption or anything like that against Gill; they just wanted to know what kind of man he was and whether he might have made enemies.

The procession pulled into the car park of the Crown and Anchor, where a buffet had been arranged in the banquet room, and the guests hurried through a heavy shower to the front doors.

II

"Bloody hell! What stone did you crawl out from under?" Burgess said when Paul Boyd walked into the front room to see what was going on.

Paul scowled. "Piss off."

Burgess strode forward and clipped him around the ear. Paul flinched and stumbled back. "Less of your cheek, sonny," Burgess said. "Show a bit of respect for your elders and betters."

"Why should I? You didn't show any fucking respect for me, did you?"

"Respect? For you?" Burgess narrowed his eyes. "What makes you think you deserve any respect? You're an ugly little pillock with a record as long as my arm. And that includes assaulting a police officer. And while we're at it, mind your tongue. There's ladies present. At least, I think there are."

Mara felt cold as Burgess ran his eyes up and down her body.

Burgess turned back to Paul, who stood in the doorway holding his hand to his ear. "Come on, who put you up to it?"

"Up to what?"

"Killing a police officer."

"I never. I wasn't even there."

"It's true, he wasn't," Mara burst out. "He was here with me all evening. Somebody had to stay home and look after the children."

She had held her tongue so far, trying to figure Burgess out. He didn't seem as mild-mannered as Banks, and she was afraid of attracting his attention. Even as she spoke, her stomach muscles tensed.

Burgess looked at her again and shook his head. His eyes were as sharp as chipped slate. "Very touching, love. Very touching. Didn't your mother and father teach you not to tell lies? He was spotted in the crowd. We know he was there."

"You must have been mistaken."

Burgess glanced at Paul, then looked at Mara again. "Mistaken! How could anyone mistake this piece of garbage for someone else? You need your mouth washing out with soap and water, you do, love."

"And don't call me love."

Burgess threw up his arms in mock despair. "What's wrong with you lot? I thought everyone called each other love up north. Anyway, I can't for the life of me see why you're defending him. He's got a limited vocabulary, and with a body like that, I doubt if he's much good in bed."

"Bastard," Mara said between clenched teeth. There was going to be no reasoning with this one, that was certain. Best just stick it out.

"That's right, love," Burgess said. "Get it off your chest. You'll feel all the better for it." He eyed her chest, as if to prove his point, and turned to Paul again. "What did you do with the knife?"

"What knife?"

"The one you used to stab PC Gill. The flick-knife. Just your kind of weapon, I'd say."

"I didn't stab anyone."

"Oh, come on! What did you do with it?"

"I didn't have no fucking knife."

Burgess wagged a finger at him. "I warned you, watch your tongue. Are you getting all this, Sergeant Hatchley? The kid's denying everything."

"Yes, sir." Hatchley was sitting on the beanbag cushions, looking, Mara thought, rather like a beached whale.

"All we need is the knife," Burgess said. "Once we trace it back to you, you'll be in the nick before your feet can touch the ground. With your record, you won't have a chance. We've already placed you at the scene."

"There were about a hundred other people there, too," Paul said.

"Count them, did you? I thought you said you weren't there."

"I wasn't."

"Then how did you know?"

"Read it in the papers."

"Read? You? I doubt you'd get past the comics."

"Very funny," Paul said. "But you can't prove nothing."

"You might just be right about that," Burgess said. "But remember, if I can't prove nothing, it means I *can* prove something. And when I do . . . when I do . . ." He left the threat hanging and turned to the room at large. They were all gathered in the house except Rick, who had taken the children to town for new clothes. "The rest of you are just as guilty," he went on. "When we build a case against dick-head here, you'll all get done for withholding information and for being accessories. So if any of you know anything, you'd best tell us now. Think about it."

"We don't know anything," Seth said quietly.

"Well, there we are then." Burgess sighed and ran his free hand through his hair. "Stalemate."

"And don't think we won't complain about the way you've treated us and how you hit Paul," Mara said.

"Do it, love. See if I care. Want me to tell you what'll happen? If you're lucky, it'll get passed down the line back to my boss at the Yard. And do you know what? He's an even bigger bastard than I am. No, your best bet's to come clean, tell the truth."

"I told you," Paul said. "I don't know anything about it."

"All right." Burgess dropped his cigar stub into a tea-cup balanced on the arm of a chair. The hot ash sizzled as it hit the dregs. "But don't say I didn't warn you. Come on, Sergeant. We'll leave these people to think about it a bit more. Maybe one of them'll come to his senses and get in touch with us."

Hatchley struggled to his feet and joined Burgess by the door. "We'll be back, don't worry," Burgess said. As they walked out of the small porch, he reached up, slapped the wind chimes and snarled, "Bloody tuneless racket."

III

Banks waited, glass of sherry in hand, until the crowd around the buffet had dwindled before he collected his own paper plateful of cold cuts and salad.

"Ee, it's a bit of all right, this, i'n't it," a grey-haired woman in a powder-blue crepe dress was saying to her friend.

"Aye," the other said. "Better'n old Ida Latham's do. Nobbut them little sarnies wi' t'crusts cut off. No bigger'n a postage stamp they weren't. Cucumber, too. It allus gives me gas, cucumber does."

"Chief inspector Banks?"

The man who suddenly materialized beside Banks was about six-two with a shiny bald head, fuzzy white hair above the ears, and a grey RAF moustache. He wore a black armband over his dark grey suit, and a black tie. Even the rims of his glasses were black. Banks nodded.

"Thought it must be you," the man went on. "You don't look like a relation, and I've never seen you around here before. Superintendent Gristhorpe sent word you were coming." He stretched out his hand. "Detective Chief Inspector Blake, Scarborough CID." Banks managed to balance his sherry glass on his plate and shake hands.

"Pleased to meet you," he said. "Shame it has to be at something like this."

They walked over to a quieter and less crowded part of the hall. Banks put down his plate on a table—after all, he couldn't eat while talking—and took out a cigarette.

"How's the investigation going?" Blake asked.

"Nothing yet. Too many suspects. Anything could

have happened in a situation like that." He looked around the hall. "Lot of people here. PC Gill must have been a popular bloke."

"Hmmm. Didn't know him well, myself. It's a big station."

"Keen, though," Banks said. "Volunteering for over-time on a Friday night. Most of our lads would've rather been at the pub."

"It's more likely he needed the money. You know how half the bloody country lives on overtime. Has to, the wages we get paid."

"True. Fond of money, was he?"

Chief Inspector Blake frowned. "Are you digging?"

"We don't know anything about Gill," Banks admit-ted. "He wasn't one of ours. Every little bit helps. I'm sure you know that."

"Yes. But this is hardly a normal case, is it?"

"Still . . ."

"As I said, I didn't really know him. I hear you've got a whiz-kid from the Yard in charge."

Banks stubbed out his cigarette and picked up his plate. He knew he wasn't going to get anything out of Blake, so he ate his lunch while exchanging small talk. From the corner of his eye, he noticed Richmond talking to one of the uniformed pallbearers, probably one of the locals who had been bussed in with Gill to the demo. They had all given statements, of course, but none had seen Gill get stabbed. He hoped that Richmond was do-ing better than he was.

Chief Inspector Blake drifted away after about five minutes, and Banks took the opportunity to refill his sherry glass. At the bar, he found himself standing next to another pallbearer.

Banks introduced himself. "Sad occasion," he said.

"Aye," PC Childers replied. He was young, perhaps in his early twenties. Banks felt irritated by his habit of looking in another direction while speaking.

"Popular bloke, PC Gill, by the look of it," Banks said.

"Oh, aye. A right card, old Eddie was."

"That right? Keen on his work?"

"You could say that. Certain parts of it, anyway."

"I'll bet the overtime came in handy."

"It's always good to have a bit extra," Childers said slowly. Banks could tell he was holding back; whether out of friendship, a sense of occasion, or out of simple duty, he couldn't be sure. But something was wrong. Childers was getting edgier, staring at the far wall. Finally, he excused himself abruptly and went to talk to his sergeant.

Banks was beginning to feel his mission had been wasted. He was also aware that very soon he would become an unwelcome guest if Childers and Blake mentioned his probings to others. Christ, he thought, they were a bloody sensitive lot here. It made him wonder if they'd got something to hide.

Back at the table for a helping of trifle, Banks manoeuvred himself next to a third pallbearer, a moon-faced lad with bright blue eyes and fine, thinning hair the colour of wheat. Taking a deep breath, he smiled and introduced himself.

"I know who you are, sir," the PC said. "Ernie Childers told me. I'm PC Grant, Tony Grant. Ernie warned me. Said you were asking questions about Eddie Gill."

"Just routine," Banks said. "Like we do in all murder investigations."

Grant glanced over his shoulder. "Look, sir," he said, "I can't talk to you here."

"Where, then?" Banks felt his heart speed up.

"Do you know the Angel's Trumpet?"

Banks shook his head. "Don't know the place well. Only been here once before."

"It'll take too long to explain," Grant said. They finished helping themselves to dessert and turned around just in time to spot one of Grant's colleagues walking towards them.

"Marine Drive, then, just round from the fun-fair," Banks said quickly out of the corner of his mouth. It was the only place he could think of offhand. "About an hour."

"Fine," Grant said as a uniformed sergeant joined them.

"Good of you to come, Chief Inspector," the sergeant said, holding out his hand. "We appreciate it."

Grant had merged back into the crowd, and as Banks exchanged trivialities with the sergeant, his mind was on the meeting ahead, and the nervous, covert way in which it had been arranged.

IV

"He made me feel dirty," Mara said to Seth. "The way he looked at me."

"Don't let it get to you. That's just his technique. He's trying to goad you into saying something you'll regret."

"But what about Paul? You saw the way he was picking on him. What can we do?"

Paul had taken off as soon as Burgess and Hatchley left. He had said he was feeling claustrophobic and needed a walk on the moors to calm down after the onslaught. He hadn't objected to Zoe's company, so Seth and Mara were left alone.

"What is there to do?" Seth said.

"But you saw the way that bastard went at him. I wouldn't put it past him to frame Paul if it came down to it. He *has* got a record."

"They'd still need evidence."

"He could plant it."

"He couldn't just plant any old knife. It'd have to be the one that fitted the wound. They have scientists work-

ing for them. You can't put things across on that lot so
easily, you know."

"I suppose not." Mara bit her lip and decided to take
the plunge. "Seth? Have you noticed that the knife's
missing? That old flick-knife from the mantelpiece."

Seth looked at her in silence for a while. His brown
eyes were sad, and the bags under them indicated lack
of sleep. "Yes," he said, "I have. But I didn't say anything. I didn't want to cause any alarm. It'll probably
turn up."

"But what if . . . what if that was the knife?"

"Oh come on, Mara, surely you can't believe that.
There are plenty of flick-knives in the country. Why
should it be that one? Somebody's probably borrowed
it. It'll turn up."

"Yes. But what if? I mean, Paul could have taken it,
couldn't he?"

Seth drummed his fingers on the chair arm. "You
know how many people were around on Friday afternoon," he said. "Any one of them could have taken it.
When did you last notice it, for example?"

"I don't remember."

"See? And it still doesn't mean it was the knife that
was used. Someone might just have borrowed it and forgot to say anything."

"I suppose so." But Mara wasn't convinced. It seemed
too much of a coincidence that a flick-knife had been
used to kill the policeman and the flick-knife from the
mantelpiece was missing. She thought Seth was grasping
for straws in trying to explain it away as he was, but
she wanted to believe him.

"There you are, then," he said. "Why assume it's Paul
just because he has a violent past? He's changed. You're
thinking like the police."

Mara wanted to, but she couldn't bring herself to tell
Seth about the blood. Somehow, along with everything
else, that information seemed so final, so damning.

She had decided to get in touch with that friend of

Dennis Osmond's, Jenny. Mara liked her, though she wasn't too sure about Osmond himself. And Jenny was a professional psychologist. Mara could put her a theoretical case, using Paul's background, and ask if such a person was likely to be dangerous. She could say it was a part of some research she was doing for a story or something. Jenny would believe her.

"Maybe he should go away," Seth said after a while.

"Paul? But why?"

"It might be best for him. For all of us. Till it's over. You can see how all this is getting to him."

"It's getting to all of us," Mara said. "You, too."

"Yes, but—"

"Where would he go? You know he hasn't got anybody else to turn to." Despite her fears, Mara couldn't help but want to protect Paul. She didn't understand her feelings, but as much as she suspected him, she couldn't just give up and send him away.

Seth stared at the floor.

"It could look bad, too," Mara argued. "The police would think he was running away because he was guilty."

"Let him stay, then. Just make up your mind."

"Don't you care about him?"

"Of course I care about him. That's why I suggested he get away. Come on, Mara, which way do you want it? If I suggest he goes, I'm being cruel, and if he stays he might have to put up with a hell of a lot more from that fascist bastard we had around this afternoon. What do you want? Do you think he can take it? Look how he reacted to today's little chat. That was a picnic compared to what'll happen if they decide to take him in for questioning. And we can't protect him. Well? How much do you think he can take?"

"I don't know." Things had suddenly got even more complicated for Mara. "I want what's best for Paul."

"Let's ask him, then. We can't make his decisions for him."

"No! We've got to stand by him. If we approach him, he might think we believe he's guilty and want him out of the way."

"But we'd have to approach him to ask if he'd like to go away for a while, until things settle down."

"So we do nothing. If he wants to stay, he stays, and we stand by him, whatever. If he goes, then it's his decision. We don't force him out. He's not stupid, Seth, I'm sure he knows he's in for a lot of police harassment. The last thing he needs is to feel that we're against him, too."

"Okay." Seth nodded and stood up. "We'll leave it at that. I've got to go and do some work on that old sideboard now. I'm already late. You all right?"

Mara looked up at him and smiled. "I'll manage."

"Good." He bent and kissed her, then went out back to his workshop.

But Mara wasn't all right. Left to herself, she began to imagine all kinds of terrible things. The world of Maggie's Farm had seemed at first to offer the stability, love and freedom she had always been searching for, but now it had broken adrift. The feeling was like that she remembered having during a mild earthquake in California, when she'd travelled around the States, with Matthew, eons ago. Suddenly, the floor of the room, the house's foundations, the solid earth on which they were built, had seemed no more stable than water. A ripple had passed fleetingly under her, and what she had always thought durable turned out to be flimsy, untrustworthy and transient. The quake had only lasted for ten seconds and hadn't registered above five on the Richter scale, but the impression had remained with her ever since. Now it was coming back stronger than ever.

On the mantelpiece, among the clutter of sea shells, pebbles, fossils and feathers, she could see the faint outline of dust around where the knife had been. As she wiped the surface clean, she thanked her lucky stars that the police had been looking for material things, not absences.

V

Banks drove along Foreshore Road and Sandside by the Old Harbour. The amusement arcades and gift shops were all closed. In season, crowds of holiday-makers always gathered around the racks of cheeky postcards, teenagers queued for the Ghost Train, and children dragged their parents to the booths that sold candy-floss and Scarborough rock. But now the prom was deserted. Even on the seaward side, there were no stalls selling cockles, winkles and boiled shrimp. A thick, high cloud-cover had set in, and the sea sloshed at the barnacle-crusted harbour walls like molten metal. Fishing boats rocked at their moorings, and stacks of lobster-pots tee-tered on the quayside. Towering over the scene, high on its promontory, the ruined castle looked like something out of a black-and-white horror film.

Banks dropped Richmond off at a pub near the West Pier and carried on along Marine Drive, parking just beyond the closed fun-fair. He buttoned up his raincoat tight and walked along the road that curved around the headland between the high cliff and the sea. Signs on the hillside warned of falling rocks. Waves hit the sea-wall and threw up spray onto the road.

Tony Grant was already there, leaning on the railing and staring out to the point where sea and sky merged in a uniform grey. He wore a navy duffle coat with the hood down, and his baby-fine hair fluttered in the wind. A solitary oil tanker was moving slowly across the horizon.

"I like it best like this," he said as Banks joined him. "If you don't mind getting a bit wet."

They both looked out over the ruffled water. Salt

spray filled the air and Banks felt the ozone freshen his lungs as he breathed deep. He shivered and asked, "What is it you want to tell me?"

Grant hesitated. "Look, sir," he said after staring at the oil tanker for half a minute, "I don't want you to get me wrong. I'm not a grass or anything. I've not been long on the force, and mostly I like it. I didn't think I would, not at first, but I do now. I want to make a career out of it." He looked at Banks intensely. "I'd like to join the CID. I'm not stupid; I've got brains. I've been to university, and I could maybe have got into teaching— that's what I thought I wanted to do—but, well, you know the job situation. Seems all that's going these days is the police force. So I joined. Anyway, as I said, I like it. It's challenging."

Banks took out a cigarette and cupped his hand around his blue Bic lighter. It took him four attempts to get a flame going long enough. He wished Grant would get to the point, but he knew he had to be patient and listen. The kid was about to go against his peers and squeal on a colleague. Listening to the justification, as he had listened to so many before, was the price Banks had to pay.

"It's just that," Grant went on, "well . . . it's not as clean as I expected."

Naïve bugger, Banks thought. "It's like anything else," he said, encouraging the lad. "There's a lot of bastards out there, whatever you do. Maybe our line of work attracts more than the usual quota of bullies, lazy sods, sadists and the like. But that doesn't mean we're all like that." Banks sucked on his cigarette. It tasted different, mixed with the sea air. A wave broke below them and the spray wet their feet.

"I know what you're saying," Grant said, "and I think you're right. I just wanted you to know what side I'm on. I don't believe that the end justifies the means. With me they're innocent until proven guilty, as the saying goes. I treat people with respect, no matter what color they are or how they dress or wear their hair. I'm not saying I approve of some of the types we get, but I'm not a thug."

"And Gill was?"

"Yes." A big wave started to peak as it approached the wall, and they both stepped back quickly to avoid the spray. Even so, they couldn't dodge a mild soaking, and Banks's cigarette got soggy. He threw it away.

"Was this common knowledge?"

"Oh, aye. He made no bones about it. See, with Gill it wasn't just the overtime, the money. He liked it well enough, but he liked the job more, if you see what I mean."

"I think I do. Go on."

"He was handy with his truncheon, Gill was. And he enjoyed it. Every time we got requests for manpower at demos, pickets, and the like, he'd be first to sign up. Got a real taste for it during the miners' strike, when they bussed police in from all over the place. He was the kind of bloke who'd wave a roll of fivers at the striking miners to taunt them before he clobbered them. He trained with the Tactical Aid Group."

The TAG, Banks knew, was a kind of force within a force. Its members trained together in a military fashion and learned how to use guns, rubber bullets and teargas. When their training was over, they went back to normal duties and remained on call for special situations—like demos and picket lines. The official term for them had been changed to PSU—Police Support Unit—as the TAGs got a lot of bad publicity and sounded too obviously martial. But it was about as effective as changing the name of Windscale to Sellafield; a nuclear-power station by another name. . . .

"Is that how he behaved in Eastvale?" Banks asked.

"I wouldn't swear to it, but I'm pretty sure it was Gill who led the charge. See, things were getting a bit hairy. We were all hemmed in so tight. Gill was at the top of the steps with a few others, just looking down at people pushing and shoving—not that you could see much, it was so bloody dark with those old-fashioned street-lamps. Anyway, one of the demonstrators chucked a bottle, and someone up there, behind me, yelled, 'Let's clobber the bastards.' I think I recognized Gill's voice. Then they charged down and . . . well, you know what happened. It needn't have—that's what I'm saying. Sure, there was a bit of aggro going on, but we could have sat on it if someone had given the order to loosen up a bit, give people room to breathe. Instead, Gill led a fucking truncheon charge. I know we coppers are all supposed to stick together, but . . ." Grant looked out to sea and shivered.

"There's a time to stick together," Banks said, "and this isn't it. Gill got himself killed, remember that."

"But I couldn't swear to anything. I mean, officially. . . ."

"Don't worry. This is off the record." At least it is for now, he told himself. If anything came of their discussion, young Grant might find himself with a few serious decisions to make. "How did the others feel about Gill?" he asked.

"Oh, most of them thought it was all a bit of a joke, a lark. I mean, there'd be Gill going on about clobbering queers and commies. I don't think they really took him seriously."

"But it wasn't just talk? You say he liked smashing skulls."

"Yes. He was a right bastard."

"Surely they knew it?"

"Yes, but . . ."

"Did they approve?"

"Well, no, I wouldn't say that. Some, maybe . . . but I didn't, for one."

"But nobody warned him, told him to knock it off?"

Grant pulled up his collar. "No."

"Were they scared of him?"

"Some of the lads were, yes. He was a bit of a hard case."

"What about you?"

"Me? Well, I wouldn't have taken him up on anything, that's for sure. I'm scarcely above regulation height, myself, and Gill was a big bugger."

A seagull screeched by them, a flash of white against the grey, and began circling over the water for fish. The tanker had moved far over to the right of the horizon. Banks felt the chill getting to him. He put his hands deep in his pockets and tensed up against the cold, wet wind.

"Did any of the others actually like him?" he asked. "Did he have any real mates at the station?"

"I wouldn't say so, no. He wasn't a very likeable bloke. Too big-headed, too full of himself. I mean, you couldn't have a conversation with him; you just had to listen. He had views on everything, but he was thick. I mean, he never really thought anything out. It was all down to Pakis and Rastas and students and skinheads and unemployed yobbos with him."

"So he wasn't popular around the station?"

"Not really, no. But you know what it's like. A few of the lads get together in the squad room—especially if they've had TAG training—and you get all that macho, tough-guy talk, just like American cop shows. He was good at that, Gill was, telling stories about fights and taking risks."

"Are there any more like him in your station?"

"Not as bad, no. There's a few that don't mind a good punch-up now and then, and some blokes like to pull kids in on a sus just to liven up a boring night. But nobody went as far as Gill."

"Did he have any friends outside the station?"

"I don't know who he went about with off duty."

"Did he have a girl-friend?"

"I don't know. He never mentioned anyone."

"So he didn't brag about having women like he did about thumping people?"

"No. I never heard him. Whenever he did talk about women it was always like they were whores and bitches. He was a foul-mouthed bastard. He'd hit them, too, at demos. It was all the same to him."

"Do you think he could have been the type to mess around with someone else's girl-friend or wife?"

Grant shook his head. "Not that I know of."

The seagull flew up towards the cliffs behind them, a fish flapping in its beak. The sea had settled to a rhythmic slapping against the stone wall, hardly sending up any spray at all. Banks risked another cigarette.

"Did Gill have any enemies that you know of?"

"He must have made plenty over the years, given his attitude towards the public," Grant said. "But I couldn't name any."

"Anyone on the force?"

"Eh?"

"You said nobody at the station really liked him. Had anyone got a good reason to dislike him? Did he owe money, cheat people, gamble? Any financial problems?"

"I don't think so. He just got people's backs up, that's all. He talked about betting on the horses, yes, but I don't think he did it that much. It was just the macho sort of thing that went with his image. He never tried to borrow any money off me, if that's what you mean. And I don't think he was on the take. At least he was honest on that score."

Banks turned his back to the choppy water and looked up towards the sombre bulk of the ruined castle. He couldn't see much from that angle; the steep cliff, where sea-birds made their nests, was mottled with grass, moss and bare stone. "Is there anything else you can tell me?" he asked.

"I don't think so. I just wanted you to know that all that crap at the funeral was exactly that. Crap. Gill was a vicious bastard. I'm not saying he deserved what happened to him, nobody deserves that, but those who live by the sword. . . ."

"Did you have any particular reason to dislike Gill?"

Grant seemed startled by the question. "Me? What do you mean?"

"What I say. Did he ever do you any harm personally?"

"No. Look, if you're questioning my motives, sir, believe me, it's exactly like I told you. I heard you were asking questions about Gill, and I thought someone should tell you the truth, that's all. I'm not the kind to go around speaking ill of the dead just because they're not here to defend themselves."

Banks smiled. "Don't mind me, I'm just an old cynic. It's a long time since I've come across a young idealist like you on the force." Banks thought of Superintendent Gristhorpe, who had managed to hang on to a certain amount of idealism over the years. But he was one of the old guard; it was a rare quality in youth these days, Banks had found—especially in those who joined the police. Even Richmond could hardly be called an idealist. Keen, yes, but as practical as the day was long.

Grant managed a thin smile. "It's nice of you to say that, but it's not exactly true. After all," he said, "I laid into them with the rest last Friday, didn't I? And do you know what?" His voice caught in his throat and he couldn't look Banks in the eye. "After a while, I even started to enjoy myself."

So, Banks thought, maybe Grant had told all because he felt ashamed of himself for acting like Gill and enjoying the battle. Getting caught up in the thrill of action was hardly unusual; the release of adrenaline often produced a sense of exhilaration in men who would normally run a mile from a violent confrontation. But it obviously bothered Grant. Perhaps this was his way of exorcising what he saw as Gill's demon inside him. Whatever his reasons, he'd given Banks plenty to think about.

"It happens," Banks said, by way of comfort. "Don't let it worry you. Look, would you do me a favor?"

They turned and started walking back to their cars.

Grant shrugged. "Depends."

"I'd like to know a bit more about Gill's overtime activities—like where he's been and when. There should be a record. It'd also be useful if I could find out about any official complaints against him, and anything at all about his private life."

Grant frowned and pushed at his left cheek with his tongue as if he had a canker. "I don't know," he said finally, fiddling in his duffle-coat pocket for his car keys. "I wouldn't want to get caught. They'd make my life a bloody misery here if they knew I'd even talked to you like this. Can't you just request his record?"

Banks shook his head. "My boss doesn't want us to be seen investigating Gill. He says it'll look bad. But if we're not seen. . . . Send it to my home address, just to be on the safe side." Banks scribbled his address on a card and handed it over.

Grant got into his car and opened the window. "I can't promise anything," he said slowly, "but I'll have a go." He licked his lips. "If anything important comes out of all this . . ." He paused.

Banks bent down, his hand resting on the wet car roof.

"Well," Grant went on, "I don't want you to think I'm after anything, but you will remember I said I wanted to join the CID, won't you?" And he smiled a big, broad, innocent, open smile.

Bloody hell, there were no flies on this kid. Banks couldn't make him out. At first he'd taken such a moral line that Banks suspected chapel had figured strongly somewhere in his background. But despite all his idealism and respect for the law, he might well be another Dirty Dick in the making. On the other hand, that damn smiling moon-face looked so bloody cherubic. . . .

"Yes," Banks said, smiling back. "Don't worry, I won't forget you."

SIX

I

In the cross-streets between York Road and Market Street, near where Banks lived, developers had converted terraces of tall Victorian family houses into student flats. In one of these, in a two-room attic unit, Tim Fenton and Abha Sutton lived.

If Tim and Abha made an unlikely-looking couple, they made an even more unlikely pair of revolutionaries. Tim had all the blond good looks of an American "preppie," with dress sense to match. Abha, half-Indian, had golden skin, beetle-black hair, and a pearl stud through her left nostril. She was studying graphic design; Tim was in the social sciences. They embraced Marxism as the solution to the world's inequalities, but were always quick to point out that they regarded Soviet Communism as an extreme perversion of the prophet's truth. Both were generally well-mannered, and not at all the type to call police pigs.

• They sat on a beat-up sofa under a Che Guevara poster while Banks made himself comfortable on a second-hand office swivel chair at the desk. The cursor blinked on the screen of an Amstrad PC, and stacks of paper and books overflowed from the table to the floor and onto any spare chairs.

After getting back from Scarborough, Banks had just had time to drop in at the station and see what Special

Branch had turned up. As usual, their files were as thin as Kojak's hair, and gathered on premises as flimsy as a stripper's G-string. Tim Fenton was listed because he had attended a seminar in Slough sponsored by *Marxism Today*, and some of the speakers there were suspected of working for the Soviets. Dennis Osmond had attracted the Branch's attention by writing a series of violently anti-government articles for various socialist journals during the miners' strike, and by organizing a number of political demonstrations—especially against American military presence in Europe. As Banks had suspected, their crimes against the realm hardly provided grounds for exile or execution.

Tim and Abha were, predictably, hostile and frightened after Burgess's visit. Banks had previously been on good terms with the two after successfully investigating a series of burglaries in student residences the previous November. Even Marxists, it appeared, valued their stereos and television sets. But now they were cautious and guarded. It took a lot of small talk to get them to relax and open up. When Banks finally got around to the subject of the demo, they seemed to have stopped confusing him with Burgess.

"Did you see anything?" Banks asked first.

"No, we couldn't," Tim answered. "We were right in the thick of the crowd. One of the cops shouted something and that was that. When things went haywire we were too busy trying to protect ourselves to see what was happening to anyone else."

"You were involved in organizing the demo, right?"

"Yes. But that doesn't mean—"

Banks held up his hand. "I know," he said. "And that's not what I'm implying. Did you get the impression that anyone involved—anyone at all—might have had more on his mind than just protesting Honoria Winstanley's visit?"

They both shook their heads. "When we got together up at the farm," Abha explained, "everyone was just so excited that we could organize a demo in a place as conservative as Eastvale. I know there weren't many people there, but it seemed like a lot to us."

"The farm?"

"Yes. Maggie's Farm. Do you know it?"

Banks nodded.

"They invited us up to make posters and stuff," Tim said. "Friday afternoon. They're really great up there; they've really got it together. I mean, Seth and Mara, they're like the old independent craftsmen, doing their own thing, making it outside the system. And Rick's a pretty sharp Marxist."

"I thought he was an artist."

"He is," Tim said, looking offended. "But he tries not to paint anything commercial. He's against art as a saleable commodity."

So that pretty water-colour Banks had noticed propped by the fireplace at Maggie's Farm couldn't have been one of Rick's.

"What about Paul Boyd?"

"We don't know him well," Abha said. "And he didn't say much. One of the oppressed, I suppose."

"You could say that. And Zoe?"

"Oh, she's all right," Tim said. "She goes in for all that bourgeois spiritual crap—bit of a navel-gazer—but she's okay underneath it all."

"Do you know anything about their backgrounds, where they come from?"

They shook their heads. "No," Tim said finally. "I mean, we just talk about the way things are now, how to change them, that kind of thing. And a bit of political theory. Rick's pissed off about his divorce and all that, but that's about as far as the personal stuff goes."

"And you know nothing else about them?"

"No."

"Who else was there?"

"Just us and Dennis."

"Osmond?"

"That's right."

"Does either of you recall seeing a flick-knife that day, or hearing anyone mention one?"

"No. That's what the other bloke went on about," Tim said, getting edgy. "Bloody Burgess. He went on and on about a flick-knife."

"He almost came right out and accused us of killing that policeman, too," Abha said.

"That's just his style. I wouldn't worry about it. Did anyone at the meeting mention PC Gill by name?"

"Not that I heard," Tim said.

"Nor me," said Abha.

"Have you ever heard anyone talk about him? Dennis Osmond, for example? Or Rick?"

"No. The only thing we knew about him," Abha said, "was that he'd trained with the TAG groups and he liked to work on crowd control. You know—demos, pickets and such."

The chair creaked as Banks swivelled sharply. "How did you know that?"

"Word gets around," Abha said. "We keep—"

Tim nudged her in the ribs and she shut up.

"What she means," he said, "is that if you're politically involved up here, you soon get to know the ones to watch out for. You lot keep tabs on us, don't you? I'm pretty sure Special Branch has a file on me, anyway."

"Fair enough," Banks said, smiling to himself at the absurdity of it all. Games. Just little boys' games. "Was this fairly common knowledge? Could anyone have known to expect Gill at the demo that night?"

"Anyone involved in organizing it, sure," Tim said. "And anyone who'd been to demos in Yorkshire before. There aren't many like him, thank God. He did have a bit of a reputation."

"Did you *know* he was going to be on duty?"

"Not for certain, no. I mean, he could have had flu or broke his leg."

"But short of that?"

"Short of that he was rarely known to miss. Look, I don't know what all this is in aid of," Tim said, "but I think you should know we're still going to do our own investigation."

"Into the murder?"

Tim gave him a puzzled glance. "No. Into the police brutality. We're all getting together again up at the farm in a few days to compare notes."

"Well, if you find anything out about PC Gill's death, let me know."

Banks looked at his watch and stood up. It was time he went and got ready for his evening out with Jenny. After he'd said goodbye and walked back down the gloomy staircase to the street, he reflected how odd it was that wherever he went, all roads seemed to lead to Maggie's Farm. More than that, almost anyone involved could have known that Gill was likely to be there that night. If Gill cracked heads in Yorkshire for a hobby, then the odds were that one or two people might hold a strong grudge against him. He wished Tony Grant would hurry up and send the information from Scarborough.

II

Mara put on her army-surplus greatcoat and set off down the track for Relton. It was dark now and the stars were glittering flecks of ice in the clear sky. Distant hills and scars showed only as muted silhouettes, black against black. The crescent moon was up, hanging lopsided like a backdrop to a music-hall number. Mara almost expected a man with a top hat, cape and cane to start dancing across it way up in the sky. The gravel crackled under her feet, and the wind whistled through gaps in the lichen-covered dry-stone wall. In the distance, the lights of cottages and villages down in the dale twinkled like stars.

She would talk to Jenny, she decided, thrusting her hands deeper into her pockets and hunching up against the chill. Jenny knew Chief Inspector Banks, too. Though she distrusted all policemen, even Mara had to admit that he was a hell of a lot better than Burgess. Perhaps she might also be able to find out what the police really thought, and if they were going to leave Paul alone from now on.

Mara's mind strayed back to the I Ching, which she had consulted before setting off. What the hell was it all about? It was supposed to be an oracle, to offer words of wisdom when you really needed them, but Mara wasn't convinced. One problem was that it always answered questions obliquely. You couldn't ask, "Did Paul kill that policeman?" and get a simple yes or no. This time, the oracle had read: "The woman holds the basket, but there are no fruits in it. The man stabs the sheep, but no blood flows. Nothing that acts to further." Did that mean Paul hadn't killed anyone, that the blood on his hand had come from somewhere else? And what about the empty basket? Did that have something to do with Mara's barren womb? If there was any practical advice at all, it was to do nothing, yet here she was, walking down the track on her way to call Jenny. All the book had done was put her fears into words and images.

At the end of the track, Mara walked along Mortsett Lane, past the closed shops and the cottages with their television screens flickering behind curtains. In the dimly lit phone booth, she rang Jenny's number. She heard a click followed by a strange, disembodied voice that she finally recognized as Jenny's. The voice explained that its owner was out, but that a message could be left after the tone. Mara, who had never dealt with an answering machine before, waited nervously, worried that she might miss her cue. But it soon came, the un-

mistakable high-pitched bleep. Mara spoke quickly and
loudly, as people do to foreigners, feeling self-conscious
about her voice: "This is Mara, Jenny. I hope I've got
this thing right. Please, will you meet me tomorrow
lunch-time in the Black Sheep in Relton? It's important.
I'll be there at one. I hope you can come." She paused
for a moment and listened to the silence, feeling that she
should add something, but she could think of nothing
more to say.

Mara put the phone back gently. It had been rather
like sending a telegram, something she had done once
before. The feeling that every word cost money was very
inhibiting, and so, in a different way, was the sense of
a tape winding around the capstan past the recording
head as she talked.

Anyway, it was done. Leaving the booth, she hurried
towards the Black Sheep, feeling lighter in spirit now
that she had at least taken a practical step to deal with
her fears.

III

Banks and Jenny sat in the bar over aperitifs while they
studied the menu. The Royal Oak was a cosy place with
muted lights, mullioned windows and gleaming copper-
ware in little nooks and crannies. Fastened horizontally
between the dark beams on the ceiling was a collection
of walking-sticks of all lengths and materials: knobbly
ashplants, coshers, sword-sticks and smooth canes, many
with ornate brass handles. On a long shelf above the bar
stood a row of toby jugs with such faces as Charles II,
Shakespeare and Beethoven; some, however, depicted
contemporaries, like Margaret Thatcher and Paul Mc-
Cartney.

Jenny sipped a vodka-and-tonic, Banks a dry sherry,
as they tried to decide what to order. Finally, after much

self-recrimination about the damage it would do to her figure, Jenny settled for *steak au poivre* with a wine-and-cream sauce. Banks chose roast leg of lamb. Much as he liked to watch the little blighters frolic around the dale every spring, he enjoyed eating them almost as much. They'd only grow up into sheep anyway, he reasoned.

They followed the waitress into the dining-room, pleased to find only one other table occupied, and that by a subdued couple already on dessert. Mozart's Clarinet Quintet played quietly in the background. Banks watched Jenny walk ahead of him. She was wearing a loose top, cut square across the collarbone, which looked as if it had been tie-dyed in various shades of blue and red. Her pleated skirt was plain rust-red, the colour of her tumbling, wavy hair, and came to midway down her calves. The tights she wore had some kind of pattern on them, which looked to Banks like a row of bruises up the sides of her legs. Being a gentleman, though, he had complimented her on her appearance.

The waitress lit the candle, took their orders and moved off soundlessly, leaving them with the wine list to study. Banks lit a cigarette and smiled at Jenny.

Despite the claims of *Playboy*, the Miss Universe contest and other promoters of the feminine image to men, Banks had often found that it was the most insignificant detail that made a woman physically attractive to him: a well-placed mole, a certain curve of the lips or turn of the ankle; or a mannerism, such as the way she picked up a glass, tilted her head before smiling, or fiddled with a necklace while speaking.

In the case of Sandra, his wife, it was the dark eyebrows and the contrast they made with her naturally ash-blonde hair. With Jenny, it was her eyes, or rather the delta of lines that crinkled their outer edges, especially when she smiled. They were like a map whose contours revealed a sense of humour and a curious mixture of toughness and vulnerability that Banks, himself, felt able to identify with. Her beautiful red hair and green eyes, her shapeliness, her long legs and full lips were all very well, but they were just icing on the cake. It was the lines around the eyes that did it.

"What are you thinking?" Jenny asked, looking up from the list.

Banks gave her the gist of it.

"Well," she said, after a fit of laughter, "I'll take that as a compliment, though there are many women who wouldn't. What shall we have?"

"They've got a nice Séguret 1980 here, if I remember rightly. And not too expensive, either. That's if you like Rhône."

"Fine by me."

When the waitress returned with their smoked salmon and melon appetizers, Banks ordered the wine.

"So what's all this decadence in aid of?" asked Jenny, her eyes twinkling in the candle flame. "Are you planning to seduce me, or are you just softening me up for questioning?"

"What if I said I was planning to seduce you?"

"I'd say you were going about it the right way." She smiled and looked around the room. "Candlelight, romantic music, nice atmosphere, good food."

The wine arrived, shortly followed by their main courses, and soon they were enjoying the meal to the accompaniment of the Flute Quartets.

Over dinner, Jenny complained about her day. There had been too many classes to teach, and she was tired of the undergraduates' simplistic assumptions about psychology. Sometimes, she confessed, she was even sick of psychology itself and wished she'd studied English literature or history instead.

Banks told her about the funeral, careful to leave out his meeting with Tony Grant. It would be useful to have something in reserve later, if he could steer her around to talking about Osmond. He also mentioned his visit to

Tim and Abha and how Burgess's approach had soured
the pitch.

"Your Dirty Dick is a real jerk," Jenny said, employ-
ing an Americanism the man himself would have been
proud of. "Dare I ask about dessert?" she asked, pushing
her empty plate aside.

"It's *your* figure."

"In that case, I think I'll have chocolate mousse. Absolutely no calories at all. And coffee and cognac."

When the waitress came by, Banks ordered Jenny's
dessert and liqueur along with a wedge of Stilton and a
glass of Sauternes for himself. "You didn't really answer
my question, you know," he said.

"What question's that?"

"The one about seducing you."

"Oh, yes. But I did. I said you were going about it
the right way."

"But you didn't say whether I'd get anywhere or not."

Jenny's eyes crinkled. "Alan! Are you feeling the itch
because Sandra's away?"

Banks felt foolish for bringing the subject up in the
first place. Flirting with Jenny might be fun, but it also
had a serious edge that neither really wanted to get too
close to. If it hadn't been for that damned incident at
Osmond's flat, he thought, he'd never have been so silly
as to start playing games like this. But when he had seen
Jenny look around Osmond's bedroom door like that—
the robe slipping off her shoulder, the tousled hair, the
relaxed, unfocused look that follows love-making—it
hadn't only made him jealous, it had also inflamed old
desires. He had felt that nobody else should enjoy what
he couldn't enjoy himself. And he couldn't; of that there
was no doubt. So he played his games and ended up
embarrassing both of them.

He lit a cigarette to hide behind and poured the last
of the Séguret. "Change the subject?"

Jenny nodded. "A good idea."

The dessert arrived at the same time as a noisy party

of businessmen. Fortunately, the waitress seated them at the far end of the room.

"This is delicious," Jenny said, spooning up the chocolate mousse. "I suppose you're going to question me now? I've got a feeling that seduction would probably have been a lot more fun."

"Don't tempt me," Banks said. "But you're right. I would like your help on a couple of things."

"Here we go. Can I just finish my sweet first?"

"Sure."

When the dishes were empty, Jenny sipped some cognac. "All right," she said, saluting and sitting up to attention. "I'm all ears."

"Were you there?" Banks asked.

"Where?"

"At the demo. You came to see me at two in the morning. You said you'd been waiting at your house for your boyfriend—"

"Dennis!"

"Yes, all right. Dennis." Banks wondered why he hated the sound of the name so much. "But you could have been at the demo, too."

"You mean I could have been lying?"

"That's not what I'm getting at. You might have just failed to mention it."

"Surely you don't think I'm a suspect now? Being seduced by Quasimodo would be more fun than this."

Banks laughed. "That's not my point. Think about it. If you were there with Osmond right up until the time he got arrested, then you'd be a witness that he didn't stab PC Gill."

"I see. So Dennis is a prime suspect as far as you're concerned?"

"He is as far as Burgess is concerned. And that's what counts."

Banks wondered if he, too, wanted Osmond to be guilty. Part of him, he had to admit, did. He was also wondering whether or not to tell Jenny about the assault charges. It would be a mean thing to do right now, he decided, because he couldn't trust his motives. Would he be telling her for her own good, or out of the jealousy he felt, out of a desire to hurt her relationship with Osmond?

"I see what you mean," Jenny said finally. "No, I wasn't at the demo. I don't know what happened. Dennis has talked to me about it, of course—and, by the way, he's going ahead with his own inquiry into the thing, you know, along with Tim and Abha. And Burgess is going to come off pretty badly. Apparently he was around again today with Hatchley."

Banks knew that. He also knew that the dirty duo had got no more out of anyone than they had the first time around. They'd probably be drowning their sorrows in the Queen's Arms by now, and with a bit of luck Dirty Dick would push it too far with Glenys and her Cyril would thump him.

"Back to the demo," Banks said. "What exactly has Dennis said?"

"He doesn't know what happened to that policeman. Do you think I'd be sitting here talking to you, answering your questions, if I wasn't trying to convince you that he had nothing to do with it?"

"So he saw nothing?"

"No. He said he heard somebody shout—he didn't catch the words—and after that it was chaos."

That seemed to square with what Tony Grant and Tim and Abha had said about the riot's origin. Banks took a sip of Sauternes and watched it make legs down the inside of his glass.

"Did he ever mention PC Gill to you?"

Jenny shrugged. "He may have done. I didn't have much to do with the demo, as I said."

"Did you ever hear the name?"

"I don't know." Jenny was getting prickly. "I can't say I pay much attention to Dennis's political concerns. And if you're going to take a cheap shot at that, forget it. Unless you want a lap full of hot coffee."

Banks decided it was best to veer away from the subject of Osmond. "You know the people at Maggie's Farm, don't you?" he asked.

"Yes. Dennis got friendly with Seth and Mara. We've been up a few times. I like them, especially Mara."

"What's the set-up there?"

Jenny swirled the cognac and took another sip. "Seth bought the place about three years ago," she said. "Apparently, it was in a bit of a state, which was why he got it quite cheaply. He fixed it up, renovated the old barn and rented it out. After Mara, Rick came next, I think, with Julian. He was having some problems with his wife."

"Yes, I've heard about his wife," Banks said. "Do you know anything else about her?"

"No. Except according to Rick her name must be Bitch."

"What about Zoe?"

"I'm not sure how she met up with them. She came later. As far as I know she's from the east coast. She seems like a bit of a space cadet, but I suspect she's quite shrewd, really. You'd be surprised how many people are into that New Age stuff these days. Looking for something, I suppose . . . reassurance . . . I don't know. Anyway, she makes a good living from it. She does the weekly horoscope in the *Gazette*, too, and takes a little booth on the coast on summer weekends for doing tarot readings and what not. You know, Madame Zoe, Gypsy Fortune Teller . . ."

"The east coast? Could it be Scarborough?"

Jenny shook her head. "Whitby, I think."

"Still," Banks muttered, "it's not far away."

"What isn't?"

The waitress brought coffee, and Banks lit another cigarette, careful to keep the smoke away from Jenny.

"Tell me about Mara."

"I like Mara a lot. She's bright, and she's had an interesting life. She was in some religious organization before she came to the farm, but she got disillusioned. She seems to want to settle down a bit now. For some reason, we get along quite well. Seth, as I say, I don't know much about. He grew up in the sixties and he hasn't sold out—I mean he hasn't become a stockbroker or an accountant, at least. His main interest is his carpentry. There's also something about a woman in his past."

"What woman?"

"Oh, it was just something Mara said. Apparently Seth doesn't like to talk about it. He had a lover who died. Maybe they were even married, I don't know. That was just before he bought the farm."

"What was her name?"

"Alison, I think."

"How did she die?"

"Some kind of accident."

"What kind?"

"That's all I know, really. I'm not being evasive. Mara said it's all she knows, too. Seth only told her because he got drunk once. Apparently he's not much of a drinker."

"And that's all you know?"

"Yes. It was some kind of motor accident. She got knocked down or something."

"Where was he living then?"

"Hebden Bridge, I think. Why does it matter?"

"It probably doesn't. I just like to know as much as I can about who I'm dealing with. They were involved in the demo, and every time I question someone, Maggie's Farm comes up."

It would be easy enough to check the Hebden Bridge accident records, though where Gill might come into it, Banks had no idea. Perhaps he had been on traffic duty at the time? He would hardly have been involved in a religious organization either, unless he felt a close friend or relation had been brainwashed by such a group.

"What about Paul Boyd?" he asked.

Jenny paused. "He's quite new up there. I can't say I know him well. To tell you the truth—and to speak quite unprofessionally—he gives me the creeps. But Mara's very attached to him, like he's a younger brother, or a son, even. There's about seventeen years between them. He's another generation, really—punk, post-sixties. Mara thinks he just needs tender loving care, something he's never had much of, apparently."

"What do you think of Paul professionally?"

"It's hard to answer that. As I said, I haven't really talked to him that much. He seems angry, antisocial. Maybe life at the farm will give him some sense of belonging. If you think about it, what reason does he have to love the world? No adult has ever given him a break, nor has society. He feels worthless and rejected, so he makes himself look like a reject; he holds it to him and shouts it out, as people do. And that," Jenny said with a mock bow, "is Dr Fuller's humble opinion."

Banks nodded. "It makes sense."

"But it doesn't make him a killer."

"No." He couldn't think of any more questions without returning to the dangerous territory of Dennis Osmond, and things had gone so well for the past half hour or so that he didn't want to risk ending the evening on a sour note. Jenny was bound to be guarded if he really started pushing about Osmond again.

Banks picked up the bill, which Jenny insisted on sharing, and they left. The drive home went smoothly, but Banks felt guilty because he was sure he was a bit over the limit, and if anyone ought to know better about drunken driving, it was a policeman. Not that he felt drunk. After all, he hadn't had much to drink, really. He was perfectly in control. But that's what they all said when the crystals changed colour. Jenny told him not to be silly, he was quite all right. When he dropped her off, there was no invitation to come in for a coffee, and he was glad of that.

Luckily, he thought as he tried to fall asleep, Jenny hadn't pushed him about his own theories. If she had, he would have told her—and trusted her to make sure it got no further—about his little chat with Tony Grant on Marine Drive, the implications of which put a different light on things.

On the one hand, what Grant had told him made the possibility of a personal motive for killing Gill much more likely. He didn't know who might have had such a motive yet, but according to what Tim and Abha had said, almost any of the demonstrators—especially the organizers or people close to them—would have known to expect Gill at the demo. And if Gill was there, wasn't it a safe bet that violence would follow?

On the other hand, Banks found himself thinking that if Gill had enemies within the force, perhaps a fellow policeman, not a demonstrator, might have taken the opportunity to get rid of him: someone whose wife or girlfriend Gill had fooled around with, for example; or a partner in crime, if he had been on the take. Tony Grant hadn't thought so, but he was only a naïve rookie, after all.

It wasn't an idea Banks would expect Burgess to entertain for a moment; for one thing, it would blow all political considerations off the scene. But another policeman would have expected Gill to cause trouble, could have arranged to be on overtime with him and could have been sure of getting away. None of which could be said for any of the demonstrators. Nobody searched the police; nobody checked their uniforms for Gill's blood.

Maybe it was the kind of far-fetched theory one usually got on the edge of sleep and would seem utterly absurd in the morning light. But Banks couldn't quite rule it out. He'd known men on the Metropolitan force more than capable of murdering fellow officers, and in many cases, the loss would hardly have diminished the quality of the human gene pool. The only way to find out about that angle, though, was to press Tony Grant even further into service. If there was anything in it, the fewer people who knew about Banks's line of investigation, the better. It could be dangerous.

And so, the Sauternes still warm in his veins and a stretch of cold empty bed beside him, Banks fell asleep thinking of the victim, convinced that someone not too far away had had a very good reason for wanting PC Edwin Gill dead.

SEVEN

I

Banks turned up the track to Gristhorpe's old farmhouse above Lyndgarth, wondering what the superintendent was doing at home on a Wednesday morning. The message, placed on his desk by Sergeant Rowe, had offered no explanation, just an invitation to visit.

Pulling up in front of the squat, solid house, he stubbed out his cigarette and ejected the Lightning Hopkins cassette he'd been listening to. Breathing in the fresh, cold air, he looked down over Swainsdale and was struck by the way Relton and Maggie's Farm, directly opposite on the south side of the dale, formed almost a mirror image of Lyndgarth and Gristhorpe's house. Like the latter, Maggie's Farm stood higher up the hillside than the village it was close to—so high it was on the verge of the moorland that spread for miles on the heights between dales.

Looking down the slope from the farmhouse, Banks could see the grey-brown ruins of Devraulx Abbey, just west of Lyndgarth. On the valley bottom, Fortford marked the western boundary of the river-meadows. Swainsdale was at its broadest there, where the River Swain meandered through the flats until it veered southeast to Eastvale and finally joined the Ouse outside York.

In summer, the lush green meadows were speckled

with golden buttercups. Bluebells, forget-me-nots and wild garlic grew by the riverside under the shade of ash and willow. The Leas, as they were called locally, were a favourite spot for family picnics. Artists set up their easels there, too, and fishermen spent idle afternoons on the riverbank and waded in the shallows at dusk. Now, although the promise of spring showed in the grass and clung like a green haze around the branches of the trees, the meadows seemed a haunted and desolate spot. The snaking river sparkled between the trees, and a brisk wind chased clouds over from the west. Shadows flitted across the steep green slopes with a speed that was almost dizzying to watch.

Gristhorpe answered the door and led Banks into the living-room, where a peat fire burned in the hearth, then disappeared into the kitchen. Banks took off his sheepskin-lined car-coat and rubbed his hands by the flames. Outside the back window, a pile of stones stood by the unfinished dry-stone wall that the superintendent worked on in his spare time. It fenced in nothing and went nowhere, but Banks had enjoyed many hours placing stones there with Gristhorpe in companionable silence. Today, though, it was too cold for such outdoors activity.

Carrying a tray of tea and scones, Gristhorpe returned and sat down in his favourite armchair to pour. After small talk about the wall and the possibility of yet more snow, the superintendent told Banks his news: the enquiry into the demo had been suspended.

"I'm on ice, as our American cousins would put it," he said. "The Assistant Chief Commissioner's been talking to the PCA about getting an outsider to finish the report. Maybe someone from Avon and Somerset division."

"Because we're too biased?"

"Aye, partly. I expected it. They only set me on it in the first place to make it look like we were acting quickly."

"Did you find anything out?"

"It looks like some of our lads over-reacted."

Banks told him what he'd heard from Jenny and Tim and Abha.

Gristhorpe nodded. "The ACC doesn't like it. If you ask me, I don't think there'll be an official inquiry. It'll be postponed till it's no longer an issue. What he's hoping is that Superintendent Burgess will come up with the killer fast. That'll satisfy everyone, and people will just forget about the rest."

"Where does that leave you?"

"I'm taking a few days' leave, on the ACC's advice. Unless anything else comes up—something unconnected to Gill's death—then that's how I'll stay. He's right, of course. I'd only get in the way. Burgess is in charge of that investigation, and it wouldn't do to have the two of us treading on each other's toes. But don't let the bugger near my office with those foul cigars of his! How are you getting on with him?"

"All right, I suppose. He's got plenty of go, and he's certainly not stupid. Trouble is, he's got a bee in his bonnet about terrorists and lefties in general."

"And you see things differently?"

"Yes." Banks told him about the meeting with Tony Grant and the possibilities it had opened up for him. "And," he added, "you'd think Special Branch would have known if there'd been some kind of terrorist action planned, wouldn't you?"

Gristhorpe digested the information and mulled it over for a few moments, then turned his light-blue eyes on Banks and rubbed his chin. "I'll not deny you might be right," he said, "but for Christ's sake keep your feet on the ground. Don't go off half-cocked on this or you could bring down a lot of trouble on yourself—and on me. I appreciate you want to follow your own nose— you'd be a poor copper if you didn't—and maybe you'd like to show Dirty Dick a thing or two. But be careful. Just because Gill turned out to be a bastard, it doesn't follow that's why he was killed. Burgess could be right."

"I know that. It's just a theory. But thanks for the warning."

Gristhorpe smiled. "Think nothing of it. But keep it under your hat. If Burgess finds out you've been pursuing a private investigation, he'll have your guts for garters. And it won't be just him. The ACC'll have your balls for billiards."

"I don't know as I've got enough body parts to go around," Banks said, grinning.

"And this conversation hasn't taken place. I know nothing about what you're up to, agreed?"

"Agreed."

"But keep me posted. God, how I hate bloody politics."

Banks knew that the superintendent came from a background of Yorkshire radicals—Chartists, the anti-Corn Laws crowd—and there was even a Luddite lurking in the family tree. But Gristhorpe himself was conservative with a small "c." He was, however, concerned with the preservation of human rights that had been fought for and won over the centuries. That was how he saw his job—as a defender of the people, not an attacker. Banks agreed, and that was one reason they got along so well.

Banks finished his tea and looked at his watch. "Talking of Dirty Dick, I'd better be off. He's called a conference in the Queen's Arms for one o'clock."

"Seems like he's taken up residence there."

"You're not far wrong." Banks explained about Glenys and put on his car-coat. "Besides that," he added, "he drinks like a bloody fish."

"So it's not only Glenys and her charms?"

"No."

"Ever seen him pissed?"

"Not yet."

"Well, watch him. Drinking's an occupational hazard with us, but it can get beyond a joke. The last thing you need is a piss-artist to rely on in a tight spot."

"I don't think there's anything to worry about," Banks said, walking to the car. "He's always been a boozer. And he's usually sharp as a whippet. Anyway, what can I do if I think he is overdoing it? I can just see his face if I suggest a visit to AA."

Gristhorpe stood by the car. Banks rolled the window down, slipped Lightning Hopkins back in the slot, and lit a cigarette.

The superintendent shook his head. "It's about time you stopped that filthy habit, too," he said. "And as for that racket you call music . . ."

Banks smiled and turned the key in the ignition. "Do you know something?" he said. "I do believe you're becoming an insufferable old fogey. I know you're tone-deaf and wouldn't know Mozart from the Beatles, but don't forget, it wasn't that long ago you gave up smoking yourself. Have you no bad habits left?"

Gristhorpe laughed. "I gave them all up years ago. Are you suggesting I should take some up again?"

"Wouldn't be a bad idea."

"Where do you suggest I start?"

Banks rolled up the window before he said, "Try sheep-shagging." But judging by the raised eyebrows and the startled smile, Gristhorpe could obviously read lips. Grinning, Banks set off down the track, the still, deserted river-meadows spread out below him, and headed for the Eastvale road.

II

Jenny was already five minutes late. Mara nursed her half of mild and rolled a cigarette. It was Wednesday lunch-time, and the Black Sheep was almost empty. Apart from the landlord reading his *Sun*, and two old men playing dominoes, she was the only other customer in the cosy lounge.

Now that the time was close, she was beginning to feel nervous and foolish. After all, she didn't know Jenny *that* well, and her story did sound a bit thin. She couldn't put the real problem into words. How could she say that she suspected Paul had killed the policeman and that she was even beginning to be afraid living in the same house, but despite it all she wouldn't give him away and still wanted to keep him there? It sounded insane without the feelings that went with it. And to tell Jenny that she just wanted information for a story she was writing hardly ranked as the important reason for the meeting she had claimed on the telephone. Perhaps Jenny wasn't going to come. Maybe Mara hadn't responded to the answering machine properly and she hadn't even got the message.

All she could hear was the sound of asthmatic breathing from one of the old men, the occasional rustling of the newspaper, and the click of dominoes as they were laid on the hard surface. She swirled the beer in the bottom of her half-pint glass and peered at her watch again. Quarter past one.

"Another drink, love?" Larry Grafton called out.

Mara flashed a smile and shook her head. Why was it that she didn't mind so much being called "love" by the locals, but when Burgess had said it, her every nerve had bristled with resentment? It must be something in the tone, she decided. The old Yorkshiremen who used the word were probably as chauvinistic as the rest—in fact, sex roles in Dales family life were as traditional as anywhere in England—but when the men called women "love," it carried at least overtones of affection. With Burgess, though, the word was a weapon, a way of demeaning the woman, of dominating her.

Jenny arrived and interrupted her train of thought.

"Sorry I'm late," she said breathlessly. "Class went on longer than I expected."

"It's all right," Mara said. "I haven't been here long. Drink?"

"Let me get them."

Jenny went to the bar, and Mara watched her, a little intimidated, as usual, by her poise. Jenny always seemed to wear the right, expensive-looking clothes. Today it was a waist-length fur jacket (fake, of course—Jenny wouldn't be caught dead wearing real animal fur), a green silk blouse, close-fitting rust cords, and well-polished knee-length boots. Not that Mara would want to dress like that—it wouldn't suit her personality—but she did feel shabby in her moth-eaten sweater and muddy wellingtons. Her jeans hadn't been artificially aged like the ones teenagers wore, either; they had earned each stain and every faded patch.

"Quiet, isn't it?" Jenny said, setting the drinks down. "You looked thoughtful when I came in. What was it?"

Mara told her her feelings about being called "love."

"I know what you mean. I could have throttled Burgess when he did it to me." She laughed. "Dorothy Wycombe once chucked her drink at a stable-lad for calling her 'love.' "

"Dorothy doesn't have much to do with us," Mara said. "I think we're too traditional for her tastes."

Jenny laughed. "You should count yourself lucky, then." She took off her fur jacket and made herself comfortable. "I heard she made mincemeat of Burgess. She gave Alan a hard time once, too. He gives her a wide berth now."

"Alan? Is that the policeman you know? Chief Inspector Banks?"

Jenny nodded. "He's all right. Why? Is that what you wanted to talk about?"

"What do you mean?"

"Don't be so cagey. I know you've come in for a lot of police attention since the demo. I just wondered if that was what was on your mind. Your message wasn't exactly specific, you know."

Mara smiled. "I'm not used to answering machines, that's all. Sorry."

"No need. You just came across as frightfully worried and serious. Are you?"

A domino clicked loudly on the board, obviously a winning move. "Not as much as I probably sounded, no," Mara said. "But it is about the demo. Partly, anyway." She had decided that, as Jenny had mentioned Banks, she might as well begin by seeing if she could find anything out about the investigation, what the police were thinking.

"Go ahead, then."

Mara took a deep breath and told Jenny about recent events at the farm, especially Burgess's visit.

"You ought to complain," Jenny advised her.

Mara sniffed. "Complain? Who to? He told us what would happen if we did. Apparently his boss is a bigger bastard than he is."

"Try complaining locally. Superintendent Gristhorpe isn't bad."

Mara shook her head. "You don't understand. The police would never listen to a complaint from people like us."

"Don't be too sure about that, Mara. Alan wants to understand. It's only the truth he's after."

"Yes, but . . . I can't really explain. What do they really think about us, Jenny? Do they believe that one of us killed that policeman?"

"I don't know. Really I don't. They're interested in you, yes. I'd be a liar if I denied that. But as far as actually suspecting anyone . . . I don't think so. Not yet."

"Then why do they keep pestering us? When's it going to stop?"

"When they find out who the killer is. It's not just you, it's everyone involved. They've been at Dennis, too, and Dorothy Wycombe and the students. You'll just have to put up with it for the time being."

"I suppose so." The old men shuffled dominoes for

another game, and a lump of coal shifted in the fire, sending out a shower of sparks and a puff of smoke. Flames rose up again, licking at the black chimney-back. "Look," Mara went on, "do you mind if I ask you a professional question, something about psychology? It's for a story I'm working on."

"I didn't know you wrote."

"Oh, it's just for my own pleasure really. I mean, I haven't tried to get anything published yet." Even as she spoke, Mara knew that her excuse didn't ring true.

"Okay," Jenny said. "Let me get another round in first."

"Oh no, it's my turn." Mara went to the bar and bought another half for herself and a vodka-and-tonic for Jenny. If only she could get away with some of her fears about Paul allayed—without giving them away, of course—then she knew she would feel a lot better.

"What is it?" Jenny asked when they'd settled down with their drinks again.

"It's just something I'd like to know, a term I've heard that puzzles me. What's a sociopath?"

"A sociopath? Good Lord, this is like an exam question. Let me think for a bit. I'll have to give you a watered-down answer, I'm afraid. I don't have the textbook with me."

"That's all right."

"Well . . . I suppose basically it's someone who's constantly at war with society. A rebel without a cause, if you like."

"Why, though? I mean, what makes people like that?"

"It's far from cut and dried," Jenny said, "but the thinking is that it has a lot to do with family background. Usually people we call sociopaths suffered abuse, cruelty and rejection from their parents, or at least from one parent, from an early age. They respond by rejecting society and becoming cruel themselves."

"What are the signs?"

"Antisocial acts: stealing, doing reckless things, cruelty to animals. It's hard to say."

"What kind of people are they?"

"They don't feel anything about what they do. They can always justify acts of cruelty—even murder—to themselves. They don't really see that they've done anything wrong."

"Can anyone help them?"

"Sometimes. The trouble is, they're detached, cut off from the rest of us through what's happened to them. They rarely have any friends and they don't feel any sense of loyalty."

"Isn't it possible to help them, then?"

"They find it very hard to give love and to trust people, or to respond to such feelings in others. If you don't give your love, then you save yourself from feeling bad if it's rejected. That's the real problem: they need someone to trust them and have some feeling for them, but those are the things they find it hardest to accept."

"So it's hopeless."

"Often it's too late," Jenny said. "If they're treated early, they can be helped, but sometimes by the time they reach their teens the pattern is so deeply ingrained it's almost irreversible. But it's never hopeless." She leaned forward and put her hand on Mara's. "It's Paul you're asking about, isn't it?"

Mara withdrew sharply. "What makes you say that?"

"Your expression, the tone of your voice. This isn't just for some story you're writing. It's for real, isn't it?"

"What if it is?"

"I can't tell you if Paul's a sociopath or not, Mara. I don't know enough about him. He seems to be responding to life at the farm."

"Oh, he is," Mara said. "Responding, I mean. He's got a lot more outgoing and cheerful since he's been with us. Until these past few days."

"Well, it's bound to get to him, all the police attention. But it doesn't mean anything. You don't think he might have killed the policeman, do you?"

"You mustn't tell anyone we've been talking like this," Mara said quickly. "Especially not Inspector Banks. All they need is an excuse to bring Paul in, then I'm sure that Burgess could force him to confess."

"They won't do that," Jenny said. "You don't have any concrete reason for thinking Paul might be guilty, do you?"

"No." Mara wasn't sure she sounded convincing. Things had gone too far for her, but it seemed impossible to steer back to neutral ground. "I'm just worried about him, that's all," she went on. "He's had a hard life. His parents rejected him and his foster parents were cold towards him."

"Well that doesn't mean a lot," Jenny said. "If that's all you're worried about, I shouldn't bother yourself. Plenty of people come from broken homes and survive. It takes very special circumstances to create a sociopath. Not every ache and pain means you've got cancer, you know."

Mara nodded. "I'm sorry I tried to con you," she said. "It wasn't fair of me. But I feel better now. Let's just forget all about it, shall we?"

"Okay, if you want. But be careful, Mara. I'm not saying Paul isn't dangerous, just that I don't know. If you do have any real suspicions . . ."

But Mara didn't hear any more. The door opened and a strange-looking man walked in. It wasn't his odd appearance that bothered her, though; it was the knife that he carried carefully in his hand. Pale and trembling, she got to her feet.

"I've got to go now," she said. "Something's come up. . . . I'm sorry." And she was off like a shot, leaving Jenny to sit and gape behind her.

III

"Bollocks!" said Burgess. "They're shit-disturbers. You ought to know that by now. Why do you think they're interested in a nuclear-free Britain? Because they love peace? Dream on, Constable."

"I don't know," Richmond said, stroking his moustache. "They're just students, they don't know—"

"Just students, my arse! Who is it tries to bring down governments in places like Korea and South Africa? Bloody students, that's who. Just students! Grow up. Look at the chaos students created in America over the Vietnam war—they almost won it for the commies single-handed."

"What I was saying, sir," Richmond went on, "is that none of them are known to be militant. They just sit around and talk politics, that's all."

"But Special Branch has a file on Tim Fenton."

"I know, sir. But he's not actually done anything."

"Not until now, perhaps."

"But what could he gain from killing PC Gill, sir?"

"Anarchy, that's what."

"With all due respect," Banks cut in, "that's hardly consistent. The students support disarmament, yes, but Marxists aren't anarchists. They believe in the class—"

"I know what bloody Marxists believe in," Burgess said. "They'll believe in anything if it furthers their cause."

Banks gave up. "Better have another try, Phil," he said. "See if you can tie any of them into more extreme groups, or to any previous acts of political violence. I doubt you'll come up with anything Special Branch doesn't know about already, but give it a try."

"Yes, sir."

"I need another drink," Burgess said.

Sergeant Hatchley volunteered to go for a round. The Queen's Arms was busy. Wednesday was farmers' market day in Eastvale, and the whole town bustled with buyers and sellers. Glenys was too busy to exchange glances with Burgess even if she wanted to.

Burgess turned to Banks. "And I'm still not happy about Osmond. He's on file, too, and I got the distinct impression he's been lying every time I've talked to him."

Banks agreed.

"We'll have another go at him," said Burgess. "You can come with me again. Who knows, that bird of his might be there. If I put a bit of pressure on her, he might appeal to you for help and let something slip."

Banks reached for a cigarette to mask his anger. The last thing he felt like was facing Osmond and Jenny together again. But in a way Burgess was right. They were looking for a cop killer, and they needed results. As each day went by, the media outcry became more strident.

When PC Craig came in and walked over to their table, he seemed unsure whom to address. After looking first to Banks and then to Burgess, like a spectator following the ball at Wimbledon, he settled on Banks.

"We've just had a call, sir, from Relton. There's a bloke in the pub there says he's found a knife. I just thought . . . you know . . . it might be the one we're looking for."

"What are we waiting for?" Burgess jumped to his feet so quickly he knocked the table and spilt the rest of his beer. He pointed at Hatchley and Richmond. "You two get back to the station and wait till you hear from us."

They picked up Banks's white Cortina from the lot behind the police station. Market Street and the square were so busy that Banks took the back streets to the main Swainsdale road.

Automatically, he reached forward and slipped a cassette into the player. "Do you mind?" he asked Burgess, turning the volume down. "Hello Central" came on.

"No. That's Lightning Hopkins, isn't it? I quite like

blues myself. I enjoyed that Billie Holiday the other day, too." He leaned back in the seat and lit a cigar from the dashboard lighter. "My father bunked with a squadron of Yanks in the last war. Got quite interested in jazz and blues. Of course, you couldn't get much of the real stuff over here at that time, but after the war he kept in touch and the Yanks used to send him seventy-eights. I grew up on that kind of music and it just seemed to stick."

Banks drove fast but kept an eye open for walkers on the verges. Even in March, the backpack brigade often took to the hills. As they approached Fortford, Burgess looked out at the river-meadows. "Very nice," he said. "Wouldn't be a bad place to retire to if it wasn't for the bloody weather."

They turned sharp left in Fortford, followed the un-fenced minor road up the daleside to Relton and parked outside the pub. Banks had been to the Black Sheep before; it was famous in the dale because the landlord brewed his own beer on the premises, and you couldn't get it anywhere else. Black Sheep bitter had won prizes in national competitions.

If beer wasn't the first thing on Banks's mind when they entered, he certainly couldn't refuse the landlord's offer of a pint. Burgess declined the local brew and asked for a pint of Watney's.

Banks knew there were shepherds in the area, but they were an elusive breed, and he'd never seen one before. Farmers who tended their own sheep were common enough, but on the south Swainsdale commons, they banded together to hire three shepherds. Most of the sheep were heughed; they grew up on the farms and never strayed far. But not all of them; winter was a hard time, and many animals got buried under drifts. The shepherds know the moors, every gully and sink-hole, better than anyone else, and to them, sheep are as different from one another as people.

Jack Crocker's face had as many lines as a tough teacher gives out in a week, and its texture looked as

hard as tanned leather. He had a misshapen blob of a
nose, and his eyes were so deeply hooded they looked
as if they had been perpetually screwed up against the
wind. His cloth cap and old, flapping greatcoat set the
final touches. His crook, a long hazel shaft with a metal
hook, leaned against the wall.

"Christ," Banks heard Burgess mutter behind him. "A
bloody shepherd!"

"I don't mind if I do," Crocker said, accepting a drink.
"I were just fetching some ewes in for lambing, like,
and I kicked that there knife." He placed the knife on
the table. It was a flick-knife with a five-inch blade and
a worn bone handle. "I didn't touch it, tha knows," he
went on, putting a surprisingly smooth and slender fore-
finger to the side of his nose. "I've seen telly."

"How did you pick it up?" Burgess asked. Banks noticed that his tone was respectful, not hectoring as usual.
Maybe he had a soft spot for shepherds.

"Like this." Crocker held the ends of the handle between thumb and second finger. He really did have beautiful hands, Banks noticed, the kind you'd picture on a
concert pianist.

Burgess nodded and took a sip of his Watney's.
"Good. You did the right thing, Mr Crocker." Banks
took an envelope from his pocket, dropped the knife in,
and sealed it.

"Is it t'right one, then? T'one as killed that bobby?"

"We can't say yet," Banks told him. "We'll have to
get some tests done. But if it is, you've done us a great
service."

" 'T'weren't owt. It's not as if I were looking fer it."
Crocker looked away, embarrassed, and raised his pint
to his lips. Banks offered him a cigarette.

"Nay, lad," he said. "In my job you need all t'breath
you can muster."

"Where did you find the knife?" Burgess asked.

"Up on t'moor, Eastvale way."

"Can you show us?"

"Aye." Crocker's face creased into a sly smile. "It's a bit of a hike, though. And tha can't take thy car."

Burgess looked at Banks. "Well," he said, "it's your part of the country. You're the nature-boy. Why don't you go up the moor with Mr Crocker here, and I'll phone the station to send a car for me?"

Yes, Banks thought, and you'll have another pint of Watney's while you're warming your hands in front of the fire.

Banks nodded. "I'd get that knife straight to the lab if I were you," he said. "If you send it through normal channels they'll take days to get the tests done. Ask for Vic Manson. If he's got a spare moment he'll dust it for prints and persuade one of the lads to try for blood-typing. It's been exposed to the elements a bit, but we might still get something from it."

"Sounds good," Burgess said. "Where is this lab?"

"Just outside Wetherby. You can ask the driver to take you straight there."

Burgess went over to the phone while Banks and Crocker drank off their pints of Black Sheep bitter and set off.

They climbed a stile at the eastern end of Mortsett Lane and set off over open moorland. The tussocks of moor grass, interspersed with patches of heather and sphagnum, made walking difficult for Banks. Crocker, always ahead, seemed to float over the top of it like a hovercraft. The higher they climbed, the harsher and stronger the wind became.

Banks wasn't dressed for the moors, either, and his shoes were soon mud-caked and worse. At least he was wearing his warm sheepskin-lined coat. Though the slope wasn't steep, it was unrelenting, and he soon got out of breath. Despite the cold wind against his face, he was sweating.

At last, the ground flattened out into high moorland. Crocker stopped and waited with a smile for Banks to catch up.

"By heck, lad, what'd tha do if tha 'ad to chase after a villain?"

"Luckily, it doesn't happen often," Banks wheezed.

"Aye. Well, this is where I found it. Just down there in t'grass." He pointed with his crook. Banks bent and poked around among the sods. There was nothing to indicate the knife had been there.

"It looks like someone just threw it there," he said.

Crocker nodded. "It would've been easy enough to hide," he said. "Plenty of rocks to stuff it under. He could've even buried it if he'd wanted."

"But he didn't. So whoever it was must have panicked, perhaps, and just tossed it away."

"Tha should know."

Banks looked around. The spot was about two miles from Eastvale; the jagged castle battlements were just visible in the distance, down in the hollow where the town lay. In the opposite direction, also about two miles away, he could see the house and outbuildings of Maggie's Farm.

It looked like the knife had been thrown away on the wild moorland about halfway or more on a direct line between Eastvale and the farm. If someone from the farm had escaped arrest or injury at the demo, it would have been a natural direction in which to run home. That meant Paul or Zoe, as Rick and Seth had been arrested and searched. It could even have been the woman, Mara, who might have been lying about staying home all evening.

On the other hand, anyone could have come up there in the past few days and thrown the knife away. That seemed much less likely, though, as it was a poor method of disposal, more spontaneous than planned. Certainly it seemed to make mincemeat of one of Banks's theories—that a fellow policeman might have committed the murder. Again, the finger seemed to be pointing at Maggie's Farm.

Banks pulled the sheepskin collar tight around his

neck and screwed up his eyes to keep the tears from
forming. No wonder Crocker's eyes were hooded almost
shut. There was nothing more to be done up here, he
decided, but he would have to mark the spot in some
way.

"Could you find this place again?" he asked.

" 'Course," the shepherd answered.

Banks couldn't see how; there was nothing to distin-
guish it from any other spot of moorland. Still, it was
Crocker's job to be familiar with every square inch of
his territory.

He nodded. "Right. We may have to get a few men
up here to make a more thorough search. Where can I
get in touch with you?"

"I live in Mortsett." Crocker gave him the address.

"Are you coming back down?"

"Nay. More ewes to fetch in. It's lambing season, tha
knows."

"Yes, well, thanks again for your time."

Crocker nodded curtly and set off further up the slope,
walking just as quickly and effortlessly as if he were on
the flat. At least, Banks thought, turning around, it would
be easier going down. But before he had even completed
the thought, he caught his foot in a patch of heather and
fell face forward. He cursed, brushed himself off and
carried on. Fortunately, Crocker had been going the
other way and hadn't seen his little accident, otherwise
it would have been the talk of the dale by evening.

He got back over the stile without further incident and
nipped into the Black Sheep for another quick pint and
a warm-up. There was nothing he could do now but wait
for Burgess to finish at the lab. Even then, there might
be no results. But a nice set of sweaty fingerprints on a
smooth surface could survive the most terrible weather
conditions, and Banks thought he had glimpsed flecks
of dried blood in the joint between blade and handle.

EIGHT

I

A sudden, heavy shower drove the merchants from the market square. It was almost time to pack up and leave anyway; market days in winter and early spring were often cold and miserable affairs. But the rain stopped as quickly as it started, and in no time the sun was out again. Wet cobblestones reflected the muted bronze light, which slid into the small puddles and danced as the wind ruffled them.

The gold hands on the blue face of the church clock stood at four-twenty. Burgess hadn't returned from the lab yet. Banks sat waiting by his window, the awkward venetian blind drawn up, and looked down on the scene as he smoked and drank black coffee. People crossed the square and splashed through the puddles that had gathered where cobbles had been worn or broken away. Everyone wore grey plastic macs or brightly coloured slickers, as if they didn't trust the sun to stay out, and many carried umbrellas. It would soon be dark. Already the sun cast the long shadow of the Tudor-fronted police headquarters over the square.

At a quarter to five, Banks heard a flurry of activity outside his office, and Burgess bounded in carrying a buff folder.

"They came through," he said. "Took them long enough, but they did it—a clear set of prints and a match with Gill's blood type. No doubt about it, that was the knife. I've already got DC Richmond running a check on the prints. If they're on record we're in business."

He lit a Tom Thumb and smoked, tapping it frequently on the edge of the ashtray whether or not a column of ash had built up. Banks went back to the window. The shadow had lengthened; across the square, secretaries and clerks on their way home dropped in at Joplin's newsagent's for their evening papers, and young couples walked hand in hand into the El Toro coffee bar to tell one another about the ups and downs of their day at the office.

When Richmond knocked and entered, Burgess jumped to his feet. "Well?"

Richmond stroked his moustache. He could barely keep the grin of triumph from his face. "It's Boyd," he said, holding out the charts. "Paul Boyd. Eighteen points of comparison. Enough to stand up in court."

Burgess clapped his hands. "Right! Just as I thought. Let's go. You might as well come along, Constable. Where's Sergeant Hatchley?"

"I don't know, sir. I think he's still checking some of the witness reports."

"Never mind. Three's enough. Let's bring Boyd in for a chat."

They piled into Banks's Cortina and headed for Maggie's Farm. Banks played no music this time; the three of them sat in tense silence as the river-meadows rolled by, eerie in the misty twilight. Gravel popped under the wheels as they approached the farm, and the front curtain twitched when they drew up outside the building.

Mara Delacey opened the door before Burgess had finished knocking. "What do you want this time?" she asked angrily, but stood aside to let them in. They followed her through to the kitchen, where the others sat at the table eating dinner. Mara went back to her half-finished meal. Julian and Luna shifted closer to her.

"How convenient," Burgess said, leaning against the

humming refrigerator. "You're all here together, except one. We're looking for Paul Boyd. Is he around?"

Seth shook his head. "No. I've no idea where he is."

"When did you last see him?"

"Last night, I suppose. I've been out most of the day. He wasn't here when I came back."

Burgess looked at Mara. Nobody said anything. "One of you must know where he is. What's it to be—now or down at the station?"

Still silence.

Burgess walked forward to pat Julian on the head, but the boy pulled a face and buried his head in Rick's side. "It'd be a shame," Burgess said, "if things got so that you couldn't look after the kids here and they had to be taken away."

"You'd never dare!" Mara said, her face flushed. "Even you can't be as much of a bastard as that."

Burgess raised his left eyebrow. "Can't I, love? Are you sure you want to find out? Where's Boyd?"

Rick got to his feet. He was as tall as Burgess and a good thirty pounds heavier. "Pick on someone your own size," he said. "If you start messing with my kid's life, you'll bloody well have me to answer to."

Burgess sneered and turned away. "I'm quaking in my boots. Where's Boyd?"

"We don't know," Seth said quietly. "He wasn't a prisoner here, you know. He pays his board, he's free to do what he wants and to come and go as he pleases."

"Not any more he isn't," Burgess said. "Maybe you'd better get Gypsy Rose Lee here to ask the stars where he is, because if we don't find him soon it's going to be very hard on you lot." He turned to Banks and Richmond. "Let's have a look around. Where's his room?"

"First on the left at the top of the stairs," Seth said. "But you're wasting your time. He's not there."

The three policemen climbed the narrow staircase. Richmond checked the other rooms while Banks and Burgess went into Paul's. There was only room for a single mattress on the floor and a small dresser at the far end, where a narrow window looked towards East-vale. Sheets and blankets lay rumpled and creased on the unmade bed; dirty socks and underwear had been left in a pile on the floor. A stale smell of dead skin and unwashed clothes hung in the air. A couple of jackets, including a parka, hung in the tiny cupboard, and a pair of scuffed loafers lay on the floor. There was nothing much in the dresser drawers besides some clean under-wear, T-shirts and a couple of moth-eaten pull-overs. A grubby paperback copy of H. P. Lovecraft's *The Shadow over Innsmouth* lay open, face down on the pillow. On the cover was a picture of a semi-transparent, frog-faced monster dressed in what looked like an evening suit. Out of habit, Banks picked the book up and flipped through the pages to see if Boyd had written anything interesting in the margins or on the blank pages at the back. He found nothing. Richmond came in and joined them.

"There's nothing here," Burgess said. "It doesn't look like he's scarpered, though, unless he had a lot more clothes than this. I'd have taken a parka and a couple of sweaters if I'd been him. What was the weather like on the night Gill was stabbed?"

"Cool and wet," Banks answered.

"Parka weather?"

"I'd say so, yes."

Burgess took the coat from the closet and examined it. He pulled the inside of each pocket out in turn, and when he got to the right one, he pointed out a faint discoloured patch to Banks. "Your men must have missed this the other day. Could be blood. He must have put the knife back in his pocket after he killed Gill. Hang on to this, Richmond. We'll get it to the lab. Why don't you two go have a look in the outbuildings? You never know, he might be hiding in the woodpile. I'll poke around a bit more up here."

Downstairs, Banks and Richmond went back into the kitchen and got Mara to accompany them with the keys.

They left by the back door and found themselves in a large rectangular garden with a low fence. Most of the place was given over to rows of vegetables—dark empty furrows at that time of year—but there was also a small square sand-box, on which a plastic lorry with big red wheels and a yellow bucket and spade lay abandoned. At the far end of the garden stood a brick building with an asphalt roof, just a little larger than a garage, and to their left was a gate that led to the barn.

"We'll have a look over there first," Banks said to Mara, who fiddled with the key-ring as she followed them to the converted barn. It wasn't a big place, no-where the size of many that had been converted into bunk barns for tourists, but it followed the traditional Dales design, on the outside at least, in that it was built of stone.

Mara opened the door to the downstairs unit first, Zoe's flat. Banks was surprised at the transformation from humble barn into comfortable living-quarters; Seth had done a really good job. The woodwork was mostly unpainted, and if it looked a little makeshift, it was cer-tainly sturdy and attractive in its simplicity. Not only, he gathered, did each unit have its own entrance, but there were cooking and bathing facilities, too, as well as a large, sparsely furnished living-room, one master bed-room, and a smaller one for Luna. But there was no sign of Paul Boyd.

The places were perfectly self-contained, Banks no-ticed, and if Rick and Zoe hadn't become friendly with Seth and Mara, they could easily have led quite separate lives there. Noting Mara's reaction to Burgess's threat, and remembering what Jenny had said at dinner, Banks guessed that Mara's fondness for the children was one unifying factor—anyone would be glad of a built-in baby-sitter—and perhaps another was their shared poli-tics.

Upstairs, the layout was different. Both bedrooms were quite small, and most of the space was taken up by Rick's studio, which was much less tidy than Zoe's large work-table downstairs, with books and charts spread out on its surface. Seth had added three skylights along the length of the roof to provide plenty of light, and canvases, palettes and odd tubes of paint littered the place. From what Banks could see, Rick Trelawney's paintings were, as Tim Fenton had said, unmarketable, being mostly haphazard splashes of colour, or collages of found objects. Sandra knew quite a bit about art, and Banks had learned from her that many paintings he wouldn't even store in the attic were regarded by experts as works of genius. But these were different, even he could tell; they made Jackson Pollock's angry explosions look as comprehensible as Constable's landscapes.

As he poked around among the stuff, though, Banks discovered a stack of small water-colour landscapes covered with an old sack. They resembled the one he'd noticed in the front room on his last visit, and he realized that they were, after all, Rick's work. So that was how he made his money! Selling pretty local scenes to tourists and little old ladies to support his revolutionary art.

Mara, who all the time had remained quiet, watching them with her arms folded, locked up as they left and led the way back to the house.

"You two go ahead," Banks said when he had closed the gate behind them. "I'm off to take a peek in the shed. It's not locked, is it?"

Mara shook her head and went back into the house with Richmond.

Banks opened the door. The shed was dark inside and smelled of wood shavings, sawdust, oiled metal, linseed oil and varnish. He tugged the chain dangling in front of him, and a naked bulb lit up, revealing Seth's workshop. Planks, boards and pieces of furniture at various stages of incompletion leaned against the walls. Spider webs hung in the dark corners. Seth had a lathe and a full set of well-kept tools—planes, saws, hammers, bevels—and boxes of nails and screws rested on makeshift wooden shelves around the walls. There was no room for anyone to hide.

At the far end of the workshop, an old Remington office typewriter sat on a desk beside an open filing cabinet. Inside, Banks found only correspondence connected with Seth's carpentry business: estimates, invoices, receipts, orders. Close by was a small bookcase. Most of the books were about antique furniture and cabinet-making techniques, but there were a couple of old paperback novels and two books on the human brain, one of which was called *The Tip of the Iceberg*. Maybe, Banks thought, Seth harboured a secret ambition to become a brain surgeon. Already a carpenter, he probably had a better start than most.

He walked back to the door and was about to turn off the light when he noticed a tattered notebook on a ledge by the door. It was full of measurements, addresses and phone numbers—obviously Seth's workbook. When he flipped through it, he noticed that one leaf had been torn out roughly. The following page still showed the faint impression of heavily scored numbers. Banks took a sheet from his own notebook, placed it on top and rubbed over it with a pencil. He could just make out the number in relief: 1139. It was hard to tell if it was in the same handwriting as the rest because the numbers were so much larger and more exaggerated.

Picking up the workbook, he turned to leave and almost bumped into Seth standing in the doorway.

"What are you doing?"

"This book," Banks said. "What do you use it for?"

"Work notes. When I need to order new materials, make measurements, note customers' addresses. That kind of thing."

"There's a page missing." Banks showed him. "What does that mean—1139?"

"Surely you can't expect me to remember that," Seth said. "It must have been a long time ago. It was probably some measurement or other."

"Why did you tear it out?"

Seth looked at him, deep-set brown eyes wary and resentful. "I don't know. Maybe it wasn't important. Maybe I'd written something on the back that I had to take with me somewhere. It's just an old notebook."

"But there's only one page missing. Doesn't that strike you as odd?"

"I've already said it doesn't."

"Did you tear out the page to give to Paul Boyd? Is it a number for him to call? Part of an address?"

"No. I've told you, I don't remember why I tore it out. It obviously wasn't very important."

"I'll have to take this notebook away with me."

"Why?"

"There are names and addresses in it. We'll have to check and see if Boyd's gone to any of them. As I understand it, he did spend quite a bit of time working with you in here."

"But it's *my* notebook. Why would he be at any of those places? They're just people who live in the dale, people I've done work for. I don't want the police bothering them. It could lose me business."

"We still have to check."

Seth swore under his breath. "Please yourself. You'd better give me a receipt, though."

Banks wrote him one, then pulled the chain to turn off the light. They walked back to the house in silence.

Seth sat down again to finish his meal and Mara followed Banks towards the front of the room. They could hear Burgess and Richmond still poking about upstairs.

"Mr Banks?" Mara said quietly, standing close to him near the window.

Banks lit a cigarette. "Yes?"

"What he said about the children . . . It's not true, is it? Surely he can't . . . ?"

Banks sat in the rocking chair and Mara pulled up a small three-legged stool opposite him. One of Zoe's tarot decks, open at "The Moon," lay on the table beside him. The moon seemed to be shedding drops of blood onto a path that led off into the distance, between two towers. In the foreground, a crab was crawling up onto land from a pool, and a dog and a wolf stood howling at the moon. It was a disturbing and hypnotic design. Banks shivered, as if someone had just walked over his grave, and turned his attention to Mara.

"They're not your children, are they?" he said.

"You know they're not. But I love them as if they were. Jenny Fuller told me she knows you. She said you're not as bad as the rest. Tell me they can't make us give the children up."

Banks smiled to himself. Not as bad as the rest, eh? He'd have to remember to tease Jenny about that back-handed compliment.

He turned to face Mara. "Superintendent Burgess will do whatever he has to to get to the bottom of things. I don't think it'll come to taking the children away, but bear in mind that he doesn't make idle threats. If you know anything, you should tell us."

Mara sucked on her bottom lip. She looked close to tears. "I don't know where Paul is," she said finally. "You can't really think he did it?"

"We've got some evidence that points that way. Have you ever seen him with a flick-knife?"

"No."

Banks thought she was lying, but he knew it was no good pushing her. She might offer him a titbit of infor-mation in the hope that it would ease the pressure, but she wasn't going to tell the full truth.

"He's gone," she said finally. "I know that. But I don't know where."

"How do you know he's gone?"

Mara hesitated, and her voice sounded too casual to be telling the truth. Before starting, she tucked her long chestnut hair behind her ears. It made her face look thin-ner and more haggard. "He's been upset these past few days, especially after your Superintendent Burgess came and bullied him. He thought you'd end up framing him because he's been in jail and because he . . . he looks different. He didn't want to bring trouble down on the rest of us, so he left."

Banks turned over the next tarot card: "The Star." A beautiful naked woman was pouring water from two vases into a pool on the ground. Behind her, trees and shrubs were blossoming, and in the sky one large, bright central star was surrounded by seven smaller ones. For some reason, the woman reminded him of Sandra, which was odd because there was no strong physical resemblance.

"How do you know why he went?" Banks asked. "Did he leave a note?"

"No, he just told me. He said last night he was thinking of leaving. He didn't say when."

"Or where?"

"No."

"Did he say anything about PC Gill's murder?"

"No, nothing. He didn't say he was running away because he was guilty, if that's what you mean."

"And you didn't think to let us know he was running off, even though there's a chance he might be a killer?"

"He's no killer." Mara spoke too quickly. "I'd no reason to think so, anyway. If he wanted to go he was quite free as far as we were concerned."

"What did he take with him?"

"What do you mean?"

Banks glanced towards the window. "It's brass-monkey weather out there; rains a lot, too. What was he wearing? Was he carrying a suitcase or a rucksack?"

Mara shook her head. "I don't know. I didn't see him go."

"Did you see him this morning?"

"Yes."

"What time?"

"About eleven or half-past. He always sleeps late."

"What time did he leave? Approximately."

"I don't know. I was out at lunch-time. I left at twenty to one and got back at about two. He'd gone by then."

"Was anyone else in the house during that time?"

"No. Seth was out in the van. He took Zoe with him because she had to deliver some charts. And Rick took the children into Eastvale."

"And you don't know what Boyd was wearing or what he took with him?"

"No. I told you, I didn't see him go."

"Come upstairs."

"What?"

Banks headed towards the staircase. "Come upstairs with me. Now."

Mara followed him up to Paul's room. Banks opened the cupboard and the dresser drawers. "What's missing?"

Mara put her hand to her forehead. Burgess and Richmond looked in at the doorway and carried on downstairs.

"I . . . I don't know," Mara said. "I don't know what clothes he had."

"Who does the washing around here?"

"Well, I do. Mostly. Zoe does some, too."

"So you must know what clothes Boyd had. What's missing?"

"He didn't have much."

"He must have had another overcoat. He's left his parka."

"No, he didn't. He had an anorak, though. A blue anorak."

Banks wrote it down. "What else?"

"Jeans, I suppose. He never wore much else."

"Footwear."

Mara looked in the closet and saw the scuffed loafers. "Just a pair of old slip-ons. Hush Puppies, I think."

"Colour?"

"Black."

"And that's it?"

"As far as I know."

Banks closed his notebook and smiled at Mara. "Look, try not to worry about the children too much. As soon as Superintendent Burgess catches Paul Boyd, he'll forget all about the threats he made. If we catch him soon, that is."

"I really *don't* know where he's gone."

"Okay. But if you come up with any ideas. . . . Think about it."

"People like Burgess shouldn't be allowed to run free," Mara said. She folded her arms tightly and stared at the floor.

"Oh? What do you suggest we should do with him? Lock him up?"

She looked at Banks. Her jaw was clenched tight and her eyes burned with tears.

"Or should we have him put down?"

Mara brushed past him and hurried down the stairs. Banks followed slowly. Burgess and Richmond stood in the front room ready to leave.

"Come on, let's go," Burgess said. "There's nothing more here." Then he turned to Seth, who stood in the kitchen doorway. "If I find out you've been helping Boyd in any way, believe me, I'll be back. And you lot'll be in more trouble than you ever dared imagine. Give my love to the kids."

II

Mara watched the car disappear down the track. She felt reassured by Banks, but wondered just how much he could do if Burgess had made his mind up about something. If the children were taken away, she thought, she could well be driven to murder the superintendent with her bare hands.

She became aware of the others behind her in the

room. She hadn't told them anything about what had happened with Paul, and none of them knew yet that he had run off for good. For one thing, she'd hardly had time to say anything. They had all drifted back close to meal-time anyway, when she was busy in the kitchen; then the police had arrived.

"What's going on, Mara?" Seth asked, coming up to her and resting his hand on her shoulder. "Do you know?"

Mara nodded. She was trying to keep the tears from her eyes.

"Come on." Seth took her hand and led her to a chair. "Tell us."

Seeing them all watching her, expectant, Mara regained her control. She reached for her tin of Old Holborn and rolled a cigarette.

"He's gone, that's all there is to it," she said, and told them about seeing old Crocker carrying the knife into the Black Sheep. "I ran back here to warn him. I didn't want the police to get him, and I thought if they'd got the knife they might find his fingerprints or something. He's been in jail, so they must be on record."

"But what made you think of Paul?" Zoe asked. "That knife was just lying around on the mantelpiece as usual, I suppose. Nobody ever paid it any mind. Any of the people here on Friday afternoon could have taken it."

Mara drew on her cigarette and finally told them about the blood she'd seen on Paul's hand when he got back from the demo. The hand that turned out to be unmarked the following morning.

"Why didn't you tell us?" Seth asked. "I don't suppose you approached Paul about it, either. There might have been a simple explanation."

"I know that," Mara said. "Don't you think I've been over it time and again in my mind? I was frightened of him. I mean, if he had done it. . . .But I wanted to stand by him. If I'd told you all, you might have asked him to leave or something."

"How did he react when you came and told him the knife had been found?" Rick asked.

"He went pale. He couldn't look me in the eye. He looked like a frightened animal."

"So you gave him money and clothes?"

"Yes. I gave him your red anorak, Zoe. I'm sorry."

"It's all right," Zoe said. "I'd have done the same."

"And I told the police he was probably wearing a blue one. He took his blue one with him, but he wasn't wearing it."

"Where's he heading?" asked Rick.

"I don't know. I didn't want him to tell me. He's a survivor; he can live out on the streets. I gave him some money, some I'd saved from working at the shop and selling my pottery. He'll have enough to get wherever he wants."

Later that evening, when the others had drifted off back to the barn and Seth had settled down with a book, Mara began to think about the few months that Paul had been around, and how alive he had made her feel. At first, he had been sullen and unresponsive, and there had come a point when Seth had considered asking him to leave. But Paul hadn't been long out of jail then; he wasn't used to dealing with people. Time and care had worked wonders. Soon, he was taking long walks alone on the moors, and the claustrophobia that had so often made his nights unbearable in jail became easier to control. Nobody forced him to, but he really took to working with Seth.

When she thought about his progress and what it had all come to, Mara couldn't help but feel sad. It would all be for nothing if he got caught and sent to prison again. When she pictured him cold and alone in the strange and frightening world beyond Swainsdale, it made her want to cry. But she told herself again that he was strong, resourceful, a survivor. It wouldn't feel the same to him as it would to her. Besides, imagined horrors were always far worse than the reality.

"I hope Paul makes it far away," Seth said in the silence that followed their love-making that night. "I hope they never catch him."

"How will we know where he is, what's happening to him?" Mara asked.

"He'll let us know one way or another. Don't you worry about it." He put his arm around her and she rested her head against his chest. "You did the right thing."

But she couldn't help but worry. She didn't think they'd hear from Paul again, not after all that had happened. She didn't know what else she could have done, but she wasn't sure she had done the right thing. As she tried to sleep, she remembered the expression on his face just before he left. There had been gratitude, yes, for the warning, the money and the clothes, but there had also been resentment and disappointment. He'd looked as if he was being sent into exile. She didn't know if he'd expected her to ask him to stay no matter what—she certainly hadn't told him he *had* to go away—but there had been a hint of accusation in his actions, as if to say, "You think I did it, don't you? You don't want me here causing trouble. You didn't trust me in the first place. I'm an outcast, and I always will be." She hadn't told Seth and the others about that.

III

Banks waited his turn at the busy bar of the Queen's Arms while Burgess sat at a round table by the Market Street entrance. It was eight-thirty. Hatchley had just left to keep a date with Carol Ellis, and Richmond had gone to a do at the Rugby Club.

Dirty Dick was clearly pleased with himself. He leaned back in his chair and positively beamed goodwill at everyone who looked his way. Nobody gave him much more than a scowl in return, though.

" 'Ey, Mr Banks," said Cyril. "A minute, if you've got one."

" 'Course. For you, Cyril, anything. And you might as well pull me a pint of bitter and a pint of Double Diamond while you're talking."

"It's about that there mate of yours." Cyril nodded his head aggressively in the direction of Burgess.

"He's not really a mate," Banks said. "More like a boss."

"Aye. Well, anyways, tell him to stop pestering my Glenys. She's got too much work to do without passing the time of day with the likes of him." Cyril leaned forward and lowered his voice. The muscles bulged above his rolled-up shirt sleeves. "And you can tell him I don't care if he is a copper—no disrespect, Mr Banks. If he doesn't keep out of my way I'll give him a bloody knuckle sandwich, so help me I will."

Glenys, who seemed to have grasped the tenor of the conversation, blushed and busied herself pulling a pint at the other end of the bar.

"I'd be delighted to pass on your message," Banks said, paying for the drinks.

"Don't forget his lordship's Double Diamond," Cyril said, his voice edged with contempt.

"You can wipe that bloody grin off your face," Burgess said after Banks had passed on Cyril's warning. "You're a long way from collecting that fiver yet. She fancies me, does young Glenys, there's no doubt about it. And there's nothing like a bit of danger, a touch of risk, to get the old hormones flowing. Look at her." True enough, Glenys was flashing Burgess a flush-cheeked smile while Cyril was looking the other way. "If we could only get that oaf out of the way. . . . Anyway, it's her night off next Monday. She usually goes to the pictures with her mates."

"I'd be careful if I were you," Banks said.

"Yes, but you're not me, are you?" He gulped down

about half of his pint. "Ah, that's good. So, we've got the bastard. Or will have soon."

Banks nodded. That, he assumed, was why they were celebrating. Burgess was on his fourth pint already and Banks on his third.

They had done everything they could. Boyd had certainly done a bunk, though Banks had no idea how he knew about the discovery of the knife. It was likely he had headed for Eastvale and taken a bus. The number forty-three ran along Cardigan Drive, on the town's western edge. He would simply have had to walk across the moors and up Gallows View to get there. Also, buses to York and Ripon passed along the same road. Somebody must have seen him. Banks had circulated his description to the bus companies and sent out his mug-shot to police around the country, paying particular attention to Leeds, Liverpool and London. As Burgess said, it was simply a matter of time before he was caught.

"Where did you get that bloody scar?" Burgess asked.

"This?" Banks fingered the white crescent by his right eye. "Got it in Heidelberg. It's a duelling scar."

"Ha bloody ha! You're a funny man, aren't you? Have you heard the one about the—" Burgess stopped and looked up at the person standing over them. "Well, well," he said, scraping his chair aside to make room. "If it isn't—"

"Dr Fuller," Jenny said. She glanced at Banks and pulled up a chair next to his.

"Of course. How could I forget? Drink, love?"

Jenny smiled sweetly. "Yes, please. I'll have a half of lager."

"Oh, come on, have a pint," Burgess insisted.

"All right. A pint."

"Good." Burgess rubbed his hands together and set off for the bar. His thigh caught the edge of the table as he stood up. Beer rippled in the glasses but didn't spill.

Jenny pulled a face at Banks. "What's with him?"

Banks grinned. "Celebrating."

"So I see." She leaned closer. "Look, I've got something to ask you—"

Banks put a finger to his lips. "Not now," he said. "He's getting served. He'll be back soon." True enough, in no time Burgess was on his way back, trying to carry three pints in his hands and slopping beer over the rims onto his shoes.

"What are you celebrating, anyway?" Jenny asked after Burgess had managed to set the drinks on the table without spilling much.

Banks told her about Paul Boyd.

"That's a shame."

"A shame! You said he gave you the creeps."

"He does. I'm just thinking of the others, that's all. It'll be a hell of a blow for Seth and Mara. They've done so much for him. Especially Mara." Jenny seemed unusually distracted at the thought of Mara Delacey, and Banks wondered why.

"You know," Burgess said, "I'm a bit sorry it turned out to be Boyd myself."

Jenny looked surprised: "You are? Why?"

"Well . . ." He moved closer. "I was hoping it might be that boy-friend of yours. Then we could get him locked up for a good long while, and you and me could . . . you know."

To Banks's surprise, Jenny laughed. "You've got some imagination, I'll say that for you, Superintendent Burgess."

"Call me Dick. Most of my friends do."

Jenny stifled a laugh. "I really don't think I could do that. Honest."

"Aren't you relieved it's all over?" Banks asked her. "I'll bet Osmond is."

"Of course. Especially if it means we won't have to put up with any more visits from him." She nodded at Burgess.

"I could still visit," Dirty Dick said, and winked.

"Oh, put another record on. So where do you think Paul is?" she asked Banks.

"We've no idea. He took off early this afternoon, before we got a positive identification. Could be anywhere."

"But you're confident you'll get him?"

"I think so."

Jenny turned to Burgess. "So your job's over, then? I don't suppose you'll want to stick around this godforsaken place much longer, will you?"

"Oh, I don't know." Burgess lit a cigar and leered at her. "It has its compensations."

Jenny coughed and waved the smoke away.

"Seriously," he went on, "I'll stay around till he's brought in. There's a lot I want to ask him."

"But that could take days, weeks."

Burgess shrugged. "It's the taxpayers' money, love. Your round again, Banks."

"Nothing for me this time," Jenny said. "I'll have to be off soon." She still had over half her drink left.

Feeling a little light-headed, Banks went to the bar.

" 'Ave you told him?" Cyril asked.

"Yes."

"Good. I just hope he knows what's best for him. Look at the bugger, he can't keep his hands off them."

Banks looked around. Dirty Dick seemed to have edged closer to Jenny, and his elbow rested on the back of her chair. She was behaving very calmly, Banks thought. It wasn't like her to take such sexist patronizing so well. Maybe she fancies him, he thought suddenly. If Glenys does, then maybe Jenny does, too. Perhaps he really does have the magic touch with women. At least he's available. And he's handsome enough, too. That casual look—the worn leather jacket, open-neck shirt— it suits him, as do the touches of grey hair at his temples.

Banks brushed the idea aside. It was ridiculous. Jenny was an intelligent, tasteful woman. A woman like her could never fall for Dirty Dick's brazen charm. But women were a mysterious lot, Banks thought glumly, carrying the drinks back. They were always falling for worthless men. He clearly recalled the beautiful Anita Howarth, object of his adolescent lust back in the third form. She had been quite oblivious to Banks's lean good looks and taken up with that spotty, good-for-nothing Steve Naylor. And Naylor hadn't seemed to give a damn about her. He gave the impression he would rather be playing cricket or rugby than go anywhere with Anita. But that just made her more crazy about him. And Banks had had to spend all his time fending off unwelcome advances from Cheryl Wagstaff, the one with the yellow buck teeth.

"I was just offering to show this lovely young lady the sights of London," Burgess said.

"I'm sure she's seen them before," Banks replied stiffly.

"Not the way I'd show her." Burgess moved his arm so that his hand rested on Jenny's shoulder.

Banks was wondering if he should act gallantly this time and defend Jenny's honour. After all, they were sort of off duty. But he remembered she was quite good at taking care of herself. Her face took on an ominously sweet expression.

"Please take your hand off my shoulder, Superintendent," she said.

"Oh, come on, love," Burgess said. "Don't be so shy. And call me Dick."

"Please?"

"Give me a chance. We've hardly even got—"

Burgess stopped abruptly when Jenny calmly and slowly picked up her glass and poured the rest of her chilled lager on his lap.

"I told you I only wanted a half," she said, then picked up her coat and left.

Burgess rushed for the gents. Luckily, Jenny had acted so naturally, and everyone around them had been so engrossed in conversation, that the event had gone largely unnoticed. Cyril had seen it, though, and his face was red with laughter.

Banks caught up with Jenny outside. She was leaning against the ancient, pitted market cross in the centre of the square with her hand over her mouth. "My God," she said, letting the laughter out and patting her chest, "I haven't had as much fun in years. That man's a positive throwback. I'm surprised you seem to be enjoying his company so much."

"He's not so bad," Banks said. "Especially after a few jars."

"Yes, you'd need to be at least half-pissed. And you'd need to be a man, too. You're all locker-room adolescents when it comes down to it."

"He's got quite a reputation as a womanizer."

"They must be desperate down south, then."

Banks's faith in women was partially restored.

It was cold outside in the deserted square. The cobbles, still wet with rain, glistened in the dim gaslight. The church bells rang half-past nine. Banks turned up his jacket collar and held the lapels close together. "What was it you wanted to ask me?"

"It's nothing. It doesn't matter now."

"Come on, Jenny, you're hiding something. You're not good at it. Is it to do with Paul Boyd?"

"Indirectly. But I told you, it doesn't matter."

"Do you know why he ran away?"

"Of course not."

"Look, I know you're a friend of Mara's. Is this to do with her? It could be important."

"All right," Jenny said, holding up her hand. "Give it a rest. I'll tell you everything you want to know. You're getting almost as bad as your mate in there. Mara just wondered how the investigation was going, that's all. They're all a bit tense up at the farm, and they wanted to know if they could expect any more visits from God's gift to women. Will you believe me now that it doesn't matter?"

"When did you talk to her?"

"This lunchtime in the Black Sheep."

"She must have seen the knife," Banks said, almost to himself.

"What?"

"The shepherd, Jack Crocker. He found the knife. She must have seen it, recognized it as Boyd's, and dashed off to warn him. That's why he took off just in time."

"Oh, Alan, surely not?"

"I thought she was lying when I talked to her earlier. Didn't you notice any of this?"

"She did take off in rather a hurry, but I'd no idea why. I left just after. You're not going to arrest her, are you?"

Banks shook his head. "It makes her an accessory," he said, "but I doubt we'd be able to prove it. And when Burgess gets Boyd, I don't think he'll spare another thought for Mara and the rest. It was just a bloody stupid thing to do."

"Was it? Would you split on a friend, just like that? What would you do if someone accused Richmond of murder, or me?"

"That's not the point. Of course I'd do what I could to clear you. But she should have let us know. Boyd could be dangerous."

"She cares about Paul. She's hardly likely to hand him over to you just like that."

"I wonder if she's told him where to run and hide as well."

Jenny shivered. "It's cold standing about here," she said. "I should go before Dirty Dick comes out and beats me up. That's just about his level. And you'd better get back or he'll think you've deserted him. Give him my love." She kissed Banks quickly on the cheek and hurried to her car. He stood in the cold for a moment thinking about Mara and what Jenny had said, then rushed back into the Queen's Arms to see what had become of the soused superintendent.

"She's certainly got spirit, I'll say that," Burgess said, not at all upset by the incident. "Another pint?"

"I shouldn't really."

"Oh, come on Banks. Don't be a party pooper." Without waiting for a reply, Burgess went to the bar.

Banks felt that he'd had enough already, and soon he would be past the point of no return. Still, he thought, after a couple more pints he wouldn't give a damn anyway. He sensed that Burgess was lonely and in need of company in his moment of triumph, and he didn't feel he could simply desert the bastard. Besides, he had only an empty house to go home to. He could leave the Cortina in the police car-park and walk home later, no matter how much he'd drunk. It was only a mile and a bit.

And so they drank on, and on. Burgess was easy enough to talk to, Banks found, once you got used to his cocky manner and stayed off politics and police work. He had a broad repertoire of jokes, an extensive knowledge of jazz and a store of tales about cock-ups on the job. On the Met, as Banks remembered, there were so many different departments and squads running their own operations that it wasn't unusual for the Sweeney to charge in and spoil a fraud-squad stake-out.

An hour and two pints later, as Burgess reached the end of a tale about a hapless drug-squad DC shooting himself in the foot, Banks suggested it was time to go.

"I suppose so," Burgess said regretfully, finishing his drink and getting to his feet.

He certainly didn't seem drunk. His speech was normal and his eyes looked clear. But when they got outside, he had difficulty walking on the pavement. To keep himself steady, he put his arm around Banks's shoulder and the two of them weaved across the market square. Thank God the hotel's just around the corner, Banks thought.

"That's my only trouble, you know," Burgess said. "Mind clear as a bell, memory intact, but every time I go over the limit my motor control goes haywire. Know what my mates call me down at the Yard?"

"No."

"Bambi." He laughed. "Bloody Bambi. You know, that little whatsit in the cartoon—the way the damn thing walks. It's not my sweet and gentle nature they're referring to." He put his hand to his groin. "Bloody hell, I still feel like I've pissed myself. That damn woman!" And he laughed.

Banks declined an invitation to go up to Burgess's room and split a bottle of Scotch. No matter how sorry he felt for the lonely bugger, he wasn't that much of a masochist. Grudgingly, Burgess let him go. "I'll drink it myself, then," were his final words, delivered at full volume in front of an embarrassed desk clerk in the hotel lobby.

As he set off home, Banks wished he'd brought his Walkman. He could be listening to Blind Willie McTell or Bukka White as he walked. He was steady on his feet, though, and arrived at the front door of the empty house in about twenty minutes. He was tired and he certainly didn't want another drink, so he decided to go straight to bed. As usual, though, when things were bothering him he couldn't get to sleep immediately. And there were plenty of things about the Gill case that still puzzled him.

Motive was a problem, unless Burgess was right and Boyd had simply lashed out indiscriminately. In this case, it seemed that knowing *who* didn't explain *why*. Boyd wasn't political as far as anyone knew, and even street punks like him weren't in the habit of stabbing policemen at anti-nuclear demos. If someone had a private reason for wanting to do away with Gill, then there was plenty to consider in the personal lives of the other suspects: Osmond's assault charges, Trelawney's custody battle, Seth's wife's accident, Mara's religious organization, and even Zoe's seaside fortune-telling. It was hard to imagine a connection at this point, but stranger things had happened. Tony Grant's report might prove useful, if it ever arrived.

Banks was also curious about the prints on the knife. Usually when a knife is thrust into a body, the fingers holding the handle slip and any impression is blurred. Boyd's prints had been perfectly clear, just as if he had carefully applied each one. It could have happened if he'd folded up the knife and carried it in his hand before throwing it away, or if he'd just picked it up after some-one else had used it. There were other prints under his, but they were too blurred to read. They could be his, too, of course, but there was no way of knowing.

Boyd had certainly carried the knife in his pocket. The stains inside the parka matched PC Gill's blood type. But if he had used it, why had he been foolish enough to pick it up after dropping it? He must have let it fall at some point, because several people had seen it being kicked around by the crowd. And if he had just left it there, it was very unlikely that it could have been traced to the farm.

But if Boyd hadn't done it, why had he picked up a knife that wasn't his? To protect someone? And who would he be more likely to protect than the people at Maggie's Farm? Or had there been someone else he knew and cared about who had access to the knife? There were a lot more questions to be asked yet, Banks thought, and Burgess was being very premature in cel-ebrating his victory tonight.

Then there was the matter of the number torn out of Seth Cotton's notebook. Banks didn't know what it meant, but there was something familiar about it, some-thing damn familiar. Boyd was close to Seth and spent plenty of time helping him in the workshop. Could the number be something to do with him? Could it help tell them where he'd gone?

It could be a phone number, of course. There were still plenty of four-digit numbers in the Swainsdale area. On impulse, Banks got out of bed and went downstairs.

It was after eleven, but he decided to try anyway. He dialled 1139 and heard a phone ring at the other end. It went on for a long time. He was just about to give up when a woman answered, "Hello. Rossghyll Guest House, bed and breakfast." The voice was polite but strained.

Banks introduced himself and some of the woman's politeness faded when it became clear that he wasn't a potential customer. "Do you know what time it is?" she said. "Couldn't this have waited till morning? Do you know what time I have to get up?"

"It's important." Banks gave a description of Paul Boyd and asked if she'd seen him.

"I wouldn't have that kind of person staying here," the woman answered angrily. "What kind of place do you think this is? This is a decent house." And with that she hung up on him.

Banks trudged back up to bed. He'd have to send a man over, of course, just to be sure, but it didn't seem a likely bet. And if it was a phone number outside the local area, it could be almost anywhere. With the dialling code missing, there was no way of telling.

Banks lay awake a while longer, then he finally drifted off to sleep and dreamed of Burgess humble in defeat.

NINE

I

The overcast sky seemed to press on Banks's nagging headache when he set off for Maggie's Farm at eleven-thirty the next morning. Burgess had called in earlier to say he was going over some paperwork in his hotel room and didn't want to be disturbed unless Paul Boyd turned up. That suited Banks fine; he wanted a word with Mara Delacey, and the less Dirty Dick knew about it, the better.

He pulled up outside the farmhouse and knocked. He wasn't surprised when Mara opened the door and moaned, "Not again!"

Reluctantly she let him in. There was no one else in the place. The others were probably working.

Banks wanted to get Mara away from the house, on neutral ground. Perhaps then, he thought, he could get her to open up a bit more.

"I'd just like to talk to you, that's all," he said. "It's not an interrogation, nothing official."

She looked puzzled. "Go on."

Banks tapped his watch. "It's nearly lunch-time and I haven't eaten yet," he said casually. "Do you fancy a trip down to the Black Sheep?"

"What for? Is this some subtle way of getting me to accompany you to the station?"

"No tricks. Honest. What I've got to say might even be of advantage to you."

She still regarded him suspiciously, but the bait was too good to refuse. "All right." She reached for an anorak to put over her sweater and jeans. "I'm going into the shop this afternoon anyway." She pulled back her thick chestnut hair and tied it in a pony-tail.

In the car, Mara leaned forward to examine the tapes Banks kept in the storage rack Brian had bought him for his birthday the previous May—his thirty-eighth. There, mixed in with Zemlinsky's *Birthday of the Infanta,* Mozart's *Magic Flute,* Dowland's *Lachrymae* and Purcell's airs, were Lightning Hopkins, Billie Holiday, Muddy Waters, Robert Wilkins and a number of blues-anthology tapes.

Picking up the Billie Holiday, Mara managed a thin smile. "A policeman who likes blues can't be all bad," she said.

Banks laughed. "I like most music," he said, "except for country-and-western and middle-of-the-road crooning—you know, Frank Sinatra, Engelbert Humperdinck and that lot."

"Even rock?"

"Even rock. Some, anyway. I must admit I'm still stuck in the sixties as far as that's concerned. I lost interest after the Beatles split up. I even know where the name of your house comes from."

Banks was pleased to be chatting so easily with Mara. It was the first time his interest in music had helped create the kind of rapport he wanted with a witness. So often people regarded it as an eccentricity, but now it was actually helping with an important investigation. A common interest in jazz and blues had also helped him to relax with Burgess a little. Still, he thought, Mara probably wouldn't stay so convivial when she followed the drift of the questions he had to ask her.

They found a quiet corner in the pub by the tiled fireplace. In a glass case on the wall beside them was a collection of butterflies pinned to a board. Banks bought Mara a half of mild and got a pint of Black Sheep bitter for himself. Maybe the hair of the dog would do the trick and get rid of his headache. He ordered a ploughman's lunch; Mara asked for lasagne.

"Ploughman's lunches were invented for tourists in the seventies," Mara said.

"Not authentic?"

"Not a bit."

"Oh well. I can think of worse inventions."

"I suppose you want to get down to business, don't you?" Mara said. "Did Jenny Fuller tell you about our meeting?"

"No, but I figured it out. I think she's worried about you."

"She needn't be. I'm all right."

"Are you? I thought you'd be worried sick about Paul Boyd."

"What if I am?"

"Do you think he's guilty?"

Mara paused and sipped some beer. She swept a stray wisp of hair from her cheek before answering. "Maybe I did at first, a bit," she said. "At least, I was worried. I mean, we don't know a lot about him. I suppose I looked at him differently. But not now, no. And I don't care what evidence you've got against him."

"What made you change your mind?"

"A feeling, that's all. Nothing concrete, nothing you'd understand."

Banks leaned forward. "Believe it or not, Mara, policemen have feelings like that, too. We call them hunches, or we put them down to our nose, our instinct for truth. You may be right about Boyd. I'm not saying you are, but there's a chance. Things aren't quite as cut and dried as they appear. In some ways Paul is too obvious."

"Isn't that what appeals to you? How easy it is to blame him?"

"Not to me, no."

"But . . . I mean . . . I thought you were sure, that you had evidence?"

"The knife?"

"Yes."

"You recognized it, didn't you, when Jack Crocker brought it in here yesterday lunch-time?"

Mara said nothing. Before Banks could speak again, the food arrived and they both tucked in.

"Look," said Banks, after polishing off the best part of a chunk of Wensleydale and a pickled onion, "let's assume that Boyd's innocent, just for the sake of argument." Mara looked at him, but her expression was hard to fathom. Suspicion? Hope? Either reaction would be perfectly natural. "If he is," Banks went on, "then it raises more questions than it answers. It's easier for everyone if Boyd turns out to be guilty—everyone but him, that is—but the easiest way isn't necessarily the true one. Do you know what I mean?"

Mara nodded and her lips curved just a little at the edges. "Sounds like the Eightfold Path," she said.

"The what?"

"The Eightfold Path. It's the Buddhist way to enlightenment."

Banks speared another pickled onion. "Well, I don't know much about enlightenment," he said, "but we could do with a bit more light on the case." He went on to tell her about the blood and prints on the knife. "That much we know," he said. "That's the evidence, the facts, if you like. Boyd was there, and we can prove that he handled the murder weapon. Superintendent Burgess thinks it's enough to convict him, but I'm not so sure myself. Given the political aspect, though, he might just be right. Finding Boyd guilty will make us look good and it'll discredit everyone who seems a bit different."

"Isn't that what you want?"

"I wish you'd stop making assumptions like that. You sound like a stoned hippie at a rock festival. Maybe you'd like to call me a pig, too, and get it over with? Either that or grow up."

Mara said nothing, but Banks saw the faint flush suffuse her face.

"I want the truth," Banks went on. "I'm not out to get any group or person, just a killer. If we assume that Boyd didn't do it, then why are his prints on the knife, and why was it found on the moors about halfway between Eastvale and Maggie's Farm?"

Mara pushed her half-eaten lasagne aside and rolled a cigarette. "I'm no detective," she said, "but maybe he picked it up and threw it away on his way home, when he realized what it was."

"But why? Would you have done something as stupid as that? Bent down at a demonstration to pick up a bloodstained knife? Think about it. Boyd had no guarantee of getting away. What if he'd been caught on the spot with the knife on him?"

"He'd probably have had time to drop it if he saw the cops closing in on him."

"Yes, but it would still have his prints on it. I doubt if he'd have been calm enough to wipe it before they grabbed him. Even if he had, there would probably have been some of Gill's blood on him."

"This is all very well," Mara said, "but I don't know what you're getting at."

"I'll tell you in a moment." Banks went to the bar and bought two more drinks. The place had filled up a bit since they'd come in, and there were even two well-wrapped hikers resting their feet by the fire.

Banks sat down and drank some beer. The hair of the dog was working nicely. "It all comes back to the knife," he said. "You recognized it; Paul Boyd must have done, too. It comes from the farm, doesn't it?"

Mara turned aside and studied the butterflies.

"You're not helping anyone by holding back, you know. I only want you to confirm what we already know."

Mara stubbed out her cigarette: "All right, so it comes from the house. What of it? If you know already, why bother to ask?"

"Because Paul might have been protecting someone, mightn't he? If he found the knife and took it away, he must have thought it was evidence pointing to someone he knew, someone at the farm. Unless you think he's just plain stupid."

"You mean one of us?"

"Yes. Who would he be most likely to protect?"

"I don't know. There were a few people up at the farm that afternoon."

"Yes, I know who was there. Could anyone have taken the knife?"

Mara shrugged. "It was on the mantelpiece, in plain view of everyone."

"Whose knife is it?"

"I don't know. It's always been there."

"Never mind, then. Let's just call it a communal flick-knife. Do you think Paul would have picked it up to protect Dennis Osmond? Or Tim and Abha?"

Mara twirled a loose strand of hair. "I don't know," she said. "He didn't know them very well."

"What part did he play that afternoon? Was he around?"

"Most of the time, yes, but he didn't say much. Paul has an inferiority complex when it comes to students and political talk. He doesn't know about Karl Marx and the rest, and he doesn't have enough confidence in his own ideas to feel he can contribute."

"So he was there but he wasn't very involved?"

"That's right. He agreed with everything in principle. I mean, he wasn't at the demo just to . . . just to . . ."

"Cause trouble?"

"No. He was there to demonstrate. He's never had a job, you know. He's got nothing to thank Thatcher's government for."

"You say the knife was usually kept on the mantelpiece. Did you see anyone pick it up that afternoon, just to fidget with, perhaps?"

"No."

"When did you notice it was missing?"

"What?"

"You must have noticed it was gone. Was it before you saw Jack Crocker walk in here with it yesterday?"

"I . . . I . . ."

Banks waved his hand. "Forget it. I think I get the gist. You had noticed it was missing, and for some reason you thought Paul might have taken it with him last Friday."

"No!"

"Then why did you run off and warn him?"

"Because I thought you'd pick on him if the knife had been found here. Jack Crocker works these moors. I knew when I saw him he couldn't have found it far away."

"Plausible," Banks said. "But I'm not convinced. You weren't at the demo, were you?"

"No. It's not that I don't believe in the cause, but somebody had to stay home and look after the children."

"You didn't put them to bed early and sneak out?"

"Are you accusing me?"

"I'm asking you."

"Well, I don't know how you'd expect me to do that. The others had taken the van and it's a good four miles' walk across the moor to Eastvale."

"So that leaves Paul, Zoe, Seth and Rick. Seth and Rick were arrested, but if Paul had picked up the knife at the demo, either one of them could have stabbed Gill, too."

"I don't believe it."

"Did Osmond or any of the others dislike you enough to want to put the blame on one of you?"

"I don't think so. Nobody had reason to hate us that much."

"If you really hadn't noticed the knife for some time,

someone else could have taken it earlier, couldn't they? Did you have any visitors during the week?"

"I . . . I don't remember."

"Do you keep the place securely locked up?"

"You must be joking. We've nothing worth stealing."

"Think about it. You see my problem, don't you? How it becomes more complicated if we leave Boyd out of it. And if someone did take the knife, there's premeditation involved. Do you know of anyone with a reason to murder PC Gill?"

"No."

"Was he mentioned that afternoon up at the farm?"

"Not that I heard. But I was in and out. You know, making tea, clearing up."

Banks drank some more Black Sheep bitter. "Does the number 1139 mean anything to you?"

Mara frowned. The lines curved down from each side of her forehead and converged at the bridge of her nose. "No," she said. "At least I don't think so. Why? Where did you find it?"

"It's not part of an address or a telephone number, for example?"

"I've told you, no. Not that I know of. It sounds vaguely familiar, but I can't place it."

"Have you ever heard of the Rossghyll Guest House?"

"Yes, it's up the dale. Why?"

Banks watched her expression closely and saw no sign that the place meant anything to her. "Never mind. Let me know if anything comes to you. It might be important."

Mara finished her drink and shifted in her chair. "Is there anything else?"

"Just one thing. It looks bad for Paul, running off like this. I know I can't ask you to turn him in, even if you do know where he is. But it really would be best for him if he gave himself up. Is there any chance of that?"

"It's unlikely. He's scared of the police, especially that bastard of a superintendent you've got." She shook her head. "I don't think he'll turn himself in."

"If you hear from him, tell him what I said. Tell him I promise he'll get a fair deal."

Mara nodded slowly. "I don't think it'll do much good, though," she said. "He won't believe me. He doesn't trust us now any more than he trusts you."

"Why not?"

"He knows I suspected him, just for a while. Paul's had so little love in his life he finds it hard enough to trust people in the first place. If they let him down, even in the slightest, then that's it."

"Still," Banks said, "if you get the chance, put in a word."

"I'll tell him. But I don't think any of us are likely to hear from Paul again. Can I go now?"

"Wait a moment and I'll give you a lift." Banks still had half a pint left and made to finish it off.

Mara stood up. "No, I'll walk. The shop's not far, and I could do with some fresh air."

"Are you sure?"

"Yes."

After she'd gone, Banks relaxed and savoured the rest of his beer. The meeting had gone better than he'd expected, and he had actually learned something about the knife. Mara had been evasive, mostly to avoid incriminating herself, but that was only to be expected. He didn't blame her for it.

Banks decided to keep his knowledge from Burgess for a while. He didn't want Dirty Dick to go charging in like a bloody elephant and frighten everyone into their corners as usual. Banks had managed to overcome some of Mara's general resentment for the police—whether through Jenny's influence, his taste in music, or sheer charm, he wasn't sure—but if Burgess turned up again, Mara's hatred for him would surely rub off on Banks as well.

By the time he set off back to Eastvale, his head had stopped aching and he felt able to tolerate some music.

But he couldn't shake off the feeling that he was missing something obvious. He had the strange sensation that two insignificant things either he or Mara had said should be joined into one truth. If they made contact, a little bulb would light up and he would be that much closer to solving the case. Billie Holiday sang on regardless:

Sad am I, glad am I
For today I'm dreaming of
Yesterdays.

II

Mara walked along the street, head down, thinking about her talk with Banks. Like all policemen, he asked nothing but bloody awkward questions. And Mara was sick of awkward questions. Why couldn't things just get back to normal so she could get on with her life?

"Hello, love," Elspeth greeted her as she walked into the shop.

"Hello. How's Dottie?"

"She won't eat. How she can expect to get better when she refuses to eat, I just don't know."

They both knew that Dottie wasn't going to get better, but nobody said so.

"What's wrong with you?" Elspeth asked. "You've got a face as long as next week."

Mara told her about Paul.

"I don't want to say I told you so," Elspeth said, smoothing her dark tweed skirt, "but I thought that lad was trouble from the start. You're best rid of him, all of you."

"I suppose you're right." Mara didn't agree, but there was no point arguing Paul's case against Elspeth. She hadn't expected any sympathy.

"Go in the back and get the wheel spinning, love," Elspeth said. "It'll do you a power of good."

The front part of the shop was cluttered with goods for tourists. There were locally knit sweaters on shelves on the walls, tables of pottery—some of which Mara had made—and trays of trinkets, such as key-rings bearing the Dales National Park emblem—the black face of a Swaledale sheep. As if that weren't enough, the rest of the space was taken up by fancy notepaper, glass paperweights, fluffy animals and fridge-door magnets shaped like strawberries or Humpty Dumpty.

In the back, though, the set-up was very different. First, there was a small pottery workshop, complete with wheel and dishes of brown and black metallic oxide glaze, and beyond that a drying room and a small electric kiln. The workshop was dusty and messy, crusted with bits of old clay, and it suited a part of Mara's personality. Mostly she preferred cleanliness and tidiness, but there was something special, she found, about creating beautiful objects in a chaotic environment.

She put on her apron, took a lump of clay from the bin and weighed off enough for a small vase. The clay was too wet, so she wedged it on a flat concrete tray, which absorbed the excess moisture. As she wedged—pushing hard with the heels of her hands, then pulling the clay forward with her fingers to get all the air out—she couldn't seem to lose herself in the task as usual, but kept on thinking about her conversation with Banks.

Frowning, she cut the lump in half with a cheese-wire to check for air bubbles, then slammed the pieces together much harder than usual. A fleck of clay spun off and hit her forehead, just above her right eye. She put the clay down and took a few deep breaths, trying to bring her mind to bear only on what she was doing.

No good. It was Banks's fault, of course. He had introduced her to speculations that caused nothing but distress. True, she didn't want Paul to be guilty, but if, as Banks had said, that meant someone else she knew had killed the policeman, that only made things worse.

Sighing, she started the wheel with the foot pedal and slammed the clay as close to the centre as she could. Then she drenched both it and her hands with water from a bowl by her side. As the wheel spun, clayey water flew off and splashed her apron.

She couldn't believe that any of her friends had stabbed Gill. Much better if Osmond or one of the students had done it for political reasons. Tim and Abha seemed nice enough, if a bit naive and gushing, but Mara had never trusted Osmond; he had always seemed somehow too oily and opinionated for her taste.

But what about Rick? He had strong political views, more so than Seth or Zoe. He'd often said someone should assassinate Margaret Thatcher, and Seth had argued that someone just as bad would take her place. But it was only a policeman who'd been killed, not a politician. Despite what Rick said about the police being mere instruments of the state, paid enforcers, she couldn't believe that would make him actually kill one of them.

She leaned forward, elbows in, and pushed hard to centre the clay. At last, she managed it, and, allowing herself a smile of satisfaction, stuck her thumb in the top and pushed down about an inch. She then filled the hole with water and began to drive deeper to where she wanted the bottom of the vase to be.

Holding the inside with one finger, she slowed the wheel and began to make a ridge from the outside bottom, raising the clay to the height she wanted. It took several times to get there, pulling just a little farther each time, watching the groove flow up the outside of the clay and disappear.

She was determined not to let Banks get to her. There was no way she was going to start suspecting Rick the way she had Paul. She had good reason for worrying about him, she told herself: his violent past; the blood he had lied about. And the knife had his fingerprints on it. She had no reason at all for suspecting anyone else. If only Paul could get far away and never be seen again. That would be best—if the police continued to believe he had done it but were never able to find him.

She could hear Elspeth out front trying to sell a sweater to a customer. "Traditional Dales pattern . . . local wool, of course . . . hand-knit, naturally. . . ."

Almost there. But her hands weren't steady, and when she'd lost her concentration she had increased the pressure with her right foot, speeding up the wheel. Suddenly the clay began to spin wildly off centre—insane shapes, like Salvador Dali paintings or plastic melting in a fire—and then it collapsed in on itself on the wheelhead. And that was that. Mara took the cheese-wire and sliced off the mess. There was enough left for an eggcup maybe, but she couldn't face starting again. That damn Banks had ruined her day.

In disgust, she tore off her wet apron and cleaned the rest of the clay from the wheel. Putting on her anorak again, she walked through to the front.

"Sorry, Elspeth," she said, "I just can't seem to concentrate today. Maybe I'll go for a walk."

Elspeth frowned. "Are you sure you're all right?"

"Yes. Don't worry, I'll be fine. Give my love to Dottie."

"Will do."

As she left the shop, the bell clanged loudly behind her.

Instead of heading back home, she climbed the stile at the end of Mortsett Lane and struck out for the moors. As she walked, she ran over the events of last Friday afternoon up at the farm.

Most of the time she'd been in the kitchen preparing a stew for dinner—something to fortify them all against the cold and rain—and making pots of tea. The children had been a nuisance, too, she remembered. Over-excited because there were so many adults around, they'd kept coming in and tugging at her apron strings, pestering her. She hadn't been paying much attention to what the others were saying or doing in the front room even when she was there, and she hadn't noticed anybody pick up anything from the mantelpiece.

The only thing that struck a chord was that number Banks had mentioned: 1139, was it? She thought that she had heard it mentioned recently. Half heard it, really, because she had been thinking about something else at the time. The ashram, that was it. She had been remembering how, after the evening meal of brown rice and vegetables (every day!), they had all sat cross-legged in the meditation room, with its shrine to the guru and the smell of sandalwood incense heavy in the air. They had talked about how their lives had been empty until they had found the True Path. How they had been searching in all the wrong places for all the wrong things. And they had sung songs together, holding hands. "Amazing Grace" had been a particular favourite. Somehow, the gathering at the farm that afternoon had made her think of those days, though it was different in almost every way.

That was what she had been thinking about when the number had been mentioned. And she had been in the kitchen, too, because she clearly recalled the earthy feel of the potatoes she'd been peeling. Wasn't it odd how the mind worked? All the components of the experience were there, clear as day, but she couldn't remember who had mentioned the number, or in what context. And people had been in and out of the kitchen all afternoon.

Worrying about Paul again, wondering where he was, she lowered her head against the wind and marched on through the rough grass and heather.

III

There was little else to do but wait for Boyd to turn up. Whatever his suspicions, Banks had nothing concrete to go on, and he wasn't likely to have until he'd questioned Boyd. Dirty Dick was still sleeping last night's beer and Scotch off in his hotel room and Richmond was running around putting together as much information as he could get on the suspects. Criminal records weren't enough; they tended to leave out the all-too-important human factor, the snippet that gives a clue to motivation and makes the pattern clear.

Mostly Banks smoked too much and stared gloomily out of his window onto the grey market square. At four o'clock, he heard a knock on his door and called, "Come in."

PC Craig stood there looking as pleased as Punch. "We've got a line on Boyd, sir," he said, ushering in a stout middle-aged woman with curlers in her hair.

Banks pulled out a chair for her.

"This is Mrs Evans," Craig said. "I went knocking on doors on Cardigan Road to find out if anyone had seen Boyd, and Mrs Evans here said she had. She kindly offered to come in with me and talk to you, sir."

"Good work," Banks said. Craig smiled and left.

Banks asked Mrs Evans what she'd seen.

"It was about three o'clock yesterday afternoon," she began. "I know the time because I'd just got back from Tesco's with the shopping and I were struggling to get off t'bus."

"Which bus was that?"

"A forty-four. Two forty-six from t'bus station."

Banks knew the route. The bus took the long way around Cardigan Road for the benefit of local passengers, then carried on to York.

"And you saw Paul Boyd?"

"I saw a lad what looked like that photo." PC Craig had taken a prison photograph of Boyd to show from door to door. "His hair's different now, but I know it was him. I've seen him before."

"Where?"

"Around town. More often than not coming out of

t'dole office. I always hold my handbag tighter when I see him. I know it's not fair to judge a book by its cover, but he looks like a bad sort to me."

"Where did you see him this time?"

"He was running up Gallows View from t'fields."

"From Relton way?"

"Aye, as t'crow flies."

"And where did he go?"

"Go? He didn't go anywhere. He were running for t'bus. Just caught it an' all. Nearly knocked me over, and me carrying two heavy shopping bags."

"What was he wearing? Do you remember?"

"Aye, that I do. A red anorak. I noticed because it looked too small for him. A bit short in t'sleeves and tight around t'armpits."

Why, Banks asked himself, wasn't he surprised that Mara had lied about Boyd's clothes?

"Was he carrying anything?"

"One of those airline bags—British Airways, I think."

"Do you remember anything else?"

"Just that he seemed in such a hurry and looked worried. I mean, as a rule, like I said, it'd be me who'd be frightened of him, but this time he looked like he were scared out of his wits."

Banks went over to the door and called Craig back. "Thanks, Mrs Evans," he said. "We appreciate your coming in like this. PC Craig here will drive you home." Mrs Evans nodded gravely and Craig escorted her out.

As soon as he was alone, Banks checked the bus timetable and found that the two forty-six from Eastvale was indeed the milk run to York; it didn't get there until 4:09. Next he phoned the York railway station and, after speaking to a succession of surly clerks, finally got put through to a pleasant woman in charge of information. From her, he discovered that Boyd could have taken a train almost anywhere between four-fifteen and five o'clock: Leeds, London, Newcastle, Liverpool, Edinburgh, plus points in between and anywhere else that connections might take him. It didn't seem much of a help, but he called Sergeant Hatchley in and put him on tracking down the train-catering crews and ticket collectors. It would mean a trip to York, and it might take a long time, but at least it was action. Of course, Hatchley pulled a long face—it seemed he had plans for the evening—but Banks ignored him. It wasn't as if Hatchley had any other work to do. Why wag your own tail when you've got a dog?

At home that evening, Banks ate a tin of Irish stew and pottered restlessly about the house waiting to hear from Hatchley. At nine o'clock, unable to concentrate on reading and almost wishing he'd gone to York himself, he turned on the TV and watched a beautiful blonde policewoman and her loud-mouthed American partner dash around spraying London with lead. It was background noise, something to fill the emptiness of the house. Finally, he could stand his own company no longer and phoned Sandra.

This time he felt even more lonely after he hung up, but the feeling didn't last as long. Twenty minutes later Hatchley phoned from York. He had managed to get the addresses of most of the ticket collectors and catering staff on the trains out of York, but none of them lived locally. All in all, the first lead seemed to be petering out. That happened sometimes. Banks told Hatchley to go over to York CID headquarters and phone as many of the crew members as he could get through to, and to call back if he came up with anything. He didn't. At eleven-thirty Banks went to bed. Maybe tomorrow morning, after Boyd's photograph appeared in all the national dailies, they would get the break they needed.

TEN

I

The big break came early Friday morning. The Rossghyll Guest House proved to be a dead end, and all the train crews out of York had been too busy to remember anyone, but an Edinburgh barber phoned to say he recognized Paul Boyd's photograph in the morning paper. Though Banks found the man's accent difficult to understand, he managed to learn what Paul's new haircut looked like. Even more important, he discovered that Paul had ditched his red anorak for a new grey duffle coat.

As soon as he hung up, Banks checked the map. Paul had headed north rather than to London or Liverpool. That had been a clever move; it had gained him time. But now that his photograph was on the front page of all the tabloid dailies, his time was running out. In addition to getting the photo in the papers as soon as possible, Banks and his men had also circulated Boyd's description to police in all major cities, ports and airports. It was routine, the best they could do with limited knowledge, but now there was somewhere concrete to start.

Assuming that Paul would ultimately want to leave the country, Banks took out his AA road map and ran his finger up the outline of the Scottish coast looking for ways out. He could find only two ferry routes north of

Edinburgh on the east coast. The first, from Aberdeen to Lerwick, on the Shetlands, could take Boyd eventually to Bergen and Torshavn, in Norway, or to Seydhisfjördhur, in Iceland. But looking at the fine print, Banks saw that those ferries ran only in summer—and as the grey sky and drizzle outside testified, it certainly wasn't summer.

Another ferry ran from Scrabster, farther north, to Stromness, on mainland Orkney, but that hardly seemed like a place to run and hide. Boyd would stand out there like an Eskimo in the tropics.

Turning to the west coast, Banks saw dozens of broken red lines leading to such places as Brodick, on the Isle of Arran; Port Ellen, on Islay; and Stornaway, on Lewis, in the Outer Hebrides. The whole map was a maze of small islands and ferry routes. But, Banks reasoned, none of those isolated places would suit Boyd. He would be trapped, as well as conspicuous, on any of Scotland's islands, especially at this time of year.

The only trip that made any sense in the area was Stranraer to Larne. Then Boyd would be in Northern Ireland. From there, he didn't need a passport to cross the border to the Republic. Boyd was from Liverpool, Banks remembered, and probably had Irish friends.

So the first call he made, after giving Richmond and Hatchley the task of informing the other Scottish ferry ports just in case, was to the police at Stranraer. He was told that there had been no sailings the previous day because of a bad storm at sea, but this morning was calm. There were sailings at 1130, 1530, 1900 and 0300, all with easy connections from Edinburgh or Glasgow. Banks gave Boyd's description and asked that the men there keep a special watch for him, especially at ferry boardings. Next he issued the new description to police in Edinburgh, Glasgow, Inverness, Aberdeen and Dundee, and passed a list of smaller places to PCs Craig and Tolliver downstairs. Then he phoned Burgess, who had been keeping a low profile in his hotel room since their drunken night, and gave him the news.

Banks knew from experience that leads like this could bring results in a matter of minutes or days. He was impatient to have Boyd in and get the truth out of him, as much to test his own theories as anything else, but he'd get nowhere pacing the room. Instead, he sent for some coffee and went over the files Richmond had put together.

Information is a policeman's life-blood. It comes in from many sources: interviews, gossip, criminal records, informers, employers, newspaper reporters, and registries of births, marriages and deaths. It has to be collated, filed and cross-referenced in the hope that one day it will prove useful. DC Richmond was the best ferret they had at Eastvale, in addition to being practically invisible on surveillance and handy in a chase. Sergeant Hatchley, though tough, tenacious and good at interrogation, was too lazy and desultory to tie everything together. He overlooked minor details and took the easy way out. Put more simply, Richmond enjoyed gathering and collating data, whereas Hatchley didn't. It made all the difference.

Banks spread out the sheets in front of him. He already knew a bit about Seth Cotton, but he had to be thorough in his revision. In the end, though, the only extra knowledge he gleaned was that Cotton had been born in Dewsbury and that in the mid-seventies he had settled in Hebden Bridge and led a quiet life, as far as the local police were concerned. Richmond had picked up the accident report on Alison Cotton, which didn't say very much. Banks made a note to look into it further.

There was nothing new on Rick Trelawney, either, apart from the name and address of his wife's sister in London. It might be worth a call to get more details on the divorce.

Zoe Hardacre was a local girl. Or near enough. As Jenny had said, she hailed from Whitby on the east coast, not far from Gill's home town, Scarborough. After

school she had tried secretarial work, but drifted away.
Employers had complained that she couldn't seem to
keep her mind on the important tasks they gave her, and
that she always seemed to be in another world. That
other world was the one of the occult: astrology, palm-
istry and tarot card readings. She had studied the sub-
jects thoroughly enough to be regarded as something of
an expert by those who knew about such things. Now
that the occult seemed to have come into fashion among
the New Age yuppie crowd, she made a living of sorts
producing detailed natal charts and giving tarot readings.
Everyone seemed to agree that Zoe was harmless, a true
flower child, though too young to have been part of the
halcyon days of the sixties. She seemed about as political as a flower, too: she supported human rights, and she
wanted the bomb banned, but that was as far as it went.

As far as Banks could make out, she had never come
into contact with PC Gill. Banks imagined him bursting
into her booth at Whitby, truncheon raised, and arresting
her for charlatanism; or perhaps she had read his palm
and told him he was a repressed homosexual. The absurdity of Banks's theories served only as a measure of
his frustration over motive. The connection between one
of the suspects and Gill's murder was there somewhere,
but Banks didn't have enough data yet to see it. He felt
as if he were trying to do a join-the-dots drawing with
too few dots.

While Banks was almost convinced that Mara Delacey
had been at the farm looking after the children at the
time PC Gill was stabbed, he glanced over her file anyway. She had started out as a bright girl, a promising
student, gaining a good degree in English, but she had
fallen in with the hippie crowd when LSD, acid rock,
bandanas and bright caftans were all the rage. The police
knew she took drugs, but never suspected her of dealing
in them. Despite one or two raids on places where she
happened to be living, they had never even been able to
find her in possession.

Like Zoe, Mara had done occasional stints of secretarial work, most often as a temp, and she had never really put her university education to practical use. She'd spent some time in the USA in the late seventies, mostly in California. Back in England, she had drifted for a while, then become involved with a guru and ended up living in one of his ashrams in Muswell Hill for a couple of years. After that, the farm. There was nothing to tie Mara to PC Gill, unless he had crossed her path during the two years she had been in Swainsdale.

Banks walked over to the window to rest his eyes and lit a cigarette. Outside, two elderly tourists, guidebooks in hand, paused to admire the Norman tower, then walked into the church.

Nothing in what Banks had read seemed to get him any further. If Gill did have a connection with someone at the farm, it was well buried and he'd have to dig deep for it. Sighing, he sat down again and flipped open the next folder.

Tim Fenton had been born in Ripon and was now in his second year at Eastvale College of Further Education. With Abha Sutton, he ran the Students Union there. It was a small one, and usually stuck to in-college issues, but students were upset about government health and education policies—especially as far as they were likely to affect grants—and took every opportunity to demonstrate their displeasure. Tim, whose father was an accountant, was only nineteen and had no blots on his copy-book except for attending the seminar that got him into Special Branch's files.

Abha Sutton was born in Bradford of an Indian mother and a Yorkshire father. Again, her upbringing had been solidly middle-class, and like Tim, as Richmond had tried to tell Burgess, she had no history of violence or involvement in extremist politics. She had been living with Tim for six months now, and together they had started the college Marxist Society. It had very few members, though; many of the college students were local farmers' sons studying agriculture. Still, the Social Sciences department and the Arts faculty were expanding, and they had managed to recruit a few new members among the literary crowd.

Banks read even more closely when he got to Dennis Osmond's file. Osmond was thirty-five, born in Newcastle-on-Tyne. His father had worked in the shipyards there, but unemployment had forced the family to move when Osmond was ten. Mr Osmond had found a job at the chocolate factory, where he'd been known as a strong union man, and he had been involved in the acrimonious and sometimes violent negotiations that marked its last days. Osmond himself, though given at first to more intellectual pursuits, had followed his father politically.

A radical throughout university, he had dropped out in his third year, claiming that the education he was being given was no more than an indoctrination in bourgeois values, and had taken up social work in Eastvale, where he'd been working now for twelve years. During that period, he had become one of the town's chief spokesmen, along with Dorothy Wycombe, for the oppressed, neglected and unjustly treated. He had also beat up Ellen Ventner, a woman he had lived with. Some of his cronies were the kind of people that Burgess would want shot on sight—shop stewards, feminists, poets, anarchists and intellectuals.

Whatever good Osmond had done around the place, Banks still couldn't help disliking the man and seeing him, somehow, as a sham. He couldn't understand Jenny's attraction to him, unless it was purely physical. And Jenny, of course, still didn't know that Osmond had once assaulted a woman.

It was after one o'clock, time for a pie and a pint in the Queen's Arms. But no sooner had Banks settled down in his favourite armchair by the fire to read the *Guardian* than PC Craig came rushing into the pub.

"They've got him, sir," he said breathlessly. "Boyd.

Caught him trying to get on the half-past-eleven ferry to Larne."

Banks looked at his watch. "It's taken them long enough to get onto us. Are they holding him?"

"No, sir. They're bringing him down. Said they should be here late this afternoon."

"No hurry, then, is there?" Banks lit a cigarette and rustled his paper. "Looks like it's all over."

But it didn't feel as if it was all over; it felt more like it was just beginning.

II

Burgess paced the office like an expectant father, puffing on his cigar and glancing at his watch every ten seconds.

"Where the bloody hell are they?" he asked for what seemed to Banks like the hundredth time that afternoon.

"They'll be here soon. It's a long drive and the roads can be nasty in this weather."

"They ought to be here by now."

The two of them were in Banks's office waiting for Paul Boyd. Scenting the kill, Burgess didn't seem able to relax, but Banks felt unusually calm. Along Market Street the shopkeepers were shutting up for the day, and it was already growing dark. In the office, the heater coughed and the fluorescent light hummed.

Banks stubbed out his cigarette and said, "I'm off for some coffee. Want some?"

"I'm jittery enough as it is. Oh, what the hell. Why not? Black, three sugars."

In the corridor, Banks bumped into Sergeant Hatchley on his way downstairs. "Anything?" he asked.

"No," said Hatchley. "Still waiting to hear. I'm on my way to check with Sergeant Rowe if there's been any messages."

Banks took the two mugs of coffee back to his office

and smiled when Burgess jumped at the sound of the door opening. "It's all right," he said. "Don't get excited. It's only me."

"Do you think the silly buggers have got lost?" Burgess asked, scowling. "Or broken down?"

"I'm sure they know their way around just as well as anyone else."

"You can never be sure with bloody Jocks," Burgess complained. Eastvale was the farthest north he had ever been, and he had already made it quite clear that he didn't care to venture any farther. "If they've let that bastard escape—"

But he was interrupted by the phone. It was Sergeant Rowe. Boyd had arrived.

"Tell them to bring him up here." Burgess took out another Tom Thumb. He lit it, brushed some ash off his shirt and picked up his coffee.

A few moments later there was a knock at the door, and two uniformed men entered with Paul Boyd between them. He looked pale and distant—as well he might, Banks thought.

"Sorry, sir," said the driver. "We had a delay setting off. Had to wait till the doc had finished."

"Doctor?" Burgess said. "Why, what's wrong? Young dickhead here didn't hurt anyone, did he?"

"Him? No." The constable gave Paul a contemptuous glance. "Fainted when they caught him, that's all, then came round screaming about walls closing in. Had to get the doc to give him a sedative."

"Walls closing in, eh?" Burgess said. "Interesting. Sounds like a touch of claustrophobia to me. Never mind. Sit him down, and you two can bugger off now."

"See the desk sergeant about expenses and accommodation," Banks said to the two Scotsmen. "I don't suppose you'll be wanting to set off back tonight?"

The driver smiled. "No, sir. Thanks very much, sir."

"Thank *you*," Banks said. "There's a good pub across the road. The Queen's Arms. You can't miss it."

"Yes, sir."

Burgess could hardly wait to close the door behind them. Paul sat facing Banks in a tubular metal chair with a wooden seat and back. Burgess, preferring a free rein and the advantage of height, chose to lean against the wall or stride around as he talked.

"Get the sergeant in, will you?" he asked Banks. "With his notebook."

Banks sent for Hatchley, who arrived red-faced and out of breath a minute later. "Those bloody stairs again," he grumbled. "They'll be the death of me."

Burgess pointed to a chair in the corner and Hatchley sat down obediently. He found a clean page in his notebook and took out his pencil.

"Right," said Burgess, clapping his hands. "Let's get cracking."

Paul looked over at him, hatred and fear burning in his eyes.

If Burgess had one professional fault, Banks thought, it was as an interrogator. He couldn't seem to take any part but that of his own pushy, aggressive self. It wouldn't prove half as effective with Boyd as the Mutt & Jeff routine Banks and Hatchley had worked out, but it would have to do. Banks knew he would be forced into the role of the nice guy, the father confessor, for the duration.

"Why don't you just tell us about it?" Burgess began. "That way we won't have to resort to the Chinese water torture, will we?"

"There's nothing to tell." Boyd glanced nervously at the window. The slats of the venetian blind were up, letting in grey light from the street below.

"Why did you kill him?"

"I didn't kill anyone."

"Did you just lose your temper, is that it? Or did someone pay you? Come on, we know you did it."

"I told you, I didn't kill anyone."

"Then how come that knife with PC Gill's blood on

it also happens to have your dabs all over it too? Are you trying to tell me you never touched it?"

"I didn't say that."

"What are you trying to say?"

Paul licked his lips. "Can I have a cigarette?"

"No, you bloody can't," Burgess growled. "Not until you've told us what happened."

"I didn't do anything, honestly. I've never killed anyone."

"So why did you run?"

"I was frightened."

"What of?"

"Frightened you'd fit me up for it anyway. You know I've done time."

"Is that how you think we operate, Paul?" Banks asked gently. "Is that really what you think? You're wrong, you know. If you just tell us the truth you've nothing to fear."

Burgess ignored him. "How did your prints get on the knife?"

"I must have handled it, I suppose."

"That's better. Now when did you handle it, and why?"

Paul shrugged. "Could've been anytime."

"Anytime?" Burgess shook his head with exaggerated slowness. "No it couldn't, sonny. No it couldn't. Want to know why? Your prints were right on top, numero uno, clear as day. You were the last person to handle that knife before we found it. How do you explain that?"

"All right, so I handled it after it'd been used. That still doesn't mean I killed anyone."

"It does unless you've got a better explanation. And I haven't heard one yet."

"How did you know we'd found the knife?" Banks asked.

"I saw that shepherd find it on the moor, so I took off."

He was lying, Banks thought. Mara had told him. But he let it go for the moment.

Paul fell silent. The floor creaked as Burgess paced the office. Banks lit a Silk Cut, his last, and leaned back in his chair. "Look, Paul," he said, "consider the facts. One: we found PC Gill's blood on the knife, and the doc tells us the blade fits the wound. Two: we found your prints on the handle. Three: we know you were at the demo—you were seen. Four: as soon as things start adding up, you bugger off to Scotland. Now you tell me what to make of it all. What would you think if you were me?"

Paul still said nothing.

"I'm getting fed up of this," Burgess snarled. "Let's just lock the bastard up now. He's in on a warrant. We've got enough evidence. We don't need a confession. Hell, we don't even need a motive."

"No!" Paul yelled.

"No what? You don't want us to lock you up? Dark down there, isn't it? Even a normal person feels the walls closing in on him down there, in the dark."

Paul was pale and sweating now, and his mouth was clamped so tight that the muscles in his jaw quivered.

"Come on," Banks said. "Why don't you just tell us. Save us all a lot of trouble. You say you've done nothing. If that's so, you've nothing to be worried about. Why hold back?"

"Stop mollycoddling him," Burgess said. "He's not going to talk, you know that as well as I do. He's guilty as sin, and he knows it." He turned to Hatchley. "Sergeant, send for a couple of men to take dick-head here down to the cells."

"No!" Paul leaned forward and gripped the edge of the desk until his knuckles turned white.

Burgess gestured to Hatchley to sit down again. The command was a bit premature, as the sergeant moved slowly and hadn't even got as far as putting his notebook away.

"Let me make it easy for you, Paul," Banks said. "I'll tell you what I think happened and you tell me if it's true. All right?"

Paul took a deep breath and nodded.

"You took the knife from the farm. It was usually just lying around the place. It didn't belong to anyone in particular. Mara used it occasionally to cut twine and wool; maybe Seth used it sometimes to whittle a piece of wood. But that day, you picked it up, carried it to the demo with you, and killed PC Gill. Then you folded the blade over again, made your way to the edge of the crowd, and escaped down an alley. You ran to the edge of town, then across the moors back to the farm—almost four miles. About halfway there, you realized what you'd done, panicked, and chucked the knife away. Am I right, Paul?"

"I didn't kill anyone," Paul repeated.

"But am I right about the rest?"

Silence.

"It's beginning to look like the thumbscrews for you, sonny." Burgess leaned forward, his face only inches from Paul's. "I'm getting bored. I'm sick of the bloody north and this miserable bloody weather. I want to get back home to London, the civilized world. Understand? And you're standing in my way. I don't like people who stand in my way, and if they do it for long enough, they get knocked down. Savvy?"

Paul turned to Banks. "You're right about everything else," he said. "But I didn't take the knife. I didn't kill the copper."

"Police officer to you, dick-head," Burgess snapped.

"How did you end up with it?" Banks asked.

"I got knocked down," Paul said. "At the demo. And I curled up, like, with my hands behind my neck and my knees up in my chest, in the . . . the . . . what do you call it?"

"Foetal position?"

"Yes, the foetal position. There were people all

around me, it was bloody awful. I kept getting booted. Then this knife got kicked towards me. I picked it up, like you said, and made off. But I didn't know it had killed anyone. I just thought it was a good knife, too good to waste, so I took it with me. Then on the moors, I saw there was blood on it, so I flung it away. That's how it happened."

"You're a bloody liar," Burgess said. "Do you think I'm an idiot? Is that what you take me for? I might be a city boy, but even I know there aren't any lights on the fucking moors. And even you're not stupid enough to lie there in the street, boots flying all around you, police everywhere, and think, 'Oh, what a pretty blood-stained knife. I must take it home with me!' You've been talking cobblers." He turned to Banks. "That's what you get for being soft with them, see. Spin you a yarn a bloody mile long."

Swiftly, he grasped the back of Paul's neck and squeezed hard. Paul hung on to the edge of the desk and struggled, almost upsetting his flimsy chair. Then, just as abruptly, Burgess let go and leaned casually against the wall.

"Try again," he said.

Paul massaged his neck and looked pleadingly at Banks, who remained impassive.

"It's true, I tell you," Paul said. "I swear it. I never killed him. I just picked up the knife."

"Let's assume we believe you," Banks said. "That still leaves us with a problem, doesn't it? And that problem is: why? Why did you pick up the murder weapon and sneak it away from the scene of the crime? See what I mean? It doesn't add up."

Paul shifted in his seat, casting nervous glances at Burgess, who stood just within his peripheral vision. "I didn't even know there was a crime," he said.

"Who are you protecting, Paul?" Banks asked.

"Nobody." But Paul had answered so quickly and loudly that even the most gullible person in the world would have known he was lying. Recognizing his slip, he turned red and stared down at his knees.

"The people at Maggie's Farm took you in and cared for you, didn't they?" Banks said. "They were probably the first people who ever did. You were lost, just out of jail, no job, nowhere to go, at the end of your tether, and then you met them. It's not surprising you'd want to protect them, Paul, but can't you see how transparent you're being? Who do you suspect?"

"I don't know. Nobody."

"Osmond, Tim Fenton, Abha Sutton? Would you go out of your way to protect them?"

Paul said nothing.

Burgess slapped the metal table. "Tell him!"

Paul jumped, startled by the sound. "I might," he said, glaring at Burgess. "I might protect anyone who killed a pig."

Burgess backhanded him across the face. Paul went with the blow and almost fell out of his chair.

"Try again, dick-head."

Banks grabbed Burgess by the elbow and led him over to the window. "Don't you think," he said between gritted teeth, "that you'd do better using your brains instead of your bloody fists?"

"What's wrong with you, Banks? Gone soft? Is that why they sent you up here?"

Banks jerked his head towards Paul. "He's used to hard knocks. They don't mean anything to him, and you bloody well ought to know that. You're satisfying your sadistic urges, that's all."

Burgess sniffed and turned back to Paul, who sat wiping the blood from his mouth with the back of his hand, sneering at both of them. He had overheard, Banks realized, and he probably thought the whole scene was staged just to throw him off balance. "You admit that when you found the knife on the ground you recognized it, right?" Banks asked.

"Yes."

"And you didn't want any of your friends at the farm to get into trouble."

"That's right."

"So you took it and threw it away."

"Yes. I went back on the moors to look for it a few times. I knew it was stupid just to throw it away without wiping it or anything, but I panicked. I should've taken it back to the farm and cleaned it up again, just like new. I know that now. I walked miles and miles looking for the bloody thing. Couldn't find it anywhere. And then that shepherd bloke turned up with it."

"So who did you think you were protecting?"

"I don't know." Paul took out a crumpled Kleenex and dabbed at the thin trickle of blood at the corner of his mouth. "I've already told you, I didn't see who took the knife and I didn't see who used it."

"We'll leave it for now, then." Banks turned to Burgess. "What do you think?"

"I still think he's lying. Maybe he's not as thick as he looks. He's trying to put the blame on his mates, subtle like."

"I'm not too sure," Banks said. "He could be telling the truth. Problem is he's got no proof, has he? I mean, he could tell us anything."

"And expect us to believe it. Let's lock him up for a while, anyway. Let him cool his heels. We'll question him again later and see if everything tallies."

Paul, who had been glancing from one to the other with his mouth open, let out a cry. "No! I've told you, it's the truth. What more do you want me to do?"

Burgess shrugged and leaned back against the wall. Banks reached for a cigarette; his pack was empty. "Well, I'm inclined to believe him," he said. "At least for the time being. Are you sure you didn't see who took the knife, Paul?"

"No. It could've been anyone."

"That gives us seven suspects, am I right?" Banks counted them off on his fingers. "Seth, Rick, Zoe, Mara,

Osmond, Tim and Abha. Was anyone else up there during the week before the demo? Anyone we don't know about?"

"No. And Mara wasn't there."

"But the others all were? Zoe was?"

He nodded.

"Did any of them have a reason for killing PC Gill?" Banks asked. "Anyone know him? Had a run-in with him before?"

Paul shook his head. "Maybe the students. I don't know."

"But I don't think you'd go out of your way to protect them, Paul, I really don't. Was Gill mentioned that afternoon?"

"Not that I heard."

"You see, it still doesn't ring true," Banks said. "Someone picking the knife up on purpose like that and taking it along, as if whoever did it knew he was going to do it. Premeditated, that is."

"I don't know what you mean."

"Oh, I think you do." Banks smiled and stood up. "I'm just off for some cigarettes," he said to Burgess. "I doubt that we'll get much more out of him."

"Maybe not," Burgess agreed. "Pick me up a tin of Thumbs, will you?"

"Sure."

"And give my love to Glenys."

Banks was grateful for the cool fresh air outside the station. He stood for a moment, breathing in and out deeply, then crossed Market Street to the Queen's Arms.

"Twenty Silk Cut and a tin of Tom Thumbs, please, Cyril," he said.

"These for that mate of yours?" Cyril asked, slapping the cigars on the counter.

"I wish you'd stop calling him my mate. You'll be getting me a bad name."

"Well, my Glenys has been acting a bit funny lately. She's an impressionable lass, if you know what I mean, and headstrong. Gets it from that bloody mother of hers. It's just little things, things only a husband notices, but if I find that your mate's behind it, I'll ... Well, I needn't spell it out for you, need I, Mr Banks?"

"Not to me, Cyril, no. Better not. I'll inform him of your concern."

"If you would."

Back outside, Banks noticed that the light had gone out in his office window. No doubt they'd sent Boyd down to the cells and gone for coffee. As he crossed the street, he heard a scream. It came from above, he was certain of that, but he couldn't pin-point it exactly. Apprehensive, he hurried back upstairs and opened the door. The office was dark, but it wasn't empty.

When he flicked on the fluorescent light, Banks saw that Sergeant Hatchley had been sent away and only Boyd and Burgess remained. The slats on the venetian blind had been completely closed, shutting out all the light from the street, a feat Banks himself had never been able to manage in all the time he'd been in Eastvale.

Boyd was whimpering in the chair, sweating and gasping for breath. He looked up in terror when Banks came back. "He turned the lights off," he said, struggling to get the words out, "and closed the blinds, the bastard."

Banks glared at Burgess, who simply flashed him a "who, me?" look and said, "I think he was telling the truth. At least, if he wasn't, he's just given the most convincing performance of his life."

"Under duress." Banks tossed him the cigars. Burgess caught the tin deftly, unwrapped it and offered Banks one. "Celebrate with me?"

"I prefer these." Banks lit a Silk Cut.

"You can have a smoke now if you want, kid," Burgess said to Paul. "Though with a breathing problem like yours, I'd watch it."

Paul lit up and coughed till he was red in the face. Burgess laughed.

"So, what now?" Banks asked.

"We lock him up and go home." Burgess looked at Paul. "You're going to have plenty of time for long chats with the prison shrink about that claustrophobia of yours," he said. "In fact, you could say we're doing you a favour. Don't they say the best way to deal with a phobia is to confront it? And the treatment's free. What more could you ask for? You'd have to wait years on National Health for that kind of service."

Paul's jaw slackened. "But I didn't do it. You said you believed me."

"It takes a lot more than that to convince me. Besides, there's tampering with evidence, accessory after the fact of murder, wasting police time, resisting arrest. You've got a lot of charges to face."

Burgess called downstairs and two constables came to escort Paul to the cells. He didn't struggle this time; he seemed to know there was no point.

When they were alone in the office, Banks turned to Burgess. "If you pull a stunt like that on my patch again," he said, "I'll kick your balls into the middle of next week, superintendent or no fucking superintendent."

Burgess held his gaze, but Banks felt that he took the threat more seriously than he had Rick Trelawney's.

After the staring match, Burgess smiled and said, "Good, I'm glad we've got that out of the way. Come on, I could murder a pint."

And he put his arm around Banks's shoulder and steered him towards the door.

ELEVEN

I

The rattle of the letter-box and the sound of mail slapping against the hall mat woke Banks early on Saturday morning. His mouth tasted like the bottom of a bird cage, and his tongue felt dry and furry from too many cigarettes and too much ale. He and Burgess had murdered more than one pint after Boyd's interrogation. It was getting to be a habit.

Banks still wasn't used to waking up alone in the big bed. He missed Sandra's warm body stirring beside him, and he missed the grumbles and complaints of Brian and Tracy getting ready for school or for Saturday morning shopping expeditions. But they'd all be back in a few days. With a bit of luck, the Gill case would be over by then and he would be able to spend some time with them.

Over coffee and burnt toast—why the toaster only burnt toast when *he* made it, Banks had no idea—he examined the mail: two bills, a letter and a new blues-anthology tape from Barney Merritt, an old friend on the Met, and, finally, just what he'd been waiting for—the package from Tony Grant.

The information, which Grant had copied in longhand from PC Gill's files, made interesting reading. Ever since picket-control duty at the Orgreave coking plant during the miners' strike in 1984, Gill had volunteered

for overtime at just about every demonstration that had
come up in Yorkshire: protests outside U.S. missile bases, marches against South Africa, National Front meetings, anything that had seemed likely to turn into a
free-for-all. Gill certainly wasn't the only one, but he
seemed to have been the kind of person who graduated
from school bully to legalized goon. Banks wouldn't
have been surprised if he had carved notches in his truncheon.

There were complaints against him, too, generally for
excessive use of force in subduing demonstrators. However, there were surprisingly few of these, and no action
had been taken on them, except perhaps a slap on the
wrist now and then. The most interesting complaint
came from Dennis Osmond, charging Gill with using
unnecessary violence during a local demonstration in
support of the Greenham Common women about two
years ago. Another familiar name on the list was Elizabeth Dale, who had accused Gill of lashing out indiscriminately against her and her friends during a peaceful
anti-nuclear march in Leeds. Banks couldn't immediately place her, as she didn't seem to belong to the pattern that included Paul Boyd and Dennis Osmond, but
he knew the name. He made a note to check it in his
files, then read carefully through the rest of the material.
No other names stood out.

But the most important piece of information Banks
gleaned from the files had nothing to do with Gill's behaviour; in fact, it was so damn simple he cursed himself
out loud for not seeing it sooner. He always thought of
his colleagues by name, even the uniformed men. Most
policemen did—especially plain-clothes detectives. But
it was a different matter for others. How could a member
of the public name a particular police officer in a complaint, or even in a letter of commendation? He couldn't.
That's why the numbers were so important. Called
"collar-numbers" because they originally appeared on
the small stand-up collars of the old police uniform, the

metal numbers are now fixed to the officer's epaulettes. And there was Gill's number staring him right in the face: PC 1139.

He remembered driving back from the Black Sheep after his lunch-time chat with Mara. He had been listening to Billie Holiday and wondering what it was he'd said that should have meant more than it did. Now he knew. He had mentioned Gill's name and, in his next question, the number. They had almost leaped together to complete the circuit, but not quite.

Banks put the papers away, grabbed his coat and hurried out to the car. It was a beautiful morning. The wind still blew cool, but the sun shone in a cloudless sky. After the miserable late-winter weather they'd been having recently, the smell of spring in the air—that strange mixture of wet grass and last autumn's decay—was almost overwhelming. As the pipes on Keats's Grecian urn appealed not to the "sensual ear" but played "spirit ditties of no tone," so this smell didn't so much titillate the sensual nose as it exhaled a scent of promise, a special feeling of anticipation, and a definite quickening of the life force. It made him want to slip the Deller Consort recording of Shakespeare's songs into his Walkman and step lightly to work. But he would need the car for the visit he had to make later in the day. Still, he thought, no reason why he shouldn't follow the musical impulse where it led him, especially on a day like this, so he made a special trip back inside and found the cassette to play in the car.

It was after nine when he got to the office. Richmond was playing with the computer, and Sergeant Hatchley was struggling over the *Daily Mirror* crossword. There was no sign of Dirty Dick. He sent for coffee and went to peer out of the window. The good weather had certainly enticed people outdoors. Tourists drifted in and out of the church, and some, wearing anoraks over warm sweaters, actually sat on the worn plinth of the market cross already eating KitKats and drinking tea from Thermos flasks.

Banks spent an hour or more staring out on the busy square trying to puzzle out why PC Gill's number had turned up in Seth Cotton's old notebook. Had it even been Cotton's handwriting? He examined the book again. It was hard to tell, because only the faint imprint remained. The numbers were exaggeratedly large, too, unlike the smaller scrawl of most of the measurements. Carefully, he rubbed a soft pencil over the page again, but he couldn't get a better impression.

He remembered Mara Delacey telling him that Paul spent a lot of time working with Seth in the shed, so the number could just as likely have been written down by him. If so, that implied premeditation. Boyd's name hadn't appeared on Grant's list of complainants, but that didn't mean they hadn't come into conflict before. A kid with a record, like Paul, would hardly walk into the nearest police station and lodge a complaint.

The only thing of which Banks could be sure, after two cups of coffee and three cigarettes, was that somebody at Maggie's Farm knew of PC Gill before the demonstration and expected him to be there. The number had been written down hard enough to press through, and that indicated some degree of passion or excitement. Who had a grudge against Gill? And who had access to Seth Cotton's notebook? Anybody, really, as he never locked the shed. Boyd was the best candidate, given the evidence against him, but Banks had a nagging suspicion that he'd been telling the truth, especially when he stuck to his story after Burgess had put the lights out on him. But if Boyd was telling the truth, who was he more likely to be protecting than Seth, Mara, Rick or Zoe?

And where, Banks asked himself, did that leave Osmond, Tim and Abha?

Tim and Abha had so far been the only ones to admit to knowing of PC Gill's existence, which probably indicated that they had nothing to hide. Banks doubted, in fact, that they had anything to do with the murder. For a start, they had no real connection with the farm people other than a mutual interest in wanting to save the human race from total obliteration.

Osmond, however, was a friend of Rick, Seth and the rest. He had been up to the farm often, and he knew Gill's number all right, because he had used it on his complaint. Perhaps he had written it in the notebook himself, or had seen it there and recognized it. Paul Boyd may have been telling the truth about not killing PC Gill, but had he been an accomplice? Had there been two people involved?

Like so many of Banks's thinking sessions, this one was raising far more questions than it answered. Sometimes he thought he could solve cases only after formulating a surfeit of questions; he reached saturation point, and the overflow produced the answers.

Before he did anything else, though, he needed something to stop the growling in his stomach. Burnt toast wasn't sufficient fuel for a detective.

On his way out to the Golden Grill for elevenses, he bumped into Mara Delacey entering the station.

"I want to see Paul," she said, brandishing the morning paper. "It says here you've caught him. Is it true?"

"Yes."

"Where is he?"

"Downstairs."

"Is he all right?"

"Of course he is. What do you think we are, the Spanish Inquisition?"

"I wouldn't put anything past Burgess. Can I see Paul?"

Banks thought for a moment. It would be unusual to grant such permission, and Burgess wouldn't like it if he found out, but there was no reason Mara shouldn't see Boyd. Besides, it would give Banks the opportunity to ask him a couple of questions in Mara's presence. Through body language and facial expressions, people often gave more away than they intended when friends or enemies were nearby.

"All right," he said, leading the way down. "But I'll have to be there."

"As you can see, I've not brought him a birthday cake with a file in it."

Banks smiled. "Wouldn't do him much good anyway. There aren't any bars on the window. He could only escape to the staircase and walk right up here."

"But his claustrophobia," Mara said, alarmed. "It'll be unbearable for him."

"We got a doctor." Banks relished his small victory over Burgess's callousness. "He's been given tranquillizers, and they seemed to help."

The four cells were the most modern part of the building. Recently overcrowded with demonstrators, they were now empty except for Paul Boyd. Mara seemed surprised to find clean white tiles and bright light instead of dark, dank stone walls. The only window, high and deep-set in the wall, was about a foot square and almost as thick. The cells always made Banks think of hospitals, so much so that he fancied he could smell Dettol or carbolic every time he went down there.

Boyd sat on his bunk and stared out through the bars at his visitors.

"Hello," Mara said. "I'm sorry, Paul."

Boyd nodded.

Banks could sense tension between them. It was due in part to his being there, he knew, but it seemed to go deeper than that, as if they were unsure what to say to each other.

"Are you all right?" she asked.

"I'm okay."

"Will you be coming back?"

Paul glared at Banks. "I don't know. They're determined to charge me with something."

Banks explained the procedure.

"So he might still be arrested for murder?" Mara asked.

"Yes."

There were tears in her eyes. Paul stared at her suspiciously, as if he wasn't sure whether she was acting or not.

Banks broke the tense silence. "Does the number 1139 mean anything to you?" he asked Boyd.

Paul seemed to consider the question, and his answer was an unequivocal no. Banks thought he was telling the truth.

"What do you know about that old notebook Seth kept in his workshop?"

Paul shrugged. "Nothing. It was just for addresses, measurements and stuff."

"Did you ever use it?"

"No. I was just an assistant, a dogsbody."

"It wasn't like that, Paul," Mara said. "And you know it."

"It doesn't matter now, does it? Except maybe it'll get me a job in the prison workshop."

"Did anybody else ever use it, other than Seth?" asked Banks.

"Why should they?" Paul was obviously puzzled by the line of questioning. "It wasn't important."

"Do you know who took the knife?"

Paul looked at Mara as he answered. "I've already told you I don't, haven't I?"

"I'm giving you another chance. If you really aren't responsible for PC Gill's death, any help you give us will count for you."

"Oh, sure!" Paul got to his feet and started pacing the narrow cell. "Why don't you just bugger off and leave me alone? I've nothing more to tell you. And tell the quack to bring me another pill."

"Is there anything we can do, Paul?" Mara asked.

"You can leave me alone, too. I curse the day I met you and the rest of them. You and your bloody protests and demonstrations. Look where you've got me."

Mara swallowed, then spoke softly. "We're still on your side, you know. It wasn't anything to do with me, with any of us, that you got caught. You can come back to the farm whenever you want."

Paul glared at her, and Banks could sense the questions each wanted to ask and the answers they hoped for. But they couldn't talk because he was there. Mara would implicate herself if she assured Paul she hadn't tipped the police off about the warning, the money and the clothes she'd given him. Paul would incriminate her if he thanked her or questioned her about these things.

"Come on." Banks took Mara's arm gently. She shook his hand off but walked beside him back upstairs. "You've seen that he's all right. No bruises."

"None that show, no."

"How did you get here?" Banks asked as they walked out of the station into the glorious day.

"I walked over the moors."

"I'll give you a lift back."

"No. I'm happy walking, thanks."

"No strings. I'm going up there anyway."

"Why?"

"Just a few questions for Seth."

"Questions, bloody questions."

"Come on."

Mara got into the Cortina beside him. She sat in silence with her hands on her lap as Banks pulled out of the car-park and set off up North Market Street for the Swainsdale road. They passed the Community Centre steps, where Gill had been stabbed. The spot looked as innocent as everywhere else that day; no signs of violence and bloodshed lingered in the grey stone. Banks pushed the tape in and the Deller Consort sang "It was a Lover and His Lass." Mara managed a weak smile at the hey-noni-nos, peering curiously at Banks as if she found it hard to connect him with the music he played.

A couple of fishermen sat under the trees in the river-meadows, and there were more walkers on the road than Banks had seen since the previous October. Even the wind chimes up at Maggie's Farm seemed to be playing a happier tune, despite the misfortune that had befallen the place. But nature is rarely in harmony with human affairs, Banks thought. It follows its predetermined natural cycles, while we fall victim to random, irrational forces, thoughts and deeds. It's natural to identify with the rain and clouds when we feel depressed, but if the sun shines brightly and we still feel depressed, we don't bother bringing the weather into it at all.

Banks found Seth in his workshop. Wearing his overalls, he was bent over the bench, planing a long piece of wood. Shavings curled and fell to the floor, releasing the clean scent of pine. Noticing his guest, he paused and put down his plane. Banks leaned against the wall near the dusty bookcase.

"What is it now?" Seth asked. "I thought you'd got your man."

"It does look like it. But I'm the kind who likes to tie up loose ends."

"Unlike your friend."

"Superintendent Burgess doesn't concern himself overmuch with little details," Banks said. "But he doesn't have to live up here."

"How is Paul?"

Banks told him.

"So, what are your loose ends?"

"It's that number in your book." Banks frowned and scratched the scar by his right eye. "I've found out what it means."

"Oh?"

"It was PC Gill's number. PC 1139."

Seth picked up his plane and began to work slowly at the pine again.

"Why was it written in your notebook?"

"It's quite a coincidence, I'll admit that," Seth said

without looking up. "But I told you, I haven't got the faintest idea what it meant."

"Did you write it down?"

"I don't remember doing so. But pick any page of the book and the odds are I'd hardly have it ingrained deeply in my memory."

"Did you know PC Gill?"

"I never had the pleasure."

"Could anyone else have scribbled it down?"

"Of course. I don't lock the place up. But why should they?"

Banks had no idea. "Why did you tear the page out?"

"I don't know that I did. I don't recall doing so. Look, Chief Inspector—" Seth put his plane aside again and leaned against the bench, facing Banks—"you're chasing phantoms. Anybody could have jotted that number down, and it could mean anything."

"Like what?"

"A phone number. They still have four digits around here, you know. Or it could be part of a measurement, a sum of money, almost anything."

"It's not a phone number," Banks said. "Do you think I haven't checked? It is PC Gill's number, though."

"Coincidence."

"Possibly. But I'm not convinced."

"That's your problem." Seth picked up the plane again and began working more vigorously.

"It could be your problem, too, Seth."

"Is that a threat?"

"No. I leave those to Superintendent Burgess. What I mean is, it would be very convenient if someone else had killed Gill—you, say—and Paul Boyd took the blame. He really doesn't have a leg to stand on, you know."

"What do you mean?" Seth paused again.

"I mean the odds are that he'll go down for it."

"Are you saying he's confessed?"

"I'm not free to talk about things like that. I'm just

saying it looks bad, and if you know of anything that might help him you'd better tell me pretty damn quick. Unless it's to your advantage that Boyd gets charged with murder."

"I don't know anything." Seth bent over the length of pine and caressed the surface. His voice was tight, and he kept his face averted.

"I can understand it if you're protecting someone," Banks went on. "Like Mara tried to protect Paul. But think about what you're doing. By covering for someone else, you almost certainly condemn Paul. Does he mean so little to you?"

Seth slammed down the plane. He turned to face Banks, his face red and eyes bright. The vein by his temple throbbed. "How can you talk like that?" he said in a shaky voice. "Of course Paul means a lot to us. He's not been tried yet, you know. It's only you bastards who've convicted him so far. If he didn't do it, then he'll get off won't he?"

Banks lit a Silk Cut. "I'm surprised you've got such faith in justice, Seth. I'm afraid I haven't. The way things are these days, he may well be made an example of."

Seth snorted. "What would you do? Fix the jury?"

"We wouldn't need to. The jury's made up of ordinary men and women—law-abiding, middle-class citizens for the most part. They'll take one look at Boyd and want to lock him up and throw away the key."

"He'll manage. And we'll stick by him. We won't let him down."

"Admirable sentiments. But it might not be enough. Where did you live before you bought this place?"

Surprised, Seth had to think for a moment. "Hebden Bridge. Why?"

"Where did you get the money from, for the farm?"

"If it's any of your business, I saved some and inherited a little from a dotty aunt. We . . . I also had a small business there, which I sold—a second-hand bookshop."

"What kind of work did you do?"

"This kind." Seth gestured around the workshop. "I was a jack-of-all-trades, showed the true Thatcherite entrepreneurial spirit. I made good money for good work. I still do."

"Who ran the bookshop, then?"

"My wife." Seth spoke between his teeth and turned back to his wood.

"There was some kind of accident, wasn't there?" Banks said. "Your wife?" He knew some of the details but wanted to see how Seth reacted.

Seth took a deep breath. "Yes, there was. But it's still none of your business."

"What happened?"

"Like you said. I had a wife. There was an accident."

"What kind?"

"She was hit by a car."

"I'm sorry."

Seth turned on him. "Why? Why the bloody hell should you be sorry? You didn't even know Alison. Just get the fuck out and let me get on with my work. I've nothing more to say to you."

Banks lingered at the doorway. "One more thing: Elizabeth Dale. Is that name familiar to you?"

"I know someone called Liz Dale, yes."

"She's the woman who ran off from the mental hospital and ended up here, isn't she?"

"Why ask if you know already?"

"I wasn't sure, but I thought so. Do you know anything about a complaint she made against PC Gill?"

"No. Why should I?"

"She used his number: 1139."

"So?"

"Bit of a coincidence, that's all: her complaint, his number in your notebook. Could she have written it?"

"I suppose so. But so could anyone else. I really don't know anything about it." Seth sounded tired.

"Have you seen her recently? Has she been up here in the past few weeks?"

"No."

"Do you know where she is?"

"We've lost touch. It happens."

Seth bent over the pine again and Banks left, avoiding the house by using the side gate. In the car, he contemplated going to the barn to talk to Rick and Zoe. But they could wait. He'd had enough of Maggie's Farm for one day.

II

Burgess winked at Glenys, who smiled and blushed. Banks was the only one to notice Cyril's expression darken. They carried their drinks and ploughman's lunches back to the table.

"How's Boyd?" Burgess asked.

"He's all right. I didn't know you cared."

Burgess spat the remains of a pickled onion into his napkin: "Bloody awful stuff. Gives me heartburn."

"I wouldn't be surprised if you're developing an ulcer," Banks said, "the way you go at life."

Burgess grinned. "You only live once."

"Are you going to stick around and see what happens?"

"I'll stay a few more days, yes." He eyed Glenys again. "I'm not quite finished up here yet."

"Don't tell me you're getting to like the north?"

"At least the bloody weather's improved, even if the people haven't."

"Friendliest lot in the country, when you get to know them."

"Tell me about it." Burgess shoved in a chunk of Wensleydale and washed it down with Double Diamond.

Banks grimaced. "No wonder you get heartburn."

Burgess pushed his plate aside and lit a cigar. "Tell me honestly, Banks. What do you make of Boyd? Guilty or not?"

"He's obviously involved. Deeply involved. But if you're asking do I think he killed Gill, the answer's no, I don't."

"You could be right. He certainly stuck to his guns under pressure, and I don't think he's that tough." Burgess prodded the air with his cigar. "Personally, I don't give a damn what happens to Boyd. I'd rather see him go down for it than no one at all. But give me some credit. I'm not a bloody idiot, and if I'm not satisfied everything's wrapped up I like to know why. I get nagging feelings like every copper."

"And you have one about Boyd?"

"A little one."

"So what are you going to do?"

"Consider the alternatives. You heard what he said last night, about the others going up to the farm on Friday afternoon. That covers just about everyone we've had our eye on since this business started. Who do you reckon?"

Banks sipped some beer to wash down his lunch. "It depends," he said. "Any of the people Boyd mentioned could have got access to the knife, and so could anyone else who went up there a few days before the demo. Nobody had noticed whether it was missing or not—at least, nobody admits to noticing. If you're convinced it was a terrorist act, then obviously you're best starting with the most politically active of them: Osmond, Trelawney and the students. On the other hand, if you accept that there could have been some other motive, then you have to rethink the whole thing in more human terms: revenge, hatred, that kind of thing. Or maybe someone was trying to put the blame on the farm people, someone who had a reason to hate them or want them off their land."

Burgess sighed. "You make it sound so bloody complicated. Do you really think that's where the answer lies?"

"It's possible, yes." Banks took a deep breath. "Gill was a bastard," he said. "He liked thumping people, bashing heads. He'd volunteered for more crowd control duties than I've had hot dinners. And another thing: Osmond made an official complaint about him for using undue force in another demo a couple of years back. So did a woman called Elizabeth Dale, in a separate incident. And she's got some connection with the farm crowd."

Burgess drank some more beer and sucked his lips. "How do you know?" he asked quietly.

Banks had been expecting this. He remembered Burgess's order not to look into Gill's record. "Anonymous tip," he said.

Burgess narrowed his eyes and stared as Banks took out a cigarette and lit it.

"I don't know if I believe you," he said finally.

"It doesn't bloody matter, does it? It's what I'm telling you that counts. Do you want to get to the bottom of this or don't you?"

"Go on."

"I'm saying we've got two options: terrorism or personal motive. Maybe they're both mixed up as well, I don't know."

"And where does Boyd come in?"

"Either he did exactly as he told us, or he was an accomplice. So we dig deeper into his political background. Richmond's doing all he can at the computer, checking people Boyd knew in jail and any others he hung about with when the local police were keeping an eye on him. He spent some time in Ireland, which is where he was heading when we caught him, and some of the people he knew had connections with the IRA. We can't prove it, but we're pretty damn sure. We also have to consider the personal motive. Gill was the kind of person to make enemies, and it looks like Osmond was one of them."

"In the meantime," Burgess said, "we hang on to Boyd."

Banks shook his head. "I don't think so."

"Let him go?"

"Yes. Why not?"

"He scarpered last time. What's to stop him doing it again?"

"I think he found out that he'd nowhere to go. If you let him out, he'll go back to the farm and stay there."

"But why let him out at all?"

"Because it might stir something up. If he's not guilty, there's still a chance he might know who is. He might slip up, set something moving."

Burgess swirled the beer in his glass. "So we charge him with tampering with evidence, wasting police time, and let him out. Is that what you're suggesting?"

"For the time being, yes. Have you got a better idea?"

"I'm not convinced," Burgess said slowly, "but I'll go along with it. And," he added, poking his cigar in Banks's direction, "on your head be it, mate. If he buggers off again, you'll answer for it."

"All right."

"And we'll keep him in another night, just so he gets the message. I'll have another little chat with him, too."

It was a compromise. Burgess was not the kind of man to give way completely to someone else's idea. It was the best deal he would get, so Banks agreed.

Burgess smiled over at Glenys. Down at the far end of the bar, a glass broke. "I'll go get us a couple more, shall I?"

"Let me." Banks stood up quickly. "It's my round." It wasn't, but the last thing they needed was a lunch-time punch-up between the landlord of the Queen's Arms and a detective superintendent from Scotland Yard.

"I'll take Osmond again, too," Burgess said, when

Banks got back. "I don't trust you when that bird of his is around. You go all gooey-eyed."

Banks ignored him.

"Can I take DC Richmond with me?" Burgess asked.

"What's wrong with Sergeant Hatchley?"

"He's a lazy sod," Burgess said. "How he ever made sergeant I don't bloody know. Every time he's been with me he's just sat there like a stuffed elephant."

"He has his good points," Banks said, surprised to find himself defending Hatchley. He wondered if the sergeant really had been nurturing a dream of Burgess's inviting him to join some elite Yard squad just because they both believed in the privatization of everything and in an England positively bristling with nuclear missiles. If he had, tough titty.

The difference between them, Banks thought, was that Hatchley just assumed attitudes or inherited them from his parents; he never thought them out. Burgess, on the other hand, really believed that the police existed to hold back the red tide and keep immigrants in their place so that the government could get on with the job of putting the Great back in Britain. He also believed that people like Paul Boyd should be kept off the streets so that decent citizens could rest easy in their beds at night. It never occurred to him for a moment that he might not pass for decent himself.

Banks followed Burgess back to the station and went up to his office. He had a phone call to make.

TWELVE

I

South of Skipton, the landscape changes dramatically.
The limestone dales give way to millstone grit country,
rough moorland for the most part, bleaker and wilder
than anything in Swainsdale. Even the dry-stone walls
are made of the dark purplish gritstone. The landscape
is like the people it breeds: stubborn, guarded, long of
memory.

Banks drove through Keighley and Haworth into open
country, with Haworth Moor on his right and Oxenhope
Moor on his left. Even in the bright sun of that springlike
day, the landscape looked sinister and brooding. Sandra
hated it; it was too spooky and barren for her. But Banks
found something magical about the area, with its legends
of witches, mad Methodist preachers, and the tales the
Brontë sisters had spun.

Banks slipped a cassette in the stereo and Robert
Johnson sang "Hellhound on My Trail." West Yorkshire
was a long way from the Mississippi delta, but the dark,
jagged edges of Johnson's guitar seemed to limn the
landscape, and his haunted, doom-laden lyrics captured
its mood.

Dominated by mill-towns at the valley bottoms and
weaving communities on the heights, the place is a prod-
uct of the Industrial Revolution. Majestic old mills with
their tall chimneys of dark, grainy millstone grit still

remain. Many have now been scoured of two hundred years' soot and set up as craft and antiques markets.

Hebden Bridge is a mill-town turned tourist trap, full of bookshops and antique shops. Not so long ago, it was a centre of trouser and corduroy manufacturing, but since the seventies, when the hippies from Leeds and Manchester invaded, it has been more of a place for arts festivals, poetry readings in pubs and other cultural activities.

Banks drove down the steep hill from the moors into the town itself. Rows of tall terraced houses run at angles diagonally along the hillside and overlook the mills at the valley bottom. They look like four-storey houses, but are actually rows of two-storey houses built one on top of the other. You enter the lower house from a street or ginnel at one level, and the upper from a higher one at the back. All of which made it very difficult for Banks to find Reginald Lee's house.

Lee, Banks had discovered from his phone call to PC Brooks of the Hebden Bridge police, was a retired shop owner living in one of the town's two-tiered buildings. Just over three years ago he had been involved in an accident on the town's busy main street—a direct artery along the Calder valley from east to west—which had resulted in the death of Alison, Seth Cotton's wife.

Banks had also discovered from the police that there had been nothing suspicious about her death, and that Mr Lee had not been at fault. But he wanted to know more about Seth Cotton's background, and it seemed that the death of his wife was a good place to start. He was still convinced that the number written so boldly in the old notebook was PC Gill's and not just part of a coincidentally similar calculation. Whether Seth himself had written it down was another matter.

Lee, a small man in a baggy, threadbare pullover, answered the door and frowned at Banks. He clearly didn't get many visitors. His thinning grey hair was uncombed, sticking up on end in places as if he'd had an electric shock, and the room he finally showed Banks into was untidy but clean. It was also chilly. Banks kept his jacket on.

"Sorry about the mess," Lee said in a high-pitched, whining voice. "Wife died two years back and I just can't seem to get the hang of housework."

"I know what you mean." Banks moved some newspapers from a hard-backed chair. "My wife's been away at her mother's for two weeks now and the house feels like it's falling apart. Mind if I smoke?"

"Not at all." Lee shuffled to the sideboard and brought an ashtray. "What can I help you with?"

"I'm sorry to bring all this up again," Banks said. "I know it must be painful for you, but it's about that accident you were involved in about three years ago."

Lee's eyes seemed to glaze over at the mention. "Ah, yes," he said. "I blame that for Elsie's death, too, you know. She was with me at the time, and she never got over it. I retired early myself. Couldn't seem to . . ." He lost his train of thought and stared at the empty fireplace.

"Mr. Lee?"

"What? Oh, sorry, Inspector. It is Inspector, isn't it?"

"It'll do," Banks said. "The accident."

"Ah, yes. What is it you want to know?"

"Just what happened, in as much detail as you can remember."

"Oh, I can remember it all." He tapped his forehead. "It's all engraved there in slow motion. Just let me get my pipe. It seems to help me concentrate. I have a bit of trouble keeping my mind on track these days." He fetched a briar from a rack by the fireplace, filled it with rubbed twist and put a match to it. The tobacco flamed up and blue smoke curled from the bowl. A child's skipping rhyme drifted in from the street:

Georgie Porgie, pudding and pie,
Kiss the girls and make them cry.

"Where was I?"

"The accident."

"Ah, yes. Well, it happened on a lovely summer's day. The sixteenth of July. One of those days when you can smell the moorland heather and the wild flowers even here in town. Not a cloud in the sky and everyone in that relaxed, dozy mood you get in summer. Elsie and I were going for a ride to Hardcastle Crags. We used to do a lot of our courting up there when we were youngsters, like. So whenever the weather was good, off we went. I wasn't doing more than thirty—and I hadn't a drop of drink in me, never touch the stuff—when I came upon this lass riding along on her bicycle on my inside." He faltered, sucked at his pipe as if it were an oxygen mask, and carried on. "She was a bit wobbly, but then a lot of cyclists are. I always took special care when there were cyclists around. Then it happened. My front wheels were a foot or two away from her back. She was over by the kerb, like, not directly in front of me, and she just keeled over."

"Just like that?"

"Aye." He seemed amazed, even though he must have told the story dozens of times to the police. "As if she'd hit a jutting stone. But there wasn't one. She might have bounced off the kerb or something. And she fell right in front of the car. I'd no time to stop. Even if I'd only been going five miles an hour I wouldn't have had time. She went right under the wheels. Keeled over, just like that."

Banks let the silence stretch. Tobacco crackled in the pipe bowl and the repetitive chant continued outside. "You said she was wobbling a bit," he asked finally. "Did she seem drunk or anything?"

"Not especially. Just like she was a learner, maybe."

"Have you ever come across a policeman by the name of Edwin Gill. PC 1139?"

"Eh? Pardon me. No, the name and number aren't familiar. It was PC Brooks I dealt with at first. Then

Inspector Cummings. I don't remember any Gill. Is he from around here?"

"Did you ever meet Seth Cotton?"

"Yes," Lee said, relighting his pipe. "I plucked up the courage to go and see him in the hospital. He knew all the details and said he didn't blame me. He was very forgiving. Of course, he was in a shocking state, still beside himself with grief and anger. But not at me. I only went the once."

"In hospital? What was he doing there?"

Lee looked surprised. "I thought you'd have known. He tried to kill himself a couple of days after the hospital phoned him about the accident. Slit his ankles. And they say he smashed the phone to bits. But someone found him before it was too late. Have you seen the lad lately?"

"Yes."

"And how is he?"

"He seems to be doing all right." Banks told him about the farm and the carpentry.

"Aye," Lee said. "He mentioned he were a carpenter." He shook his head slowly. "Terrible state he were in. Bad enough losing the lass, but the baby as well. . . ."

"Baby?"

"Aye. Didn't you know? She were pregnant. Five months. The police said she might have fainted, like, had a turn, because of her condition. . . ."

Lee seemed to drift off again, letting his pipe go out. Banks couldn't think of any more questions, so he stood up to leave. Lee noticed and snapped out of his daze.

"Off, are you?" he said. "Sure you won't stay for a cup of tea?"

"No, thank you, Mr Lee. You've been very helpful. I'm sorry I had to put you through it all again."

"There's hardly a day goes by when I don't think on it," Lee said.

"You shouldn't keep torturing yourself that way," Banks told him. "Whichever way you look at it, no blame can possibly attach itself to you."

"Aye, no blame," Lee repeated. And his piercing inward gaze put Banks in mind of the actor Trevor Howard at his conscience-stricken best. There was nothing more to say. Feeling depressed, Banks walked back out to the street in the chilly spring sunshine. The children paused and stared as he passed by.

It was after five o'clock and the people down in the town were hurrying home from work. All Banks had to look forward to was a tin of ravioli on toast—which he would no doubt burn—and another evening alone.

Looking up the hillside to the west, he thought of Heptonstall, a village at the summit. He'd heard that the pub there served Timothy Taylor's beer, something he'd never tried. It had been a wasted and depressing afternoon as far as information was concerned, so he might as well salvage it somehow.

Alison Cotton's death had obviously been a tragic accident, and that was all there was to it. She had either rubbed against the kerb and lost her balance, or she had fainted, perhaps due to the effects of her pregnancy. Banks could hardly blame Seth for not wanting to talk about it.

He got in his car and drove up the steep hill to Heptonstall. It was a quiet village at that time of day: narrow winding terraces of small dark cottages, many with the tell-tale rows of upper windows where weavers had once worked.

He lingered over his food and beer in the window seat of the Cross Inn, planning what to do next. The Timothy Taylor's bitter was good, smooth as liquid gold. Shadows lengthened and the fronts of the gritstone houses over the narrow street turned even darker.

It was late when he got home—almost ten—and he'd hardly had time to put his slippers on and sit down before the phone rang.

"Alan, thank God you're back. I've been trying to call you all evening." It was Jenny.

"Why? What's wrong?"

"It's Dennis. His flat has been broken into."

"Has he reported it?"

"No. He wants to see you."

"He should report it."

"I know, but he won't. Will you go and see him? Please?"

"Was he hurt?"

"No, he was out when it happened. It must have been sometime earlier this evening."

"Was anything taken?"

"He's not clear about that. Nothing important, I don't think. Will you see him? Please?"

Banks could hardly refuse. In the first place, Jenny was clearly distraught on Osmond's behalf, and in the second, it might have a bearing on the case. If Osmond refused to come to him, then he would have to go to Osmond. Sighing, he said, "Tell him I'll be right over."

II

"You don't like me very much, do you, Chief Inspector?" said Osmond as soon as Banks had made himself comfortable.

"I'm not bowled over, no."

Osmond leaned back in his armchair and smiled. "You're not jealous, are you? Jenny told me how close you two got during that Peeping Tom business."

She did, did she? Banks thought angrily. Just how much had she told him? "Could you just get on with it, please?" he said. "I'm here, at Jenny's request, to investigate a break-in you haven't reported officially. The least you can do is stop trying to be so fucking clever."

The smile disappeared. "Yes, all right. For what good it'll do me."

"First off, why didn't you report it?"

"I don't trust the police, certainly not the way I've

been treated since the demonstration. Burgess was around here again this afternoon tossing insults and accusations about. And I don't want my apartment done over by a bunch of coppers, either."

"Why not? What have you got to hide?"

"Nothing to hide, not in the way you mean it. But I value my privacy."

"So why am I here?"

Osmond crossed his legs and paused before answering. "Jenny persuaded me."

"But you don't really want to talk about it?"

"What's the point? What can you do?"

"We could do our job if you'd let us. Check for fingerprints, interview neighbours, try to get a description. Was anything stolen?"

"A book."

"What?"

"A book. Most of my books were pulled off the shelves, scattered on the floor, and I noticed when I put them back that one was missing."

"Just one?"

"That's right. Marcuse's *One Dimensional Man*. Do you know it?"

"No."

Osmond smiled smugly. "I didn't think you would. It doesn't matter. Anyway, that's all."

"That's all that was taken?"

"Yes."

"How did they get in? The lock doesn't seem broken."

"It's easy enough to open. They probably used a credit card or something. I've had to do that myself more than once."

"And it works?"

"Yes. Unless the catch is on from the inside. Obviously, as I was out at the time, it wasn't."

"Then I'd suggest the first thing you do is get a new lock. Preferably a deadlock."

"I've already called the locksmith. He's coming on Monday."

"Did you get the impression that they were looking for something? Or was it just vandalism?" Banks had his cigarette packet in his hand without thinking before he realized Osmond was a rabid non-smoker.

"Oh, go on, Chief Inspector." Osmond allowed himself another superior smile. "Pollute the atmosphere if you must. You're doing me a favour; it's the least I can do in return."

"Thanks, I will." Banks lit up. "What might they have been looking for? Money?"

"I don't think so. There was a little cash in the dresser drawer, but they left it. There was also some quite valuable jewellery—it used to be my mother's—and they left that, too. The only things disturbed were the books and some papers—nothing important—but there was no damage. I don't think it was vandalism."

"But it was clear they'd seen the money and jewellery?"

"Oh, yes. The drawer was open and the contents of the jewellery box were spilled on the bed."

"What do you think they were looking for?"

Osmond scratched his cheek and frowned. Noticing Banks's half inch of ash, he fetched an ashtray from the kitchen. "In case of emergencies," he said. "Stolen property, I'm afraid. Courtesy of the Bridge, Helmthorpe."

Banks smiled. Having got over his initial nervousness that, as with so many people, manifested itself in the form of rudeness, Osmond was making an attempt at least to smooth the waters. He still wasn't comfortable around the police, but he was trying.

"Would you like a drink?"

"Scotch, if you've got it." Osmond was prevaricating, making time to think. That meant his answer would be at best a blend of truth and falsehood, and it would be damn difficult for Banks to sort out which was which. But there was no point pushing him. Osmond liked being in control, and any challenge at this point would just make him clam up. Best wait for a gap in his defences and leap right through. Let him take his own sweet time.

Finally, drink in hand, Banks repeated his question.

"I don't want to appear unduly paranoid, Chief Inspector," Osmond began slowly, "but I've been involved with the CND and a number of other organizations for some years now, so I think I can speak from experience. I take it you know, of course, that I once made a complaint against the policeman who was killed?"

Banks nodded. "You'd have saved us a lot of trouble if you hadn't lied in the first place."

"That's easy for you to say. Anyway, your charming superintendent knew. He wouldn't let it drop. So I assume you know about it, too. Anyway, we come to expect that kind of thing. The CND doesn't take sides, Chief Inspector. Believe it or not, all we want is a nuclear-free world. But some members bring along strong political beliefs, too, I won't deny it. I'm a socialist, yes, but that doesn't have anything to do with the CND or its aims."

He paused and fingered his small gold crucifix. As Banks looked at him slouching on the sofa with his long legs crossed and his arms spread out along the back, the word languid came to mind.

"Have you noticed how things seem to come in packages?" Osmond went on. "If you're anti-nuclear, people also expect you to be pro-choice, pro-union, pro-gays, anti-American, anti-apartheid and generally left wing. Most people don't realize that it's perfectly possible to be, say, anti-nuclear and anti-apartheid without being pro-gay and pro-choice—especially if you're a Catholic. Oh, the permutations might differ a bit—some packages are more extreme and dangerous than others, for example—but you can pretty well predict the kind of things our members value. The point is that what we stand for is politically hot, and that draws attention to us from all sides. The government thinks we're in league with the Russians, so they raid our offices periodically and go over our files. The communists think we're allies in overthrowing a decadent capitalist government, so they woo us and infiltrate us with their own. It's a bloody mess, but we manage, through it all, to stick to our aims."

"Are you saying you think the break-in was politically motivated?"

"That's about it." Osmond lifted the Scotch bottle and raised his eyebrows. Banks held out his glass. "And the theft of the book was a sort of calling card, or warning. So do you see what I mean about not expecting much help from the police? If Special Branch or M15 or whoever are involved, you'd get your wrists slapped, and if it's the other side, you'd never catch them anyway."

"But what were they looking for?"

"I don't know. Anyway, I don't keep my files here. Most of the important ones are at the CND office, and some of the stuff is at work."

"The Social Services Centre?"

"Yes. I've got an office there. It's convenient."

"So they didn't find what they were looking for because they didn't look in the right place."

"I suppose so. The only current thing is the inquiry I'm making into the demo. I've already told you about that—and Superintendent Burgess, too. I've talked to quite a lot of people involved, trying to establish exactly what happened and how it could have been avoided. Tim and Abha are helping, too. They've got most of the info at their place. We're having a meeting up at the farm tomorrow to decide what to do about it all. Ever since your boss was taken off the job, we've been carrying on for him, and our results will be a hell of a lot less biased."

"You're wrong," Banks said, lighting another cigarette. "The trouble with people like you, despite all your talk about packages, is that you tar everyone with the same brush. To you, all police are pigs. Superintendent

Gristhorpe would have done a good job. He wouldn't have swept it all under the carpet."

"Maybe that's why he was taken off," Osmond said. "I read in the paper that they were going to appoint an impartial investigating commission—which, I suppose, means a bunch of high-ranking policemen from somewhere other than Eastvale—but most of us think they're just going to forget about the whole embarrassing affair. Once the killer is convicted—and it looks like you're well on your way to doing that—the anti-nuke lefties will be shown up for exactly what you all think we are— a gang of murderous anarchists—and the police will gain a lot of very useful public sympathy."

Banks put his empty glass down and walked over to the window. "Tell me about Ellen Ventner."

Osmond paled. "You certainly do your homework, don't you?"

"Ellen Ventner."

"If you think I'm going to admit to those ludicrous charges against me, you must be crazy."

"Much as it saddens me to say so, I'm not here to investigate those old charges. So you like to beat up women. That's your privilege."

"You bastard. Are you going to tell Jenny?"

"I honestly don't know. Ellen Ventner didn't pursue the charges. God knows why, but a lot of women don't. Maybe she thought you were still a really sweet fellow underneath it all. But that doesn't alter what happened. You might think you're a very important man in the political scheme of things, but personally I doubt it. On the other hand, a woman you once assaulted might bear a grudge."

"After four years?"

"It's possible."

"Forget it. She wouldn't. Besides, she emigrated not long after we split up."

"I can understand why she might have wanted to get

as far away from you as possible. Just checking all the angles."

Osmond glared, then looked into his glass and started to fiddle with his crucifix again. "Look, it was only the once. . . . She . . . I was drunk. I didn't mean to. . . ."

Banks sat down opposite him again and leaned forward. "When you made your complaint about PC Gill," he asked, "how did you do it?"

Osmond floundered. It was so easy, Banks thought. Stir up a man's emotions, then change the subject and you're in control again. He'd had enough of Osmond's lectures and his arrogance.

"What do you mean, how did I do it? I wrote a letter."

"How did you refer to him?"

"By his number. How else?"

"1139?"

"Yes, that's it."

"You still remember it?"

"Obviously."

"So how did you know his name?"

"Look, I don't—"

"When I first asked you if you knew Gill, you said no. I didn't use his number, I used his name, and you recognized it when you lied to me."

"He told me," Osmond said. "When I tried to stop him from hitting a woman at a demo once, he pulled me aside and told me to keep out of it. I told him I'd report him, and he said go ahead. When I looked at his number, he told me his name, as well. Spelled it out, in fact. The bastard was proud of what he was doing."

So Osmond defended women in public and only hit them in private. Nice guy, Banks thought, but he kept his questions factual and direct. "When you were up at Maggie's Farm on the afternoon of the demonstration, did you mention that number to anyone?"

"I don't know. I can't remember."

"Think. Did you write it in a notebook, or see it written in a notebook?"

"No, I'd remember something like that. But I might have mentioned it. Really, I can't say."

"How might you have mentioned it? Just give me a sense of context."

"I might have said, 'I wonder if that bastard PC 1139 will be out tonight.' I suppose I'd have warned people about him. Christ, you can't be involved in demos around this part of the world and not know about PC bloody 1139."

"So I gather." Banks remembered what Tim and Abha had told him.

There was nothing more to ask. Banks said good night and Osmond slammed the door behind him. In the corridor, he decided to try the flats on that floor to see if anyone had noticed the housebreaker. There were only ten—five on each side.

At the third door, a man who had been nipping out to the off-licence at about a quarter to eight said he'd seen two men walking along the corridor on his way back. They had seen him, too, but had made no move to run off or turn away. The description was average—most people are about as observant as a brick wall, Banks had discovered over the years—but it helped.

They were both tall and burly, and they both wore dark blue pants, a bit shiny, probably the bottom part of a suit; one had on a black overcoat, fake leather, while the other wore a light trench coat; one had black hair, the other none at all; and neither wore a hat or glasses. About facial features, the man remembered nothing except that both men had two eyes, a nose, a mouth, and two ears. They had walked confidently and purposefully, as if they knew where they were going and what they were about, not furtively, as he imagined criminals would have done. So, no, he hadn't seen any need to call the police. He was sorry now, of course. His speech was slurred, as if he'd already drunk most of what he'd bought at the off-licence. Banks thanked him and left.

Over the next four doors, Banks found himself told

to piss off by a writer whose concentration he had disturbed and asked in for a cup of tea by a lonely military-type who wanted to show off his medals. As yet, there had been no temptress in a négligé.

It wasn't until the ninth door that he found anyone else who knew anything. Beth Cameron wore tight, checked slacks, which hardly flattered her plump hips and thighs, and a maroon cardigan over a shiny white blouse. Her curly brown hair showed traces of a recent perm, and she had the most animated face that Banks had ever seen. Every comment, every word, was accompanied by a curled lip, a raised eyebrow, a wrinkled nose, a deep frown or a mock pout. She was like one of those sponge hand-puppets he remembered from his childhood. When you put your hand inside it, you could wrench the face into the most remarkable contortions.

"Did you see anyone coming in or out of Mr Osmond's flat this evening?" Banks asked.

"No, no, I can't say I did. Wait a minute, though, I did notice *something* odd. Not up here but down in the garage. It struck me as a bit strange at the time, you know, but I just brushed it off. You do, don't you?"

"What did you see?"

"A blue Escort. And it was parked in Mr Handley's spot. He's often out during the evening—he's the entertainment reporter for the Eastvale *Gazette*—but still, I thought, that's no reason to steal the man's parking spot, is it? See, there's places for visitors outside. We don't encourage non-residents to park underground. It could lead to all sorts of trouble, couldn't it?"

"What time was this?" Banks asked.

"Oh, about eight o'clock. I was just bringing Lesley—that's my daughter—back from her piano lesson."

"Did you see if there was anyone in the car?"

"Two men, I think. Sitting in the front."

"Did you get a good look at them?"

"No, I'm sorry. They looked big, but I mean, you just don't look at people, do you? Especially not in places like that. It doesn't do to make eye contact with strangers in an underground garage, does it?"

"No," Banks said, "I don't suppose it does. You didn't recognize either of the men, then?"

"No. Whatever happened, anyway?" Mrs Cameron suddenly frowned. "There wasn't nobody assaulted, was there? I've been saying all along that place is too dark. Just asking for trouble it is."

"Nobody was hurt," Banks assured her. "I'm just interested in that Escort. Have you ever noticed it before?"

"No, never. I did think of calling the police, you know. It did cross my mind they might be up to no good. But you don't want to cause a fuss, do you? It might all be perfectly innocent and there you'd be with egg on your face looking a proper fool. But I'd never forgive myself if someone got hurt."

"Don't worry, it's nothing like that. You didn't get the number, by any chance?"

"No." She laughed, then put her hand to her mouth. Her fingernails were painted pale green. "I'm sorry, Mr Banks, but I always think it's so funny when the police go asking people that on telly. I mean, you don't go around collecting car numbers, do you? I don't think I even know my own."

"Is there anything else you can think of?" Banks asked, without much hope.

Beth Cameron chewed her lower lip and frowned for a moment, then shook her head. "No. Not a sausage. I didn't pay it much mind, really. They weren't doing nothing. Just sitting there like they were waiting to leave. . . . Wait a minute!" Her eyebrows shot up almost to her hairline. "I think one of them was bald. There was a light on the pillar by the car, you see. Dim as can be, but I could swear I saw a bald head reflecting the light." Then her lips curved down at the edges. "I don't suppose that's much help, though, is it?"

"Everything helps." Banks closed his notebook and put it back into his inside pocket. At least he was certain now that the two men in the blue Escort were the same two who had been seen in the corridor near Osmond's flat. "If you see the car again," he said, handing her a card, "would you please let me know?"

"Yes, of course I will, Mr Banks," she said. "Glad to be of use. Good night."

At the last door Banks turned up nothing new. It had been a long time since he'd made door-to-door enquiries himself, and he had enjoyed it, but now it was going on for half-past eleven and he was tired. Outside, the crisp, cold air woke him up a bit. He stood by his car for a few moments and smoked a cigarette, thinking over what had happened that evening.

However much he had ridiculed the man's pretensions, he had to admit that Osmond was the type who made waves politically. Banks had a lot of sympathy for the CND and its goals, but he knew that, like so many peace-loving, well-meaning groups, it sometimes acted as a magnet for dangerous opportunists. Where there was organization there was politics, and where there was politics there was the aphrodisiac of power. Maybe Osmond *had* been involved in a plot to do with the demonstration. Perhaps his masters didn't trust him to keep his trap shut, and what had happened this evening had been intended as a kind of warning.

Banks found it hard to swallow all the cloak-and-dagger stuff, but the mere possibility of it was enough to send a shiver of apprehension up his spine. If there really was anything in the conspiracy theory, then it looked like these people—Russian spies, *agents provocateurs*, or whoever they were—meant business.

If that was true, Osmond might get hurt. That didn't concern Banks very much, but it did cause him to worry about Jenny. It was bad enough her being involved with a man who had beat up a previous girl-friend, but much worse now there was a strong possibility that some very dangerous and cold-blooded people were after him too.

None of it concerned Jenny directly, of course; she was merely an innocent bystander. But since when did governments or terrorists ever give a damn about innocent bystanders?

THIRTEEN

I

Maybe it was the spring weather, but the toasted tea-cakes in the Golden Grill tasted exceptionally good to Banks on Sunday morning. Burgess chose a doughnut filled with raspberry purée and dusted with icing sugar, which he dipped into his coffee. "A taste I developed in America," he explained, as Banks watched, horrified. "They've got a place there called Dunkin' Donuts. Great."

"What's happening with Boyd?" Banks asked.

"I had another chat with him. Got nowhere. Like you said, I let him go this morning, so we'll see what turns up now."

"What did you do? Torture him again?"

"Well, there's not many can keep on lying when faced with their greatest fear. The way things stand now, I think we could get a conviction on Boyd, no problem, but we'd probably get chucked out of court if we tried to fit one of the others up—Osmond, for example. I say if we turn up nothing more in a couple of days, let's just charge Boyd with murder and I'll bugger off back to the Smoke a happy man."

"What about the truth?"

Burgess treated Banks to a slit-eyed glance. "We don't know Boyd didn't do it, do we? The Burgess Test not-withstanding. It's not infallible, you know. Anyway, I'm getting a bit sick of your moralizing about the truth all the bloody time. The truth's relative. It depends on your perspective. Remember, we're not judge and jury. It's up to them to decide who's guilty and who's not. We just present the evidence."

"Fair enough, but it's up to us to make a charge that sticks, if only to stop us looking like prize berks in court."

"I think we're solid on Boyd if we need to be. Like I say, give it a couple of days. Find anything interesting on the funny-farm lot?"

"No."

"Those students puzzled me. They're only bloody kids—cheeky bastards, mind you—but their little minds are crammed full of Marx, Trotsky, Marcuse and the rest. They even have a poster of Che Guevara on the wall. I ask you—Che fucking Guevara, a vicious, murdering, mercenary thug got up to look like Jesus Christ. I can't understand what they're on about half the time, honest I can't. And I don't think they've got a clue, either. Pretty gutless pair, though. I can't see either of them having the bottle to stick a knife between Gill's ribs. Still, the girl's not bad. Bit chubby around the waist, but a lovely set of knockers."

"Osmond's place was broken into yesterday evening," Banks said.

"Oh?"

"He didn't report it officially."

"He should have done. You talked to him?"

"Yes."

"Then you should have made a report. You know the rules." He grinned. "Unless, of course, you think rules are only for people like me to follow and for Jack-the-lads like you to ignore?"

"Listen," Banks said, leaning forward, "I don't like your methods. I don't like violence. I'll use it if I have to, but there are plenty more subtle and effective ways of getting answers from people." He sat back and reached for a cigarette. "That aside, I never said I was any less ruthless than you are."

Burgess laughed and spluttered over a mouthful of recently dunked doughnut.

"Anyway," Banks went on, "Osmond didn't seem to give a damn. Well, maybe that's too strong. At least, he didn't think we would do anything about it."

"He's probably right. What *did* you do?"

"Told him to change his lock. Nothing was stolen."

"Nothing?"

"Only a book. They'd searched the place, but apparently they didn't find what they were looking for."

"What was that?"

"Osmond thinks they might have been after some papers, files to do with his CND stuff. He's got a touch of the cloak-and-dagger about him. Anyway, he keeps most of his files at the local office, and Tim and Abha have all the stuff on the demo. It seems they're having a meeting up at the farm this afternoon to plan their complaint strategy. It looks like the thieves wasted their time, whoever they were."

"Who does he think it was? KGB? M15? CIA?"

Banks laughed. "Something along those lines, yes. Thinks he's a very important fellow does Mr Osmond."

"He's a pain in the ass," Burgess said, getting up. "But I'll trip the bastard up before I'm done. Right now I'm off to catch up on some paperwork. They want everything in bloody quadruplicate down at the Yard."

Banks sat over the rest of his coffee wondering why so many people came back from America, where Burgess had been to a conference a few years ago, full of strange eating habits and odd turns of phrase—"pain in the ass" indeed!

Outside on Market Street tourists browsed outside shop windows full of polished antiques and knitted woollen wear. The bell of the Golden Grill jangled as people dropped in for a quick cup of tea.

Banks had arranged to meet Jenny for lunch in the

Queen's Arms at one o'clock, which left him well over an hour to kill. He finished his drink and nipped over to the station. First, he had to enlist Richmond's aid on a very delicate matter.

II

Mara was busy making scones for the afternoon meeting when Paul walked into the kitchen. Her hands were covered with flour and she waved them about to show she'd embrace him if she could. Seth immediately threw his arms around Paul and hugged him. Mara could see his face over Paul's shoulder, and noticed tears in his eyes. Rick slapped Paul on the back and Zoe kissed his cheek. "I did the cards," she told him. "I knew you were innocent and they'd have to let you go." Even Julian and Luna, caught up in the adults' excitement, did a little dance around him and chanted his name.

"Sit down," Seth said. "Tell us about it."

"Hey! Let me finish this first." Mara gestured at the half-made scones. "It won't take a minute. And it was your idea in the first place."

"I tell you what," Paul said. "I could do with a cup of tea. That prison stuff's piss-awful."

"I'll make it." Seth reached for the kettle. "Then we'll all go in the front room."

Mara carried on with the scones, readying them for the oven, and Seth put the kettle on. The others all wandered into the front room except for Paul, who stood nervously behind Mara.

"I'm sorry," he said. "You know . . ."

She turned and smiled at him. "Forget it. I'm just glad you're back. I should never have doubted you in the first place."

"I was a bit . . . well, I did lie. Thanks for tipping me off, anyway. At least I had a chance."

The kettle started boiling, and Seth hurried back in to make tea. Mara put the tray of scones in the oven and washed her hands.

"Right," she said, drying them on her apron. "I'm ready."

They sat down in the living-room and Seth poured tea.

"Come on, then," he urged Paul.

"Come on, what?"

"Tell us what happened."

"Where do you want me to start?"

"Where did you go?"

Paul lit a Players and spat a strand of loose tobacco from his upper lip. "Edinburgh," he said. "Went to see an old mate, didn't I?"

"Did he help you?" Mara asked.

Paul snorted. "Did he fuck. Bastard's changed a lot. I found the building easy enough. It used to be one of those grotty old tenements, but it's all been tarted up now. Potted plants in the stairwell and all that. Anyway, Ray answers the door, and he doesn't recognize me at first—at least he pretends he doesn't. I hardly knew him, either. Wearing a bloody suit, he was. We say hello and then this bird comes out—hair piled up on top of her head and a black dress slit right down the front to her belly button. She's carrying one of those long-stemmed wineglasses full of white wine, just for the effect. 'Who's this, Raymond?' she says, right lah-de-dah, like, and I head for the stairs."

"You didn't stay?" Mara said.

"Are you joking?"

"Do you mean your old friend wouldn't let you in?"

"Gone up in the world has old Raymond. Seems he was entertaining the boss and the wife—he's in computers—and he didn't want any reminders of his past. Used to be a real wild boy, but . . . Anyway, I left. Oh, I reckon he might have let me in if I'd pushed hard enough, stuck me in the cupboard or somewhere out of the way. But I wasn't having any."

"So where did you go?" Seth asked.

"Just walked around for a while till I found a pub."

"You didn't walk the streets all night, did you?" Mara asked.

"Like hell. It was colder than a witch's tit up there. This is bloody Scotland we're talking about. First thing the next morning I bought myself a duffle coat just to keep from freezing to death."

"What did you do then, after you left the pub?"

"I met this bloke there," Paul said, reddening. "He said I could go back to his place with him. Look, I know what you're thinking. I'm not a fucking queer. But when you're on the streets, just trying to survive, you do what you have to, right? He was a nice enough bloke, anyway, and he didn't ask no awkward questions. Careful, he was, too, if you know what I mean.

"Next day I was going to head for Glasgow and look up another old mate, but I thought fuck that for a lark, best thing to do is get straight to Ireland. I've got mates there, and I don't think they've changed. If I'd got to Belfast, *nobody* would have found me."

"So what went wrong?" Seth asked.

Paul laughed harshly. "Bloody ferry dock. I goes up to this shop-bloke to buy some fags and when I walk away he shouts after me. I can't understand a bleeding word he's saying on account of the Jock accent, like, but this copper sees us and gives me the look. I get nervous and take off and the bastards catch me."

"Did the shopkeeper recognize you?" Mara asked. "Your picture was in the papers, you know."

"Nah. I'd just given him too much bloody money, that's all. He was shouting he wanted to give me my fucking change." Paul laughed and the others laughed with him. "It wasn't so funny at the time," he added.

"What did the police do?" asked Rick.

"They've charged me with being an accessory. I'll have to go to court."

"Then what?" Mara asked.

Paul shrugged. "With my record I'll probably end up doing porridge again. That copper with the scar seems to think I might get off if they get a sympathetic jury. I mean, sometimes you respect people for standing by their mates, right? He says he might be able to get the charge reduced to giving false information and wasting police time. I'd only get six months max, then. But the other bloke tells me I'm looking at ten years. Who do you believe?"

"If you're lucky," Mara said, "Burgess might be gone by then and Banks'll take it easy on you."

"What's wrong with him? He soft or something?"

Seth shook his head. "Somehow I don't think so, no. He just has a different technique."

"They're all bastards when you get right down to it," Rick added.

Paul agreed. "So what's been happening here?" he asked.

Seth filled him in on the police visits. "Apart from that, not much really. We've all been worrying about you most of the time." He ruffled Paul's hair. "Glad you're back, kid. Nice new haircut, too."

Paul blushed. "Fuck off. Anyway, nothing's changed, has it?"

"What do you mean?" Mara asked.

"Well, they still don't have their killer and they're not going to stop till they do. And if they don't get someone else, I'm still their best bet. That Burgess bastard made that quite clear."

"Don't worry about it," Seth said. "We won't let them blame it on you."

Paul looked at his watch. "Nearly opening time," he said. "I could do with a pint and some nosh."

"We'll have to eat at the pub today, anyway," Mara

said. "I've not made any dinner. What with that meeting and all. . . ."

"What meeting?" Paul asked.

"We're getting together to talk about the demo this afternoon," Rick said. "Dennis is bringing Tim and Abha up about three. We want to look over statements and stuff to prove police brutality."

"Well you can count me out," Paul said. "I've had enough of that bleeding demo, and those fucking do-gooders. Sod 'em all."

"You don't have to stick around," Mara told him. "Not if you don't want."

"I think I'll go for a walk," Paul said, calming down. "Being cooped up in that cell hasn't done my head much good."

"And I've got work to do," Seth said. "I've got to finish that bureau today. It's already overdue."

"What's this?" Rick said. "Is everybody copping out on us?"

"I'll put my two penn'orth in, first, don't worry," Seth said. "Then I'll get some work done. As for now, I think Paul's right. They do a nice Sunday lunch at the Black Sheep and I'm starving."

Seth put his arm around Paul. The others stood up and went for their coats. In the fresh spring air, the seven of them walked down the track to Relton, happy together for the last time.

Except for Mara. The others might realize it, too, she thought, but nobody's saying anything. If Paul isn't guilty, then someone else here is.

III

Jenny was already waiting when Banks came into the Queen's Arms at lunch-time. Hungry, he arranged with Cyril for a few slices of roast leg of lamb. Glenys wasn't around, and Cyril, though he said nothing, seemed distracted.

"So," Jenny said, resting her elbows on the table and cupping her chin in her hands, "what's new? Dennis told me you dropped by. Thanks for going."

"*He* didn't thank me."

Jenny smiled. "Well, he wouldn't, would he?"

"You didn't tell me it was you who persuaded him to talk to me in the first place."

The lines around her eyes crinkled. "Didn't I? Sorry. But did you find anything out?"

"Not really."

"What does that mean?"

"It means no, I suppose. Have you ever noticed a blue Escort with two burly men in it hanging around Osmond's place?"

"No. Haven't you got *any* ideas, Alan?"

"Maybe one. It seems a bit far-fetched, but if I'm right. . . ."

"Right about what?"

"Just an idea, that's all."

"Can you tell me?"

"I'd rather not. Best wait and see. Richmond's working on it."

"When will you know?"

"Tomorrow, I hope."

The food arrived. "I'm starving," Jenny said, and the two ate in silence.

When he'd finished, Banks bought another round of drinks and lit a cigarette. Then he explained his doubts about Paul Boyd's guilt.

"Are you any closer to catching the real killer?" Jenny asked.

"It doesn't look like it. Boyd's still the closest we've got."

"I can't believe that Dennis is a murderer, you know."

"Are you speaking as a psychologist?"

"No. As a woman."

"I think I'd trust that opinion more if it came from a professional."

Jenny arched her eyebrows. "What do you mean by that?"

"Don't bristle, it doesn't suit you. I mean that people—men and women—tend to be very protective about whoever they get involved with. It's only natural—you know that as well as I do. And not only that, but they deliberately blinker themselves sometimes, even lie. Look what Boyd did. If he really is innocent of murder, then he sure as hell risked a lot. And think about how Mara behaved. Whichever way you look at it now, it comes down to Seth, Rick or Zoe—with Mara, Tim and Abha, *and* your Dennis running close behind."

"All right. As a professional, I don't think Dennis did it."

"Just how much do you know about him?"

"What do you mean?"

"Never mind."

"What? Come on. Out with it. If there's something I should know, tell me."

Banks took a deep breath. "Would you say Osmond is the kind of person to hit women?"

"What?"

Haltingly, Banks told her about Ellen Ventner. The more he said, the paler she became. Even as he told her, Banks wasn't sure of his motives. Was he doing it because he was worried about her association with Osmond, or was it out of pure vindictive jealousy?

"I don't believe it," she whispered.

"Believe it. It's true."

"Why are you telling me this?"

"I didn't want to tell you. You pushed me into it."

"It was you who made me push you. You must have known how bloody humiliated it would make me feel."

Banks shrugged. He could feel her starting to turn her anger against him. "I'm sorry, that's not what I intended. He could be dangerous, Jenny. And I don't know about you, but I have problems understanding a person who rescues defenceless women from police brutality in public and beats them up in private."

"You said it only happened once. There's no need to go making him into a monster. What do you expect me to do? Chuck him over just because he made a mistake?"

"I expect you to be careful, that's all. Osmond hit a woman once, put her in hospital, and he's also a suspect in a murder investigation. In addition, he seems to think the CIA, the KGB and MI5 are all after him. I'd say that merits a little caution, wouldn't you?"

Jenny's eyes glittered. "You've never liked Dennis right from the start, have you? You've never even given him a chance. And now as soon as you find a bit of dirt on him, you sling it at me. Just what the bloody hell do you hope to achieve, Alan? You're not my keeper. I can take care of myself. I don't need a big brother to look out for me."

She picked up her coat and swept out of the pub, knocking over her glass as she went. Faces turned to stare and Banks felt himself flush. Good one, Alan, he said to himself, you handled that really well.

He followed her outside, but she was nowhere in sight. Cursing, he went back to his office and tried to occupy his mind with work.

After a couple of false starts, he finally got through to Rick's wife's sister at her home in Camden Town. She sounded cagey and Banks first had to assure her that his call had nothing at all to do with the custody battle. Even then, she didn't sound as if she believed him.

"I just need some information about Rick's wife, that's all," he said. "Were you always good friends?"

"Yes," the sister answered. "Our ages are close, so we always supported one another, even after she married Rick. I don't want you to think I've anything against him, by the way. He's selfish and egotistical, but then most men are. Artists even more so. And I'm sure he's a good father. Pam certainly wasn't capable of taking care of Julian when they split up."

"And now?"

"She's getting there. It's a long road, though, alcoholism."

"Did Pam ever have any connections up north?"

"Up north? Good Lord, no. I don't think she's ever been farther north than Hendon."

"Not even for a visit?"

"No. What's there to visit, anyway? It's all canals and slag heaps, isn't it?"

"So she's spent most of her life in either London or Cornwall?"

"Yes. They had a few months in France some years ago. Most painters seem to gravitate towards France at one time or another. But that's all."

"Have you ever heard her mention a policeman called Gill—PC Edwin Gill, number 1139?"

"I've never heard her mention any policemen. No, I tell a lie. She said the local pub in Cornwall stayed open till all hours when the bobby was there. But I don't think that'd be your PC Gill."

"No," Banks said, "it wouldn't. Did she ever attend political demonstrations—Greenham Common, the Aldermaston march, that kind of thing?"

"Pam's never been very political. Wisely so, if you ask me. What's the point? You can't trust one lot more than the other. Is that all, Chief Inspector?"

"Is she there? Can I talk to her?"

There was a short pause and Banks heard muffled sounds from the other end of the line. Finally, he could hear the phone changing hands and another voice came on—husky and weary, as if doped or ill.

"Yes?"

Banks asked her the same questions he'd asked her sister, and the answers were the same. She spoke hesitantly, with long pauses between each sentence.

"Are the police involved in this custody battle?" Banks asked.

"Uh, no," she answered. "Just . . . you know . . . lawyers."

Naturally, Banks thought. "And you've never heard of PC Gill?"

"Never."

"Has your sister visited Yorkshire recently?" Banks asked the question as soon as it came to him. After all, the sister might have got herself involved somehow.

"No. Here . . . looking after me. Can I go now? I've got to . . . I don't know anything."

"Yes," Banks said. "That's all. Thanks for your time."

He hung up and made notes on the conversation while it was fresh in his mind. The one thing that struck him as odd was that neither of the women had asked about Julian, about how he was. Why, he wondered, did Rick's wife want custody if she didn't even care that much about the child? Spite? Revenge? Julian would probably be better off where he was.

Next he called the Hebden Bridge police and asked for PC Brooks.

"Sorry to bother you again, Constable," he said. "I should probably have asked you all this before, but there's been rather too much going on here. Can you tell me anything about Alison Cotton, the woman who was killed in the car accident?"

"I remember her all right, sir," Brooks said. "It was my first accident and I . . . well . . . I, er . . ."

"I know what you mean. It happens to us all. Did you know her before the accident?"

"Oh, aye. She'd been here a few years, like, ever since the artsy types discovered us, you might say."

"And Alison was artsy?"

"Aye. Helped organize the festival, poetry readings, that kind of thing. She ran the bookshop. I suppose you already know that."

"What kind of a person was she?"

"She were a right spirited lass. Proper bonny, too. She wrote things. You know, poems, stories, stuff like that. I tried reading some in the local paper but I couldn't make head nor tail of it. Give me 'Miami Vice' or 'Dynasty' any day."

"Was she ever involved in political matters—marches, demos, things like that?"

"Well," PC Brooks said, "we never had many things like that here. A few, but nowt much. Mostly 'Save the Whales' and 'Ban the Bomb.' I don't know as she was involved, though she did sometimes write bits for the paper about not killing animals for their fur and not making laboratory mice smoke five hundred fags a day. And about them women outside that missile base."

"Greenham Common?"

"That's the one. When it comes down to it, I dare say she was like the rest, though. If some bandwagon came along, they jumped on it."

"Ever heard of a PC Gill, 1139, from Scarborough?"

"Only what I've read in the papers, sir. I hope you catch the bastard who did it."

"So do I. What about a friend of Cotton's called Elizabeth Dale? Heard of her?"

"Oh, aye. Liz Dale hung around with the Cotton crowd all right. Thick as thieves. I felt sorry for her, myself. I mean it's like a sickness, isn't it, when you get so you need something all the time."

"Was she a registered addict?"

"Aye. She never really gave us any trouble. We just like to keep an eye on them, that's all, make sure they're not selling off half their prescriptions."

"What kind of person is she?"

"Moody," Brooks said. "She got off drugs, but she were never really right afterwards. One day she'd be up, the next down. Right bloody yo-yo. But there was a lass with strong political opinions."

"Liz Dale was political?"

"Aye. For a while, at least. Till she got it out of her system. Like I said, bandwagon."

"But she was keener than the rest?"

"I'd say so, yes. Now Seth, he was never much more than partly interested. Rather be slicing up a piece of wood. And Alison, like I said, well, she had a lot of energy and she had to put it somewhere, but she was more your private, artistic type. But Liz Dale, she was up to her neck in everything at one time."

"Were Liz Dale and Alison Cotton especially close?"

"Like sisters."

Banks thought of the complaint Dale had made against PC Gill. From that, he already knew she had attended at least one demonstration and come across him. Perhaps there had been others, too. Alison Cotton could have been with her. Perhaps this was the link he was looking for. But so what? Alison was dead; Reginald Lee had run her over by accident. It still didn't add up, unless everyone was lying and Liz Dale *had* been at Maggie's Farm and at the Eastvale demonstration. Banks didn't know her, but if she did have a history of drug abuse, there was a chance she might be unbalanced.

"Thanks a lot," Banks said. "You've been a great help."

"I have? Oh, well—"

"Just one more thing. Do you know where Liz Dale lives?"

"Sorry, I can't help you there, sir. She's been away from here a few years now. I've no idea at all."

"Never mind. Thanks anyway."

Banks broke the connection and walked over to the window. At the far side of the square, just outside the National Westminster bank, a rusty blue Mini had slammed into the back of a BMW, and the two drivers were arguing. Automatically, Banks phoned downstairs and asked Sergeant Rowe to send someone over. Then he lit a cigarette and started thinking.

He certainly needed to know more about Liz Dale. If

he could prove that she had been in the area at the time of the demo, then he had someone else with a motive for wanting to harm Gill. The Dale woman could easily have visited the farm one day earlier that week and taken the knife—Mara said that no one paid it any mind as a rule. If nobody had seen her, perhaps she had walked in and taken it while everyone was out. But was she at the demo? And why use Seth's knife? Did she have some reason other than revenge for wanting Gill dead? Obviously the best way to get the answer to that was to find Dale herself. Surely that couldn't prove too difficult.

As PC Craig approached the two drivers in the market square, Banks walked over to his filing cabinet.

IV

Mara stood inside the porch with Rick and Zoe and waved goodbye to Dennis Osmond and the others as they drove off. The sky was darkening in the west, and that early-evening glow she loved so much held the dale in its spell, spreading a blanket of silence over the landscape. Flocks of birds crossed the sky and lights flicked on in cottages down in Relton and over the valley in Lyndgarth.

"What do you think?" she asked Rick, as they went back inside. The evening was cool. She hugged herself, then pulled on a sweater and sat in the rocking chair.

Rick's knees cracked as he knelt at the grate to start the fire. "I think it'll work," he said. "We're bound to get the newspapers interested, maybe even TV. The police might try and discredit us, but people will get the message."

Mara rolled a cigarette. "I'll be glad when it's all over," she said. "The whole business seems to have brought us nothing but trouble."

"Look on the bright side," Rick said, turning to look

at her. "It's a blow against the police and their heavy-handed tactics. Even that woman from the Church for Peace group has started calling them pigs."

"Still," Mara said firmly, "it would have been better for all of us if none of it had ever happened."

"Everything's all right now," Zoe said. "Paul's back, we're all together again."

"I know, but . . ."

Mara couldn't help feeling uneasy. True, Paul's return had cheered them up no end, especially Seth, who had been moping around with a long face the whole time he'd been away. But it wasn't the end. The police weren't going to rest until they'd arrested someone for the murder, and they had their eyes on the farm. Paul might still end up in jail as an accessory, a serious charge, Mara now realized. She wondered if Banks was going to charge her, too. He wasn't stupid; he must know she had warned Paul about Crocker's finding the knife. Everything felt fragile. There was a chance she might lose it all, all the peace of mind and stability she had sought for so long. And the children, too. That didn't bear thinking about.

"Cheer up." Rick crawled over and tilted her chin up. "We'll have a party to celebrate Paul's release. Invite everyone we can think of and fill the place with music and laughter, eh?"

Mara smiled. "I hope you're right."

"Where is Paul, anyway?" Zoe asked.

"He went walking on the moors," said Mara. "I suppose he's just enjoying his freedom." She almost added "while it lasts," but decided that Rick was right; she at least ought to try to enjoy herself while things were going well.

"Seth didn't want much to do with us this afternoon, either," Rick complained.

"Don't be like that, Rick," Mara said. "He's been getting behind in his work. This business with the police has been bothering him, too. Haven't you noticed how upset he's been? And you know what a perfectionist he is, what he's like about deadlines. Besides, I think he's just relieved Paul's back. He's as fed up with the aftermath of this bloody demonstration as I am."

"We have to try and bring some good out of it," Rick argued, placing the coal on top of the layered newspaper and wood chips. "Don't you see that?"

"Yes, I do. I just think we all need a rest from it, that's all."

"The struggle goes on. There is no rest." Rick lit the fire in several places and stood the piece of plywood in front of the fireplace to make it draw. Behind the board the flames began to roar like a hurricane, and Mara could see red around the edges.

"Be careful," she said. "You know how wildly it burns with the wind up here."

"Seriously," Rick said, keeping an eye on the plywood shield, "we can't stop now. I can understand your lack of enthusiasm, but you'll just have to shake yourself. Seth and Paul, too. You don't get anywhere against the oppressors by packing it in because you're fed up."

"I sometimes wonder if you ever get anywhere," Mara muttered.

She was aware that now she had found her home, Maggie's Farm, she was less concerned about the woes of the world. Not that she didn't care—she would be quite happy to write letters for Amnesty International and sign petitions—but she didn't want to make it her whole life, attending rallies, meetings and demonstrations. Compared to the farm, the children and her pottery, it all seemed so distant and pointless. People were going to go on being as cruel to one another as they always had been. But here was a place where she could make room for love. Why should it be contaminated by the sordid world of politics and violence?

"Penny for them?"

"What? Oh, sorry, Zoe. Just dreaming."

"It's okay to dream."

"As long as you don't expect them to come true without hard work," Rick added.

"Oh, shut up!" Mara said. "Just give it a rest, can't you, Rick? Let's pretend everything's all right for a few hours at least."

Rick's jaw dropped. "Isn't that what I said at first?" Then he shook his head and muttered something about women. Mara couldn't be bothered to take him to task for it.

Just then, the kitchen door flew open and Paul stood there, white and trembling. Mara jumped to her feet. "Paul! What is it? What's wrong?"

At first he couldn't speak. He just leaned against the door jamb and tried to force the words out. Rick was beside him by then, and Zoe had reached for his hand.

"What is it, Paul?" she asked him softly. "Take a deep breath. You must try to tell us."

Paul followed her advice and went to slump down on the cushions. "It's Seth," he said finally, pointing towards the back garden. "I think he's dead."

FOURTEEN

I

Banks and Burgess rushed through the dark garden to Seth's workshop, where a bare bulb shone inside the half-open door. Normally, they would have been more careful on their approach to the scene, but the weather was dry and a stone path led between the vegetable beds to the shed, so there was no likelihood of footprints.

Burgess pushed the door open slowly and they walked in. Mixed with the scents of shaved wood and varnish was the sickly metallic smell of blood. Both men had come across it often enough before to recognize it immediately.

At first, they stood in the doorway to take in the whole scene. Seth was just in front of them, wearing his sand-colored smock, slumped over his work-bench. His head lay on the surface in a small pool of blood, and his arms dangled at his side. From where Banks was standing, it looked as if he had hit his head on the vice clamped to the bench slightly to his left. On the concrete floor over in the right-hand corner stood a small bureau in the Queen Anne style, its finish still wet, a rich, glistening nut-brown. At the far end of the workshop, another bare light bulb shone over the area Seth used for office work.

It was only when Banks moved forward a pace that he noticed he had stepped in something sticky and slippery. The light wasn't very strong and most of the floor space around Seth was in semi-darkness. Kneeling, Banks saw that what he had first taken for shadow was, in fact, more blood. Seth's feet stood at the centre of a large puddle of blood. It hadn't come from the head wound, though, Banks realized, examining the bench again. There hadn't been much bleeding and none of the blood seemed to have dribbled off the edge. Bending again, he caught sight of a thin tubular object, a pen or a pencil, perhaps, half-submerged in the pool. He decided to leave it for the forensic team to deal with. They were on their way from Wetherby and should arrive shortly after Dr Glendenning and Peter Darby, the young photographer, neither of whom had as far to travel.

Leaving the body, Banks walked cautiously to the back of the workshop where the old Remington stood on its desk beside the filing cabinet. There was a sheet of paper in the typewriter. Leaning forward, Banks was able to read the message: "I did it. I killed the policeman Gill. It was wrong of me. I don't know what came over me. I'm sorry for all the trouble I caused. This is the best way. Seth."

He called Burgess over and pointed out the note to him.

Burgess raised his eyebrows and whistled softly between his teeth. "Suicide, then?"

"Looks like it. Glendenning should be able to give us a better idea."

"Where the hell is this bloody doctor, anyway?" Burgess complained, looking at his watch. "It can't take him that long to get here. Everywhere's within pissing distance in this part of the country."

Burgess and Glendenning hadn't met yet, and Banks was looking forward to seeing Dirty Dick try out his aggressive arrogance on the doctor. "Come on," he said, "there's nothing more to do in here till the others arrive. We'll only mess up the scene. Let's go outside for a smoke."

The two of them left the workshop and stood in the

cool evening air. Glendenning, Banks knew, would smoke wherever he wanted and nobody had ever dared say a word to him, but then he was one of the top pathologists in the country, not a lowly chief inspector or superintendent.

From the doorway of the shed, they could see the kitchen light in the house. Someone—Zoe, it looked like—was filling a kettle. Mara had taken the news very badly, and Rick had called the local doctor for her. He had also phoned the Eastvale station, which surprised Banks, given Rick's usual hostility. Still, Seth Cotton was dead, there was no doubting that, and Rick probably knew there would be no way of avoiding an investigation. It made more sense to start out on the right foot rather than have to explain omissions or evasions later. Banks wondered whether to go inside and have a chat with them, but decided to give them a bit longer. They would have probably got over the immediate shock by the time Glendenning and the scene-of-crime team had finished.

At last, the back door opened and the tall, white-haired doctor crossed the garden, a half-smoked cigarette hanging from the corner of his mouth. He was closely followed by a fresh-faced lad with a camera bag slung over his shoulder.

"About bloody time," Burgess said.

Glendenning gave him a dismissive glance and stood in the doorway while Darby did his work. Banks and Burgess went back into the workshop to make sure he photographed everything, including the blood on the floor, the pen or pencil, the Queen Anne bureau and the typewriter. When Darby had finished, Glendenning went in. He was so tall he had to duck to get through the door.

"Watch out for the blood," Banks warned him.

"And there's no smoking at the scene," Burgess added. He got no answer.

Banks smiled to himself. "Ease up," he said. "The doc's a law unto himself."

Burgess grunted but kept quiet while Glendenning felt for a pulse and busied himself with his stethoscope and thermometer.

About fifteen minutes later, while Glendenning was still making calculations in his little red notebook, the forensic team arrived, headed by Vic Manson, the fingerprints man. Manson was a slight, academic-looking man in his early forties. Almost bald, he plastered the few remaining hairs over the dome of his skull, creating an effect of bars shadowed on an egg. He greeted the two detectives and went inside with the team. As soon as he saw the workshop, he turned to Banks. "Bloody awful place to look for prints," he said. "Too many rough surfaces. And tools. Have you any idea how hard it is to get prints from well-used tools?"

"I know you'll do your best, Vic," Banks said. He guessed that Manson was annoyed at being disturbed on a Sunday evening.

Manson snarled and got to work alongside the others, there to take blood samples and anything else they could find.

Banks and Burgess went back outside and lit up again. A few minutes later, Glendenning joined them.

"What's the news, doc?" Burgess asked.

Glendenning ignored him and spoke directly to Banks. "He's dead, and that's about the only fact I can give you so far."

"Come on, doc!" said Burgess. "Surely you can tell us more than that."

"Can you ask your pushy friend here to shut up, just for a wee while?" Glendenning said to Banks in a quiet, nicotine-ravaged voice redolent of Edinburgh. "And tell him not to call me doc."

"For Christ's sake." Burgess flicked the stub of his cigar into the vegetable patch and stuck his hands deep in his pockets. He was wearing his leather jacket over an open-necked shirt, as usual. The only concession he had made to the cold was a V-necked sweater. Now that darkness had come, their breath plumed in the air, lit by the eerie glow of the bare bulb inside the workshop.

Glendenning lit another cigarette and turned back to Banks, who knew better than to rush him. "It doesn't look to me," the doctor said slowly, "as if that head wound was serious enough to cause death. Don't quote me on it, but I don't think it fractured the skull."

Banks nodded. "What do you think was the cause?" he asked.

"Loss of blood. And he lost it from his ankles."

"His ankles?"

"Aye," Glendenning went on. "The veins on the insides of each ankle were cut. I found a blade—most likely from a plane—lying in the blood, and it looks like it might have been used for the job. I'll have to make sure, of course."

"So was it suicide?" Burgess asked.

Glendenning ignored him and went on speaking to Banks. "Most suicides with a penchant for gory death," he said, "slit their wrists. The ankles are just as effective, though, if not more so. But whether he inflicted the wounds himself or not, I canna say."

"He's tried that way before," Banks said. "And there was a note."

"Aye, well, that's your department, isn't it?"

"Which came first," Banks asked, "the head wound or the cut ankles?"

"That I can't say, either. He could have hit his head as he lost consciousness, or someone could have hit it for him and slit his ankles. If the two things happened closely in succession, it won't be possible to tell which came first, either. It looks like the head wound was caused by the vice. There's blood on it. But of course it'll have to be matched and the vice compared with the shape of the wound."

"How long has he been dead?" Banks asked. "At a guess."

Glendenning smiled. "Aye, you're learning, laddie," he said. "It's always a guess." He consulted his notebook. "Well, rigor's not much farther than the neck, and the body temperature's down 2.5 degrees. I'd say he's not been dead more than two or three hours."

Banks looked at his watch. It was six o'clock. So Cotton had probably died between three and four in the afternoon.

"The ambulance should be here soon," Glendenning said. "I called them before I set off. I'd better just bag the head and feet before they get here. We don't want some gormless young ambulance driver spoiling the evidence, do we?"

"Can you do the post-mortem tonight?" Banks asked.

"Sorry, laddie. We've the daughter and son-in-law down for the weekend. First thing in the morning?"

Banks nodded. He knew they'd been spoiled in the past by Glendenning's eagerness to get down to the autopsy immediately. It was more usual to be asked to wait until the next day. And to Glendenning, first thing in the morning was probably very early indeed.

The doctor went back inside, where Manson and his team were finishing up. A short while later, the ambulance arrived, and two white-coated men bearing a stretcher crossed to the workshop. Seth looked oddly comical now, with his head in a plastic bag. Like some creature out of a fifties horror film, Banks thought. The ambulance men tagged him, zipped him into a body bag and laid him on the stretcher.

"Can you leave by the side exit?" Banks asked, pointing to the large gate in the garden wall. "They're shook up enough in the house without having to see this."

The ambulance men nodded and left.

Manson came out five minutes later. "Lots of prints," he grumbled, "but most of them a mess, just as I thought.

At first glance, though, I'd say they belong to only two or three people, not dozens."

"You'll get Seth's, of course," Banks said, "and probably Boyd's and some of the others. Could you get anything from the blade?"

Manson shook his head. "Sorry. It was completely covered in blood. And the blood had mixed to a paste with the sawdust on the floor. Very sticky. You'd have to wipe it all off to get anywhere, and if you do that . . ." He shrugged. "Anyway, the doc's taken it with him to match to the wounds."

"What about the typewriter?"

"Pretty smudged, but we might get something. The paper, too. We can treat it with graphite."

"Look, there's a handwriting expert down at the lab, isn't there?"

"Sure. Geoff Tingley. He's good."

"And he knows about typewriting, too?"

"Of course."

Banks led Manson back into the workshop and over to the old Remington. The suicide note was now lying beside it. Also on the desk was a business letter Seth had recently written and not posted. "Dear Mr Spelling," it read, "I am most grateful for your compliments on the quality of my work, and would certainly have no objection to your spreading the word in the Wharfedale area. Whilst I always endeavour to meet both deadlines and quality standards, I am sure you realize that, this being a one-man operation, I must therefore limit the amount of work I take on." It went on to imply that Mr Spelling should seek out only the best jobs for Seth and not bother him with stacks of minor repairs and commissions for matchbox-holders or lamp stands.

"Can you get Mr Tingley to compare these two and let us know if they were typed by the same person?"

"Sure." Manson looked at the letters side by side. "At a pinch I'd say they weren't. Those old manual typewriters have all kinds of eccentricities, it's true, but so do typists. Look at those 'e's, for a start."

Banks looked. The 'e's in Seth's business letter had imprinted more heavily than those in his suicide note.

"Still," Manson went on, "better get an expert opinion. I don't suppose his state of mind could be called normal, if he killed himself." He placed each sheet of paper in an envelope. "I'll see Geoff gets these first thing in the morning."

"Thanks, Vic." Banks led the way outside again.

Burgess stood with his hands still in his pockets in the doorway beside Peter Darby, who was showing him the polaroids he'd taken before getting down to the real work. He raised his eyebrows as Banks and Manson joined him. "Finished?"

"Just about," Banks said.

"Time for a chat with the inmates, then." Burgess nodded towards the house.

"Let's take it easy with them," Banks said. "They've had a hell of a shock."

"One of them might not have had, if Cotton was murdered. But don't worry, I won't eat them."

In the front room, Zoe, Rick, Paul and the children sat drinking tea with the doctor, a young female GP from Relton. A fire blazed in the hearth and candles threw shadows on the whitewashed walls. Music played quietly in the background. Banks thought he recognized Bach's Third *Brandenburg* Concerto.

"Mara's under sedation," Rick said. "You can't talk to her."

"That's right," the doctor agreed, picking up her bag and reaching for her coat. "I just thought I'd wait and let you know. She took it very badly, so I've given her a sedative and put her to bed. I'll be back in the morning to check."

Banks nodded, and the doctor left.

"How about some tea?" Burgess said, clapping his

hands together and rubbing them. "It's real brass-monkey weather out there."

Rick scowled at him, but Zoe brought two cups and poured the steaming liquid.

Burgess smiled down at her. "Three lumps and a splash of milk, love, please."

"What happened?" Zoe asked, stirring in the sugar. Her eyes were red and puffy from crying.

"That's for you to tell us, isn't it?" Burgess said. He really was being quite polite, Banks noticed. "All we know is that Seth Cotton is dead and it looks like suicide. Has he been depressed lately?" He took a sip of tea and spluttered. "What the fuck is this?"

"It's Red Zinger," Zoe said. "No caffeine. You shouldn't really have milk and sugar with it."

"You're telling me." Burgess pushed the tea aside. "Well, was he?

"He was upset when Paul was in jail," Zoe answered. "But he cheered up this morning. He seemed so happy today."

"And he never said anything about ending it all?"

"Never." Zoe shook her head.

"I gather you had some kind of meeting this afternoon," Banks said. "Who was here?"

Rick eyed him suspiciously but said nothing.

"Just Dennis Osmond, Tim and Abha, that's all," Zoe answered.

"What time were they here?"

"They arrived about half-two and left around five."

"Were you all present?"

Zoe shook her head. "Seth stayed for a few minutes then went to . . . to work."

"And I went for a walk," Paul said defiantly. "I needed some fresh air after being cooped up in your bloody jail for so long."

"Not half as long as you will be if you don't knock off the cheek, sonny," said Burgess.

"Was it you who found the body?" Banks asked.

"Yes."

"Don't be shy. Tell us about it," Burgess prompted him.

"Nothing to tell, really. I just got back from my walk and decided to look in on Seth and see how he was doing. I helped him, you know. I was sort of an apprentice. When I opened the door—"

"The door was closed?" Burgess asked.

"Yes. But it wasn't locked. Seth never locked it."

"And what did you see?"

"You know what I saw. He was sprawled out on the bench, dead."

"How did you know he was dead? Did you feel his heart?"

"No, of course I didn't. I saw the blood. I called his name and he didn't answer. I just knew."

"Did you touch anything?" Banks asked.

"No. I ran in here and told the others."

"Did you go near the typewriter?"

"Why should I? I didn't even notice the bloody thing. All I saw was Seth, dead."

It was hard to know whether or not he was telling the truth. The shock of what he'd seen made his responses vague and defensive.

"So you left everything just as you found it?" Banks said.

"Yes."

"This afternoon, during the meeting," Burgess asked, "did anyone leave the room for any length of time?"

"We all left at one time or another," said Zoe. "You know, to go to the toilet, stretch our legs, whatever."

"Was anyone gone for a long time?"

"I don't know. We were talking. I don't remember."

"So someone could have been away for, say, ten minutes?"

"I suppose so."

"I know you were all busy playing at being concerned

citizens," Burgess said, "but surely one of you must have noticed if anyone was gone too long?"

"Look," Rick cut in, "I thought you said it was suicide. What are you asking these questions for?"

"I said it *looked* like suicide," Burgess answered coldly. "And I'll ask whatever bloody questions I think necessary, without any comments from you, Leonardo, thank you very much."

"Did any of you hear the typewriter at any time this afternoon?" Banks asked.

"No," Zoe answered. "But we wouldn't anyway. The walls are thick and the workshop's right at the far end of the garden. Well . . . you've seen where it is. We were all here in the front room. We could never even hear Seth sawing or using his drill from here."

Banks glanced at Burgess. "Anything else?"

"Not that I can think of right now," the superintendent said, subdued again after his exchange with Rick. "I don't want any of you buggering off anywhere, hear me?" he added, wagging his finger and giving Paul a particularly menacing look. "There'll be more questions when we've got the results of the post-mortem tomorrow, so be available, all of you."

Banks and Burgess left them to their grief. Down the valley side, the lights of Relton looked inviting in the chilly darkness.

"Pint?" Burgess suggested.

"Just what I had in mind," said Banks. They got into the Cortina and bumped away down the track towards the Black Sheep.

II

The pillow felt like a cloud, the bed like cotton wool. Mara lay on her back, drifting, but not quite asleep. When she had first heard the news, she had lost control completely. The tears seemed to spurt from her eyes, her heart began to beat wildly, and the breath clogged in her throat. But the doctor's injection had taken care of all that, trading spasms and panic for clouds and cotton wool.

She could hear the muffled voices downstairs, as if from a great distance, and they made her think of those times when Seth and Liz Dale had stayed up late talking. How jealous she had been then, how insecure. But Liz was long gone, and Seth, they told her, was dead.

Dead. The thought didn't register fully through the layers of sedative. She thought she should still be crying and gasping for breath, but instead her body felt as heavy as iron and she could hardly move. Her mind seemed to have a life of its own, wandering over events and picking them out like those miniature mechanical cranes that dipped into piles of cheap trinkets and sweets at seaside arcades. You put your penny in—a real penny, large and heavy—and off the crane went, with its artic-ulated grip, inside the glass case. You held down a but-ton to make it swing over and pressed another to make it drop onto the heap of prizes. If you were lucky, you got a chocolate bar, a cigarette lighter or a cheap ring; if not, the metal claw came up empty and you'd wasted your money. Mara had never won anything. Just as well, her father had always said: chocolate is bad for teeth; you're too young to smoke; and those rings will turn your finger green inside a week.

But her mind felt like one of those machines now, one she could not control. It circled her life, then swooped and snatched up the memory of the first time she and Seth had met. Just out of the ashram and eager to escape London, Mara had taken on a friend's flat in Eastvale when the friend emigrated to Canada.

She needed a job and decided to seek craft-work be-fore falling back on her secretarial skills, which were pretty rusty by then. Luckily, she heard of Elspeth's shop in Relton and went out to see her. Dottie had just become too ill to work—the pottery workshop was hers—and Mara got the job of helping out in the shop and the use of the facilities. It didn't bring in much money, but it was enough, along with the commission on the pottery. Her rent wasn't very high and she lived cheaply. But she was lonely.

Then one day after work, she had dropped in at the Black Sheep. It was pay-day and she had decided to treat herself to a glass of lager and a cheese-and-onion sandwich. No sooner had she started to eat than Seth walked in. He stood at the bar, tall and slim, his neatly trimmed dark hair and beard frosted with grey at the edges. And when he turned around, she noticed how deep and sad his eyes were, how serious he looked. Something passed between them—Seth admitted later that he'd noticed it, too—and Mara felt shy like a teenager again. He smiled at her and she remembered blushing. But when he came over to say hello, there was no phoney coyness on her part; there were never any silly games between them.

He was the first person she'd met in the area with a background similar to her own. They shared tastes in music and ideas about self-sufficiency and the way the world should be run; they had been to the same rock festivals years ago, and had read the same books. She went back with him to the farm that night—he was the only one living there at that time—and she never really left, except to give her notice to her landlord and move her meagre belongings.

It was a blissful time, a homecoming of the spirit for Mara, and she thought she had made Seth happy, too, though she was always aware that there was a part of him she could never touch.

And now he was dead. She didn't know how, or what had killed him, just that his body had ceased to exist. Her spiritual beliefs, which she still held to some extent, told her that death was merely a beginning. There would be other worlds, other lives perhaps, for Seth's spirit, which was immortal. But they would never again drink wine together in bed after making love, he would never kiss her forehead the way he did before going to the workshop, or hold her hand like a boy on his first date on the way down to the Black Sheep. And that was what hurt: the absence of living flesh. The spirit was all very well, but it was far too nebulous an idea to bring Mara much comfort. The miniature crane withdrew from the heap of prizes and held nothing in its metal claw.

Downstairs, the voices droned on, more like music, a *raga*, than words with meaning. Mara felt as if her blood had thickened to treacle and darkened to the colour of ink. Her body was getting heavier and the lights in the glass case were going out; it was half in shadows now, the prizes indistinguishable from one another. And what happens when the lights go out in the fun-house? Mara began to dream.

She was alone on the moors. A huge full moon shone high up, but the landscape was still dark and bleak. She stumbled over heather and tussocks of grass, looking for something.

At last she came to a village and went into the pub. It was the Black Sheep, but the place was all modern, with video games, carpets and bare concrete walls. A jukebox was playing some music she didn't understand. She asked for the farm, but everyone turned and laughed at her, so she ran out.

This time it was daylight outside, and she was no longer in Swainsdale. The landscape was unfamiliar, softer and more green, and she could smell a whiff of the ocean nearby.

In a hollow, she saw an old farmer holding wind chimes out in front of him. They made the same music as the jukebox and it frightened her this time. She found her voice and asked him where Maggie's Farm was. "Are you the marrying maiden?" he asked her, smiling toothlessly. "The basket is empty," he went on, shaking the wind chimes. "The man stabs the sheep. No blood flows. Misfortune."

Terrified, Mara ran off and found herself in an urban landscape at night. Some of the buildings had burned out and fires raged in the gutted shells; flames licked around broken windows and flared up high through fallen roofs. Small creatures scuttled in dark corners. And she was being followed, she knew it. She hadn't been able to see anyone, just sensed darting movements and heard rustling sounds behind her. For some reason, she was sure it was a woman, someone she should know but didn't.

Before the dream possessed her completely and turned her into one of the scavengers among the ruins, before the shadow behind tapped her on the shoulder, she struggled to wake up, to scream.

When she opened her eyes, she became conscious of someone sitting on the bedside pressing a damp cloth to her forehead. She thought it must be Seth, but when she turned and looked closely it was Zoe.

"Is it morning?" she asked in a weak voice.

"No," said Zoe, "it's only half-past nine."

"He really is dead, isn't he, Zoe?"

Zoe nodded. "You were having a nightmare. Go to sleep now." Mara closed her eyes again. The cool cloth smoothed her brow, and she began to drift. This time there was only darkness ahead, and the last thing she felt before she fell asleep was Zoe's hand gripping hers tightly.

III

"Anything wrong?" Larry Grafton asked, pulling Banks a pint of Black Sheep bitter.

Banks glanced at Burgess, who nodded.

"Seth Cotton's dead," he answered, and felt ears prick up behind him in the public bar, where most of the tables were occupied.

Grafton turned pale. "Oh no, not Seth," he said. "He was only in here this lunch-time. Not Seth?"

"How did he seem?" Banks asked.

"He was happy as a pig in clover," Grafton said. "That young lad was back and they all seemed to be celebrating. You're not telling me he killed himself, are you?"

"We don't know yet," Burgess said, picking up his pint of Watney's. "Anywhere quiet the chief inspector and I can have a little chat? Police business."

"Aye, you can use the snug. There's no one in there."

The snug was aptly named. Hidden away behind a partition of smoked glass and dark wood, there was room for about four people, and even that would be a tight squeeze.

Banks and Burgess made themselves comfortable, both of them practically draining their drinks before even reaching for smokes.

"Have a cigar," Burgess said, offering his tin.

"Thanks." Banks took one. He didn't enjoy cigars as a rule, but thought that if he tried them often enough he might eventually come to like them.

"And I think I'd better get a couple more drinks in before we start," Burgess said. "Thirsty work, this."

He was back in a moment carrying another pint of bitter for Banks and, this time, a pint of draught Guinness for himself.

"Right," he said, "I can tell you're not happy about this. Don't clam up on me, Banks. What's bothering you?"

"Let's take it at face value, for a start," Banks suggested. "Then maybe we can see what's wrong."

"Suicide?"

"Yes."

"But you don't think so?"

"No. But I'd like to play it through and see if I can pin down my ideas."

"All right. Cotton murdered Gill, then he was overcome with remorse and slit his ankles. Case closed. Can I go back to London now?"

Banks smiled. "But it's not as simple as that, is it? Why would Cotton murder PC Gill?"

Burgess ran a hand through his greying, Brylcreemed hair. "Bloody hell, I thought we'd been through all this before. We're talking about a political crime; call it an act of terrorism. Motive as such doesn't apply."

"But Seth Cotton was perhaps the least political of the lot of them," Banks argued. "Except maybe for Mara, or Zoe Hardacre. Sure, he was anti-nuclear, and he no doubt believed in social equality and the evils of apartheid. But so do I."

Burgess sniffed. "You might be the murder expert around here, but I know about terrorism. Believe me, anyone can get involved. Terrorists play on people's ideals and warp them to their own ends. It's like the brainwashing religious cults do."

"Do you think Gill's death was calmly planned and executed, or was it a crime of passion?" Banks asked.

"A bit of both. Things aren't so clear-cut in this kind of crime. Terrorists are very emotional about their beliefs, but they're cold and deadly when it comes to action."

"The only thing Seth Cotton cared passionately about was his carpentry, and perhaps Mara. If he did commit suicide, I doubt it was anything to do with politics."

"We have his note, don't forget. It's a confession."

"Let's leave that for later. Why did he kill himself? If he's the kind of person you're trying to make out he is, why would he feel remorse after succeeding in his aim? Why would he kill himself?"

Burgess doodled in the foam of his Guinness. "You expect too many answers, Banks. As often as not, there just aren't any. Can't you leave it at that?"

Banks shook his head and stubbed out the cigar. It tasted like last week's tea-leaves. He swigged some more Black Sheep bitter to get rid of the taste and lit a

Silk Cut. "It's because there's too many questions," he said. "We still don't know much about Cotton's political background before he came to the farm, though if there'd been any subversive activity I'm sure Special Branch would have a record of it. And what about his behaviour over the last few days? How do you read that?"

"They said he seemed happy when Boyd was released. Is that what you mean?"

"Partly."

"Well, of course he'd be happy," Burgess said. "If he knew the kid wasn't guilty."

"Why should he care? It'd be better for a cold-blooded terrorist to let someone else go down for what he'd done. So why kill himself?"

Burgess shrugged. "Because he knew we'd get to him soon."

"So why didn't he just disappear? Surely his masters would have taken care of him in Moscow or Prague or wherever."

"More likely Belfast. But I don't know. It's not unusual for suicides to appear happy once they've decided to end it all."

"I know that. I'm just not sure that he was happy because he'd decided to kill himself."

Burgess grunted. "What's your theory, then?"

"That he was killed, and it was made to look like a suicide."

"Killed by who?"

Banks ignored the question. "We won't know anything for certain until the doc does his post-mortem," he said, "but there's a few things that bother me about the note."

"Go on."

"It just doesn't ring true. The damn thing's neither here nor there, is it? Cotton confesses to killing Gill, but doesn't say why. All he says is, 'I don't know what came over me.' It doesn't square with what we know of him."

"Which is?"

"Precious little, I admit. He was a closed book. But I'd say he was the kind who'd either not bother with a note at all, or maybe he'd explain everything fully. He wouldn't come out with such a wishy-washy effort as the one we saw. I think he'd have used Gill's number, too, not his name. And I don't know if you had a good look, but it seemed very different from that business letter on the desk. The pressure on the characters was different, for a start."

"Yes," Burgess said, "but don't forget the state of mind he must have been in when he typed it."

"I'll grant you that. Still . . . and the style. Whoever wrote that suicide note had only very basic writing skills. But the business letter was more than competent and grammatically correct."

Burgess slapped the table. "Oh, come on Banks! What's the problem? Is it too easy for you? Business letters are always written in a different style; they're always a bit stuffy and wordy. You wouldn't write to a friend the same way you would in a business letter, would you, let alone a suicide note. A man writing his last words doesn't worry about grammar or how much pressure he puts on each letter."

"But that's just it. Those things are unconscious. Someone used to writing well doesn't immediately become sloppy just because he's under pressure. If anything, I'd have expected a more carefully composed message. And you don't think about how each finger hits the keys when you're typing. It's something you just do, and it doesn't vary much. Why leave it over in the typewriter, too? Why didn't he put it on the bench in front of him?"

"And what I'm saying," Burgess argued, "is that his state of mind could account for all your objections. He must have been disturbed. Contemplation of suicide has an odd effect on a man's character. You can't expect everything to be the same as usual when a bloke's on the verge of slitting his bloody ankles. And remember, you said he'd tried that before."

"That is a problem," Banks agreed. "Whoever did it must have known about the previous attempt and copied it to make it look more like a genuine suicide."

"That's assuming somebody else did it. I'm not sure I agree."

Banks shrugged. "We'll see what forensic says about the note. But I'm not happy with it at all."

"What about the bureau?"

"What about it?"

"He'd obviously just finished it, hadn't he? The coat of varnish was still fresh. And he'd moved it to the corner of the workshop. Doesn't that imply anything?"

"That he was tidying things up behind him, you mean? Tying up loose ends?"

"Exactly. Just like a man on the point of suicide. He finished his last piece of work, put it carefully aside so he wouldn't get blood all over it, then he slit his fucking ankles. When he got weak and passed out, he hit his head on the vice, accounting for the head wound."

Banks stared into the bottom of his glass. "It could have happened that way," he said slowly. "But I don't think so."

"Which brings us back to the big question again," Burgess said. "If we're to follow your line of reasoning, if you are right, then who killed him?"

"It could have been any of them, couldn't it? Zoe said as much."

"Yes, but she might have said that to get herself and her mates off the hook. I'm thinking of one of them in particular."

"Who?"

"Boyd."

Banks sighed. "I was afraid you'd say that."

"I'll bet you bloody were." Burgess leaned forward

so suddenly that the glasses rattled on the table. Banks could smell the Guinness and cigar smoke on his breath. "If we play it your way, there's no getting around the facts. Boyd was missing all afternoon, unaccounted for. We only have his word that he was walking on the moors. I shouldn't think anybody saw him. It would have been easy for him to get in by the side gate and visit Seth while everyone in the house was wrapped up in their own little games. Nothing odd about that. He helped Seth a lot, and the shed would be full of his fingerprints anyway. They talk, and he kills Seth— pushes his head forward to knock him out on the vice, then slits his ankles." Burgess leaned back again, satisfied, and folded his arms.

"All right," Banks said. "I agree. It fits. But why? Why would Boyd kill Seth Cotton?"

Burgess shrugged. "Because he knew something to link Boyd to Gill's murder. It makes sense, Banks, you know it does. Why you're defending that obnoxious little prick is beyond me."

"Why was Cotton so miserable when Boyd was in jail," Banks asked, "and so happy when he came out?"

Burgess lit another Tom Thumb. "Loyalty, perhaps? He knew something and was worried he might be called on to give evidence. He wasn't sure he could carry on with his lies and evasions under pressure. Boyd gets out, so Cotton feels immediate elation. They talk. Cotton tells Boyd what he knows and how glad he is he won't have to testify under oath, so Boyd gets worried and kills him. Remember, Boyd knew he wasn't quite off the hook, whatever Cotton might have made of his release. And you know how terrified the kid is of enclosed spaces. He'd do anything to avoid a life sentence."

"And the note?"

"Let's say you're right about that. Boyd typed it to clear himself, put the blame on someone who isn't able to defend himself. It's a cowardly kind of act typical of someone like him. That explains the pressure on the keys and the literacy level. Boyd wasn't very well educated. He was spending most of his time on the streets by the time he was thirteen. And he couldn't explain anything about Cotton's motives because he killed Gill himself. So," Burgess went on, "even if we see it your way, I still come out right. Personally, I don't give a damn whether it was Boyd or Cotton. Either way, we've cracked it. Which way do you want to go? Toss a coin."

"I'm still not convinced."

"That's because you don't want to be."

"What do you mean by that?"

"You know damn well what I mean. You've argued yourself into a corner. It was your idea to let Boyd out and see what happened. Well, now you've seen what's happened. No sooner is he out than there's another death. That makes you responsible."

Banks took a deep breath. There was too much truth for comfort in what Burgess was saying. He shook his head. "Somebody killed Seth," he said, "but I don't think it was Boyd. For all the kid's problems, I believe he genuinely cared. The people at Maggie's Farm are the only ones who have ever done anything for him, gone out on a limb."

"Come off it! That sentimental bullshit doesn't work on me. The kid's a survivor, an opportunist. He's nothing more than a street punk."

"And Cotton?"

Burgess sat back and reached for his glass. The chair creaked. "Good actor, accomplice, innocent bystander, conscience-stricken idealist? I don't bloody know. But it doesn't matter now, does it? He's dead. It's all over."

But Banks felt that it did matter. Somehow, after what had happened that afternoon, it seemed to matter more now than it ever had before.

"Is it?" he said. Then he stubbed out his cigarette and drained his glass. "Come on, let's go."

FIFTEEN

I

Eastvale General Infirmary stood on King Street, about half a mile west of the police station, not far from the comprehensive school. Because the day was warming up nicely, Banks decided to walk. As he left the station, he turned on his Walkman and listened to Muddy Waters sing "Louisiana Blues" as he made his way through the warren of narrow streets with their cracked stone walls, gift shops and overpriced pubs.

The hospital itself was an austere Victorian brick building. About its high draughty corridors hung an air of fatalistic gloom. Not quite the hospital I'd choose if I were ill, Banks thought, fiddling with the Walkman's off-switch in his overcoat pocket.

The mortuary was in the basement, which, like the police station's cell area, was the most modern part of the building. The autopsy room had white-tiled walls and a central metal table with guttering around its edges to channel off the blood. A long lab bench, complete with Bunsen burners and microscopes, stretched along one wall, with shelving above it for jars of organs, tissue samples and prepared chemical solutions.

Fortunately, the table was empty when Banks entered. A lab assistant was in the process of scrubbing it down, while Glendenning stood at the bench, a cigarette dangling from his mouth. Everyone smoked in the mortuary;

they did it to keep the stench of death at bay.

The lab assistant dropped a surgical instrument into a metal kidney bowl. Banks winced at the sound.

"Let's go into the office," Glendenning said. "I can see you're a bit pink around the gills."

Glendinning's office was small and cluttered, hardly befitting a man of his stature and status, Banks thought. But this wasn't America; health care was hardly big business, despite private insurance plans. Glendenning took his white lab coat off, smoothed his shirt and sat down. Banks shifted some old medical journals from the only remaining chair and placed himself opposite the doctor.

"Coffee?"

Banks nodded. "Yes, please."

Glendenning picked up his phone and pressed a button. "Molly, dear, do you think you could scrape up two cups of coffee?" He covered the mouthpiece and asked Banks how he liked his. "One black no sugar, and the usual for me. Yes, three sugars, that's right. What diet? And don't bring that vile muck they drink at reception. What? Yes. I know you'd run out yesterday, but that's no excuse. I haven't paid my coffee money for three weeks? What is this, woman, the bloody Inquisition?" He hung up roughly, ran a hand through his white hair and sighed. "Good help is hard to find these days. Now, Mr Banks, let's see what we have here." He riffled through the stack of papers on his desk.

He probably knew it all off by heart, Banks thought, but needed the security of his files and sheets of paper in front of him, just as Richmond always liked to read from his notebook what he knew perfectly well in the first place.

"Seth Cotton, aye, poor chappie." Glendenning took a pair of half-moon reading glasses from his top pocket and held the report at arm's length as he peered down his nose at it. Having done with that, he put it aside, took off his glasses and sat back in his chair with his large but delicate hands folded on his lap. The coffee arrived, and Molly, giving her boss a disapproving glance on the way, departed.

"Last meal about three hours before death," Glendenning said. "And a good one, too, if I may say so. Roast beef, Yorkshire pudding. What better meal could a condemned man wish for?"

"Haggis?"

Glendenning wagged his finger. "Dinna extract the urine, Mr Banks."

Banks sipped some coffee. It was piping hot and tasted good. Clearly it wasn't the "vile muck" from reception.

"No evidence of poisoning, or indeed of any other wounds bar the external. Mr Cotton was in perfectly good health until the blood drained out of his body."

"Was that the cause of death?"

"Aye. Loss of about five pints of blood usually does cause death."

"What about the blow to the head? Was it delivered before or after the cuts to the ankles?"

Glendenning scratched his head. "That I can't tell you. The vital reaction was quite consistent with a wound caused before death. As you saw for yourself, there was plenty of blood. And the leucocyte count was high—that's white blood cells to you, the body's little repairmen. Had the blow to the head occurred some time after death, then of course there would have been clear evidence to that effect, but the two wounds happened so closely together that it's impossible to say which came first. Cotton was certainly alive when he hit his head—or when someone hit it for him. But how long he survived after the blow, I can't tell. Of course, the head wound may have caused loss of consciousness, and it's very difficult to slash your ankles when you're unconscious, as I'm sure you're aware."

"Could he have hit his head while bending down to make the cuts?"

Glendenning pursed his lips. "I wouldn't say so, no. You saw the blood on the bench. None of it had trickled onto the floor. I'd say by the angle of the wound and the sharp edges of the vice that his head was resting exactly where it landed after the blow."

"Could someone have come up behind him and pushed his head down onto the vice?"

"Now you're asking me to speculate, Mr Banks. All I can tell you is that I found no signs of scratching or bruising at the back of the neck or the head."

"Does that mean no?"

"Not necessarily. If you come up behind someone and give his head a quick push before he has time to react, then I doubt it would show."

"So that means it must have been someone he knew. He'd have noticed anyone else creeping up on him. Whoever did it must have been in the workshop already, someone he didn't mind having around while he carried on working."

"Theories, theories," Glendenning said. "I don't know why you're not satisfied with suicide. There's absolutely no evidence to the contrary."

"No medical evidence, perhaps."

"I'm sorry," said Glendenning. "I'd like to be able to help you more, but those are the facts. While the blow to the head may well have caused complications had Mr Cotton lived, it was in no way responsible for his death."

"Complications? What complications?"

Glendenning frowned and reached for another cigarette from the box on his desk. It looked antique, and Banks noticed some words engraved in ornate italics on the top: "To Dr C. W. S. Glendenning, on Successful Completion of . . ." He couldn't read the rest. He assumed it was some kind of graduation present.

"All kinds," Glendenning answered. "We don't know a great deal about the human brain, Mr Banks. A lot more than we used to, of course, but still not enough. Certain head wounds can result in effects far beyond the power of the blow and the extent of the apparent damage. Bone chips can lodge in the tissue, and even bruising can cause problems."

"What problems?"

"Almost anything. Memory loss—temporary or permanent—hearing and vision problems, vertigo, personality change, temporary lapses of consciousness. Need I go on?"

Banks shook his head.

"But in the case of Mr Cotton, of course, that's something we'll never know."

"No." Banks got to his feet. "Anyway, thank you very much, doctor."

Glendenning inclined his head regally.

On the way back to the station, Banks hardly heard Muddy Waters. According to Glendenning, Cotton could have been murdered, and that was enough for Banks. Of course, the doctor wouldn't commit himself—he never did—but even an admission of the possibility was a long way for him to go. If Burgess was right, there was a good chance Boyd had done it, and that left Banks with Seth's blood on his hands.

As if that weren't enough, something else nagged at him: one of those frustrating little feelings you can't quite define, like having a name at the tip of your tongue, or an itch you can't scratch. He didn't want to be premature, but it felt like the familiar glimmer of an idea. Disparate facts were coming together, and with a lot of hard thinking, a bit of help from the subconscious and a touch of luck, they might actually lead to the answer. He was still a long way from that as yet, and when Muddy Waters started singing "Still a Fool," Banks believed him.

It was after eleven o'clock, according to the church clock, and Burgess would be out questioning Osmond and the students. In his office, Banks called the forensic lab and asked for Vic Manson. He had to wait a few minutes, but finally Vic came on the line.

"The prints?" Banks asked.

"Yes. Four sets. At least four identifiable sets. One belongs to the deceased, of course, another to that Boyd character—the same as the ones we found on the knife—and two more."

"They'll probably be Mara's and one of the others'," Banks said. "Look, thanks a lot, Vic. I'll try and arrange to get the others fingerprinted for comparison. Is Geoff Tingley around?"

"Yep. Just a sec, I'll get him for you."

Banks could hear distant voices at the end of the line, then someone picked up the receiver and spoke. "Tingley here. Is it about those letters?"

"Yes."

"Well, I'm almost positive they weren't typed by the same person. You can make a few allowances for changes in pressure, but these were so wildly different I'd say that's almost conclusive. I could do with a few more samples of at least one of the writers, though. It'll give me more variables and a broader scope for comparison."

"I'll see what I can do," Banks said. There were probably other examples of Seth's typing in the filing cabinet. "Would it do any good if we got a suspect to type us a sample?" he asked.

"Hmmm. It might do. Problem is if he knew what we were after it wouldn't be too difficult to fake it. I'd say this chap's a plodder, though. You can tell it's been pecked out by the overall high pressure, each letter very deliberately sought and pounced on, so to speak. Hunt-and-peck, as I believe they call the technique. The other chap was a better typist, still two fingers, I'd say, but fairly quick and accurate. Probably had a lot more practice. And there's another thing, too. Did you notice the writing styles of the letters were—"

"Yes," Banks said. "We spotted that. Good of you to point it out, though."

Tingley sounded disappointed. "Oh, it's nothing."

"Thanks very much. I'll be in touch about the samples and testing. Could you put Vic on again? I've just remembered something."

"Will do."

"Are you still there?" Manson asked a few seconds later.

"Yes. Look, Vic, there's a couple more points. The typewriter for a start."

"Nothing clear on that, just a lot of blurs."

"Was it wiped?"

"Could have been."

"There was a cloth on that table, wasn't there? One of those yellow dusters."

"Yes, there was," said Manson. "Do you want me to check for fibres?"

"If you would. And the paper?"

"Same, nothing readable."

"What about that pen, or whatever it was we found on the floor. Have you had time to get around to that yet?"

"Yes. It's just an ordinary ball-point, a Bic. No prints of course, just a sweaty blur."

"Hmmm."

The pen had been found in the puddle of blood, just below Seth's dangling right arm. If he was right-handed, as Banks thought he was, he could have used the pen to write a note before he died. It could have just fallen there earlier, of course, but Seth had been very tidy, especially in his final moments. Perhaps he had written his own note, and whoever killed him took it and replaced it with the second version. Why? Because Seth hadn't murdered Gill and had said so clearly in his note? That meant he had committed suicide for some other reason entirely. Had he even named the killer, or was it an identity he had died trying to protect?

Too many questions, again. Maybe Burgess and Glendenning were right and he was a fool not to accept the easy solutions. After all, he had a choice: either Seth

Cotton was guilty as the note indicated and had really killed himself, or Paul Boyd, fearing discovery, had killed him and faked the note. Banks leaned closer towards the second of these, but for some reason he still couldn't convince himself that Boyd had done it—and not only because he took the responsibility for letting the kid out of jail. Boyd certainly had a record, and he had taken off when the knife was discovered. He could be a lot tougher and more clever than anyone realized. If he was faking his claustrophobia, for example, so that even Burgess was more inclined to believe him because of his fear of incarceration, then anything was possible. But so far they had nothing but circumstantial evidence, and Banks still felt that the picture was incomplete. He lit a cigarette and walked over to look down on the market square. It brought no inspiration today.

Finally, he decided it was time to tidy his desk before lunch. Almost every available square inch was littered with little yellow Post-it notes, most of which he had acted on ages ago. He screwed them all up and dropped them in the waste basket. Next came the files, statements and records he'd read to refresh his memory of the people involved. Most information was stored in the records department, but Banks had developed the habit of keeping brief files on all the cases he had a hand in. At the top was his file on Elizabeth Dale. Picking it up again, he remembered that he had just pulled it out of the cabinet, after some difficulty in locating it, when Sergeant Rowe had called with the news of Seth Cotton's death.

He opened the folder and brought back to mind the facts of the case—not even a case, really, just a minor incident that had occurred some eighteen months ago.

Elizabeth Dale had checked herself into a psychiatric hospital on the outskirts of Huddersfield, complaining of depression, apathy and general inability to cope with the outside world. After a couple of days' observation and treatment, she had decided she didn't like the service and ran off to Maggie's Farm, where she knew that Seth

Cotton, an old friend from Hebden Bridge, was living. The hospital authorities informed Eastvale that she had spoken about her friend with the house near Relton, and they asked the local social services to please check up and see if she was there.

She was. Dennis Osmond had been sent to the farm to try to convince her to return to the hospital for her own good, but Ms Dale remained adamant: she was staying at the farm. Osmond also had the nerve to agree that the place would probably do her good. In anger and desperation, the hospital sent out two men of its own, who persuaded Elizabeth to return with them. They had browbeaten her and threatened her with committal, or so Seth Cotton and Osmond had complained at the time.

Because Elizabeth Dale also had a history of drug addiction, the police were called out when the hospital employees said they suspected the people at the farm were using drugs. Banks had gone out there with Sergeant Hatchley and a uniformed constable, but they had found nothing. Ms Dale went back to the hospital, and as far as Banks knew, everything returned to normal.

In the light of recent events, though, it became a more intriguing tale. For one thing, both Elizabeth Dale and Dennis Osmond were connected with PC Gill via the complaints they had made independently. And now it appeared there was yet another link between Osmond and Dale.

Where was Elizabeth Dale now? He would have to go to Huddersfield and find her himself. He'd learned from experience that it was absolutely no use at all dealing with doctors over the phone. But that would have to wait until tomorrow. First, he wanted to talk to Mara again, if she was well enough. Before setting off, he considered phoning Jenny to try to make up the row they'd had on Sunday lunch-time.

Just as he was about to call her, the phone rang.

"Chief Inspector Banks?"

"Speaking."

"My name is Lawrence Courtney, of Courtney, Courtney and Courtney, Solicitors."

"Yes, I've heard of the firm. What can I do for you?"

"It's what I might be able to do for you," Courtney said. "I read in this morning's newspaper that a certain Seth Cotton has died. Is that correct?"

"That's right, yes."

"Well, it might interest you to know, Chief Inspector, that we are the holders of Mr Cotton's will."

"Will?"

"Yes, will." He sounded faintly irritated. "Are you interested?"

"Indeed I am."

"Would it be convenient for you to call by our office after lunch?"

"Yes, certainly. But look, can't you tell me—"

"Good. I'll see you then. About two-thirty, shall we say? Goodbye, Chief Inspector."

Banks slammed the phone down. Bloody pompous solicitor. He cursed and reached for a cigarette. But a will? That was unexpected. Banks wouldn't have thought such a nonconformist as Seth would have bothered making a will. Still, he did own property, and a business. But how could he have had any idea that he was going to die in the near future?

Banks jotted down the solicitor's name and the time of the meeting and stuck the note to his desk. Then he took a deep breath, phoned Jenny at her university office in York, and plunged right in. "I'm sorry about yesterday. I know what it must have sounded like, but I couldn't think of a better way of telling you."

"I over-reacted." Jenny said. "I feel like an idiot. I suppose you were only doing your job."

"I wasn't going to tell you, not until I realized that being around Osmond really might be dangerous."

"And I shouldn't have mistaken your warning for interference. It's just that I get so bloody frustrated. Damn men! Why do I never seem able to choose the right one?"

"Does it matter to you, what he did?"

"Of course it matters."

"Are you going to go on seeing him?"

"I don't know." She affected a bored tone. "I was getting rather tired of him, anyway. Have there been any developments?"

"What in? The break-in or the Gill murder?"

"Well, both, seeing as you ask. What's wrong? You sound a bit tense."

"Oh, nothing. It's been a busy morning, that's all. And I was nervous about calling you. Have you read about Seth Cotton?"

"No. I didn't have time to look at the paper this morning. Why, what's happened?"

Banks told her.

"Oh God. Poor Mara. Do you think there's anything I can do?"

"I don't know. I've no idea what state she's in. I'm calling on her later this afternoon. I'll mention your name if you like."

"Please do. Tell her how sorry I am. And if she needs to talk . . . What do you think happened, or can't you say?"

"I wish I could." Banks summed up his thoughts for her.

"And I suppose you're feeling responsible? Is that why you don't really want to consider that Boyd did it?"

"You're right about the guilt. Burgess would never have let him go if I hadn't pressed him."

"Burgess hardly seems like the kind of man to bow to pressure. I can't see him consenting to do anything he didn't want to."

"Perhaps you're right. Still . . . it's not just that. At least, I don't think so. There's something much more complex behind all this. And don't accuse me of over-complicating matters—I've had enough of that already."

"Oh, we are touchy today, aren't we? I had no such thing in mind."

"Sorry. I suppose it's getting to me. About the break-in. I've got something in the works and we'll probably know by tonight, tomorrow morning at the latest."

"What's it all about?"

"I'd rather not say yet. But don't worry, I don't think Osmond's in any kind of danger."

"Are you sure?"

"Absolutely."

"If you're right?"

"Am I ever wrong? Look, before you choke, I've got to go now. I'll be in touch later."

Though where he had to go he wasn't quite certain. There was the solicitor, but that wasn't until two-thirty. Feeling vaguely depressed, he lit another cigarette and went over to the window. The Queen's Arms, that was it. A pie and a pint would soon cheer him up. And Burgess had made a tentative arrangement to meet there around one-thirty and compare notes.

II

Banks found the offices of Courtney, Courtney and Courtney on Market Street, quite close to the police station. Too close, in fact, to make it worthwhile turning on the Walkman for the journey.

The firm of solicitors was situated in what had once been a tea-shop, and the new name curved in a semicircle of gold lettering on the plate-glass window. Banks asked the young receptionist for Mr Lawrence Courtney, and after a brief exchange on the intercom, was shown through to a large office stacked with legal papers.

Lawrence Courtney himself, wedged behind a large executive desk, was not the prim figure Banks had expected from their phone conversation—three-piece suit, gold watch chain, pince-nez, nose raised as if perpetually exposed to a bad smell—instead he was a relaxed, plump man of about fifty with over-long fair hair, a broad, ruddy face and a fairly pleasant expression. His jacket hung behind the door. He wore a white shirt, a red and green striped tie and plain black braces. Banks noticed that the top button of the shirt was undone and the tie had been loosened, just like his own.

"Seth Cotton's will," Banks said, sitting down after a brisk damp handshake.

"Yes. I thought you'd be interested," said Courtney. A faint smile tugged at the corners of his pink, rubbery lips.

"When did he make it?"

"Let me see. . . . About a year ago, I think." Courtney found the document and read off the date.

"Why did he come to you? I'm not sure how well you knew him, but he didn't seem to me the kind of person to deal with a solicitor."

"We handled the house purchase," Courtney said, "and when the conveyance was completed we suggested a will. We often do. It's not so much a matter of touting for business as making things easier. So many people die intestate, and you've no idea what complications that leads to if there is no immediate family. The house itself, for example. As far as I know, Mr Cotton wasn't married, even under common law."

"What was his reaction to your suggestion?"

"He said he'd think about it."

"And he thought about it for two years?"

"It would appear so, yes. If you don't mind my asking, Chief Inspector, why all this interest in his reason for making a will? People do, you know."

"It's the timing, that's all. I was just wondering why then rather than any other time."

"Hmmm. I imagine that's the kind of thing you people have to think about. Are you interested in the contents at all?"

"Of course."

Courtney unfolded the paper fully, peered at it, then put it aside again and hooked his thumbs in his braces. "Not much to it, really," he said. "He left the house and what little money he had—somewhere in the region of two thousand pounds, I believe, though you'll have to check with the bank—to one Mara Delacey."

"Mara? And that's it?"

"Not quite. Oddly enough he added a codicil just a few months ago. Shortly before Christmas, in fact. It doesn't affect the original bequest, but merely specifies that all materials, monies and goodwill relating to his carpentry business be left to Paul Boyd, in the hope that he uses them wisely."

"Bloody hell!"

"Is something wrong?"

"It's nothing. Sorry. Mind if I smoke?"

"If you must." Courtney took a clean ashtray from his drawer and pushed it disapprovingly towards Banks. Undeterred, Banks lit up.

"The way I see things, then," Banks said, "is that he left the house and the money to Mara after he'd only known her for a year or so, and the carpentry business to Paul after the kid had only been at the farm for a couple of months."

"If you say so, Chief Inspector. It would indicate that Mr Cotton was quick to trust people."

"It would indeed. Or that there was nobody else he could even consider. I doubt that he'd have wanted his goods and chattels to go to the state. But who knows where Boyd might have got to by the time Cotton died of natural causes? Or Mara. Could he have had some idea that he was in danger?"

"I'm afraid I can't answer that," Courtney said. "Our business ends with the legal formalities, and Mr Cotton certainly made no mention of an imminent demise. If there's anything else I can help you with, of course, I'd be more than willing."

"Thank you," said Banks. "I think that's all. Will you be informing Mara Delacey?"

"We will take steps to get in touch with beneficiaries in due course, yes."

"Is it all right if I tell her this afternoon?"

"I can't see any objection. And you might ask her—both of them, if possible—to drop by the office. I'll be happy to explain the procedure to them. If you have any trouble with the bank, Chief Inspector, please refer them to me. It's the National Westminster—or NatWest, as I believe they call themselves these days—the branch in the market square. The manager is a most valued client."

"I know the place." Know it, Banks thought, I practically stare at it for hours on end every day.

"Then goodbye, Chief Inspector. It's been a pleasure."

Banks walked out into the street more confused than ever. Before he got back to the station, however, he'd managed to put some check on his wild imaginings. The will probably didn't come into the case at all. Seth Cotton had simply had more foresight than many would have credited him with. What was wrong with that? And it was perfectly natural that, with his parents both dead and no close family, he would leave the house to Mara. And Paul Boyd was, after all, his apprentice. It was a gesture of faith and confidence on Seth's part.

Even if Mara and Paul had known what they had coming to them, neither, Banks was positive, would have murdered Seth to get it. Life for Mara was clearly better with Seth than without him, and whatever ugliness might be lurking in Boyd's character, he was neither stupid nor petty enough to kill for a set of carpenter's tools. So forget the will, Banks told himself. Nice gesture though it was, it is irrelevant. Except, perhaps, for the date. Why wait till two years after Courtney had suggested it before actually getting the business done? Procrastination?

It also raised a more serious question: had Seth felt that his life was in danger a year ago? If so, why had it taken so long for the danger to manifest itself? And had that fear somehow also renewed itself around Christmas time?

Before returning to his office, he nipped into the National Westminster and had no problem in getting details of Seth's financial affairs, such as they were: he had a savings account at £2343.64, and a current account, which stood at £421.33.

It was after three-thirty when he got back to the station, and there was a message from Vic Manson to the effect that, yes, fibres matching those from the duster had been found on the typewriter keys. But, Manson had added with typical forensic caution, there was no way of proving whether the machine had been wiped before or after the message had been typed. The pressure of fingers on the keys often blurs prints.

Banks's brief chat with Burgess over lunch had revealed nothing new, either. Dirty Dick had seen Osmond and got nowhere with him. Early in the afternoon he was off to see Tim and Abha, and he was quite happy to leave Mara Delacey to Banks. As far as Burgess was concerned, it was all over bar the shouting, but he wanted more evidence to implicate Boyd or Cotton with extremist politics. Most of the time he'd had his eye on Glenys, and he'd kept reminding Banks that it was her night off that night. Cyril, fortunately, had been nowhere in sight.

Banks left a message for Burgess at the front desk summarizing what Lawrence Courtney had said about Seth's will. Then he called Sergeant Hatchley, as Richmond was busy on another matter, to accompany him and to bring along the fingerprinting kit. He slipped the Muddy Waters cassette from his Walkman and hurried out to the car with it, a huffing and puffing Hatchley in tow. It was time to see if Mara Delacey was ready to talk.

"What do you think of Superintendent Burgess?" Banks asked Hatchley on the way. They hadn't really had a chance to talk much over the past few days.

"Off the record?"

"Yes."

"Well . . ." Hatchley rubbed his face with a hamlike hand. "He seemed all right at first. Bit of zip about him. You know, get up and go. But I'd have thought a whiz-kid like him would have got a bit further by now."

"None of us have got any further," Banks said. "What do you mean? The man's only flesh and blood after all."

"I suppose that's it. He dazzles you a bit at first, then . . ."

"Don't underestimate him," Banks said. "He's out of his element up here. He's getting frustrated because we don't have raving anarchists crawling out of every nook and cranny in the town."

"Aye," said Hatchley. "And you thought I was right wing."

"You are."

Hatchley grunted.

"When we get to the farm, I want you to have a look in Seth's filing cabinet in the workshop," Banks went on, pulling onto the Roman road, "and see if you can find more samples of his typing. And I'd like you to fingerprint everyone. Ask for their consent, and tell them we can get a magistrate's order if they refuse. Also make sure you tell them that the prints will be destroyed if no charges are brought." Banks paused and scratched the edge of his scar. "I'd like to have them all type a few lines on Seth's typewriter, too, but we'll have to wait till it comes back from forensic. All clear?"

"Fine," Hatchley said.

Zoe answered the door, looking tired and drawn.

"Mara's not here," she said in response to Banks's question, opening the door only an inch or two.

"I thought she was under sedation."

"That was last night. She had a good long sleep. She said she felt like going to the shop to work on some pots, and the doctor agreed it might be good therapy. Elspeth's there in case . . . just in case."

"I'll go down to the village, then," Banks said to Hatchley. "You'll have to manage up here. Will you let the sergeant in, Zoe?"

Zoe sighed and opened the door.

"Are you coming back up?" Hatchley asked.

Banks looked at his watch. "Why not meet in the Black Sheep?"

Hatchley smiled at the prospect of a pint of Black Sheep bitter, then his face fell. "How do I get there?"

"Walk."

"Walk?"

"Yes. It's just a mile down the track. Do you good. Give you a thirst."

Hatchley wasn't convinced—he had never had any problems working up a thirst without exercise before— but Banks left him to his fate and drove down to Relton.

Mara was in the back bent over her wheel, gently turning the lip of a vase. Elspeth led him through, muttered, "A policeman to see you," with barely controlled distaste, then went back into the shop itself.

Mara glanced up. "Let me finish," she said. "If I stop now, I'll ruin it." Banks leaned against the doorway and kept quiet. The room smelled of wet clay. It was also hot. The kiln in the back generated a lot of heat. Mara's long brown hair was tied back, accentuating the sharpness of her nose and chin as she concentrated. Her white smock was stained with splashed clay.

Finally, she drenched the wheel-head with water, sliced off the vase with a length of cheese-wire, then slid it carefully onto her hand before transferring it to a board.

"What now?" Banks asked.

"It has to dry." She put it away in a large cupboard at the back of the room. "Then it goes in the kiln."

"I thought the kiln dried it."

"No. That bakes it. First it has to be dried to the consistency of old cheddar."

"These are good," Banks said, pointing to some finished mugs glazed in shades of orange and brown.

"Thanks." Mara's eyes were puffy and slightly unfocused, her movements slow and zombie-like. Even her voice, Banks noticed, was flatter than usual, drained of emotion and vitality.

"I have to ask you some questions," he said.

"I suppose you do."

"Do you mind?"

Mara shook her head. "Let's get it over with."

She perched at the edge of her stool and Banks sat on a packing crate just inside the doorway. He could hear Elspeth humming as she busied herself checking on stock in the shop.

"Did you notice anyone gone for an unusually long time during the meeting yesterday afternoon?" Banks asked.

"Was it only yesterday? Lord, it seems like months. No, I didn't notice. People came and went, but I don't think anyone was gone for long. I'm not sure I would have noticed, though."

"Did Seth ever say anything to you before about suicide? Did he ever mention the subject?"

Mara's lips tightened and the blood seemed to drain from them. "No. Never."

"He'd tried once before, you know."

Mara raised her thin eyebrows. "It seems you knew him better than I did."

"Nobody knew him, as far as I can tell. There was a will, Mara."

"I know."

"Do you remember when he made it?"

"Yes. He joked about it. Said it made him feel like an old man."

"Is that all?"

"That's all I remember."

"Did he say why he was making it at that time?"

"No. He just told me that the solicitor who handled

the house, Courtney, said he should, and he'd been thinking about it for a long time."

"Do you know what was in the will?"

"Yes. He said he was leaving me the house. Does that make me a suspect?"

"Did you know about the codicil?"

"Codicil? No."

"He left his tools and things to Paul."

"Well, he would, wouldn't he. Paul was keen, and I've got no use for them."

"Did Paul know?"

"I've no idea."

"This would be around last Christmas."

"Maybe it was his idea of a present."

"But what made him think he was going to die? Seth was what age—forty? By all rights he could expect to live to seventy or so. Was he worried about anything?"

"Seth always seemed . . . well, not worried, but pre-occupied. He'd got even more morbid of late. It was just his way."

"But there was nothing in particular?"

Mara shook her head. "I don't believe he killed himself, Mr Banks. He had lots to live for. He wouldn't just leave us like that. Everyone depended on Seth. We looked up to him. And he cared about me, about us. I think somebody must have killed him."

"Who?"

"I don't know."

Banks shifted position on the packing crate. Its surface was hard and he felt a nail dig into the back of his right thigh. "Do you remember Elizabeth Dale?"

"Liz. Yes, of course. Funny, I was just thinking about her last night."

"What about her?"

"Oh, nothing really. How jealous I was, I suppose, when she came to the farm that time. I'd only known Seth six months then. We were happy but, I don't know, I guess I was insecure. Am."

"Why did you feel jealous?"

"Maybe that's not the right word. I just felt cut out, that's all. Seth and Liz had known each other for a long time, and I didn't share their memories. They used to sit up late talking after I went to bed."

"Did you hear what they were talking about?"

"No. It was muffled. Do smoke if you want."

"Thanks." She must have noticed him fidgeting and looking around for an ashtray. He took out his pack and offered one to Mara.

"I think I will," she said. "I can't be bothered to roll my own today."

"What did you think about Liz Dale?"

Mara lit the cigarette and inhaled deeply. "I didn't like her, really. I don't know why, just a feeling. She was messed up, of course, but even so, she seemed like someone who used people, leaned on them too much, maybe a manipulator." She shrugged wearily and blew smoke out through her nose. "She was Seth's friend, though. I wasn't going to say anything."

"So you put up with her?"

"It was easy enough. She was only with us three days before those SS men from the hospital took her back."

"Dennis Osmond came up first, didn't he?"

"Yes. But he was too soft, they said. He didn't see why she shouldn't stay where she was, especially as she hadn't been committed or anything, just checked herself in. He argued with the hospital people, but it was no good."

"How did Osmond and Liz get along?"

"I don't know really. I mean, he stuck up for her, that's all."

"There wasn't anything between them?"

"What do you mean? Sexual?"

"Anything."

"I doubt it. They only met twice, and I wouldn't say she was his type."

"And that was the first time Seth met Osmond?"

"As far as I know."

"Did you get the impression that Osmond had known Liz before?"

"No, I didn't. But impressions can be wrong. What are you getting at?"

"I'm not sure myself. Just following my nose."

"Mr Banks," Mara whispered suddenly, "do you think Dennis Osmond killed Seth? Is that it? I know Seth couldn't have done it himself, and I . . . I can't seem to think straight. . . ."

"Steady on." Banks caught her in his arms as she slid forward from the stool. Her hair smelled of apples. He sat her on a stiff-backed chair in the corner, and her eyes filled with tears. "All right?"

"Yes. I'm sorry. That sedative takes most of the feeling out of me, but . . ."

"It's still there?"

"Yes. Just below the surface."

"We can continue this later if you like. I'll drive you home." He thought how pleased Hatchley would be to see the Cortina turning up again.

Mara shook her head. "No, it's all right. I can handle it. I'm just confused. Maybe some water."

Banks brought her a glass from the tap at the stained porcelain sink in the corner.

"So are we," he said. "Confused. It looked like a suicide in some ways, but there were contradictions."

"He wouldn't kill himself, I'm sure of it. Paul was back again. Seth was happy. He had the farm, friends, the children. . . ."

Banks didn't know what to say to make her feel better.

"When he tried before," she said, "was it because of Alison?"

"Yes."

"I can understand that. It makes sense. But not now. Someone must have killed him." Mara sipped at her water. "Anyone could have come in through the side gate and sneaked up on him."

"It didn't happen like that, Mara. Take my word for it, he had to know the person. It was someone he felt comfortable with. Have you seen or heard anything from Liz Dale since she left?"

"I haven't, no. Seth went to visit her in the hospital a couple of times, but then he lost touch."

"Any letters?"

"Not that he told me about."

"Christmas card?"

"No."

"Do you know where she is now?"

"No. Is it important?"

"It could be. Do you know anything about her background?"

Mara frowned and rubbed her temple. "As far as I know she's from down south somewhere. She used to be a nurse until . . . Well, she fell in with a bad crowd, got involved with drugs and lost her job. Since then she just sort of drifted."

"And ended up in Hebden Bridge?"

"Yes."

"Did you see her do any drugs at the farm?"

"No. And I'm not just saying that. She was off heroin. That was part of the problem, why she was unable to cope."

"Was Seth ever an addict?"

"I don't think so. I think he'd have told me about that. We talked about drugs, how we felt about them and how they weren't really important, so I think he'd have told me."

"And you've no idea where Liz is now?"

"None at all."

"What about Alison?"

"What about her? She's dead."

A hint of bitterness had crept into her tone, and Banks wondered why. Jealousy? It could happen. Plenty of people were jealous of previous lovers, even dead ones. Or was she angry at Seth for not making her fully a part of his life, for not sharing all his feelings? She unfastened her hair and shook her head, allowing the chestnut tresses to cascade over her shoulders.

"Can I have another cigarette?"

"Of course." Banks gave her one. "Surely Seth must have told you something," he said. "You don't live with someone for two years and find out nothing about their past."

"Don't you? And how would you know?"

Banks didn't know. When he had met Sandra, they had been young and had little past to talk about, none of it very interesting. "It just doesn't make sense," he said.

The shop bell clanged and broke the silence. They heard Elspeth welcoming a customer, an American by the sound of his drawl.

"What are you going to do now?" Banks asked.

Mara rubbed her eyes. "I don't know. I'm too tired to throw another pot. I think I'll just go home and go to bed early."

"Do you want a ride?"

"No. Really. A bit of fresh air and exercise will do me good."

Banks smiled. "I wish my sergeant felt the same way."

"What?"

Banks explained and Mara managed a weak smile.

They walked out together, Banks collecting a sour look from Elspeth on the way. Outside the Black Sheep, Mara turned away.

"I am sorry, you know, about your loss," Banks said awkwardly to her back.

Mara turned around and stared at him for a long time. He couldn't make out what she was thinking or feeling.

"I do believe you are," she said finally.

"And Jenny sends her condolences. She says to give her a call if you ever need anything . . . a friend."

Mara said nothing.

"She didn't betray your confidence, you know. She was worried about you. And you went to her because you were worried about Paul, didn't you?"

Mara nodded slowly.

"Well, give her a call. All right?"

"All right." And tall though she was, Mara seemed a slight figure walking up the lane in the dark toward the Roman road. Banks stood and watched till she was out of sight.

Hatchley was already in the Black Sheep—halfway through his second pint, judging by the empty glass next to the half-full one in front of him. Banks went to the bar first, bought two more and sat down. As far as he was concerned, Hatchley could drink as much as he wanted. He was a lousy driver even when sober, and Banks had no intention of letting him anywhere near the Cortina's driving seat.

"Anything?" the sergeant asked.

"No, not really. You?"

"That big bloke with the shaggy beard put up a bit of an argument at first, but the little lass with the red hair told him it was best to co-operate."

"Damn," Banks said. "I knew there was something I'd forgotten. Mara's prints. Never mind, I'll get them later."

"Anyway," Hatchley went on, "most of the letters in the cabinet were carbons, but I managed to rescue a couple of drafts from the waste bin."

"Good."

"You don't sound so pleased," Hatchley complained.

"What? Oh, sorry. Thinking of something else. Let's drink up and get your findings sent over to the lab."

Hatchley drained his third pint with astonishing speed and looked at his watch. "It's going on for six-thirty," he said. "No point rushing now; they'll all have buggered off home for the night." He glanced over at the bar. "Might as well have another."

Banks smiled. "Unassailable logic, Sergeant. All right. Better make it a quick one, though. And it's your round."

III

At home, Banks managed to warm up a frozen dinner—peas, mashed potatoes and veal cutlet—without ruining it. After washing the dishes—or, rather, rinsing his knife and fork and coffee cup and throwing the metal tray into the rubbish bin, he called Sandra.

"So when do I get my wife back?" he asked.

"Wednesday morning. Early train," Sandra said. "We should be home around lunch-time. Dad's a lot better now and Mum's coping better than I'd imagined."

"Good. I'll try and be in," Banks said. "It depends."

"How are things going?"

"They're getting more complicated."

"You sound grouchy, too. It's a good sign. The more complicated things seem and the more bad-tempered you get, the closer the end is."

"Is that right?"

"Of course it is. I haven't lived with you this long without learning to recognize the signs."

"Sometimes I wonder what people do learn about one another."

"What's this? Philosophy?"

"No. Just frustration. Brian and Tracy well?"

"Fine. Just restless. Brian especially. You know Tracy, she's happy enough with her head buried in a history book. But with him it's all sports and pop music now. American football is the latest craze, apparently."

"Good God."

Brian had changed a lot over the past year. He even seemed to have lost interest in the electric train that Banks had set up in the spare room. Banks played with it himself more than Brian did, but then, he had to admit, he always had done.

To keep the emptiness after the conversation at bay, he poured out a glass of Bell's and listened to Leroy Carr and Scrapper Blackwell while he tried to let the information that filled his mind drift and form itself into new patterns. Bizarre as it all seemed, a number of things began to come together. The problem was that one theory seemed to cancel out the other.

The doorbell woke him from a light nap just before ten o'clock. The tape had long since ended and the ice had melted in his second Scotch.

"Sorry I'm so late, sir," Richmond said, "but I've just finished."

"Come in." Banks rubbed his eyes. "Sit down. A drink?"

"If you don't mind, sir. Though I suppose I am still on duty. Technically."

"Scotch do? Or there's beer in the fridge."

"Scotch will do fine, sir. No ice, if you don't mind."

Banks grinned. "I'm getting as bad as the Americans, aren't I, putting ice in good Scotch. Soon I'll be complaining my beer is too warm."

Richmond fitted his long athletic body into an armchair and stroked his moustache.

"By the way you're playing with that bit of face fungus there," Banks said, "I gather you've succeeded."

"What? Oh, yes, sir. Didn't know I was so obvious."

"Most of us are, it seems. You'd not make a good poker player—and you'd better watch it in interrogations. Come on then, what did you find?"

"Well," Richmond began, consulting his notebook, "I did exactly as you said, sir. Hung around discreetly near Tim and Abha's place. They stayed in all afternoon."

"Then what?"

"They went out about eight, to the pub I'd guess. And about half an hour later that blue Escort pulled up and two men got out and disappeared into the building. They looked like the ones you described. They must have been waiting and watching somewhere nearby, because they seemed to know when to come, allowing a bit of a safety margin in case Tim and Abha had just gone to the shop or something."

"You didn't try to stop them from getting in, did you?"

Richmond seemed shocked. "I did exactly as you instructed me, sir, though it felt a bit odd to sit there and watch a crime taking place. The front door is usually left on the latch, so they just walked in. The individual flats are kept locked, though, so they must have broken in. Anyway, they came out about fifteen minutes later carrying what looked like a number of buff folders."

"And then what?"

"I followed them at a good distance, and they pulled into the car-park of the Castle Hotel and went inside. I didn't follow, sir—they might have noticed me. And they didn't come out. After they'd been gone about ten minutes, I went in and asked the desk clerk about them and got him to show me the register. They'd booked in as James Smith and Thomas Brown."

"How imaginative. Sorry, carry on."

"Well, I rather thought that myself, sir, so I went back to the office and checked on the number of the car. It was rented by a firm in York to a Mr Cranby, Mr Keith J. Cranby, if that means anything to you. He had to show his licence, of course, so that's likely to be his right name."

"Cranby? No, it doesn't ring any bells. What happened next?"

"Nothing, sir. It was getting late by then so I thought I'd better come and report. By the way, I saw that barmaid, Glenys, going into the hotel while I was waiting outside. Looked a bit sheepish, she did, too."

"Was Cyril anywhere in sight?"

"No. I didn't see him."

"You've done a fine job, Phil," Banks said. "I owe you for this one."

"What's it all about?"

"I'd rather not say yet, in case I'm wrong. But you'll be the second to find out, I promise. Have you eaten at all?"

"I packed some sandwiches." He looked at his watch. "I could do with a pint, though."

"There's still beer in the fridge."

"I don't like bottled beer." Richmond patted his flat stomach. "Too gassy."

"And too cold?"

Richmond nodded.

"Come on, then. We should make it in time for a jar or two before closing. My treat. Queen's Arms do you?"

"Fine, sir."

The pub was busy and noisy with locals and farm lads in from the villages. Banks glanced at the bar staff and saw neither Glenys nor Cyril in evidence. Pushing his way to the bar, he asked one of the usual stand-in bar-maids where the boss was.

"Took the evening off, Mr Banks. Just like that." She snapped her fingers. "Said there'd be three of us so we should be able to cope. Dead cagey, he was too. Still, he's the boss, isn't he? He can do what he likes."

"True enough, Rosie," Banks said. "I'll have two pints of your best bitter, please."

"Right you are, Mr Banks."

They stood at the bar and chatted with the regulars, who knew better than to ask too many questions about their work. Banks was beginning to feel unusually pleased with himself, considering he still hadn't found the answer. Whether it was the chat with Sandra, the nap, Richmond's success or the drink, he didn't know. Perhaps it was a combination of all four. He was close to the end of the case, though, he knew that. If he could solve the problem of two mutually exclusive explanations for Gill's and Seth's deaths, then he would be home and dry. Tomorrow should be an interesting day. First he would track down Liz Dale and discover what she knew; then there was the other business. . . . Yes, tomorrow should be very interesting indeed. And the day after that, Sandra was due home.

"Last orders, please!" Rosie shouted.

"Shall we?" Richmond asked.

"Go on. Why not," said Banks. He felt curiously like celebrating.

SIXTEEN

I

Dirty Dick was conspicuous by his absence the following morning. Banks took the opportunity to make a couple of important phone calls before getting an early start.

Just south of Bradford, it started to rain. Banks turned on the wipers and lit a cigarette from the dashboard lighter. On the car stereo, Walter Davis sang, "You got bad blood, baby, / I believe you need a shot."

It was so easy to get lost in the conurbation of old West Yorkshire woollen towns. Built in valleys on the eastern edges of the Pennines, they seemed to overlap one another, and it was hard to tell exactly where you were. The huge old textile factories, where all the processes of clothes-making had been gathered together under one roof in the last century, looked grim in the failing light. They were five or six storeys high, with flat roofs, rows of windows close together, and tall chimneys you could see for miles.

Cleckheaton, Liversedge, Heckmondwike, Brighouse, Rastrick, Mirfield—the strange names Banks usually associated only with brass bands and rugby teams—flew by on road signs. As he drew nearer to Huddersfield, he slowed and peered out through his rain-spattered windscreen for the turn-off.

Luckily the psychiatric hospital was at the northern end of the town, so he didn't have to cross the center.

When he saw the signpost, he followed directions to the left, down a street between two derelict warehouses.

The greenery of the hospital grounds came as a shock after so many miles of bleak industrial wasteland. There was a high brick wall and a guard at the gate, but beyond that, the drive wound its way by trees and a well-kept lawn to the modern L-shaped hospital complex. Banks parked in the visitors' lot, then presented himself at reception.

"That'll be Dr Preston," said the receptionist, looking up Elizabeth Dale in her roll file. "But the doctor can't divulge any information about his patients, you know."

Banks smiled. "He will see me, won't he?"

"Oh, of course. He's with our bursar right now, but if you'll wait he should be finished in ten minutes or so. You can wait over in the canteen if you like. The tea's not too bad."

Banks thanked her and walked towards the cluster of bright orange plastic tables and chairs.

"Oh, Mr Banks?" she called after him.

He turned.

She put her hands to the sides of her mouth and spoke quietly and slowly, mouthing the words as if for a lip-reader. "You won't wander off, will you?" She flicked her eyes right and left as if to indicate that beyond those points lay monsters.

Banks assured her that he wouldn't, bought a cup of tea and a Penguin biscuit from the pretty teenage girl at the counter and sat down.

There was only one other person in the canteen. A skinny man with a pronounced stoop and hair combed straight back from his creased brow, he was dressed as a vicar. Seeing Banks, he brought his cup over and sat down. He had a long, thin nose and a small mouth. The shape of his head, Banks noticed, was distinctly odd; it was triangular, and the forehead sloped sharply backwards. With his hair brushed straight back, standing at forty-five degrees, he looked as if his entire face had been sculpted by a head-on wind.

"Mind if I join you?" he asked, smiling in a way that screwed up his features grotesquely.

"Not if you don't mind my smoking," Banks replied.

"Go ahead, old chap, doesn't bother me at all." His accent was educated and southern. "Haven't seen you here before?"

It should have been a comment, but it sounded like a question.

"That's not surprising," Banks said. "I've never been here before. I'm a policeman."

"Oh, jolly good!" the vicar exclaimed. "Which one? Let me guess: Clouseau? Poirot? Holmes?"

Banks laughed. "I'm not as klutzy as Clouseau," he said. "Nor, I'm afraid, am I as brilliant as Poirot and Holmes. My name's Banks. Chief Inspector Banks."

The vicar frowned. "Banks, eh? I haven't heard of him."

"Well, you wouldn't have, would you?" Banks said, puzzled. "It's me. I'm Banks. I'm here to see Dr Preston."

The vicar's expression brightened. "Dr Preston? Oh, I'm sure you'll like him. He's very good."

"Is he helping you?"

"Helping me? Why, no. I help him, of course."

"Of course," Banks said slowly.

A nurse paused by the table and spoke his name. "Dr Preston will see you now," she said.

The vicar stuck out his hand. "Well, good luck, old boy."

Banks shook it and muttered his thanks.

"That man back there," he said to the nurse as she clicked beside him along the corridor, "should he be wandering around freely? What's he in for?"

The nurse laughed. "That's not a patient. That's the Reverend Clayton. He comes to visit two or three times a week. He must have thought *you* were a new patient."

Bloody hell, Banks thought, you could soon go crazy hanging around a place like this.

Dr Preston's office lacked the sharp polished instruments, kidney bowls, hypodermics and mysterious odds and ends that Banks usually found so disconcerting in Glendenning's lair. This room was more like a comfortable study with a pleasant view of the landscaped grounds.

Preston stood up as Banks entered. His handshake was firm and brief. He looked younger than Banks had expected, with a thatch of thick, shiny brown hair, a complexion as smooth as a baby's bottom, and cheeks just as chubby and rosy. His eyes, enlarged behind spectacles, were watchful and serious.

"What can I do for you, er, Chief Inspector?" he asked.

"I'm interested in an ex-patient of yours called Elizabeth Dale. At least, I think she's an ex-patient."

"Oh, yes," Preston said. "Been gone ages now. What exactly is it you wish to know? I'm sure you realize that I'm not at liberty to—"

"Yes, doctor, I understand that. I don't want the details of her illness. As I understand it, she was suffering from depression."

"Well"—the doctor unbent a paper-clip on his blotter—"I suppose in layman's terms . . . But you said that's not what you came about?"

"That's right. I just want to know where she is. Nothing confidential about that, is there?"

"We don't usually give out personal information."

"It's important. A murder inquiry. I could get a court order."

"Oh, I don't think that will be necessary," Preston said quickly. "The problem is, though, I'm afraid we don't know where Miss Dale is."

"No idea?"

"No. You see, we don't keep tabs on ex-patients as a rule."

"When did she leave here?"

Preston searched through his files. "She stayed for two months." He read off the dates.

"Is that usual? Two months?"

"Hard to say. It varies from patient to patient. Miss Dale was ... well, I don't think I'm giving too much away if I tell you she was difficult. She'd hardly been here a couple of days before she ran off."

"Yes, I know." Banks explained his involvement. "As far as I understand, though, she admitted herself in the first place, is that right?"

"Yes."

"Yet you treated her as if she had escaped from a high-security prison."

Preston leaned back in his chair and his jaw muscles twitched. "You have to understand, Chief Inspector, that when anyone arrives here, they are given a whole range of tests, and a complete physical examination. On the basis of these, we make a diagnosis and prescribe treatment. I had examined Miss Dale and decided she required treatment. When she disappeared we were naturally worried that she ... Well, without the proper treatment, who knows what might have become of her? So we took steps to persuade her to come back."

"Doctor knows best, eh?"

Preston glared at him.

"How was she when she'd completed her treatment?" Banks asked.

"Given your hostile attitude, I don't know that I care to answer that."

Banks sighed and reached for a cigarette. "Oh, come on doctor, don't sulk. Was she cured or wasn't she?"

Preston passed an ashtray as Banks lit up. "That'll kill you, you know." He seemed to take great pleasure in the observation.

"Not before I get an answer from you, I hope."

Preston pursed his lips. "I imagine you know about Elizabeth Dale's drug problem?"

"Yes."

"That was part of the cause of her mental illness. When she came to us she said she'd been off heroin for about a month. Naturally, we're not equipped to deal with addicts here, and if Miss Dale had been still using drugs we would have had to send her elsewhere. However, she stayed, on medication I prescribed, and she made some progress. At the end of two months, I felt she was ready to leave."

"What did *she* feel?"

Preston stared out of his window at the landscaped garden. A row of topiary shrubs stood close to the building, cut in the shapes of birds and animals.

"Miss Dale," Preston started slowly, "was afraid of life and afraid of her addiction. The one led to the other, an apparently endless circle."

"What you're saying is that once she'd got used to the idea she'd have been happy to stay here forever. Am I right?"

"Not just here. Any institution, anywhere she didn't have to make her own decisions and face the world."

"And that's the kind of place I'm likely to find her in?"

"I'd say so, yes."

"Can you be any more specific?"

"You might try a DDU."

"DDU?"

"Yes. A Drug-Dependency Unit, for the treatment of addicts. Elizabeth had been in and out of one a couple of times before she came to us."

"So she hadn't been cured?"

"How many are? Oh, some, I agree. But with Elizabeth it was on and off, on and off. The cure worked for a while—Methadone hydrochloride in gradually decreasing doses. It's rather like chewing nicotine gum when you're trying to stop smoking. Helps with some of the severe physical symptoms, but—"

"That's not enough?"

"Not really. Many addicts get hooked again as soon as the opportunity for a fix arises. Unfortunately, given the network of friends they have, that can be very soon."

"So you think this DDU might have Liz as a patient, or might know where she is?"

"It's likely."

"Where is it?" Banks slipped out his notebook.

"The only local one is just outside Halifax, not too far away." Preston continued to give directions. "I hope she's not in any trouble," he said finally.

"I don't think so. Just need her to help us with our inquiry."

Preston adjusted his glasses on the bridge of his nose. "You do have a way with words, you policemen, don't you?"

"I'm glad we've got something in common with doctors." Banks smiled and stood up to leave. "You've been a great help."

"Have I?"

Banks beat a hasty retreat from the hospital back onto the rainswept roads and headed for Halifax. He soon found the DDU, using the Wainhouse Tower as a landmark, as Dr Preston had suggested. Originally built as a factory chimney, the tall, black tower was never used as one and now stands as a folly and a lookout point, its top ornamented in a very unchimneylike pointed Gothic style.

Banks found the DDU up a steep side street. It was set back from the road at the top of a long sloping lawn and looked like a Victorian mansion. It also had an eerie quality to it, Banks felt. He shivered as he made his approach. Not the kind of place I'd want to find myself in after dark, he thought.

There were no walls or men at the gate here. Banks walked straight inside and found himself standing in a spacious common room with a high ceiling. On the walls hung a number of paintings, clearly the work of patients, dominated by an enormous canvas depicting an angel plummeting to earth, wings ablaze and neck contorted so that it looked straight at the viewer, eyes red and wild, raw muscles stretched like knotted ropes. It could have been Satan on his way to hell. Certainly the destination, impressionistically rendered in the lower half of the painting, was a dark and murky place. He shuddered and looked away.

"Can I help you?" A young woman came up to him. It wasn't clear from her appearance whether she was a member of staff or a patient. She was in her early thirties, perhaps, and wore jeans and a dark-brown jacket over a neck-high white blouse. Her long black hair was plaited into wide braids and pinned at the back.

"Yes," Banks said. "I'm looking for Elizabeth Dale. Is she here, or do you know where I can find her?"

"Who are you?"

Banks showed her his identification.

The woman raised her eyebrows. "Police? What do you want?"

"I want to talk to Elizabeth Dale," he repeated. "Is she here or isn't she?"

"What's it about?"

"I'm the one who asks the questions," Banks said, irritated by her brusque, haughty manner. Suddenly, he realized who she must be. "Look, doctor," he went on, "it's nothing to do with drugs. It's about an old friend of hers. I need some information to help solve a murder case, that's all."

"Elizabeth's been here for the past month. She can't be involved."

"I'm not saying she is. Will you just let me talk to her?"

The doctor frowned. Banks could see her brain working fast behind her eyes. "All right," she said finally. "But treat her gently. She's very fragile. And I insist on being present."

"I'd rather talk to her alone." The last thing Banks

wanted was this woman watching over the conversation like a lawyer.

"I'm afraid that's not possible."

"How about if you remained within calling distance? Say, the other end of this room?" The room was certainly large enough to accommodate more than one conversation.

The doctor smiled out of the side of her mouth. "A compromise? All right. Stay here while I fetch Elizabeth. Take a seat."

But Banks felt restless after being in the car. Instead, he walked around the room looking at the paintings, almost all of which illustrated some intense level of terror: mad eyes staring through a letter-box; a naked man being dragged away from a woman, his features creased in a desperate plea; a forest in which every carefully painted leaf looked like a needle of fire. They sent shivers up his spine. Noticing plenty of pedestal ashtrays around, he lit up. It was warm in the room, so he took off his car-coat and laid it on a chair.

About five minutes later, the doctor returned with another woman. "This is Elizabeth Dale," she said, introducing them formally, then walked off to the far end of the room, where she sat facing Banks and pretended to read a magazine. Liz took a chair on his left, angled so they could face one another comfortably. The chairs were well-padded, with strong armrests.

"I saw you looking at the paintings," Elizabeth said. "Quite something, aren't they?" She had a melodic, hypnotic voice. Banks could easily imagine its persuasive powers. He had a feeling, however, that it would probably become tiresome after a while: whining and wheedling rather than beautiful and soft.

Elizabeth Dale smoothed her long powder-blue skirt over her knees. Her slight frame was lost inside a baggy mauve sweater with two broad white hoops around the middle. If she was Seth's contemporary, that made her about forty, but her gaunt, waxy face was lined like that of a much older woman, and her black hair, hacked, rather than cut, short was liberally streaked with grey. It was a face that screamed of suffering; eyes that had looked deep inside and seen the horror there. Yet her voice was beautiful. So gentle, so soothing, like a breeze through woods in spring.

"They're very powerful," Banks said, feeling his words pathetically inadequate in describing the paintings.

"People see those things here," Elizabeth said. "Do you know what this place used to be?"

"No."

"It was a hospital, a fever-hospital, during the typhoid epidemics in the last century. I can hear the patients screaming every night."

"You mean the place is haunted?"

Elizabeth shrugged. "Maybe it's me who's haunted. People go crazy here sometimes. Break windows and try to cut themselves with broken glass. I can hear the typhoid victims screaming every night as they're burning up and snapping bones in convulsions. I can hear the bones snap." She clapped her hands. "Crack. Just like that."

Then she put her hand over her mouth and laughed. Banks noticed the first and second fingers of her right hand were stained yellow with nicotine. She rummaged inside her sweater and pulled out a packet of Embassy Regal and a tarnished silver lighter. Banks took out a cigarette of his own, and she leaned forward to give him a light. The flame was high and he caught a whiff of petrol fumes as he inhaled.

"You know," Elizabeth went on, "for all that—the ghosts, the screaming, the cold—I'd rather be here than . . . than out there." She nodded her head towards the door. "That's where the real horror is, Mr Banks, out there."

"I take it you don't keep up with the world, then. No newspapers, no television?"

Elizabeth shook her head. "No. There is a television here, next door. But I don't watch it. I read books. Old books. Charles Dickens, that's who I'm reading now. There's opium-taking in *Edwin Drood*, did you know that?"

Banks nodded. He had been through a Dickens phase some years ago.

"Have you come about the complaint?" Elizabeth asked.

"What complaint?"

"It was years ago. I made a complaint about a policeman for hitting people with his truncheon at a demonstration. I don't know what became of it. I never heard a thing. I was different then; things seemed more worthwhile fighting for. Now I just let them go their way. They'll blow it up, Mr Banks. Oh, there's no doubt about it, they'll blow us all up. Or is it drugs you want to talk about?"

"It's partly about the complaint, yes. I wanted to talk to you about Seth Cotton. Seth and Alison."

"Good old Seth. Poor old Seth. I don't want to talk about Seth. I don't have to talk to you, do I?"

"Why don't you want to talk about him?"

"Because I don't. Seth's private. I won't tell you anything he wouldn't, so it's no good asking."

Banks leaned forward. "Elizabeth," he said gently, "Seth's dead. I'm sorry, but it's true."

At first he thought she wasn't going to react at all. A little sigh escaped her, nothing more than a gust of wind against a dark window. "Well, that's all right, then, isn't it?" she said, her voice softer, weaker. "Peace at last." Then she closed her eyes, and her face assumed such a distant, holy expression that Banks didn't dare break the silence. It would have been blasphemy. When she opened her eyes again, they were clear. "My little prayer," she said.

"What did you mean, poor Seth?"

"He was such a serious man, and he had to suffer so

much pain. How did he die, Mr Banks? Was it peaceful?"

"Yes," Banks lied.

Elizabeth nodded.

"The problem is," Banks said, "that nobody knew very much about him, about his feelings or his past. You were quite close to Seth and Alison, weren't you?"

"I was, yes."

"Is there anything you can tell me about him, about his past, that might help me understand him better. I know he was upset about Alison's accident—"

"Accident?"

"Yes. You must know, surely? The car—"

"Alison's death wasn't an accident, Mr Banks. She was murdered."

"Murdered?"

"Oh yes. It was murder all right. I told Seth. I made him believe me."

"When?"

"I figured it out. I used to be a nurse, you know."

"I know. What did you figure out?"

"Are you sure Seth's dead?"

Banks nodded.

She eyed him suspiciously, then smiled. "I suppose I can tell you, then. Are you sitting comfortably? That's what they say before the story on 'Children's Hour,' you know. I used to listen to that when I was young. It's funny how things stick in your memory, isn't it? But so much doesn't. Why is that, do you think? Isn't the mind peculiar? Do you remember Uncle Mac and 'Children's Favourites'? 'Sparky and the Magic Piano'? Petula Clark singing 'Little Green Man'?"

"I'm sorry, I don't remember," Banks said. "But I'm sitting comfortably."

Elizabeth smiled. "Good. Then I'll begin."

And she launched into one of the saddest and strangest stories that Banks had ever heard.

II

What Liz Dale told him confirmed what he had been beginning to suspect. His theories were no longer mutually exclusive, but he felt none of his usual elation on solving this case.

He drove back to Eastvale slowly, taking the longest, most meandering route west through the gritstone country away from the large towns and cities. There was no hurry. On the way, he listened to scratchy recordings of the old bluesmen: gamblers, murderers, ministers, alcoholics, drug addicts singing songs about poverty, sex, the devil and bad luck. And the signs flashed by: Mytholmroyd, Todmorden, Cornholme. In Lancashire now, he skirted the Burnley area on a series of minor roads that led by the Forest of Trawden, then he was soon back in Craven country around Skipton, where the grass was lush green with limestone-rich soils.

He stopped in Grassington and had a pub lunch, then cut across Greenhow Hill by Pateley Bridge and got back to Eastvale via Ripon.

Burgess was waiting in his office. "You owe me a fiver," he said. "A couple of glasses of Mumm's and she was all over me."

"There's no accounting for taste," Banks said.

"You'll have to take my word for it. I'm not crass, I don't go in for stealing knickers as a trophy."

Banks nodded towards the superintendent's swollen, purplish cheek. "I see you've got a trophy of a kind."

"That bloody husband of hers. Mistrustful swine." He fingered the bruise. "But that was later. He's lucky I didn't pull him in for assaulting a police officer. Still, I suppose he deserved a swing at me, so I let him. All nice and quiet."

"Very magnanimous of you." Banks pulled a five-pound note from his wallet and dropped it on the desk.

"What's wrong with you today, Banks? Sore loser?" Burgess picked up the money and held it out. "Fuck it, you don't have to pay if you're that hard up."

Banks sat down and lit a cigarette. "Ever heard of a fellow called Barney Merritt?" he asked.

"No. Should I?"

"He's an old friend of mine, still on the Met. He's heard of you. He's also heard of DC Cranby. Keith J. Cranby."

"So?" The muscles around Burgess's jaw tightened and his eyes seemed to turn brighter and sharper.

Banks tapped a folder on his desk. "Cranby and a mate of his—possibly DC Stickley—rented a blue Escort in York a couple of days ago. They drove up to Eastvale and checked into the Castle Hotel—the same place as you. I'm surprised you didn't pass each other in the lobby, it's not that big a place."

"Do you realize what you're saying? Maybe you should reconsider and stop while the going's good."

Banks shook his head and went on.

"The other day they broke into Dennis Osmond's flat. They didn't find what they were looking for, but they took one of his political books to put the wind up him. He thought he had every security force in the world after him. Yesterday evening they broke into Tim and Abhà's apartment and took away a number of folders. That was after I told you where the information they'd collected on the demo was kept."

Burgess tapped a ruler on the desk. "You have proof of all this, I suppose?"

"If I need it, yes."

"What on earth made you think of such a thing?"

"I know your methods. And when I mentioned the Osmond break-in you didn't seem surprised. You didn't even seem to care very much. That was odd, because my first thought was that it might have had a bearing on the Gill case. But, of course, you already knew all about it."

"And what are you going to do?"

"I just don't understand you," Banks said. "What the

bloody hell did you hope to achieve? You used the same vigilante tactics they did in Manchester after the Leon Brittan demo."

"They worked, though, didn't they?"

"If you call hounding a couple of students out of the country and drawing national attention to the worst elements of policing good, then yes, they worked."

"Don't be so bloody naïve, Banks. These people are all connected."

"You're paranoid, do you know that? What do you think they are? Terrorists?"

"They're connected. Union leaders, Bolshy students, ban-the-bombers. They're all connected. You can call them misguided idealists if you want, but to me they're a bloody menace."

"To who? To what?"

Burgess leaned forward and gripped the desk. "To the peace and stability of the nation, that's what. Whose side are you on, anyway?"

"I'm not on anyone's side. I've been investigating a murder, remember? A policeman was killed. He wasn't a very good one, but I don't think he deserved to end up dead in the street. And what do I find? You bring your personal bloody goon squad from London and they start breaking and entering."

"There's no point arguing ethics with you, Banks—"

"I know—because you don't have a leg to stand on."

"But let me remind you that I'm in charge of this case."

"That still doesn't give you the right to do what you did. Can't you bloody understand? You with all your talk about police image. This vigilante stuff only makes us end up looking like the bad guys, and bloody stupid ones at that."

Burgess sat back and lit a cigar. "Only if people find out. Which brings us back to my question. What are you going to do?"

"Nothing. But you're going to make sure those files

are returned and that the people involved are left alone from now on."

"Am I? What makes you so sure?"

"Because if you don't, I'll pass on what I know to Superintendent Gristhorpe. The ACC respects his opinion."

Burgess laughed. "You're not very well-connected, you know. I don't think that'll do much good."

"There's always the press, too. They'd love a juicy story like this. Dennis Osmond has a right to know what was done to him, too. Whatever you think, I don't believe it would do your future promotion prospects much good."

Burgess tapped his cigar on the rim of the ashtray. "You're so bloody pure of heart, aren't you, Banks? A real crusader. Better than the rest of us."

"Don't come that. You were out of line and you know it. You just thought you could get away with it."

"I still can."

Banks shook his head.

"You're forgetting that I'm your superior officer. I can order you to hand over whatever evidence you've got."

"Balls," said Banks. "Why don't you send Cranby and Stickley in to steal it?"

"Look," Burgess said, reddening with anger, "you don't want to cross me. I can be a very nasty enemy. Do you really think anyone's going to take any notice of your accusations? What do you think they'll do? Kick me off the force? Dream on."

"I don't really care what they do to you. All I know is that the press will make a field-day of it."

"You'd be sawing off the branch you're sitting on. Think about where your loyalty lies. We do a difficult enough job as it is without taking an opportunity to set everyone against us. Have you considered that? What effect it would have on you lot up here if it did get out? I don't have to live here, thank God, but you do."

"Damn right I do," said Banks. "And that's the point.

You can come here and make a bloody mess then bugger off back to London. I have to live and work with these people. And I like it. It took me long enough to get accepted as far as I have been, and you come along and set back relations by years. Take it or leave it. Give back the files, call off your goons, and it's forgotten, another unsolved break-in."

"Oh, what a bleeding hero we are! And what if I put on a bit more pressure, got a couple of higher-ups to order you to hand over your evidence? What then, big man?"

"I've already told you," Banks said. "It's not me you need to worry about, it's the press, Osmond and the students."

"I can handle them."

"It's up to you."

"That's it?"

"That's it. Take your pick."

"Who's going to believe a couple of loony lefties anyway? And everyone knows the press is biased."

Banks shrugged. "Maybe nobody. We'll see."

Burgess jerked to his feet. "I won't forget this, Banks," he snarled. "When I make my report on this investigation—"

"It's over," Banks said wearily.

"What is?"

"The investigation." Banks told him briefly about his conversation with Elizabeth Dale.

"So what happens now?"

"Nothing. Except maybe you piss off back home."

"You're not going to go blabbing the whole bloody story to the press?"

"No point, no. But I think Mara and the others have a right to know."

"Yes, you would." Burgess strode over to the door. "And don't think you've won, because you haven't. You won't get out of it as easily as all that."

And he left, the threat hanging in the air.

Banks stretched out his hands in front of him and noticed they were shaking. Even though the office was cool, his neck felt sweaty under the collar. His legs were weak, too, as he found out when he grabbed another cigarette and walked over to the window. It wasn't every day you got the chance to be high-handed with a senior officer, especially a whiz-kid like Dirty Dick Burgess. And it was the first time Banks had ever seen him ruffled.

Maybe he *had* made a dangerous enemy for life. Perhaps Burgess had even been right and he was overplaying the crusader role. After all, he played it a bit close to the edge himself sometimes. But to hell with it, he thought. It wasn't worth dwelling on. He picked up his coat, pocketed his cigarettes and set off for the car-park.

III

The rain had stopped and the afternoon sun was charming wraiths of mist from the river-meadows and valley-sides. Banks's Cortina crackled up the track and pulled up outside the farmhouse.

Mara answered the door on his second knock and let him in.

"I suppose you want to sit down?" she asked.

"It might take a while." Banks made himself comfortable in the rocking chair. The children sat at the table colouring, and Paul slouched on the beanbag cushions reading a science-fiction book.

"Where are Rick and Zoe?" Banks asked.

"Working."

"Can you go get them, please? I'd like to talk to all of you. And would it be too much to ask for some tea?"

Mara put the kettle on first, then went out to the barn

to fetch the others. When she came back, she saw to the tea while Rick and Zoe sat down.

"What the bloody hell is this?" Rick demanded. "Haven't we had enough? Where's your friend?"

"He's packing."

"Packing?" Mara said, walking in slowly with the teapot and mugs on a tray. "But—"

"It's all over, Mara. Almost over, anyway."

Banks poured himself some tea, lit a cigarette and turned to Paul. "You wrote that suicide note, didn't you?"

"I don't know what you're talking about."

"Come off it, the time for messing around is over. The pressure on the keys was different from that on the letters Seth typed, and his style was a hell of a lot better than yours. Why did you do it?"

"I've told you, I didn't do anything." They were all staring at him now and he began to turn red.

"Shall I tell you why you did it?" Banks went on. "You did it to deflect the blame from yourself."

"Wait a minute," Mara said. "Are you accusing Paul of killing Seth?"

"Nobody killed Seth," Banks said quietly. "He did it himself."

"But you said—"

"I know. And that's what we thought. It was the note that confused me. Seth didn't write it; Paul did. But he didn't kill anyone. When Paul found him, Seth was already dead. Paul just took the opportunity to type out a note of confession, hoping it would get him off the hook. It didn't seem like such a bad thing to do, I'm sure. After all, Seth was dead. Nothing could affect him any more. Isn't that right, Paul?"

Paul said nothing.

"Paul?" Mara turned to face him sternly. "Is it true?"

"So what if it is? Seth wouldn't have minded. He wouldn't have wanted us to go on being persecuted. He was dead, Mara. I swear it. All I did was type out a note."

"Had he written anything himself?" Banks asked.

"Yes, but it said nothing." He pulled a scrap of paper out of the back pocket of his jeans and passed it over. It read, "Sorry, Mara." Just that. Banks passed it to Mara, and tears filled her eyes. She wiped them away with the back of her hand. "How could you, Paul?" she said.

Paul sat forward and hugged his knees. "It was for all of us," he said. "Can't you see? To keep the police off our backs. It's what Seth would have done."

"But he didn't," Banks said. "Seth had no idea that Paul would forge a note. As far as he was concerned, his suicide would be accepted for what it was. He'd never imagined that we'd see it as murder. If his death led us to the truth, so be it, but he wasn't going to explain. He never did while he was alive, so why should he when he was about to die?"

"The truth?" Mara said. "Is that what you're going to tell us now?"

"Yes. If you want me to."

Mara nodded.

"You might not like it."

"After all we've been through," she said, "I think you owe it to us."

"Very well. I think Seth killed himself out of shame, among other reasons. He felt he'd let everyone down—including himself."

"What do you mean?"

"I mean that Seth stabbed PC Gill and he couldn't live with what he'd done. Paul had already suffered for it. Seth would never have let him take the blame. He'd have confessed himself rather than that. When Paul was released, he was happy for him. What it meant for Seth, though, was that the police would get even closer to him now. It was just a matter of time. I'd already seen PC Gill's number in his notebook, and those books in his workshop. I knew it was his knife, too. I'd asked him about Elizabeth Dale, and he knew how unstable she was. All I had to do was find her and get her to talk. Seth knew all this. He knew it would soon be all over for him."

Mara was pale. Her hands trembled as she tried to roll a cigarette. Banks offered her a Silk Cut and she took it. Zoe went around and poured tea for everyone.

"I can't believe this, you know," Mara said, shaking her head. "Not Seth."

"It's true. I'm not saying that he intended to kill PC Gill. He couldn't be sure that the demo would turn nasty, even though Gill was supposed to be there. But he went prepared. He knew very well the kind of things that were likely to happen if Gill was around. That's why I asked you if you'd heard anyone mention Gill's number that afternoon. Someone had it in for him and knew he'd be there."

"I thought it sounded vaguely familiar," Mara said, speaking quietly as if to herself. "I was in the kitchen, I think, with Seth."

"And Osmond mentioned the number."

"I . . . It could have been like that. But why Seth? He wasn't like that. He was a gentle person."

"I agree, on the whole," Banks said. "But the circumstances are very unusual. I had to find Liz Dale to put it all together. She told me a very curious thing, and that was that Alison, Seth's wife, was murdered. Now that didn't make sense to me, because I'd spoken to the local police and to the man who ran her over. It was an accident. He hadn't killed her deliberately. It had ruined his life, too.

"Seth tried to commit suicide after Alison's death, but he failed. He got on with his life but he never got over his grief, and that's partly because he never expressed it. You know he didn't like to talk about the past, he kept it all bottled up inside, all those feelings of grief and guilt. We always blame ourselves when someone we love dies, because maybe, just in a fleeting moment, we've wished them dead, and we tell ourselves that if things had been just a little different—if Seth had ridden to the shops that day instead of Alison—then the tragedy would never have happened. Liz was the only one who really knew about what went on, and that was only because she was a close friend of Alison's. According to the Hebden Bridge police, Alison was more outgoing, spirited and communicative than Seth. Because he was the 'strong silent type,' everyone thought he was really in control, calm and cool, but he was torturing himself inside."

"I still don't see," Mara said. "What does all this have to do with that policeman who got killed?"

Banks blew gently on the surface and sipped some tea. It tasted of apple and cinnamon. "Liz Dale filed a complaint about PC Gill's vicious behaviour during a demo she went to with Alison Cotton. Seth hadn't been there himself. During the demo, Liz told me, Alison was struck a glancing blow on her temple by Gill. It was just one of many such incidents that afternoon. Alison didn't want to make a fuss and attract police attention by making a complaint, but Liz was far more political at that time. She made a complaint about Gill's behaviour in general. When nothing came of it, she didn't pursue it any further. She'd lost interest by then—heroin made her forget politics—and like you, she assumed that the police wouldn't listen to someone like her."

"Can you blame her?" Rick said. "They obviously didn't, did they? It hardly seems that—"

"Shut up," Banks said. He spoke quietly, but forcefully enough to silence Rick.

"Over the next few months," he went on, "Alison started to show some unusual symptoms. She complained of frequent headaches, she was becoming forgetful, and she suffered from dizzy spells. Shortly afterwards, she became pregnant, so she put her other troubles out of her mind for a while.

"One time, though, she really scared Seth and Liz. She started speaking as if she were a fourteen-year-old girl. Her family had been on holiday in Cyprus then, staying with an army friend of her father's who was stationed there, and she started describing a warm evening walk by the Mediterranean in Famagusta in great detail. Apparently, even her voice was like that of a fourteen-year-old. Finally she snapped out of it and recalled nothing. She just laughed when the others told her what she'd been talking about.

"But that did it as far as Seth was concerned. He was worried she might have a brain tumour or something, so he insisted she tell the doctor. According to Liz, the doctor had nothing much to say except that pregnancy can do strange things to a woman's mind as well as her body. Alison told him that the symptoms started *before* she got pregnant, but he just said something about people having funny spells, and that was that.

"A few weeks later, she went to the local shop one evening and got lost. It was about a two-minute walk away, and she couldn't find her way home. Seth and Liz found her wandering the streets an hour later. Anyway, things didn't get much better and she went to see the doctor again. At first, he tried to blame the pregnancy again, but Alison stressed the terrible headaches, lapses of memory, and slipping in and out of time. He said not to worry, but he arranged for a CAT scan, just to be on the safe side. Well, you know the National Health Service. By the time her appointment came around, she was already dead. And they couldn't do a proper autopsy later because of the accident—her head was crushed.

"Seth had his breakdown, attempted suicide, put himself back together and bought the farm, where he lived in isolation for a while—until you came along, Mara. He proved himself capable of moving on, but he carried all the weight of the past with him. He was always a serious person, a man of strong feelings, but there was a new darker dimension to him after the shock of Alison's death."

"It doesn't make sense," Mara said. "If all that's true, why did he wait so long before doing what you say he did?"

"Two reasons really. First, he wasn't convinced until about a year ago. That's around the time he made his will. According to Liz, about eighteen months ago he'd read an article in a magazine about a similar case. A woman showed symptoms like Alison's after receiving a relatively mild blow to the head, and she later crashed her car. Just after he'd read this and started thinking about the implications, Liz ran off from the hospital and came to stay. He talked to her about it, and she agreed it was a definite possibility. After all, Alison's attacks only began to occur shortly after the demo. Liz hadn't been a very good nurse—not good enough to come up with a diagnosis at the time—but she knew something about the human body, and once Seth had put the idea into her head, she helped to convince him."

"That's when they were up talking all the time," Mara said. "Is that what they were talking about?"

"Mostly, yes. Next, Seth went on to study the subject himself. I even saw two books on the human brain in his workshop, though I'd no idea what significance they had. One was called *The Tip of the Iceberg*. Seth just left them there; he never really tried to cover his tracks at all. And then there was PC Gill's number in his notebook. Liz said she wrote it down for him the last time she was here. He must have torn it out in anger after he'd heard Gill would be at the demo."

"You said there were two reasons he didn't act straight away," Mara said. "What's the other one?"

"Seth's character, really. You know he wasn't normally quick-tempered or impatient. Far from it, he needed lots of patience in his line of work. He wasn't the type to go out seeking immediate vengeance, either. And remember, he'd never really got over his grief and his guilt. I imagine he repressed his anger in the same way, and it all festered together, under the surface, and finally turned into hatred—hatred for the man who had robbed him of his wife and child. And it wasn't just a man, it was a policeman, an enemy of freedom." He glanced at Rick, who was listening closely and sucking on a strand of his beard.

"But there was nothing he could do. It had happened so long ago, and there was no evidence—even if he had believed that the police would listen to his story. I don't think he really considered revenge, but when Osmond mentioned the number that afternoon, something gave. The whole business had been eating away at him for so long, and he felt so impotent.

"He snatched up the knife, expecting trouble. I shouldn't imagine he really believed he would kill Gill, but he wanted to be prepared. When he dropped the knife later and it got kicked away, he must have been surprised to find no blood on him. Most of Gill's bleeding was internal. So he kept quiet. There were over a hundred people at that demo. As far as Seth was concerned, that seemed to mean we hadn't a snowball in hell's chance of finding the killer. Besides, we'd be after the politicos, and he wasn't especially active that way." Banks paused and sipped some more tea. "If Paul hadn't taken the knife and thrown it away, we might never have known where it came from. None of you would ever have told us it was missing, that's for certain. Liz had described Gill to him as well—a big man with his teeth too close to his gums—and he was easy to spot up there on the steps. That's where the most light was, above the doors. And Seth was near the front of the crowd. When they got close in the scuffles, Seth saw the number on Gill's epaulette and—"

"My God!" Zoe said. "So that's it. . . ."

"What?"

"When the police started to charge, I was next to Seth, right at the front, and the first thing that policeman did was lash out at a woman standing on my other side. She looked a bit like you, Mara."

"What happened next?" Banks asked.

"I didn't really see. I was frightened. I got pushed away. But I looked up at Seth and I saw an expression on his face. It was . . . I can't really describe it, but he was pale and he looked so different . . . so full of hate."

They all remained silent as they digested what Zoe had said. She couldn't have known at the time, but what Seth was seeing was a replay, an echo of what happened to Alison. Given that, Banks thought, what Seth had done was even more understandable. He had been pushed far beyond the breaking point.

"Liz Dale told you all about his background?" said Mara finally.

"Yes. Everything else made sense then: Seth's behaviour, the knife, the number, the books."

"If . . . if you'd found her earlier, talked to her, would that have saved Seth?"

"I don't think so. It's not as easy as that. It was actually carrying out the crime that finished him. He'd spent all his hate and anger, and he felt empty. He might have committed suicide sooner if he hadn't been lucky and got away from the demo clean. I imagine he thought he could live with what he'd done at first, but as the investigation went on, he realized he couldn't. I don't think he could have faced prison, either, and he knew that we'd find him. All that talking to Liz Dale has done is put things in perspective and make the motive clear.

"And Liz is a difficult person. Her grasp on reality is pretty tenuous, for a start. She knew nothing of the demo or of Gill's murder. And I honestly don't think she'd have told me about Seth unless I'd told her he was dead. I probably wouldn't even have known the right questions to ask. I'm not making excuses, Mara. We make mistakes in this job, and usually someone suffers for them. But the rest of you lie, evade and treat us with hostility. There's good and bad on both sides. You can't look back and say how things might have been. That's no good."

Mara nodded slowly. "Do you think Seth was right?"

"Right about what?"

"About Gill being responsible for Alison's death."

"I think there's a good chance, yes. I've spoken to the police doctor about it, too, and he agrees. But we'll never know for sure. Liz Dale was wrong, though— Alison wasn't murdered. Gill might not have been a good policeman, but he didn't *intend* to kill her.

"But look at it from Seth's point of view. He'd lost everything he valued—in the most horrible way—and he'd lost it all to a man who abused the power the state gave him. Seth came of age in the late sixties and early seventies. He was anti-authoritarian, and he lost his wife and unborn child to a representative of what he saw as oppressive authority. It's no wonder he had to hit back eventually, especially considering what Zoe just told us, or go mad. That's why he made the will when he did, I think, because knowing what had happened to Alison— knowing the real cause of her death—changed things, and he wasn't sure he could be responsible for his actions any more. He wanted to make certain you got the house."

Mara covered her face with both hands and started to cry. Zoe went over to comfort her and the children looked on, horror-stricken. Paul and Rick seemed rooted where they sat. Banks rose from the chair. He'd done his job, solved the crime, but it didn't end there for Mara. For her, this was only the beginning of the real pain.

"But why couldn't he be happy here?" she cried from behind her hands. "With me?"

Banks had no answer to that.

He opened the door and late-afternoon sunshine flooded in. At the car, he turned and saw Mara standing in the doorway watching him, arms folded tightly across her chest, head tilted to one side. The sunlight caught the tears in her eyes and made them sparkle like jewels as they trickled down her cheeks.

All the way home through the wraiths of mist, Banks could hear the damn wind chimes ringing in his ears.

NOVELS of SUSPENSE from
NEW YORK TIMES BESTSELLING AUTHOR

PETER
ROBINSON

A DEDICATED MAN
978–0–380–71645–6

A NECESSARY END
978–0–380–71946–4

BLOOD AT THE ROOT
978–0–380–79476–8

PAST REASON HATED
978–0–380–73328–6

GALLOWS VIEW
978–0–380–71400–1

COLD IS THE GRAVE
978–0–380–80935–6

WEDNESDAY'S CHILD
978–0–380–82049–8

THE HANGING VALLEY
978–0–380–82048–1

INNOCENT GRAVES
978–0–380–82043–6

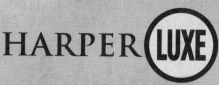